PLAN A

ALSO BY DEB CALETTI

PLAN A

Her choice.

DEB CALETTI

LABYRINTH ROAD | NEW YORK

Text copyright © 2023 by Deb Caletti
Jacket art copyright © 2023 by Maeve Norton

Visit us on the Web! GetUnderlined.com

Educators and librarians, for a variety of teaching tools,
visit us at RHTeachersLibrarians.com

Library of Congress Cataloging-in-Publication Data
Names: Caletti, Deb, author.
Title: Plan A / Deb Caletti.
Description: First edition. | New York: Labyrinth Road, [2023] | Audience: Ages 14 and up. | Summary: Sixteen-year-old Ivy's road trip across the country to get an abortion becomes a transformative journey of vulnerability, strength, and, above all, choice.
Identifiers: LCCN 2023012459 (print) | LCCN 2023012460 (ebook) | ISBN 978-0-593-48554-5 (trade) | ISBN 978-0-593-48555-2 (lib. bdg.) | ISBN 978-0-593-48557-6 (ebook)
Subjects: CYAC: Abortion—Fiction. | Reproductive rights—Fiction. | Automobile travel—Fiction. | Self-actualization—Fiction.
Classification: LCC PZ7.C127437 Pl 2023 (print) | LCC PZ7.C127437 (ebook) | DDC [Fic]—dc23

The text of this book is set in 11.5-point Sabon LT Pro.
Interior design by Megan Shortt

Printed in the United States of America
10 9 8 7 6 5 4 3 2 1
First Edition

To Liesa Abrams, for four hundred and two pages of reasons. I am so very lucky to have you as my editor, friend, and fellow traveler on this Labyrinth Road. Love and gratitude always.

1

WHEN I'M NOT AT SCHOOL, YOU CAN FIND ME AT Euwing's Drugs, and so that's where I am that day, in the staff break room, surrounded by a shipment of pain relievers. It's not the most pleasant place to be, I admit. There's a permanent burnt smell in there after my manager, Maureen, once left the Mr. Coffee on all night, and it has twitching fluorescent lights that make you feel like you're in one of those futuristic movies where someone implanted a microchip in your brain. Still, it's what we've got, so I set my water bottle on a box that reads THIS END UP and try for the hundredth time to start *Tess of the D'Urbervilles* for Advanced English III. I'm so far behind that it's becoming one of those things that grow bigger and bigger the longer you don't do them. I've never been this far behind in any of my schoolwork, and we've got a final coming up soon, but I just can't get through the beginning. You wouldn't believe how many pages there are before that thing actually starts. There's a foreword, and then an explanatory note to the first edition, and then a preface to the fifth and later editions. I'm not even kidding. You practically expect an introduction to the 109th edition.

Blah, blah, blah, preface. If you ask me, they ought to be outlawed, the pages before the pages. And if they're in italics, forget it.

You have a lot of opinions, Ivy, my mom always says.

Which is, of course, an opinion.

She has a lot of them, too—opinions about music and men, guitars and rom-coms—and so does Grandma Lottie, about everything from shit cars to fast food. It's a thing in my family, especially among the DeVries women, to see yourself as strong-minded and willful, fierce. Also, that old-fashioned word *plucky*. But I can tell you one thing—right then, I don't feel very fierce, and you'd need way more boxes of pain relief to fix the hurt swirling around in my head. *Swirl*—my stomach, too. Forget about eating.

To get to the actual beginning of the book, I just skip all of it, all those pages that seem so meaningless. Fine, whatever, get to page seventeen, where the thing actually starts. You know what's funny? The first line. *On an evening in the latter part of May,* it reads, and right at that moment, it's actually an evening in the latter part of May. Something about this makes me think of our dog, Wilson, chasing his tail. Going around and around only to end up at the same place.

Stop being a preface, Ivy, I tell myself. *Get on with it.*

I sigh long and loud, even if no one hears it, and take off my blue vest with my name tag pinned on. In order to reveal my future, I open the book to a random spot to see what it says. Pages 142 and 143. *My life looks as if it had been wasted for want of chances!* Wow, thanks. Come on, book, you can do better! I close my eyes, move my finger down the page, and stop. *What's the use of learning that I am one of a long row only?*

Oh my God. Or oh somebody's God. I *wish* he were mine, but the way people around here talk about God, he too often seems like the worst bad boyfriend—moody, mean, and impossible to please.

Ms. La Costa did say that *Tess of the D'Urbervilles* was the most depressing book ever as she handed out the copies in class, her legs *shush-shush*ing from her nylons. How can it *not* be? It's about a woman in the 1870s who gets raped and has a baby, and then her whole town basically ostracizes her. When Olivia Kneeley said, *Why do we have to read it, then?* Ms. La Costa said, *We still have to* look.

I wrap up the second triangle-half of my peanut butter sandwich, tucking it into a plastic-wrap swaddle. It's one of those awful times when everything seems to be telling you something, even a peanut butter sandwich. Mini fridge, checkered linoleum, the curve of an orange peel in the trash, goodbye. I gather my things. Bending down, I tie my shoes even though they're already tied, like you do for a marathon.

My opinions—they don't have the power to wreck lives, though. They don't have the ability to make you so scared and so ashamed that you'll do what people want you to do, even if it destroys you.

This all could be so easy, since I'm right there at Euwing's Drugs, where I've worked three days a week after school for two years now, and all day in the summer. Those very boxes are right in reach. But it's not easy. It's not Tess hard, but it's hard enough that I haven't slept for days. A scary dread keeps popping out at unexpected times, same as Diesel, our neighbor Mr. Sykes's dog, who snarls and flings his body against the chain-link fence whenever anyone or anything passes by.

"Be right back," I say to Maureen, who pinches her lips together and adjusts her own blue vest with the name tag that reads MAUREEN and, under that, in print so small you practically have to have your face in our boobs to read it, HOW CAN I HELP YOU? She hates me. She absolutely hates me. I hate her daily tuna, how the smell of it merges with the old burnt coffee, but I try really hard to see the good in her. Whenever I relay all the thrilling drama at Euwing's Drugs for my best friends, Peyton and Faith, Peyton says for the millionth time, *She's just jealous—you know that.*

I know that. I'm the youngest assistant manager Euwing's has ever had, according to Mr. Euwing. Bob. *Call me Bob. No more of this Mr. Euwing business. You're making me feel old!* Promoted to management in only two years. While I'm still in *high school.* It took Maureen, who's, like, forty or fifty, something like fifteen years to be assistant manager, and two more to make manager after Flo died. I get it. I'd be jealous, too. I keep trying to be nice to her to make up for it, offering her a mint, giving her compliments about her hair or her latest manicure design, but there's no going back to the days when she'd pat my shoulder and say, *How you doing,*

Ives? Mr. Euwing tapped the magic wand on my head because I'm his favorite, and who likes a favorite? I'd hate me if I were Maureen, trudging in to work all those years and then hearing Mr. Euwing say stuff to me like, *I want to support your goals!* I don't even know what my goals actually are. Go to college. Make money. Definitely see some places beyond Paris, Texas. Definitely see the real Paris someday, the real lots of cities in lots of countries, even. That's as far as I've gotten.

I try to walk casually across the store, past the aisles labeled FIRST AID and BEAUTY and SEASONAL. I don't look at that wire cage by the door with those two lovebirds inside, Buddy and Missy, with their orange heads and curved red beaks and those black bead eyes on a circle of white that look like the plastic eyes you can find in a bin at Shelley's Craft and Quilt. Those eyes are so creepy and lifeless that you better make a joke about them, fast. *Euwing Opaline Lovebird,* Mr. Euwing will tell you. *That's right! They have my last name! How can I not want to own them?* He'll tell you much more than that, too—how they're a mutation of two mutations, Euwing and Opaline, how you can pair two birds to actually design the bird you want. *You can change its color. You can stop it from flying, even.* "Birds don't belong in cages" is another opinion I have. What a life, to be forced inside, the door shut on all the possibilities that are right out there for you to see but not have. I hate the way those birds lift their feathers and peck at their small fat bodies and screech and scream. They make me so uneasy, I always try to avoid them, unless Mr. Euwing is watching.

Outside, I stroll all casual until I'm sure I'm out of sight of Maureen and Evan, who's at the register. Then I take off. I run so hard, my backpack bangs against my side until I'm practically falling at the automatic doorstep of Euwing's archenemy, CVS. Giant corporation, forcing out the little guy. "Everything always seems to be about power" is another opinion I have. I step on the black mat, and the door whooshes open, which seems so upscale compared to our regular old door that you have to actually push. Everyone pulls, even though there's a sign right on it. Customers who have been coming for years do it, because, let me tell you, the force of habit is strong. If you watch Wilson go outside to pee, you even wonder if habit is inborn. Sniff the same two bushes, lift leg on tree, repeat for years, even when I try really hard to get him to view the yard in a new way.

Inside CVS, air-conditioning hits, and a wall of cool suddenly surrounds me. Goose bumps prickle up my arms as I face the display of Pump-Up Max protein powder on sale that greets you as you walk in. The store is bright and clean and new, and so big that it's almost hard to see the anything in the everything. I glance around like a spy. My heart beats a guilty gallop, as if I'm about to rob the place. I didn't imagine how this would actually feel. Well, it feels bad. Really bad. Like a shame python is wrapping itself around me and squeezing.

No cart, just a basket, the kind with the metal handles covered in a thin roll of red plastic. I get a hairbrush, on sale, protected in its transparent dome. A bottle of Suave shampoo, strawberry. A box of Red Vines for a dollar twenty-five. A box of Junior Mints for ninety-nine cents. A cheap mascara. When I get to *that* aisle, my face flushes. It's mid-May and warm, eighty-two. Paris doesn't get hot like the Texas desert where my dad lives. It once got to be one twenty in Odessa. But I'm perspiring even in that air-conditioning. Still, I wish I had a sweatshirt or something to cover my bare arms in my sundress. My skin feels all exposed, because when you're in that aisle, the one way in the back, it's the aisle of disgrace, where you stand there and publicly admit that you had sex or are about to have sex or that you get your period or can't control your bladder.

Past the adult diapers and the tampons and the pads and the K-Y Jelly and the condoms and the urinary tract whatevers, there they are, the pink boxes. Pink says, *These are for you, ladies. Not your business, dudes.* I was hoping for a sale, because those things are expensive. Why are they so expensive? I get the cheaper CVS brand, then worry about getting the cheaper CVS brand. I put it back, then grab the more expensive one, then put that back and choose the CVS one again. Cheaper doesn't mean it won't work as well, does it? Because there must be some law or something that protects you, where they make sure the product has to be good or something, right? *They.* The *They* you count on.

Come on! Just decide, Ivy, and get out of that fucking aisle! Literally the fucking aisle, haha! Which is not even a word I use. My dad hates swearing, *hates,* and my best friend Faith says, *Cussing is a sin and a dishonor to God.* Once when our friend Nate jokingly said, *Fuck you,* she said, *God isn't laughing,* and he blushed. I try to be respectful of other people's feelings, so the word stays in my head, but the whole subject matter makes me sad, to be honest. Here we are, talking about God again, because I just hoped that he would have a sense of humor and that he was maybe someone who kept his priorities straight, like thinking guns and cruelty and little kids with cancer were the sins, not certain words. Also, swear words are a minefield. My other best friend, Peyton, used the words *fanny pack* when we went out to Pat Mayse Lake with her cousin from the UK, and he burst out laughing, since *fanny* is apparently a crass word there. I have no idea what God would do in a case like that.

Anyway, right then, some part of me separates from the body me and sees me down there in the fucking aisle. I look awful. My face is blotchy, and my eyes have a haze of shock and disbelief. Honestly, it's way worse than that. I look paralyzed and full of horror. No way, not in a million years, a jillion, more, would I ever have imagined me here. I don't even really understand *how* I'm here. The only possible way—I can't even think about it.

Wait, is that Faith's mom? I see her styled blond hair, sprayed into an unmoving helmet, a flash of turquoise, the color she always wears. I get out of that aisle fast, the test badly hidden under the pile of beauty products and candy. The turquoise disappears around the corner toward the pharmacy. Seriously, I could be the worst criminal ever for how nervous and guilt-ridden I am. That song you always hear in grocery stores is playing. *I can feel it coming in the air tonight, oh Lord*. I think it's Bill Collins—my mom went to his concert once, she told me. But it makes you feel like something bad is about to happen.

Something bad *is* about to happen. A lot of somethings.

Hurry. At the checkout counters: a middle-aged woman, an old guy, a college-aged girl. Three registers! In Paris! I choose the college-aged girl, but as she's ringing me up, a sense of doom rides in on a wave of regret. She could be someone's sister. She might recognize my name on the Visa I applied for to *build credit,* as my dad suggested. She runs each item over the scanner, holding it in her long white fingers with the perfect red nails. *Bleep. Bleep. Bleep.* I am fearing the nightmare scene you'd see in a movie, where she has to call over the intercom for a price check. That doesn't happen. But something else does. Her face gets very still, and her eyebrows rise just a fraction when she sees the test. I'm not imagining it. I can see the little muscle in her cheek tighten. *Bleep.* It's on the other side. Now comes the mascara. My stomach is a rope, pulled at both ends. The checker can't get the bar code to work. She has to take the scanner off the holder and do it manually. Her eyes narrow slightly as she looks at the neon-pink wand and the flashy eyelash promises on the package. And then—I know for sure I'm not imagining this—one corner of her mouth goes up slightly. It looks . . . smug. Sarcastic.

I put the Visa in the chip reader. A chip reader! So fancy. "Need a bag?"

Oh, come on.

I don't go around hating people. I don't even go around hating things. According to my brother, Mase, I'm too forgiving, of bad food and scratchy fabrics, even. I want, I really want, to try to see everyone like the shit cars Grandma talks about. *Show respect to that old Honda with the bashed fender and the fluff coming out the seats, because you don't know where it's been or what it's been through. You can't assume you know things just by looking at them.* But something bitter rises up my throat. I mean, *of course* I need a bag. Overhead, all around, Bill Collins breaks out into the dark, dramatic drum sequence.

"Yes, please," I manage to say.

Why are people so mean to each other? Why, why, why?

I don't want her touching my stuff, but in it goes. Righteousness is in there, too. I take the bag and walk past the row of candy bars and breath mints and gum. I walk past that display of Pump-Up Max, right in front. It's the kind of stuff Jason Maxwell and his friends would drink. A powder to make you bigger and more powerful, and it's definitely not hidden in the back. Ego, bulk-mass, muscle-guy drink mix, beauty products, surface—it's all okay to be seen. Cover-up, concealer, men's aftershave and vitamins, feast your eyes. Go farther back, farther in, to get to the truth. The truths of a body, its betrayals and pleasures and disasters, periods and sex and failures of your lower half.

What isn't seen at all, anywhere: contraception a female can use. I didn't even notice this until my own cousin Savannah pointed it out when she and her family were visiting, bringing the news from another foreign land (Oregon). Apparently, there, even if she's underage, and even if she's unmarried, a female can just get birth control. Here, if you're not married before you're eighteen, you need to be brave enough to tell your parents you want pills or whatever, and they have to be brave enough to tell your doctor. *But, hey, the dudes can protect themselves. With options,* Savannah had said, pointing to the wide choice of condoms, purple foil, gold, red cellophane, ribbed, glow-in-the-dark, even. It made me feel defensive and protective of Paris, and of our whole state. I don't always love everything about it, but I've never lived anywhere else, and this is my home. And there's stuff I *do* love, a lot. The fountain in the middle of town. The whole town square, actually. The yearly tree lighting and decorations, and the pumpkin festival. My friends, our school, old Mrs. Peony, with her pink windbreaker and tennis shoes. And our state, too. Souped-up trucks, barbecue, boots, and Whataburger. Giant crickets and *y'all*. Football fans, rodeos, big welcomes, big everything, state pride. My dad, in Odessa, even has one of those waffle makers in the shape of Texas.

Outside, I reach into the bag. I pull out the mascara to see what the cashier thought was so amusing.

Wet n Wild Mega Length.

My face flushes again. Whatever. Anything can sound sexual if you want it to.

Now I shove that bag into my backpack. It bulges guiltily. There's ten minutes left of my break, and I don't want to be late. I don't want anything to mess up what I've got going there. No one makes this kind of money at my age, and by next year when I graduate, I'll have enough saved for two years at Paris Junior College, and two more at Texas State. If I'm careful, I'll maybe even get to take a trip to South Padre Island, or a Colorado mountain town. If I work really hard *and* I'm careful, maybe I'll get to see more than that. The world, even.

If I'm careful, God.

I run.

2

WE HAVE A SHIT CAR OURSELVES, A BROWN CHRYSLER
Sebring. I don't think they even make that model anymore.
The one good thing about it is that it's got a happy-looking
grille, so we call it Mr. Smiley. After work, when Maureen
finally dims the lights and locks up, I head to the back lot,
where Mr. Smiley's parked. It's starting to get dark, and
under the lone streetlight Mrs. Euwing waits in the back
seat of their giant fancy truck for Mr. Euwing while their
son, Drake, sits behind the wheel. They do this all the time
now that Drake got his permit. The grille of that thing is big
and menacing. Another opinion I have is that you can tell a
lot about a person by how friendly their car looks. I pretend
I don't see them, though who could miss that monstrous vehicle. I hurry to unlock my door.

I slip inside, and thankfully, the sometimes-ugly world is
shut out. I try to breathe calmly, but this whole day is making my hands shake. I inhale Mr. Smiley's usual scent—the
fake pine smell of some long-ago Christmas tree air freshener,

with back notes of ancient fast-food French fries. Like most bad smells and bad things in general, you just sort of get used to it and stop noticing it after a while, but not today. Today, it makes me feel like an elevator is rushing upward inside. I try to exhale slowly to make the nausea go away, but there's no getting rid of the dread.

Mr. Smiley might be lentil-soup brown and running on prayers, but I'm really lucky I get to use it. My mom gets a ride to work with her friend and boss, Shelley from Shelley's Craft and Quilt, so I can bring my brother home from school and stuff. *And stuff* is supposed to mean activities and friends, but Mason is kind of a loner, and seventh grade is rough even when you fit in. Junior high is pretty much like an army boot camp, weeding out the weakest members through a system of rigorous humiliation. The army only prepares you for being in the army and not the real world, though; that's what I keep telling him, and I think Mase is going to be a shining talent if he can just get through it. Lately, he mostly likes to stay home and read and do homework, but he also plans these awesome, elaborate dinners for us from my mom's *Elegant Entertaining on a Budget* cookbook. Recipes he finds on the internet, too, like Pasta Aglio e Olio, which is a name we thought he made up until he proved it.

The lights are all on when I pull up into our parking strip. Our neighborhood is basically one long road, off 286, not far from my high school. Our house—small, brick, blue shutters—is at the end of that road, which pretty much just stops at an endless and weedy dirt lot. Mase and I used to pretend it was part of our yard. The real yard is small, with a telephone pole in the bottom half, and we don't have grass per se, but a dry bit of once-lawn. The Bransons, our neigh-bors, somehow always have green grass (and an actual car-port), and Wilson goes over there and rolls on his back in it, like he's found the luxury spa. From our roof you can see the Paris, Texas, Eiffel Tower with the cowboy hat on it; don't ask me how I know.

It's nine-thirty, but when I open the door, Wilson leaps up and scurries around, trying to convince me he was on duty the whole time. He's getting older, and his hearing isn't what it used to be. Mom got him from Shelley when I was in first grade and she and Dad got divorced. I wanted to name him Flower and Mase wanted to name him Doggie, so Mom wisely took the reins and named him Wilson Phillips, after another music group she saw in concert when she was younger. She still wears the (pretty ratty, honestly) concert T-shirt to bed—CALIFORNIA REUNION TOUR 2004. She said this was right after a boy named Donny Osmond broke up with her, which is supposed to be the funny part. I guess it's the real name of a superstraight religious boy singer who was popular a long time ago, and her Donny was skinny and cruel and smoked pot. This isn't as funny to me as it is to her, but I like the part of the story where she's at the concert and the three women are singing "Hold On." Their high, clear voices bring her to her feet, and she's singing with her girlfriends and with the whole crowd, and she's suddenly happier than she's ever been in her life until then.

The house still smells like dinner. Something meat, some-thing onion. I don't get the rising-elevator feeling on that one, only a rush of supreme hunger. No smell makes me actually race to the bathroom to puke like you see in the movies.

One day I want to see a movie where puking does not mean being pregnant or drunk, just something normal, like the flu or a bad burrito. I also want to see someone throw up without another person holding their hair back. I personally have never experienced this clearly popular phenomenon and would hate it if someone did it to me, but this is apparently a sign of True Love. Over these past two weeks, I *have* felt a little queasy when I've woken up, though. But couldn't this just be my mind being afraid after no period, no period, no period? This lack of throwing up is one thing that gives me hope. Also, my periods are irregular sometimes. A lot of times. The internet says this could be stress, and yeah, what a hamster wheel *that* is—no period causes stress causes no period. I don't feel transformed. I don't look transformed. I keep checking, but my body looks pretty much like it always does.

"Hey, Ives!" Mom calls.

"Hey! Just a sec!" I race to my room before Mom or Mason sees me, and I shove my backpack in my closet. The TV is on. I hear the microwave door open and slam and the hum of the glass plate circling around. I pull my sundress off over my head and unhook my bra first thing, like any reasonable person. But ow. Ow, ow. The putting on and taking off of the bra is painful, and the tingling at the sides of my breasts shoots zaps of alarm and kills all hope just like that because, sure, breasts hurt before you get your period, but not like *this*.

Loose pajamas on. I walk down the flat, dingy carpet in the hall, past the mark on the wall where Mase once threw a Frisbee, and I cross the cool, chipped linoleum of the kitchen floor. Mom removes the plate from the microwave. "Mediterranean kebabs." She smiles.

"Thanks for dinner, Mase!" I yell to my brother, who's been swallowed by our old floral couch. He's listening to three contestants prepare meals with challenging ingredients. I hear the words "fermented scallops" and "reindeer pâté" and hope to never hear those words again.

"No problemo," he shouts back. It's a leftover phrase from the year he got into magic and called himself Mr. Mysterioso. He wore an old satin pillowcase for a cape and made things disappear with a flourish, using words like *hoco poco* and *abrocadabro,* putting his own spin on tradition.

"It's really good," Mom says. "More rice in the fridge, if you want."

Mom sets the plate down in front of me on the laminated place mat featuring a map of the world. It's a funny thing to look down at every night, since I've lived my whole life in this house. Same yellow clock in the kitchen that runs five minutes behind, even with new batteries. Same floral couch, same coffee table with the white ghost-rings from various glasses and cups. Same salt and pepper shakers that no one uses, in the shape of chef heads. A house in a town where I can count the exact number of seconds—*tick tick tick*—for the stoplights on Main Street to turn from red to green. Where I think the very same thoughts at the very same places: how cool it would be if the Grand Theater still showed movies, and how sad that there's only a blank circle instead of a clock on the tower of the R.F. Scott Building. I know the exact week in late August that our air conditioner will breathe a sigh of exhaustion and quit, causing my mom to say, *God, I miss the ocean.*

What would it be like to be one of those kids whose parents move every few years, like my boyfriend, Lorenzo? He and his dad moved here from Southern California last fall, and before that, Idaho, and before that, Montana. He says it's hard to make friends, and they kept him back a year when they moved to California, which was embarrassing, but he seems so self-sufficient. He's as quietly capable as those tools you get at the army surplus store on Main, with various little foldout knives and a screwdriver and a bottle opener. If those tools had gorgeous eyes and a mouth you couldn't stop staring at.

My mom and dad came to Paris after they got married. To my dad, Texas is home, but Mom grew up in Oregon, where they met. When my dad's parents died and left him some money, he bought a T-Mobile store over on Lamar, where he worked when Mase and I were little. I only remember a spinning stool and how boring it was when we had to visit. He and Mom got divorced just before the store shut and he went bankrupt. He needed a *fresh start* and moved to Odessa, and my mom got *stuck* here, her word. We started using her last name to make things easier, since the three of us were together. *Easy* is a point of view, though, because the name change is something my dad might never forgive us for, even if we were just kids. Now we only see him for a few weeks in the summer and over Thanksgiving weekend, so sometimes he forgets what grade we're in, and sometimes we forget that he used to tuck us in at night.

Paris is a funny place for Mom to end up. Grandma Lottie, Mom, that whole side of my family—they aren't religious, and here, Christianity is as common as hot sauce. And just like hot sauce, it can either add a nice touch or be overpowering enough to make your eyes water. *They've got us surrounded,* Mom says, which is literally true. Heading toward our street, you pass City of Hope Church of God, Life Horizons Baptist Church, and Fellowship Pointe Christian, and just beyond us is New Redeemer Christian. I sometimes feel like I'm faking it when I say people-pleasing stuff like *I'm blessed* or *yeah, absolutely* when anyone advises me to *just pray about it,* even if I *am* blessed and I *do* pray about it. Me, I *want* to believe. I try to. Belief is so great and reassuring; a *team* of believers is, too, especially last year when Mom had breast cancer and everyone kept telling us, *We're praying for you.* The ladies of New Redeemer brought us all this food after her surgery, and Rick and Jeanie Branson sat with Mason and me at the hospital.

Belief can be hard, though. Maybe especially here, because things keep wrecking it. Like Faith and Nate and the swearing, or the times during Mom's illness when Mrs. Euwing would say, *Just give it to God.* This was honestly confusing, in my opinion, since if we're going that route, he's the one who gave it to her. So giving it back—it's basically cancer hot potato.

The biggest thing that makes believing hard is other believers. *That* thought—it sends a bunch of images through my mind like my dad's old slide projector, so I unplug that machine in my head, and fast.

The kebabs have squares of chicken and a translucent

chunk of onion and a slice of zucchini all layered up on a chopstick from the collection of them jammed in the back of the silverware drawer, along with cellophane packages of plastic forks and fast-food napkins. You have to work hard to get them off, but finally, success. "Yum," I say, loud enough for Mason to hear. Dad would tell me not to talk with my mouth full, but Mom doesn't. She plunks some ice in a glass for me and stands at the sink to fill it, looking out the kitchen window at the moon. You can really see the stars out here, too, not like in Dallas or Fort Worth or even Odessa.

"I can get that," I tell her.

"I want to." She smiles again.

We used to have twin dark ponytails that reached our shoulders, but her hair is only recently long enough to pull back again. It's a baby ponytail laced with silver. She wipes her hands on her sweatpants, and she's wearing her old Madonna concert T-shirt, with the swirling word RE-INVENTION on it. Madonna is on her hands and knees like a cat, and she has the tall, elaborate hair of a Renaissance queen. The T-shirt lies flat against my mom's chest now, and that silver in her hair seems to be increasing by the day, along with those envelopes of medical bills. I can't tell her what's going on. If this is the situation I'm in . . . I just can't. She's been through so much. She still looks so tired.

"What's wrong?" she asks.

"Nothing," I answer, but my eyes water. I open my mouth to speak, but no words come out. I feel so emotional, though this isn't unusual, not at all, not for any of us after last year. The way I was just looking at her, with care and worry—that isn't unusual, either.

"Oh, honey." Mom puts her arms around me. Her shirt still smells a little like bacon from Mason's festive Breakfast for Dinner last night. "It's okay. I'm fine. It's all good."

It's such a *fragile* thing to say. *All good,* a soap bubble, lasting seconds if you're lucky. I look down at my kebab, and below that, my plate, and below that, the world. All those continents and countries and cities, not just Paris. Is it so much to ask, to want to see the planet you were born on? "You miss the ocean so much. We should just move," I say. Think of it. Think of all the *choices* out there. Available, you know. Right there, just because you're human and deserve them.

"Ives . . . you don't have to fix any longings of mine."

"I'm not. It's just always so fun when we go."

"Yeah . . ." The word drifts away like a dream. "I can't afford to move, Ives. You know that. This house isn't worth much, but it's paid for. And foolish me did not finish college, which will all be different for *you.*" Did not finish college because she met my dad. He played guitar, and *if I had a dime for every woman whose life was yanked off track by a guy playing guitar, I'd have enough money to get us out of Paris.* Me going to college is her deepest desire, too. She wants it bad, for me to fulfill my dreams of maybe seeing some other places besides here. Music was her world, but she wants me to have the real one. And my job at Euwing's is a freeway heading straight toward it, no detours. Minimum wage somewhere else is an unpaved road that could take me years, if ever.

"Grandma Lottie *wants* us out there with her. How many times has she offered to help?"

Mom makes a face. Help is rescue is weakness is no self-respect. That's not who we are. *We,* especially the females of our family.

I think of Grandma Lottie's house on the beach, and Aunt Betts's house, too, on that river, which we've visited a few times. It feels so wide open there. "Hey, maybe you'd walk into Rockaway Auto Supply and Repair and meet the love of your life."

Mom scoffs. "Right."

It's a joke, and I knew she'd do that very thing—scoff and roll her eyes. Rockaway Auto Supply and Repair was the shop Grandma Lottie and Grandpa Larry owned before Grandpa Larry died. Usually, that's all I have to say, and people know what it is. Yep, that cute place covered in hub-caps in *Rockaway Weekend,* the megahit romantic comedy from nineteen ninety-whatever. The very one in that iconic scene where Julia Jane Ford walks in and spots Jon J. Roberts wearing that leather jacket. He's suggestively cranking a wrench on the engine of a motorcycle as their eyes meet. Everyone *loves* that scene. People make memes of it, so it's kind of fun to brag about, and Grandma Lottie has the framed film poster in her house. Their shop became a tourist spot afterward, and still is. That movie is super corny if you watch it now. But I've got to admit, even though she's wearing that dress with the hilarious shoulder pads and her hair is nineties big and crimped, and even though he'd get fired in real life for staring at her like that, not saying a word, you feel something. You understand why that scene has *lasted* when so many others have just disappeared. There's this deep and magnetic energy between them, magic, and for a few moments you're certain that love is the one most powerful and forever thing.

Still, a lot of the jokes in that movie are just plain offensive now, about boobs, and women, and what women really want, and guy characters who make you wonder why it's only called sexual "harassment," a word that makes it sound like a pesky annoyance instead of a nightmare. Every time we watch it, Mom reminds us that movies aren't real life, especially not romantic comedies.

"Movies aren't real life, especially not romantic comedies," she says now.

I groan the way you do when you know someone too well. Besides, I figured that out on my own, trust me.

"And, what, honestly? You'd move to Oregon and leave *Lorenzo*?" She pats her heart as if it's throbbing. She wasn't sure about him at first, mostly because he's a senior and already eighteen and I'm a junior, but now she adores him.

I wave my hand in front of my face like it's too hot, because damn, Lorenzo. I mean, come on. Those dark curls of his, let alone those brown eyes, pools of sweetness. You know when people claim that nice guys can't be sexy? Are you kidding? Who thought that up? It's some BS fed to us by not-nice guys, probably. Plus, I'm sorry to say, nice guys are equally capable of breaking your heart. Dread rises again, because I think of the conversation Lorenzo and I have to have, and fast.

In the living room a commercial plays. A new drug to ask your pharmacist about. Warnings about things going from bad to worse. I change the subject before Mom sees any truth in my eyes. "Madonna, huh," I say.

" 'Like a virgin!' " She sings into her fist microphone, shimmies her shoulders. " 'Touched for the ve-ry first time!' " She does an impressive slide in her ankle socks. Her hands and feet are always cold now, no matter how hot it is.

Virgins and mothers and sex and its troubles. It's everywhere.

"She looks scary." I point at Madonna.

"Rawr," my mom says, and claws the air. "Fierce."

It's two-seventeen a.m. Two-eighteen. Two-twenty-five. I can practically hear that box in the bag in my backpack in my closet, sending out silent radar rings of distress. I make two fists and dig my nails into my skin, because how, how, how could I have let this happen? Thoughts of Tess and the pages I forced myself to read before bed loop in my mind. *Why, I danced and laughed only yesterday! To think that I was such a fool!*

I've finally reached the point where I can't stand another hopeful and then disappointing trip to the bathroom. Or another moment where I'm sure that I feel some cinch of a cramp, some dull ache in my lower back, and (TMI here) shove one finger up, but nope.

I open my mom's secondhand, thirdhand laptop with the Arcade Fire sticker on it and read how to do the test for the hundredth time. You're supposed to wait to pee on the stick until morning.

This *is* morning. Two-thirty-eight is morning. If I wait until seven, is it more morning? But I'll have privacy now, no Mase suddenly knocking on the door to brush his teeth and floss, which he does with the diligence of an overachieving dental hygienist. This is how he is about most things.

A wave of nausea most definitely hits. Nerves, but who knows. I could be making myself nauseous thinking about being nauseous. I swear, hands have memories, because I feel it in my palm and on my fingers, cold and slippery, relief and disgust then, horror and disgust now. Over and over in my head, horror and disgust.

I better not wake anyone up, that's all I can say, and my mother is a light sleeper. I step carefully to the closet. The zipper of my pack sounds like a train coming down a track, and the cellophane of that box like a crackling, blazing fire. I ignore the booklet. If there were a quiz on it at school tomorrow, I'd ace it. All I need is the stick.

When the stick is in my hand, when I'm stepping oh so quietly down the hall, a tiny door opens in a distant corner of my mind, and an awful and humiliating scene spills out. I just feel so mad, furious, at myself mostly. I slam that mental door shut because I can't deal with all the feelings, only the one I'm having now, pure anxiety.

Our bathroom is a vision in pink—the countertop is white tiles with a pink edge, and the tub is pink, a favorite color, obviously, of the former owners, and now we just have to forget to notice. The shower curtain features a row of cheerful penguins, and there are too many bottles of shampoo with only one squirt left. Mom and maybe Mase and I, too, have a hard time throwing them away. It's probably nicer to see lots of choices and options, even if some are basically empty.

I hike up my sleep shirt. It has a cartoon corgi riding a whale on it. Faith gave it to me for Christmas a few years ago, after the Great Corgi Dispute, where she said they were animals favored by royalty, and I said they were bread loaves with legs. I yank down my underwear. Nothing noteworthy to report about those. From where I sit, I can read the cross-stitched serenity prayer above the light switch, with some of the important words in bold swirls. *GOD, grant me the SERENITY to accept the things I cannot change, the COURAGE to change the things I can,* et cetera. I think they use it in Alcoholics Anonymous, though none of us are alcoholics (maybe my mom's last boyfriend, Terry), and, as I said, not particularly religious. But Shelley made it for Mom last year during her breast cancer treatment, and Mom says that stuff people make by hand is love you can touch.

I focus on the penguins, and for a moment I close my eyes and imagine a life where everything turns out okay.

I pee. A stream of pee to tell my future. Then I turn the stick facedown on the counter, and I wait. Maybe it's not supposed to be upside down. A new worry. I wash my hands and dry them on my towel for the week, the big beach one with a palm tree.

I retch into the toilet, but this is definitely nerves.

Sometimes you have to wait for it, that moment when the delaying becomes more painful than the doing.

I turn it over.

I knew it.

I knew it, I knew it.

I did. I'm just so mad, mad, *mad* at myself for all that wasted hope. Wasted hope is the worst, like you've been duped and tricked and betrayed by your own horrible self. I was right, so right, to feel that doom-dread because, yes, it's mine. Here it is, the truth, sinking like a stone. There's no doubt. It says it right on the stick—a minus sign means not pregnant; a plus sign means pregnant. And what I'm seeing is a big blue plus.

I hurry back to my room and close my door on Wilson, who woke up to see if I was okay. Dog worry will only make me feel worse. God, grant me REAL ANSWERS and SOLUTIONS and A PLAN, but, yeah, COURAGE, too.

Touching that stick is gross, but I can't throw it away, not now. I can't risk Mom or Mase seeing it. I hide it in my *Tess* book and stuff that in my backpack. I hate myself so much, I can barely stand it. I make those two tight fists and squeeze again, my nails digging into my palms, the way Missy the lovebird grips her perch.

3

LUCKILY, MY MOM IS IN THE SHOWER WHEN WE LEAVE in the morning, so I only have to shout a goodbye. Her laser eyes that can spot a problem or a sadness or a bad mood a mile away are safely behind the bathroom door and the penguin shower curtain, but not forever. And Mason is too busy trying to annoy me by messing around with our shit car's shit radio to notice that I am different now. When I whack his arm to get him to stop, I do it too hard, and it feels kind of good, I hate to admit.

But only for a second, because Mase says, "God, Ivy," and his eyes look hurt. He rubs his arm. Guilt is everywhere, in everything you do. Shit person in a shit car, I tell myself.

"Just stop, okay?" I say to Mase, like he's done something awful, when only one of us has. We ride the rest of the way in silence. When we pull up to the drop-off curb of New Jefferson Junior High, he gets out, then ducks his head back into Mr. Smiley to retrieve his backpack. He quickly checks my face for forgiveness and doesn't see any. My face is hard and unsmiling because I am a crappy and horrible person, and selfish, and just generally awful, letting him think any of this is because of him. He does something totally, one-hundred-percent Mason DeVries: he unzips his backpack and takes out his new gel pen—the one he bought with his own money, the one I said I really liked because it wrote so smooth—and he tosses it onto the seat.

"You can have it," he says, and then shuts the door, and when I watch the vulnerable back of his head with that piece of hair that won't stick down descending into the mean, viper-filled halls of junior high, I burst into tears. I mean, I'm sobbing there in the drop-off lane, and I'm not sure if I've ever cried this hard in my whole life, except when Mom told us about her cancer. I'm practically bent over the steering wheel when some parent honks, and a parent volunteer in a neon vest comes striding over, because you're not supposed to linger there. They police their little turf like it's the airport and we're potential bombers.

Power, power everywhere. Like, everyone wants power over someone or something, somehow. I wave my hand, like, *okay, okay,* and move on. God, I've got to go to school now, how, how? My face is a mess, mascara streaking down, looking like one of the singers in that oldies band KISS that my mom likes. Back in the day, they were a heavy-metal band, supposedly. This is hard to imagine when she plays their songs and dances around singing, *I was made for loving you, bay-bee,* and sticks her tongue out like a lizard, which the lead singer apparently used to do. *Not a* lizard, she says. *It's supposed to be* sexy, and I shrug because I don't get this at all, maybe because I'm inexperienced, in spite of the current state of affairs.

I pull over into New Jefferson Junior High's visitors' parking and fix my face. Is that even me in the mirror? I think those are my eyes, but I'm not sure. I have "a bundle of cells" (according to some sites online) inside me, and it makes me think of the bundle of cells inside my mom last year, and suddenly, bundles of cells seem like the most important things on earth, even if you don't necessarily want them in you. Bundles of cells are life-or-death. It feels a bit like an alien invasion, something happening in me without my permission, full steam ahead, whether I want it or not, same as The Beast, which is what we called my mom's cancer.

I get myself together enough to drive the few blocks to New Jefferson High, with its big steps flanked by two flags, American and Texas. The choir is getting onto a school bus for a field trip, and the parking lot has a ton of shit cars. *Most* cars, you don't know where they've been or what they've been through, like Grandma Lottie says. So I try not to ever bully some poor vehicle by laughing at it or writing *Wash Me* on it with my finger. Well, Jason Maxwell's car isn't shit. It's an Acura FLT. I just made those initials up, if I'm being honest, but it has initials after the name, and probably has seats that warm your butt. It sits there all shiny gold, reminding you of coins and jewelry and the faucets in his house. His dad is a big shot at City of Hope Church of God, and his house is fancy, too. The one time I was in there, I saw the TV, as big as a movie theater screen, and his parents' huge bed, so tall that it had steps to climb up to it, like they're the Paris, Texas, king and queen. It reminded me of that story "The Princess and the Pea," where the princess can still feel a tiny pea under a ton of mattresses, because even though Jason has all the money a person could need, he still seems constantly irritated. That story always bugs me for some unknown reason. Maybe because it makes me think of those clothing tags that make you itch, the ones you try to cut off while you're still wearing the shirt.

After I get out, I peek inside Lorenzo's truck, and love whooshes through me. There's a Stephen King novel he's been reading forever, and a crushed can of Orange Crush, and *I* have a crush, at the very least. I spot that hoodie that's always in the back, the zip-up kind. *In case you need it?* I joked once on some eighty-five-degree day. Where he lived in Southern California, it could get cold at night, and he didn't even get my joke. *No, in case you need it,* he said. There's also that solo, beat-up Converse on the back-seat floor, rescued roadside because it looked so lonely. Yes, Lorenzo is the type of guy who feels sorry for an abandoned shoe and the single lost sock and the mushed grape no one eats. He once broke down crying at a flattened gray fox we saw on the highway. *They find a partner when they're young, and they mate for life,* he said, though he could barely speak. He knows a lot about a lot of things, maybe from living in so many places. We just looked at each other, love flowing between us, and grief, too, for that other fox out there somewhere, alone now.

All of this . . . Well, it makes my heart burst but squeeze with anguish, too. In a matter of hours, I may lose him.

I basically zone out during first period. Statistics—it's easy for your mind to go numb anyway. I willingly drown in the white noise of Mr. Bryson's voice, *blah blah blah sampling distributions,* and in the M. C. Escher poster behind him. It's called *Relativity,* and it just might be one of the most distressing pieces of art ever, with all of these staircases leading to nowhere and faceless figures trying to get somewhere. Up one set of stairs, Lorenzo ditches me. Down another, he stays. It's all anxious disconnection.

Period two, Advanced Plant and Soil Science (don't ask), and period three, Anatomy and Physiology, which tick past in a similar haze. Peyton is in anatomy, though, so I force myself to talk to her like normal. It's hard work, pretending your life isn't falling apart. We've known each other practically forever, but we've been best friends since sixth grade, when we both had the scary Mr. Tremain with the mean mouth and beetle eyes. Peyton got close with Faith in ninth grade, when Peyton's parents started going to their same church, and now the three of us hang out. Peyton seems closer to Faith than to me lately, but I'm closer to Lorenzo, so I try not to mind.

We have a quiz coming up on the nervous system, and it's going to be easy to remember that there are more nerve cells in the human brain than stars in the Milky Way, because all of mine are ablaze. Luckily, Shayna Julio and I already did our final oral report, so we can kick back while Peyton and Noah Alvarez, who Peyton likes, are up today. Apparently, gray matter versus white matter is a pretty racy topic, judging by their body language. I can't understand why she likes him, honestly. He makes fart noises whenever he sees Fiona Sanchez sit down because she farted during the second-grade play a million years ago. It's cruel, and he hangs out with cruel people, like Jason Maxwell. Another opinion I have is that cruelty always has minions, individuals who are secretly mean but get the courage to show who they really are because some creep makes them feel brave.

At lunch I finally get to see him, Lorenzo. God, the sight of him is a relief and a panic both. He's wearing his softest pair of Levi's, and that American flag shirt that his dad gave him to help him fit in. Lorenzo's not sure how he feels about that flag. *When you see me wear it,* he told me, *know I wear it ironically,* which is something he shouldn't say to anyone else.

He smiles so big when he sees me in the cafeteria. He already has his tray with the burger and the Tater Tots and the small grassy hill of salad, damp with Italian dressing. We sit with my friends (now his friends), even though he's a senior and I'm a junior. He doesn't care about that stuff; he just doesn't. It's probably all that moving around and the fact that he's graduating in two weeks, but I really admire that, how he doesn't worry about what other people think.

"Ironic," I say to Lorenzo, and tug his sleeve after he sits down next to me. Our friends leave us two spots at the end of the table, because *no one likes that much PDA with their food,* according to Megan. I've known most of the people at this table since elementary school. Megan still drinks the same chocolate milk she's had since second grade, and Madeleine still sticks her carrots in her yogurt like it's dip. Over at another table are the drinker-partyers like Quentin Giles and Emory Elias and their friends, who look bored and hungover as they slump over their sack lunches. Shawna Casings and Fiona Sanchez and a few other quiet kids sit closest to the exit, and Jason Maxwell, Hope Mathias, Chase Winston, Noah Alvarez, Olivia Kneeley, and their friends are at the table by the window, farthest from the trash cans. We pretty much all stay on our own ice floes in the Arctic of New Jefferson High, and we rarely mingle outside of them, either, aside from some rare event like Jason Maxwell's party. Peyton was sure Noah got us invited to that, but I think they just wanted as many people as possible to pay the ten bucks they were charging.

Peyton might make it onto the other ice floe, though. She's a penguin and they are polar bears, but she's still hanging around and talking to Noah. Her cheeks are pink. Faith has second lunch, so she'll have to be filled in on these recent developments.

"Hey, you," Lorenzo says. He slips an arm around me and rests his hand low on my hip, but I take it off. He doesn't seem bothered by that. With Lorenzo, not much can cause a fight, unlike my mom's ex-boyfriend Terry, who used to get pissed off at every little rejection. He once bought Mom a Subway sandwich and got all threatened when she took the pickles out. *You said you liked pickles, and now you don't like pickles?* When a guy is insecure about a condiment, you know you're in trouble.

Then again, maybe Lorenzo and I don't fight *yet*. We've only been officially together for a month. I've known him since March, the night of the New Jefferson Junior High Science Fair. Mase made a battery out of a potato, and Lorenzo's little sister, Chloe, made a fingerprint kit, and when Lorenzo and I met at the treats table, reaching for oatmeal cookies at the same time, our hands grazed, and our hearts became two baking-soda volcanoes, for sure. Especially after he said, *Anything but the lemon ones,* and I said, *I am in one-hundred-percent agreement.* We started texting and being kind of flirty afterward, and then a month ago, he kissed me at Peyton's track meet, and we became a couple.

Peyton finally shows up at our table, all red-faced and embarrassed, and Madeleine says, "I love when love is all around me." Peyton shoves her shoulder and says "noooo" in a way that means *yessss.* The smell of burger plus some hard-boiled-egg gross sandwich thing Nate is eating makes me scrunch up my nose. I pick off parts of my bagel. I make a bagel river heading to a Saran Wrap mountain.

"You okay?" Lorenzo asks.

I look into his brown eyes, and I fall. I fall *into* them, and they, he, catches me. I say a bunch of stuff with *my* eyes without saying a word.

"Oh no. Is it The Beast? Is it back?" he whispers.

The Beast is a name that happened accidentally. Last year, when Mason was in sixth grade, he had to do one of those assignments that are both thoughtless and snoopy if you ask me, a total ruse to find out the dirt on your crappy homelife: one page on The Hardest Thing You've Had to

Overcome. He wrote about Mom: *She has beast cancer.* We were deep in it then. Mom's skin looked yellowish, and a chunk of her hair actually fell onto our take-out pizza, one of the only times I saw her cry, and hard. Mase's teacher, Mrs. Kay, underlined the word in red as a misspelling, but when he brought it home, Mom told him that, somehow, he'd given it the best name ever, and that she was calling it that from now on. He felt proud, you could tell. Mom was mad about that red line.

I give my head a little shake, and then I stare into Lorenzo's endless-pool again and make mine say, *It's serious.*

He looks so worried, my heart breaks. "You're not working today, right?" he asks.

"Yeah."

"Meet at the tower to talk? After we drop the kids off?"

After we drop the kids off . . . For one second I imagine us married and doing regular life together, even though he means Chloe and Mase. We'd drop the kids—where? At school or soccer practice or something, and maybe we'd go back to our own home, and take our clothes off and get in bed together. All I can picture as "home" is the one I've always lived in, and then I erase that and somehow make it much fancier, like Jason Maxwell's. Which is how you definitely know it's a fantasy, because if we got married now, there wouldn't likely be college for either of us. We'd both be working at We Pack and living in some tiny apartment, if we were lucky, like Faith's sister, Harmony, and her husband, Abraham. It's funny to call him "husband" when I can still just remember him standing around by his locker. They got married right out of school and had a baby, like, six months after, though no one ever mentions that part. Apparently, God thinks premarital sex isn't so bad if you marry the guy. Now they all live at the Belle Vista apartments, the ones that used to be a motor inn long ago. The sign out front still says HEATED POOL, COLOR TV, A/C.

"Okay," I say. Lorenzo rubs his hand up my leg underneath the table. Only a few weeks ago, it was amazing when he did that. No one could see, and it was thrilling, and I wanted him so bad. That was the secret I had then, wanting him, same as the song lyrics that rhyme *desire* with *fire*. But now I just take his hand and hold it and notice that Peyton's looking at me funny. She knows me so well, and now her eyebrows are down, like *What's going on?* I try to look relaxed and smile, and then make a face at her, eyes open as wide as I can, sticking my tongue out, and she shakes her head like I'm being immature.

Lorenzo feels my distance and removes his hand again. He dunks one of his Tater Tots into a splotch of ketchup distractedly. He thinks it's strange that no one really kisses in the halls here, or by their locker, or whatever. Even in Montana in junior high, and definitely in California, they did, and it was no big deal, he says. Except maybe that time the vice-principal caught him and his girlfriend Marissa in the stairwell, her shirt unbuttoned, thanks so much for telling me. I prefer not to think about Marissa (blond, pretty, her house on some horsey ranch—an actual ranch, wow, spotted on social media), given how close they were until he moved out here. We're so unequal that way, Marissa and me, but Lorenzo and me, too—him being my first real boyfriend, if you don't count Caleb Baylor. Caleb and I hung out for a while and went to homecoming together. He also asked me to go to a concert, which turned out to be a Jesus concert at his church, and not a concert-concert, like Mom loves. At the intermission the preacher got all pumped and excited, asking who wanted to be saved. People started hurrying down the aisles, like there wasn't a minute to lose, and, I've got to say, I almost went. You get all taken up in the energy, same as a football game, when the band's playing *We will, we will, rock you!* and you're clapping and screaming and stomping so hard the stands shake, even though you don't honestly care who wins. Those concerts, they're very popular around here. It wasn't the last one I went to.

I shake that image away, and fast. I peel my orange and take a few bites. Suddenly, I could eat ten of them. It's cool and juicy and, ugh, this must be hormones, because I almost feel all choked up about the beauty of life, how we get to have oranges and dogs and clouds, and friends like these, real friends, sitting around this table. Peyton and Madeleine are debating whether the Game of Thrones books are better than the shows, and Megan says she can't watch those because of the sloshy sounds the swords make every time they go in someone's body, and Ian is bragging to Nate about his parents going to the Bahamas, and Nate has a stomach-flopping splotch of mayonnaise at the corner of his mouth. The bell rings, and Peyton says, *Nate!* and rubs her finger at her own mouth like she's his mother.

Mother.

Parents.

Sloshy sounds of swords in bodies. The words don't stop.

Beside me Lorenzo's face is serious. He looks like he's doing everything in his power to remain seated and not run away.

"It's still there, Nate! Geez, you're a pig," Peyton says as we gather up our trash and head to class.

"You're so mean to pigs, Pey," I joke. It just pops out, and, wow, it's such a relief. Parts of you must stay in there, no matter what. Maybe the me I am won't be gone forever, though she feels like she's disappearing fast.

"The place they're staying even has a swim-up bar," Ian brags to Nate.

A swim-up bar. Man, would I ever like to see something like that. The world can seem so big and so small at the same time. Sometimes, you can get to wondering if all those other places are really even out there.

❤️

I manage to get through the next period, Floral Design. Floral Design is what happens when you have trouble signing on during your registration hour and have to go visit Miss Marvelle to fix your schedule—ditto for Advanced Plant and Soil Science. After that, Advanced English III, my favorite class. Ms. La Costa still wears nylons (we love you, but it's time to move on from those) and a prim, often disapproving smile, but she's my favorite. Sometimes she taps her fingertips on my desk as she passes and smiles at me like we have a shared secret. She writes compliments like *Wow!* and

Excellent writing! on my papers, too, and even asked me to stay after class one day to tell me she thought I had *real potential* in a writing field. I almost started to cry, it was so nice. I pretty much just stood there because it was hard to even talk.

Ms. La Costa is maybe like a book herself, where you only see the cover, even if that's true of most of us. You can tell, though, that there's more to her than her serious skirts and layered gray hair and sensible shoes. Last year she got in huge trouble for hanging a pride flag in her room— parents complained, and she had to take it down. And she drives a shit car, too. I saw her once in the parking lot with a dead battery. Our vice-principal, the Rock, used her own jumper cables to get Ms. La Costa's car going again.

"Okay, peons," Ms. La Costa says. She's handing back a quiz we took two days ago about the book's symbols. She makes a scrunched *What happened?* face when she places mine on my desk. I got three right out of eight. I feel so tired. I want to rest my head right down on the desk and sleep.

"Pee on," Noah Alvarez says.

Peyton's jealous that he lives on my street and that we have this class together, but all I can see is Noah in Jason Maxwell's rec room that night at the party. You wouldn't think that something like a plate of nachos could change the course of your life, but it can. That's what Jason was holding when he walked in. He didn't see my sandal and tripped. He actually went flying, like in those movies where someone stumbles while carrying a wedding cake or something, only it was a slab of nachos. It slid right off and landed upside down on the carpet, and Jason practically did a face-plant, his elbow landing in sour cream. Noah laughed so hard, he was bent over, and Hope Mathias was laughing, too, and Jason's face turned the shade of a bad sunburn. *What the fuck?* Jason said, and glared at me. *What the actual fuck?* I apologized and said it was an accident, but he was seething as he and Hope mopped up the red stain of salsa on his parents' carpet. I felt bad, and Noah kept pretending to fall to get laughs. Jason looked like he was going to punch him. He looked *pissed* as he stood there, holding a glob of wet paper towels stained pink. Peyton wanted to stay when Faith and I left. On our way out the door, Jason looked at me with utter hatred and said, *You're going to regret this.*

I regretted this.

Oh, how I regretted this. Here's what I know for sure. When a guy with a big ego gets humiliated, you better watch out.

Ms. La Costa writes *THEMES* on the whiteboard, and under that the numbers one, two, three, and four. I unzip my pack and reach in to retrieve the book. There's no big teen pregnancy movie scene right then, where the stick falls out and everyone sees and I become a pariah like Tess and have to escape to fight for my life. No, I'm just a regular girl, sick with dread, stuck in a crisis that feels unsolvable. That *is* unsolvable. I slide the stick out carefully, and when class is over, I tuck it back into the book.

· I'm scared that I'm like Tess, ruined forever. More of a problem than a person, already broken, her future sealed.

Those themes, those words on the whiteboard next to

the numbers—they could be written on my own skin, with a piece of barbed wire and drops of blood.

Pride.

Purity and Fallen Women.

Injustice.

Fate.

4

IT'S ACTUALLY KIND OF NICE OUT THERE BY THE EIFFEL Tower. Peyton's cousin from the UK thought it was laughable when we brought him, because it's so much shorter than the real thing. He said it's ten times smaller than the one in Las Vegas, too, which was pretty rude, if you ask me. Another opinion I have—if you visit someone, you should remember that their town is their home. And, okay, it's only about two and a half flagpoles high, but so what.

The tower has a red cowboy hat on top, and there's a long brick walkway leading to it, and trees all around, and well-kept grass. There's a war memorial nearby, and the convention center is there, too. It's all on the outskirts of town, which is why we like to meet there. You mostly only see tourists taking photos, and not even many of those. When you lie on your back and gaze skyward, if you ignore the red cowboy hat perched at a carefree angle at the top, you can almost imagine that you're in the real, actual Paris, in spite of the fact that you're surrounded by a huge parking lot where kids come to spin out and burn rubber in their fathers' trucks.

I'm there first, so I head to our favorite tree at the far-right leg of the tower. In an oblong circle of shade, I spread out the blue-and-orange Houston Astros blanket, the one that Dad left behind when he and Mom got divorced. He's the only one in our family who likes sports. Some part of my brain refuses to remember whether the Astros are basketball or baseball, the way Mom can forget east and west, and Mason can forget how to spell *friend*. Then again, I don't watch any games, Mom misses the Oregon Coast, and Mase is an introverted kid, even though he always says, *Alone doesn't mean lonely.*

I hear Lorenzo's truck before I see it. That Avalanche rumbles like an avalanche. Lorenzo parks next to Mr. Smiley. I wave to him when he spots me, but he only lifts one hand, like he's swearing to tell the whole truth and nothing but the truth.

He lopes across the grass, a goofy gazelle. Lorenzo is tall, and sometimes his limbs seem to have a mind of their own. Damn, it's so awkward and sexy, and I feel so sad because I'm about to destroy him.

Lorenzo is carrying two Gatorade bottles, still united in beverage matrimony by their plastic rings, and it's my favorite flavor, orange. He's also got a package of those expensive Pepperidge Farm cookies, the ones that sit in fancy, ruffly paper cups. They're my favorite kind, too, Geneva, oval crunchies with chocolate and nuts, but I like all the ones named after cities, Brussels and Milano, too. Lorenzo's face, though—it looks strained. His eyes are some mix of horror and pleading.

And I don't know how to explain it, but I suddenly feel a calm resolve. Maybe it's just relief that someone else will finally know and that I won't be alone in this circle of hell. I remember after my mom told me and Mase about The Beast, she said, *I was so afraid to tell you both, but I feel so much better now that you know,* and I totally see what she meant.

"Hey," he says.

"Hey."

Lorenzo folds his legs underneath him and sits on the Astros blanket. "I brought . . ." He swallows. He's having a hard time speaking, like maybe he might burst into tears. He's not one of those guys who think they shouldn't cry. He thinks it shows strength not to have to show strength.

"Um," I say. Not a particularly strong start. I pull a blade of grass and then examine it. It's beautiful, with its grass spine and grass wings. Nature is so symmetrical and perfect in ways humans never are. "I have to tell you something."

Lorenzo shakes his head, stares at the metal grid of the tower because he can't look at me. So, at first, I tell his profile, until he can't help it, and his eyes study my face. When I'm done, he flings himself up, knocking over the Gatorade bottles and scrunching up his side of the blanket. He's more upset than I've ever seen him before. Well, in the short while I've known him.

He stalks away, paces in front of the tower. Way over

here, I can still hear him. "Fuck, man! *Fuck!*" he rants, going back and forth like that old guy who hangs out by the court-house, carrying the sign that says HE IS COMING.

But then Lorenzo returns. I could understand if he didn't, but he does. I feel weirdly calm, though maybe *numb* is the better word. "Are you mad at me?" I ask.

"At *you*? No. No, of course not! I just—"

"I'm so sorry. How could I let this happen? How, how? I don't know what's wrong with me. What is *wrong* with me?" My head is in my hands. My palms make deep, dark cups, a little hand cave. I squinch my eyes hard so my mind doesn't see things I don't want it to.

"Ivy! Ives. Stop it. Stop! Do you hear me?" Lorenzo is jiggling my shoulder. Then he gently takes my chin and lifts it, and we look at each other. "I thought you were going to break up with me," he says.

"I thought *you'd* break up with *me*."

"Ives." His voice is all wobbly. "I *love* you."

"Lorenzo! No! Don't!" We've never said it before, not outright like that. We're still at the casual end of expressing our feelings, the "love yous" minus the *I*. Why does the *I* make all the difference? No idea, but it does. I don't want a pity *I*. "You don't have to say that!"

"I know I don't have to say that! It's the truth, okay? Fuck! I want you to know I'm not going anywhere. I'm here. Whatever you want, whatever you need. We'll handle this."

"We will?" I never expected a *we*. I mean, I did this. He shouldn't have to stick around.

"Yeah. We will. Have you told your mom?"

"No. Not yet."

"You've got to tell your mom! *At least.*"

"I'm going to! Okay? I thought you should know first. And I hear what you're saying, but forget it. I don't want anyone else to know. *Promise* me."

He shakes his head like I'm asking something impossible, but he says, "Promise." He puts his arms around me, and the calm slips away, and the numbness does, and maybe even a little of the fear, and a sob rises. Tears have just been piling up against that stone wall of alarm, and now they've stormed the castle. I'm soaking his T-shirt, that flag, and he keeps saying, "It's okay, it's okay," even though it isn't okay, not by a long shot.

I wipe my face with the back of my hand and stare at him hard. "I don't want to be your Converse."

"I have no idea what you're talking about."

"The one shoe. In the back of your car."

"Okay, Ives. I still don't get it, but okay."

"I don't need to be rescued. Maybe I do. I don't think so. I don't know." We sit there in silence for a second. I'm a DeVries, though. "No. *Hell* no, I don't."

"Hey, I'm way more that Converse than you are, Ives. I didn't want it to just be sitting out there, you know, alone. Lonely, whatever. I've felt that way for so long. If you're a Converse, if you're worried you are, so the fuck what. We're a pair now."

Back at our cars, he kisses me, sweet and gentle, like I'm newly breakable, which is wrong. I don't like that, because I'm me and this is temporary. I tell him this.

"Is that what you want?"

I nod. I can't say anything more. I can't even say it—*abortion*. The land is so flat here, the word might escape, roll across the ground, lift skyward and flow through every kitchen window, whispering and whispering.

He doesn't grill me or ask a million questions or give me a million of his own opinions, which he has every right to do. He only says, "Your mom would let you, right?"

"Yeah, but . . ." I shake my head because it's impossible.

"Six weeks," he says. Abortion is against the law here after that amount of time.

"Six weeks and, like, a day. At first I didn't even wonder about being late, you know? Who would even do it? It'd be a *felony*." I can't even imagine *felony*. Actually, I don't even really know what that word means compared to other crime words. I mean, I'm usually guilty of taking the last piece of leftover pizza, but that's about it.

"Then we'll figure it out. I don't know *how*. I mean, look where we are." He doesn't mean this big field with an Eiffel Tower in the middle of it. He means Texas. "I would take you . . . wherever we needed to go."

"Thank you. Really."

"Baby, you don't have to *thank* me." He's never called me *Baby* before, either, and I see him flinch after he says it. Now there are two of us in the world who'll be shot with little word arrows.

I don't answer, but I *am* thankful. Jason Maxwell, with his important dad at City of Hope Church of God, would never say, *We'll figure it out,* and neither would Jason's friend Chase Winston, or Caleb Baylor, or even our friend Ian, or a million other people. When Faith finds out, she might never speak to me again. I have no idea what Lorenzo's parents would think.

"You won't tell your parents, right?" I plead. Lorenzo's living situation is the opposite of mine—he lives with his dad, and his mom lives in San Jose. I met her once. We had dinner at Olive Garden, and she told us to order whatever we wanted, but she only got a salad. Lorenzo claims she's hard to get along with, but she was nice to me, and his dad is so quiet, I get uncomfortable around him. Once, Peyton said, *You should get your mom and Lorenzo's dad together,* but we both laughed nervously, since it was one of those ideas that's cute in the movies but would be creepy in real life.

"I promised, Ives. I always keep my promises." Lorenzo runs his hand through his hair, though, anxious. The biggest problem he had before now was not knowing what he was going to do after graduation. College, no college, job—he has no idea, and hates having no idea.

The cookies—well, you never hear what happens to the food. In the movies there's always all this extravagant-looking food, and no one ever eats. They're in a restaurant, and they order, and then someone stalks out after some fight, but what about that glorious steak or lobster or burger that'll be arriving any moment? Even if it's just a made-up movie, I worry about who will pay.

So here's what happens: Lorenzo hands me the cookies.

Everything is bad right now, so bad, but there are still nice things like cookies in ruffled cups. On my worst days I like to try to remember what's still good. He hands me the orange Gatorade, too.

"Thank you. Thank you so, so much," I say. I've been given way more than I deserve. I can only imagine how he feels about what I did.

It's hard to believe, but when Lorenzo shuts the door of his truck, I feel closer to him than ever. When he drives away, though, when he's out on the main road, I can still see him, even if he doesn't see me. One elbow sticks out from his window like a dog on his best day, but Lorenzo's face—it's stony and troubled.

5

THAT NIGHT MASE COOKS BUCATINI CARBONARA
with bacon. It's so good that I don't even drop any down to
Wilson Phillips no matter how hard he stares. At first Mase
tries to tell us that the meat is pancetta, but I know bacon
when I see it. He also doesn't like it when we say "cooks"—he
wants us to say "prepares." A few weeks ago I heard Mase
crying in his room, and when I went in and asked him what
was wrong, he said that no one in Paris understands him,
and he doesn't understand them. This other old singer my
mom likes, Leonard Cohen, sings a song called "Anthem"
that sounds kind of sad and religious, though it's hard to tell.
There's a line that says something like *Cracks are how the
light gets in.* But maybe how the light gets out, too, because
that not-understanding is a crack, and Mase is the light, and
he's going to get out of Paris, Texas, one day; I'm sure of that.

That song is playing right now as I clear the table, Leonard Cohen's voice sounding like a great old leather chair, if
a leather chair could sing. In our house, the rule is "Cooks

don't do dishes," though Mase asks us to please say *chefs* instead. I'm jamming the rest of the bucatini into a plastic container for Mom's lunch tomorrow when she waltzes into the kitchen and takes my hands for a dance.

"Mooooommmmm, stop. I want to get this done."

I also don't want her to really see me. Thankfully, Mase held the floor all during dinner, going on about one of his biggest life problems, PE. How the hurdles in the track unit are going to kill him, how Henderson Maxwell (Jason's little brother, it figures) made fun of him because Mase got a leg cramp during the long-distance run and had to sit out. How Henderson kept singing *cra-amps,* like they were period cramps. How no one ever stands up to Henderson because his dad is so important.

Period cramps. Ugh! Mom said, *Nothing is wrong with period cramps, and if he's making fun of them, he's a mean little misogynist, and tell him* that *next time.* Like anyone would. Jason and Henderson are the two little princes of the king and queen of City of Hope Church of God, the popular group of Paris. The Euwings go there, our principal does, and a bunch of our teachers do, too. The church gives money for the annual tree lighting in town and buys the uniforms for our school's sports teams and band. If I could have stood up to Jason during those post-nacho weeks when he tormented me, I wouldn't even be in this mess. Still, at dinner, Mom looked toward me for backup, and I nodded, my cheeks full of pasta because I've been so hungry. We all know Mase won't be telling Henderson that or anything else.

Now, though, danger, danger, because Mom says, "Get *this* done, my girl," and takes my hands and sways me. And, oh man, that sad old song about light sends goose bumps up my arms because it might be religious or it might not, but it definitely has that ALL OF LIFE, capital-letters feeling, where you're suddenly aware of beauty and grief and nature's majesties. And love, too. Love like the kind in that scene from *Rockaway Weekend,* which is totally corny but hits your heart anyway. Hormones swirl, and I get all emotional. My eyes fill. It's not just awfulness that's filling me, but also the swelling hope of overcoming large obstacles, and a golden wave of all that I'm grateful for right now. Life has somehow given me Lorenzo, and The Beast is in retreat, and my mom is smiling a little, her eyes closed. She's just swaying with me and listening to the music, and her small hands are in my small hands. I'm a mess because I feel their fragility, too. I'm so scared that I'm going to be what breaks her. The Beast didn't, but I might.

I also have a crack in me now, and the thought that it might ever let any light in is just too good and beautiful to be true, but what if.

That's when she pops her eyes open. It's like in the movies when someone is supposed to be dead and wakes up right in the casket. I even flinch because they seriously *pop* open, like she's been jolted with electricity. She probably has—a current of emergency has probably traveled through our hands. She always knows when something is wrong, but then again, so do we, Mase and I, with her. We're all connected like a rope, or a wire, intertwined, coiled, and this thought basically destroys me when I think about the bundle of cells and what could be but won't be.

My mother folds her eyebrows down in distrust and fear and confusion. Yeah, eyebrows can say a lot.

"Ivy?"

I don't answer.

"Ivy." Her face is serious. "Ivy, what?"

I want to lie to buy time, but we also have to hurry. And the moment is here, the one I've been dreading. It's over—at least, the secret is.

"Okay," I say.

And let me tell you, when I look in her eyes, when mine tell her that this is bad, bad, and that I am falling, she catches me, too, same as Lorenzo did. I am that slab of nachos flying in midair, and she is a plate sliding into place at just the right second. Or else she's got the biggest roll of paper towels, letting me know with a quiet determination that the mess won't be permanent. That's the way it is with us. We are family. I get it, that family can mean love, yeah, but also suffocation, or dark, buried secrets, or just plain loneliness and distance, an endless road of longing. But for us, the three DeVrieses plus Wilson Phillips, it means *I'm here.*

"Oh, honey," Mom says for the hundredth time. We've been in her bedroom for hours. She's been through the five stages of grief we learned about in health: denial, anger, bargaining, going to the kitchen, and pounding ice cream. In the movies people always eat ice cream when they're stressed or depressed, but this is one thing that actually happens in real life, too, and she even brings a spoon and the carton of Blue Bell Pecan Pralines 'n Cream—really just the last slimy, icy blob of it—into her room. Any flavor of pecan or praline is long gone, and I'm pretty sure it only tastes like old cold.

She is *sad*, God. So sad, trying to hold it together but just looking like all the work she's done from the time I was born, all the feeding and chin-wiping and crayon-drawing and show-and-telling and nightmare-soothing and sore-throat Tylenol-ing, has been a waste. Mostly like my future is gone. At least that's what I'm imagining she's thinking.

And I am guilty. So guilty. Disappointing your parents can feel horribly permanent, I'll tell you that much. Right now as I sit at the edge of my mom's bed on a bedspread of flowers, and she sits beside me, rubbing and rubbing the bridge of her nose, I feel *made* of guilt. My head is guilt and so is my heart, and my arms and legs are guilt, and if you wrung them out, guilt would drip from them like dirty water.

"I'm sorry," I say. "I'm so sorry."

"Ives, no," she says. "Stop." She holds my hand.

"I wrecked everything."

"You haven't wrecked anything. I just feel awful that you're going through this. I feel awful about how it happened. It's so many things, but it's so *unfair*, too. I would take it away if I could. That's a mother thing to say, but it's true."

My terrible mind flashes on my hand releasing its grasp

on the chain link, doing what I'd hoped would free me but instead causing the opposite. I squeeze my eyes shut, make two fists, and dig my fingernails into my palms again.

"Ives?" Mom shakes my shoulder. I don't want to open my eyes, but that's one of the problems with memory. It's a movie that plays right in front of you no matter what screen you're looking at. Mom uncurls one of my hands. "Ives . . ."

I shake my head. "I just can't stop *thinking*. . . ."

"I know."

I twirl my hand near my head, indicating how it goes on and on. "The uglies. That's what I call them, those thoughts."

"That's a perfect name." She nods. "Ives, we need to take you to a doctor."

"No way. We can't. People will *know*."

The thing is, she doesn't even argue. She only shakes her head. I look out the window at the night sky, and the electrical pole looming in our yard, and our neighbors' windows, squares of light, a row of them, marching the length of our street. I worry that someone can see us, or hear us. The curtains are still open, and we would be illuminated like two actors, the audience watching in the darkness.

Three actors, because now there's a knock.

"Mase, we're—"

He barges in, and my mom doesn't even get a chance to finish. "You think I can't hear every single word?" He's right—there are no secrets in a house this small. *Four* actors—Wilson Phillips, looking worried, trots in, too.

"Damn it, you people and dog . . . ," I say. It's already spilling out of control, that's what it feels like. Lorenzo and my mom and now Mase . . . Everyone knows that criminals always get caught when they just can't stand it, when they unburden their conscience and tell someone. The more people who hear the truth, the more likely it is to get out.

Mase sits at the head of the bed like he's the one who's watching a riveting drama, and Wilson Phillips hops up next to him, then circles himself into a dog bagel and sighs.

"Maybe his parents should be—"

"No," I say. "*No.*"

"Your dad . . ."

"No, Mom. *Please.*"

"You don't think you should tell your dad?"

I think of him, how when we visit, we have fun going to the Odessa Meteor Crater, or goofing around at the Stonehenge replica at the university, or having picnics by Jack Ben Rabbit, an eight-foot-tall statue of a jackrabbit (don't ask). But we also watch his favorite sci-fi movies even though Mase and I don't like sci-fi movies. We shoot hoops in his driveway because he likes basketball and says it's good for us. When he has a new girlfriend, she's the one who makes us dinner. He has very distinct ideas about things, like how guys should be tough enough to take stuff, and how girls should act like ladies, and how Mase and I should be . . . *better.* Right that minute Mase is giving me the big *Emergency! Emergency!* eyes of siblings who understand the big picture, silently screaming, *NO! DON'T TELL HIM, IVY!*

"Forget it. If I change my mind, I'll let you know," I say.

We're all silent for a long while. If an audience *were* watching this, they'd be gathering up their coats and heading for the exit. Wait, no. This audience, the one in Paris,

Texas—if they saw what was happening, it'd be over for me. Some might even storm the theater with blazing pitchforks.

Unless this became a different movie. The kind where a girl in my "situation" decides to keep the baby. She and her teen boyfriend get married and somehow make it, or she becomes a scrappy young mom who heroically manages to support her kid. Even better, the best yet—she bonds with a couple who become surrogate parents to the troubled teen and eventually adopt the baby. The wife will be successful and warm, a capable and financially well-off woman who has longed for a baby for years, and the husband will be eccentric enough to be charmingly quirky. He'll forge a closeness with the girl that remains platonic but might make you wonder in real life. The kind of movie where she's good and you root for her. I'd be forgiven then.

But none of this is going to happen.

"Is there any part of you that doesn't want to have the, uh . . . ?" My mom trails off and then shrugs in a helpless *How can I put this?* way. *"Procedure?"* She can't say the word, either. "I mean, is there any part of you that wants to keep . . . ?"

"I know what you mean," I snap. "No. Of course not. No." The thought of it—my eyes squeeze shut again. I could be sick. My hands feel gross, and I wipe them on my shorts. It would be so wrong, and not just for me. No one should have a beginning like that.

"Well, we'll go to Oregon. We can stay with Grandma Lottie. We'll do it there."

"You can't take that kind of time off from work," I say. "What will you tell Shelley?"

"I can tell her a hundred things. Visiting my mom . . ."

"You keep saying how you've taken so much time off of work already."

"You come first."

"Lorenzo . . ." I shouldn't even mention it. I shouldn't even tell her that this is what I'd really want, Lorenzo and me going to Oregon together.

"Lorenzo *what?*" Her tone is a shut door.

"He offered to, you know, go with me. Wherever. Handle it together."

"Honey, no. Absolutely not! I mean, I understand how you feel about him, but you've only known him a few *months*. This is a situation for a *parent*."

"Shouldn't she get a choice about *that* at least?" Mason says. He raises one eyebrow, a trick from the Mr. Mysterioso days.

"You need to shut up if you're going to be here," I say.

"I'm on your side," he says.

"*I'm* on your side," my mom says.

"I am," Mason makes Wilson Phillips say by moving his lips up and down. He's the kind of dog that takes this sort of abuse—talking lips, amusing things put on his head, Halloween costumes, et cetera—with patience and with his dignity intact. He has a generous soul, unlike Diesel, the neighbor dog, whose need for dominance makes him mean.

"Lorenzo . . . This isn't . . . He's a *boy*. You need an adult. Your mom. *Me*."

"He's not a boy. He *is* an adult. It's not like he's *thirteen*."

"Hey!" Mason says.

"What would his parents say, huh?" my mom says.

"He's eighteen. He doesn't even have to tell them."

"Ivy, do you hear yourself? This plan sounds like two kids making a plan."

"God, Mom . . ."

"Yeah, maybe it's a bad idea," Mason interjects. "They might get married on the way." He's seen those movies, too.

"Would you just quit!" I glare at him.

"Mason." My mom has got her *stop this right now* voice on. "Until you have some actual experience in anything you're speaking about, I suggest you keep your mouth closed or go directly to your room."

Mason shuts up and holds a pillow.

"When do we go?" I hate how I sound. Like a child. The furthest thing from fierce. "I just want this over. And . . ." I gesture toward my middle. "Fast."

"I was just thinking. . . . School's out in a week and a half. Maybe we should wait until then."

"I'm like a bomb ticking!" I say. I looked, okay? I opened Mom's secondhand, thirdhand laptop with the Arcade Fire sticker on it, and saw the grain of rice inside me, and read about the cells multiplying by the minute. There's no time to lose. But then I realize what my mom is saying. She's not worried about me finishing up the semester. She's worried about people *guessing*. "Oh. You mean the whole *felony* thing."

My mother puts her head in her hands.

"I'm sorry. I'm so sorry," I say again.

"Ivy, honey. Don't keep apologizing."

"Why are you being so understanding, though? *Why?*" I was expecting . . . I don't know. She's usually pretty understanding, but I've never been this disappointing. The worst thing I've done so far was skipping school with Peyton when we were in ninth grade, and all we did was hang out at her house and make cookies and watch TV. I expected some yelling at least.

"I've seen a lot of life, Ivy. And this whole thing that happened to you a few weeks ago . . . I've done that very same thing, for the same reasons."

"Really?" These are not things you want to visualize, but it's still a small relief.

"More than once. I wish I hadn't. I wish *you* hadn't. But probably every female has experienced a version of this. You know what else? I get the uglies, too, when I remember those times." Maybe disappointing your parents *isn't* forever, because her eyes are soft and kind.

"I'm so sorry," I say again. I don't know how many "sorrys" I'm going to need to give before I stop. I also don't know how many I deserve.

"Ives, I told you . . . this is not your fault."

"I didn't even know you could get pregnant that way," I say.

6

OVER THE NEXT FEW DAYS, I TRY TO TRICK MY MIND into believing everything is normal, but anyone with a mind knows that those things have a will of their own. At school I try to focus on Tess of the D'Urbervilles and Angel (who's no angel, I'll tell you that much), and on flowers and plants and soil—growing things, living things, all hope and sorrow. I try to listen to the details of Peyton's locker-side talk with Noah, and share Faith's glee at her new Instagram account after her parents finally gave her permission to have one. I try to avoid Jason Maxwell and his minions, though he seems to be done with me since that concert, mission accomplished, the score settled.

Lorenzo—he's trying to show up, even if he's sort of lost about how to do that. He's sad we won't be going to Oregon together, but I keep telling him it's maybe not right to have actual fun heading out to do what I'm going to do. So instead he looks at me too long with sad eyes, and keeps texting *How are you?* when we're away from each other, to the point that Madeleine said, *Are you two fighting* already? as she stuck that carrot stick into her yogurt and licked it off. If you ask me, it's not particularly thoughtful to make observations about other people's business, especially when you don't have all the facts. These facts . . . Well, when I look around that cafeteria, I feel lonely beyond words, that single Converse in a sea of boots and heels, because no one else there has gone through this exact thing, that's for sure.

I pick up Mase after school and then go to work. I try to concentrate on vitamins and bath salts and pain relievers. I hold old Mrs. Peony's fragile elbow, a small knot on a thin tree branch, and lead her back to the Fleet enema boxes for the hundredth time. I tell Maureen she smells good, and I keep smiling even when she says, *It's just my* shampoo, like, *How annoying can a person be.* I go out to my car and avoid the eyes of Drake Euwing behind the wheel of that truck as it sits in the circle of streetlight. And then I am home again, finally, where I can wallow in what's real. I go to the bathroom and lift up my shirt, checking for changes. Only my breasts so far, fuller, like water balloons. My pants, harder to button, though the internet says it's "just bloat" this early, the "just" sounding like a warning. And my hand—it's maybe different, too, because when I look down at it, I'm so full of hatred that I imagine chopping it right off, same as Tess with the roots of those turnips when she works on the farm. Slice, slice, her hand in that leather glove when Alec D'Urberville asks her to marry him and she says no. For an old guy, that Thomas Hardy can make you feel like you're right there, once you're through the foreword and the explanatory note to the first edition and the preface to the fifth and later editions.

And then somehow, at last, there are only five days left until Mom and I and Mase and Wilson Phillips head to Oregon and Grandma Lottie's house, and less than two weeks until the appointment Grandma Lottie made for me. Grandma Lottie—she's someone you want in your corner. She's someone you can trust. *I* can trust. When Mom told her the story, the whole story, she responded with her usual *I protect my people, damn it* demeanor, according to Mom. She said, *Get my girl here, pronto.* I felt all choked up when Mom told me that.

Five days until we leave, and only four days left of school, too.

I'm almost there. I've almost made it.

If you've watched any film, any film at all, you know what a line like that means.

We're at the point in the school year where teachers are showing movies because it's almost summer. We watch *Kiss the Ground,* a soil documentary (I know, but it's better than you think), in Advanced Plant and Soil Science, and *Love Happens* in Floral Design, a romantic comedy where Jennifer Aniston plays a florist, which is nowhere near as good as *Rockaway Weekend,* if you ask me. There's no moment where you feel a true and lasting love with all its complications, just that pretend hate that supposedly means she actually loves him. This is something I can never imagine happening in real life, because you usually hate someone for very good reasons.

Now Ms. La Costa aims the remote at the big TV so we can see the description of the *Tess of the D'Urbervilles* movie, the 1998 version. " 'A dramatic and timeless tale of romance,' " she reads. She makes this sound like: *A dramatic and timeless tale of romance?!* Then, she pushes *play.*

The music is all anguished, and I wish they hadn't made Alec and Angel so handsome and appealing when they're both so horrible. The scenery is all beautiful and everything, but somehow I missed it in the reading, how young Tess is. Sixteen. My age. It loops around my brain as the movie plays, sixteen, sixteen. Sixteen loops around in my sixteen-year-old body, now holding the teeniest collection of multiplying cells. Ten minutes before class ends, we stop right at that very scene, the one that I—by chance, by fate—placed my finger on in Euwing's Drugs. Where Tess says she doesn't understand the point of learning history, since it just makes her sad to find out there's only a line of people just like her, going through the same things she has.

Chase Winston flicks the lights on since his desk is closest to the switch. Ms. La Costa is at the whiteboard. She usually writes like she's attacking something, same as now. *Why does history matter?*

"There's only ten minutes left," Jace Huett whines.

"A paper," Ms. La Costa says. "Due on the last day.

However long it needs to be. Mandatory. Surprise, friends, *this* is your final." Everyone groans, because honestly? There are books on that, entire books, and I hate to say it, because I *want* to get a good education, but we're at the end of the year and who cares. "Please mark and reference the quote, page one forty-two."

"So, wait. There's no test?" Jace perks up.

"Nope. Like I said, this is your final."

"How many pages?" Olivia Kneeley asks.

"However long it needs to be," Ms. La Costa repeats.

"Oh, come *on*," Chase says. "Haven't we had enough of her? Tess was a *bimho*." Throughout this whole unit, he's become weirdly more and more aggressive, and I'm worried he's going to tell his parents about the things Ms. La Costa says in class. More than once, she's talked about men using their power to make "God" say things that serve them, like how they're the head of the household. She actually made air quotes with her fingers, which seems dangerous. People around here believe those things. And after the pride flag, she's probably on thin ice.

Ms. La Costa's face gets a hard, stony expression, like she's maybe clenching her teeth. "*Not okay,*" she says to Chase. She means it. I have no idea what she's going to do about it, but you can tell she's *pissed*. Everyone's unzipping their packs and getting out their books to mark page 142, even though we've got, like, six minutes left, but everyone's also keeping their eyes fixed on Chase, because, oh my God, he's suddenly standing, and, geez, is he going to grab her by her blouse, or what? He's got that look that some guys get, same as Mom's old boyfriend Terry whenever he didn't feel like he was the number one top guy in the room, the veins in his temples pulsing almost to the point of bursting. Ms. La Costa puts her hands on her hips, even though she's a head shorter than Chase. "Sit. Down," she says. And Chase is about to blow, because if there's anything worse to guys like that than not being the number one dude in a room, it's being number two to a female.

It's all shocking and awful and sort of thrilling, to be honest, since nothing that exciting has happened since Raymond Pace Jr. threw a chair across the room in Concepts of Chemistry, shattering a row of test tubes. It's so involving that I'm not watching what I'm doing at all, like when your hands are eating popcorn during the movie, just doing their own thing. I unzip my bag, and I get the book out, and as I set it down, the test, that little thermometer-like wand, slips out and clatters to the floor and actually slides under Olivia Kneeley's chair.

I watch this all happen as if it's *not* happening. It's surreal—a slow-motion slide into disaster, and now this thing that I was imagining as a scene in a movie that would never occur in real life is occurring in real life. The stick stops. I have a moment where I'm sure I can rescue this, where I can snatch it up before anyone sees, and where this will all turn out fine. And then another moment of horror where I'm pleading, *Please, please, please, I promise I will be a good person for the rest of my life if no one sees,* and then another where I am absolutely furious with myself for keeping that stick in my book. What was I possibly thinking? I wasn't, that's what. I suddenly realize that the five stages of grief can all happen in seconds, and can happen even before the loss. In a moment, utter despair fills me, because Olivia Kneeley heard it, that tiny little clatter that to me sounded like a building falling. She sees me hopping up, panicked, and she leans over and looks under her chair.

I watch her face change. Olivia, ex-girlfriend to Chase himself, though they're only friends now. Friends, too, with Jason Maxwell, and Hope Mathias, and their whole group. The stick has landed faceup, the plus sign blazing like a neon light. Why, why, why did I even keep it? Honestly, how reckless can you get? "Very" is the answer. So very reckless. No criminal keeps the murder weapon around unless they want to get caught.

Olivia's eyes meet mine. I beg her silently, girl to girl, woman to woman. I mean, we should protect each other, right? We should be on each other's side, no matter what, because we share the same vulnerabilities of the body, right? It could happen to anyone, right? Not if you kept your legs closed, not if you stayed a virgin. Being a virgin was all the birth control you needed, according to Jason Maxwell's dad and the leaders of City of Hope Church of God, Life Horizons Baptist Church, Fellowship Pointe Christian, and New Redeemer Christian. We heard them say this on TV and saw it in political pamphlets left on our doorstep during all the debate before the six-week abortion law came into effect. We needed to keep our legs closed, but guys could get condoms, boys will be boys, and this was confusing, you know, because a lot of the time, they were having sex with us.

Please, I beg Olivia.

Please, because Olivia is more than just a popular girl who might judge me. She's someone who isn't only one thing, too, even if it seems like it, her with her shiny hair and new outfit after new outfit. Even if she's always set solidly in the center of her group of friends, a group that moves as a whole, same as bees, from one sweet thing to another, she has secrets. I saw her getting in a fight with her dad once as they drove up to school. Olivia was shouting, and her mouth was ugly and twisted, and her dad looked mean, and later I walked in on her crying in the bathroom when she thought she was alone. Her eyes were all puffy, and her nose was dripping, and at first I thought, *What could possibly be that wrong for someone like Olivia Kneeley?* But then I remembered what Grandma Lottie always says, how you shouldn't compare people's tragedies. And I thought about how every person is a shit car, where you don't know what they've been through, and how human beings always have kindness to give, at least, if they choose to. I handed her a wad of TP and a peppermint Life Savers, because you don't always want to talk when you're going through something rough. She gave me a little smile and said, *Shit,* and I said *Shit* back.

Now her mouth makes the shape of the word *wow.* It's a sarcastic wow, a disgusted wow. Her lips, slick with peach gloss, purse in disapproval. She looks at me like she now knows everything she needs to about me, like she knows exactly who I am. Mostly, a girl she will never be.

"I'm not touching that thing," she says.

Quentin Giles, no innocent himself, he who trails the smell of pot like that *Peanuts* character with the dirt—I can never remember his name—looks in the direction of Olivia and me and the stick, and he snorts. Ms. La Costa says something to Chase, which I don't even hear, and I snatch the test. It's burning my hand. My body is radioactive with shame. My face flushes so hot, I can feel the redness traveling down my neck.

The bell rings. Everyone gathers up their stuff and pushes their chairs back, and Chase is the first out the door. He gets out of there so fast, his Nikes squeak. Ms. La Costa is in her own world, looking at the question on the whiteboard.

"Wow," Olivia says again, out loud now. She makes a face, like she's viewing something revolting that she will never understand. I stay behind, rummaging in my backpack as a way to hide, since I don't know who else saw. I don't know who else saw, but I can guess that in minutes, my *no one can know*, my privacy, my secret story, my pain, my guilt, these traumatic, horrible weeks, will be fun, fun for everyone to talk about and be appalled by. Jason Maxwell will boil with glee. Someone else's trauma can be such a great spectator sport. Judgment can make any boring day exciting and pump you up in the process, because when you compare that loser with your own amazing self, you're a superstar.

I should warn Lorenzo, because, poor guy. But I don't. The last week has been exhausting. Holding a weighty secret is grueling. But the escape of it in this unsafe place is a spilled acid. I suddenly think of that awful Dr. Seuss book, the one that always scared me, where the Cat in the Hat leaves a pink goo that rapidly covers everything—shoes, rug, bed, the entire snowy, pristine property outside. I need to get away.

When the classroom is nearly empty, I scoot out, and

I don't even stop at my locker. I am filled with such panic that I can barely see or hear anything. There's just a blur of kids and classroom doors and lockers slamming and people shouting. Lorenzo doesn't deserve what I do next.

I get in my car and go.

I don't *go* go, like leave forever, though I wish I could. I want out of there, out of whatever might come next, because it's going to be bad. That's one thing I can be sure of—it's going to be really, really bad. I remember what happened to Bethany Jayne Grigg; everyone does. *B.J.* Grigg, Bethany *More Than a B.J.* Grigg, Bethany *Grigg-Grigg-Grigg* (insert pumping hips here, and make sure her name, her father's name, and his father's, sounds like a moan). Bethany Jayne Grigg, who couldn't take it. Who got bullied to the point of despair.

And wait. Macie Dutton. We were inseparable in sixth grade, but junior high changed that. She got pregnant in ninth grade and dropped out of school, and after the baby was born, I went to visit because I felt *sorry* for her. I wanted to show that I still cared about her, no matter what. Her mom let me in, and there was Macie on the couch in the living room, holding a baby. An actual baby. I don't know what I was expecting, but the space between us was like a canyon. She had done and gone through adult things, things I couldn't imagine, and I felt silly and childish being there. My offering of myself felt naive and self-serving, and it was the most awkward visit ever. I never saw her again after that. We never heard about a father, a boy, a man; that part was a mystery, safely hidden in ways Macie could never be. She wasn't bullied—she was just forgotten, even by me, until now.

The point is, when I remember Bethany and Macie, I know my future. In other people's minds, in my own, they became the thing that happened to them.

When I start up Mr. Smiley and drive to New Jefferson Junior High, my heart is beating hard. I wait in the pickup line for Mason. I watch for his brown hair and bright orange T-shirt, too bright, too orange, like a target. I roll down the passenger window, lean over, and stick my head out.

"Would you hurry up?" I hiss. Damn, *he* doesn't deserve this, either. I'll have some serious making-up to do to him after, if there's an after. To him, and to Lorenzo, and to Mom. I feel like I'm digging a hole, regret, regret, regret. With each push of the shovel, the dirt piles up.

Mason gets in, fastens his seat belt like the responsible person he is. He looks at me then. "Ivy? Are you okay? You're all, like, *white*."

I feel light-headed. Stress dizzy, pregnant dizzy, *get me the heck out of here* dizzy. I start the engine.

"Ivy? Ives? Shit, slow down." We fly over the speed bumps. My chin hits my chest. "No one's chasing us." But then he looks over his shoulder to make sure. I feel his eyes boring into me, but I don't dare turn my head. "Someone found out," he guesses.

"I hate myself. Hate, hate, hate." I pound the wheel with my palms.

He doesn't even ask what happened. He just says, "You don't have to go back to school. There're only three days left.

We can go home and pack up right now." I think that's what he says. Something along those lines. My mind is a tornado, and it only picks up his words and tosses them around.

When we pull up to our house, our neighbor Mrs. Branson is unloading groceries. She gives a wave, and I wave back, and it hits me suddenly, *all* of the people who will know. Not just kids at school, but teachers. Mrs. Branson, and our whole block, adults who matter to me. Mrs. Peony, even. Ones I've always tried to impress with my grades and politeness.

With my *diligence*. With my bright future. "I can't believe this! I have to go to *work*."

"Call in sick!" Mason pleads. "How can you even *go* there?" We're inside the house now, and I'm rushing around, trying to find my blue vest. It's gone missing, same as me. I find it under my bed, where I'd like to be, too. Good job, vest. Nice try on the hiding.

"I *have* to go there, Mase. Don't you get it? Don't you understand? If I want a life where I maybe actually see the world, I need a good job. A *really* good job. And to get a really good job, I have to go to *college*. And for that I need *money*, and there's no possible way I'll make enough money for college with most of the jobs around here, which means I won't get a really good job one day! I won't ever go anywhere beyond Paris. *Do you understand?* I *need* Euwing's Drugs!"

"There's got to be other ways besides that one, Ives," Mase says. "You shouldn't have to go in there."

What does a thirteen-year-old know about money, huh?

He hasn't even gotten that first paycheck, the one where you work hours and hours for minimum wage, and then they take all the stuff out, taxes, whatever, and you look down at the amount, sure that there's been a mistake. "Yeah? Like what other ways?"

"I don't know. Just, when you don't have pancetta, you use bacon."

I glare at him because I'm mad at life. Taking things out on people is something I'm going to have to work on, if this is ever over and I have a minute to breathe. "No one at Euwing's will know."

Mase stares at me and only lifts his eyebrows. And yes, I realize there are a lot of eyebrows doing a lot of talking in this awful story, but this is what they do; these are the facts of life, whether you've been previously aware of them before or not. His eyebrows, they are saying one word, and the word hits me with the most unjust finality.

"Yet."

No one will know anything there *yet*. Which means all of this has been for nothing. The outcome I was desperately hoping to avoid is exactly where I've ended up anyway. It's a circle, a Tess circle, where fate forces an inevitable end, where society grinds its heel into you to keep you in place.

I picture Maureen, smug with the news, gloating down at her glittery yellow nails. (*They're so summery!* I'd complimented.) I think of Mr. Euwing, Bob, and all of his help and attention and praise, his belief in me, teaching me how to make the schedules, how to manage customer complaints, how to deal with the cash if Maureen is out, which

Maureen never is. Giving me a salary that'll help make my dreams come true. I think of him sometimes touching the small of my back, or my arm, in ways a different generation of men don't know they shouldn't, or something. I think of Mrs. Euwing, with her little gold cross necklace, coming into Euwing's with Drake, picking up Mr. Euwing on their own Family Dinner Night Out, when they walk down the street to Leon's for Steak Thursdays and fried cheesecake. And I think of Drake, too, the way Mrs. Euwing fixes his hair or adjusts his collar, beaming. The way she says, *Drake has asthma,* as if it's a delicate health condition that excuses any bad behavior. Drake's a sophomore, but he looks like he's in junior high, with his bony shoulders and babyish face, his polo shirts picked out by his mom, probably, to match his dad's. Mrs. Euwing's pride and joy—he's had a reputation since elementary school for being the kind of guy who's always talking about "tits," and who draws pictures of naked girls in his notebook, and stares at your boobs, and gets "crushes" that mean you can't get rid of him. *Crush, crushed*—I'm sure that's how our friend Megan felt when he followed her (and us) around for a good three months last year. He'd brush up against her and accidentally bump into her until she finally told him that her (nonexistent) boyfriend was going to make him regret it if he didn't leave her alone. And then he moved on to Ava Surrey, and then to Brie Chen.

Crush, crushed. I dig my nails into my fists. The uglies wash over me, a shower of self-hatred.

"Just quit, Ives. It's not worth it."

Mason doesn't say what we both are thinking, that it's over anyway.

I do go to work, though. I go because I'm on the schedule. I go because I don't want to leave Evan or Maureen in the lurch. I go because being responsible is something I can't shake, even if I'd love to, even if being irresponsible sounds so freeing and fantastic. God, it sounds amazing. But I just don't think you should be an asshole like that, do stuff that causes other people more work or trouble. Force something on someone else because you just plain decide to. If I didn't show, Evan would have to stay late and miss judo, and he loves judo. Maureen would have to work the register until closing and wear that arm brace because of carpal tunnel whatever. Evan calls it *carpet tunnel,* which sounds like a cozy expressway to a plush land.

When I push open the door of Euwing's Drugs, I try to act as normal as possible. I try to act better than ever, like the last few weeks have never happened. I want to leave a lasting impression that's larger than what they're about to find out. Since the lovebirds mean so much to Mr. Euwing, I stick my finger in Missy and Buddy's cage when he's looking, trying to show I care about them when I really think they're creepy. I ask Maureen if she's lost weight. I'm extra friendly to every customer, taking old Mrs. Peony directly back to the Fleet enema boxes like it is the very first time and not the hundredth. I show Mr. Avery, still in his postal uniform, where the Ace bandages are after he holds up his wrist and rotates it slowly. I sniff several lotions to help Mrs. Ivers, with her snowball of white hair and shaky hands, decide on gardenia.

It's not all that different from what I do every day, but I try to infuse it with extra meaning.

On my break Mr. Euwing crooks his finger to say, *Come here.* He asks me how I like the new cage. I tell him I love it, but honestly, I didn't even notice. It looks just like the old one to me.

7

I KEEP MY PHONE OFF AT WORK BECAUSE *MAUREEN*.
I once accidentally left it on, and it rang while I was behind
the register, and Maureen read me the riot act. *Read me
the riot act* is one of those expressions you go around using
until one day you realize it's sort of strange, look it up on
the internet to see where it came from, and then promptly
forget what you read. Anyway, Mr. Euwing overheard her
and said, *Easy, Maureen. You're talking to my little go-
getter,* and winked at me, which did not go over well, as you
can imagine. The minute he was out of the room, Maureen
said, *You're always the teacher's pet, I bet,* which was a jab
disguised as a compliment, and far from the truth, besides.
My teachers, aside from Ms. La Costa, don't seem to know
I exist, though going unnoticed is a highly underrated super-
power, if you ask me. When Maureen said that, I didn't have
a good comeback, so I said, *Hey! Pet, I bet!* like she made
an accidental and humorous poem. I have no idea why I
said that. It will probably be one of those odd moments you

remember forever, like the time Mom's old boyfriend asked me what my sign was, and I said, *Stop*. Maureen, she just gave me a look to indicate what a huge task it was to tolerate me.

The point is, my phone is off.

The point is, I don't see all the texts and calls until I'm shoving my vest in my pack and Maureen's locking up. The cold phone is in my hand, a long row of messages filling the screen. The clock in the break room goes *tick tick tick*. Missy is making that screeching sound that sends goose bumps of alarm up my arms, no matter how many times I hear it.

All afternoon that sick heaviness known as dread was with me wherever I went, same as one of our shopping baskets on my arm getting heavier and heavier by the hour. The scene played in my mind again and again: that test sliding across the floor, Olivia's voice saying, *Wow*, with such disgust. How fast can news get around, news of someone not many people even really care about? *Fast* is the answer. Very fast. No one really cared about Tess, either. But they sure cared about the news.

Outside now, Maureen tucks the key ring into her bag. "Have a great night," I tell her. The night smells like heat and fried chicken from Leon's. The moon is a hanging chair. Maureen holds the padded bag of cash against her chest, guarding the bank deposit like it's the most important thing she'll ever do.

"Well, if you-know-who isn't just giving me back talk the whole time, maybe," she says. You-know-who is her daughter, Cheyenne. Cheyenne is twenty-something and has some "issues" with drugs and alcohol. She lives with Maureen and Harv, Maureen's second husband, who's on disability for some mysterious reason she won't disclose. If you looked up *ungrateful* in the dictionary, you'd see a picture of Cheyenne, according to Maureen.

I give an encouraging smile even though panic is clawing my insides. I watch my shoes walk to my car because if I glance up, I'll see that truck with Drake behind the wheel. As soon as I'm out of that parking lot, I've got my phone on my leg. With twelve seconds at the first stoplight on Main, I look down. Four voicemail messages from Peyton, which I don't listen to, and four texts from her, too. The first: *Call me.* And then: *We need to talk.* And then: *It's urgent!* And then: *Olivia told Noah what . . .* The light changes.

I drive, passing Très Jolie Boutique and the hardware store. I pass the library and Bywaters Park, where they hold the outdoor concerts in the summer and the Winter Wonderland at Christmastime, with its cutouts of nativities and other holiday scenes. I make it all the way to the beautiful street where that incredible white Victorian house sits, the Sam Bell Maxey House State Historic Site, before I hit another red light where I can read again. *Olivia told Noah what happened in class. CALL ME RIGHT NOW.* Then two texts from Faith: *Some very bad stuff is going around about you!* Scream emoji, crying emoji, red-faced angry emoji. *Call me.* And then: *It's not TRUE, is it?* I listen to the voicemail from Lorenzo. *Hey, you okay? I heard from Ian what happened in class. Faith asked him if I told him already, and he couldn't believe I hadn't. I said, "It's private, dude," and he backed off, but . . . Well, just call me. I'm worried, since you weren't there after school. I was going to swing by work, but I didn't*

*want to get you in trouble. I, uh . . . Well, anyway. Just . . .
let me know you're all right.*

I make it until I get home, and then I run inside to the
bathroom. I retch and puke, and I'm seriously unconvinced
this has to do with pregnancy at all, because terror does this
to me, too. I learned this after we heard Mom's diagnosis.
Terror—it makes demands, and the first and most urgent
one is that it wants *out.* The vomiting does nothing, because
there is no out. Terror fills my whole body, and I sit down
there, right on the cold tiles of the bathroom floor, because
my legs are shaky and I'm sweating like mad.

My mom knocks and then cracks the door open. "Oh,
honey. You okay?" She's already getting a washcloth and
running it under the cool water. The smell of gravy drifts in,
and I groan.

She puts the cloth on my forehead. She knows this trick
from her treatment, and it *is* soothing, a cool reprieve, a
small comfort. I shut my eyes. I wish I could stay there, in
that dark *away,* where no one can come in, no one.

"The worst thing happened," I say. I mean the stick, but
not just.

"You're going to get through this," she says.

It's weird because we said that to her, too, and there are
these strange overlaps, the unwanted cells and the unwanted
cells, each on the opposite ends of existence, life and death.
There's the fear and the physical changes, too, being thrust
into something that overtakes you, consumes you, separates you from everyone else. Separates you from yourself,
even, your body becoming your enemy and destroyer instead
of your usual and mostly ignored companion.

It's hard not to think of the way people also celebrate those cells, the kind I have. *Long* for them and do every possible thing to have those very cells dividing inside of them. *Of course* I think about this. *Of course* I think *baby*, even though the word is *embryo*. I want to summon and keep some sort of clinical scientific remove, but it's not possible, not all the way. The best I can do is have this wall, this *I can't, I can't*. I just need them, they, everyone out there, to please, please understand that I can't, I can't, I can't. *Please.*

It would be wrong. Awful. Just awful, for anyone to have fifteen-year-old Drake Euwing as a father.

Oh God, oh God.

"I can't go back there," I say behind the safe darkness of my eyes, under the cool wetness of the cloth. "To school."

She doesn't argue. Now I hear the clink of ice cubes against glass.

"Here," Mason says. I peek my eyes open to see the tall glass of water, something else we learned to bring Mom after a bout of sickness. I get suddenly worried about the boy, my brother, who knows how to take care of two females falling apart right in front of him.

A glass of water isn't much up against the war of dividing cells. And neither is a cool washcloth. But I suddenly understand why those things were such a help to my mother. It's about the person holding the glass. It's about the person holding the washcloth.

I shut my phone off. I don't eat the boeuf bourguignon (winner of the all-time hardest-to-spell food), just a peanut-butter-and-honey sandwich and a glass of milk, something I remember my mom making for me and Mase when we were little. The phone feels like that heart in the Edgar Allan Poe story we read earlier in the semester, beating under the floorboards. When I can't stand the loudness of the silence, I turn the phone on, just for a second. I see that Lorenzo has called again and again, but I'm too tired to talk. My whole body is aching with fatigue. One night not long ago, Mom looked especially spent, and I asked her if she'd had a hard day. She said, *I'm just tired. Like,* life *tired.* I'm life tired. And maybe pregnant tired, too, a different kind of tired entirely, I see now, way larger than me.

But I do text Faith. *It's not TRUE, is it?* her text read, and that question is a fire surrounding our house. God, I'm desperate to put it out, so I answer. *THAT TEST WASN'T MINE,* I type. *Zoop,* it sends, and the lie is so bad, and so obviously a lie, that my face gets red and hot from shame and embarrassment even though I'm in my own room and no one is there to see me. And then I suddenly realize that *WASN'T MINE* might implicate someone *else,* Peyton, maybe, and then I panic because I'm horrible but not that horrible. I try to think about how to get out of this and can't, so I shut off my phone again. I stick it under my pillow so I can't hear its guilty beat. The other lie, the one I tell myself about being a fierce girl of the indomitable DeVries family, waggles its tongue out and teases, *nah nah,* like an elementary school bully. It's another Grandma Lottie word, *indomitable,* and it makes you think of those movies where some girl survives on a prairie during a long winter. I wouldn't know the first thing about getting maple syrup from a tree.

Around nine the doorbell rings. I hear them talking in the other room—Lorenzo and my mom. They're not arguing, but their voices are intense and insistent. It sounds like they're deciding things for me, and this makes me so mad, I can barely stand it. It also feels really, really good. Like maybe all I have to do is sit on this bed while they plan, and then follow instructions. I stay in there, in my room. I'm too pissed-reassured to move. After a while my mom taps on the door and peeks her head in. "Lorenzo's here," she says.

I'm life tired times a jillion. "I can't" shoots out from me like rays of radiation, with one big, blazing *I can't* in the center. It's all too much, and my star burns out, and I'm made of ashes, and I just look at her with dead eyes.

"I'll tell him," she says. "It's been a hard day."

It's so kind that I want to cry. I mean, when is she going to yell at me like I would yell at me? But she just closes the door softly, and I sink into my covers, even though my clothes are still on.

I hear the front door shut, and Diesel, Mr. Sykes's dog, starts barking and snarling at the sound of Lorenzo's footsteps. He's still out there, always out there, even though it's late now. There's that rattle of chain-link fence, the *clang clang* sound of a body thrust against that net of metal. God, it's scary every single time. I hear Lorenzo's truck start up. I see the two headlight beams flare, and then I jump out of bed and race to the window, which is already open. Open, because the air-conditioning of our house is constantly working too hard and then not at all.

"Lorenzo!" I shout, and wave my arms. I'm doing that thing I hate, hate, hate in movies, where the girl (mostly the girl) chases after the guy she's turned away. Where she makes a big dramatic scene when there didn't need to be one, not in my opinion. Those scenes always make me yell at the TV. *Run*, I say to him. *Get the heck away*. It always makes her look so needy and unhinged, and for God's sake, *get it together*. Just *stop*. But there I am, waving my arms. I might as well be chasing after his car in my bare feet, or driving wildly to stop him before he boards a plane.

Ugh! Maybe we can all be that girl if we hit the right level of despair. You shouldn't go around congratulating yourself just because you've had it good.

Lorenzo yanks the brake, I guess, because he opens the truck door and gets out. He stands beside it, those two beams still on. He looks up at me. It's probably the wrong time to notice how adorable he is, but God, look at him with the moonlight on his hair.

"I'm sorry!" I hope I won't one day run out of apologies.

He holds up one flip-flop and then the other. But what he shouts is "Converse!"

I can't even speak. I just grip that sill, my neck craned out.

He shouts again. "We're a pair!"

My heart fills with bursting love and then collapses. I don't deserve him, that's for sure.

8

A *FAMILY EMERGENCY* ISN'T A LIE. WITH THREE DAYS left of school, everything is mostly done anyway: the finals in Statistics and Anatomy and Physiology, the analysis for Plant and Soil Science ("How Hydrogels Impact the Environment"). And there's no real urgency in Floral Design, if there ever was. (Florists might disagree.) The only thing unfinished is my Tess final, the paper on why history matters. The email finally arrives from Ms. La Costa, giving me permission to turn it in later. *If you need anything or want to talk . . . ,* she writes. My face heats up, flushes red. By now she's definitely heard about what happened in class yesterday. The way she used to meet my eyes said we understood each other, that we were on the same side, and I've wrecked that by becoming the messed-up kid.

I spend the day at home, alone. It's like those times some celebrity commits a crime and hides out in their house, with the paparazzi just waiting for them to leave, except I'm not a celebrity and there's no paparazzi. What I mean is, I'm in here, and "they" are all out there, ready to pounce. Ready, too, to make me and my private tragedy their entertainment. Nothing seems out of the ordinary, though. Nothing else. Mr. Sykes goes to work, and Diesel flings himself against the fence, teeth bared, even if it's just a squirrel that passes, and Mrs. Branson is outside, planting little flowers along her walkway. It's too hot, and those plants always die, but Mrs. Branson, according to my mother, is an *eternal optimist*. Last year when we all heard her scream, *If that's what you think I'm doing, Rick, you need to get your eyes bleeping checked*, I said, *She's not being an eternal optimist now*, and Mase said, *Maybe an eternal optometrist*. We all laughed, even though we heard their front door slam and Mr. Branson's car screech away. Now I hear the clink of the trowel when she sets it down, and the *whoosh* of her garden hose turning on and off.

The only one who's having an unusual day is Wilson Phillips, who keeps following me around as if we're about to do something exciting. After a while he seems to get the idea that pacing doesn't mean we're going for a walk. He curls up on the couch and sighs through his nose but keeps one eye open, as if I might blow at any minute. Actual pacing feels better than just sitting there, pacing in your mind. I need a plan, bad. If my mom and Lorenzo made one last night, no one has told me yet. The lack of answers gnaws like a lost thing does—your keys, or your favorite ChapStick, or that disappearing coin case from Mase's magic kit that actually disappeared. Man, you sure can get unhinged over a ChapStick or a disappearing coin case. Clothes tossed from the laundry basket, couch cushions dislodged, hands meeting the dust balls under furniture or the coffee grounds in the garbage, all for a little peace of mind.

But, of course, I do have a plan. One plan and one plan only. Plan A.

Plan A. It makes me think about that other famous fallen girl we read about last year, Hester Prynne, with her scarlet letter. An *A* forced on her chest for a different reason.

I guess we're not done wearing those.

Luckily, it's my day off at Euwing's, so I have endless hours to torment myself with something else I need to do: ask Maureen for vacation time. I should have done it the minute I knew we were going to Oregon, but it's one of those things that get scarier the more you put them off. No one really has vacation time at Euwing's Drugs. Evan once took a long weekend to go camping, and we heard *It must be nice*–type comments from Maureen for weeks, and Mrs. Euwing had to come fill in. She kept screwing up and calling for Maureen over the intercom to fix the register errors. Mr. Euwing also said, *Evan is not a go-getter.* I wish a silly little compliment wouldn't make me work so hard to get another one.

I also have endless hours to fight off every horrible and complicated thought about the Euwings and my job. Every time I think I can't stand it another second, having to see Drake in that truck or in the store, having to wonder in a sick endless loop what Mr. Euwing would do if he knew, what Mrs. Euwing, with her little cross necklace, would want or even demand if *she* knew, I think of my paycheck, a big zero. I think of my dream of the world, being in it and seeing it, gone. Maybe it's denial, not the most successful coping mechanism, that's for sure, but I keep thinking I can make this turn out okay. If they can only not find out about me, I might have a chance. I'd just have to stomach the rest. The uglies, whenever I see Drake's skinny shoulders and baby face. The narrow escape from being intertwined in their lives forever.

Of course, the denial isn't working all that well, since I am right now hiding out in my own house. The finding-out is spreading, like our weeds into Mrs. Branson's perfect lawn.

I lie down and fall into the weird, deep sleep I've been having lately. When I wake up, I'm still me, and my body is still no longer mine, and that stick still dropped, and everyone still knows. I read the Tess book for a while, then put it down and pick it up again, but she's sixteen, and this isn't helping. The only coping mechanism that works for sure is to give yourself a little treat of comfort, so I make myself a box of Kraft Macaroni & Cheese, and I pour in the milk and the butter and the cheese dust, and I eat it out of the pan. Oh, the other coping mechanism I know is to do one useful thing, so I also tidy up the drawer with the silverware in it, spooning the spoons and the forks, and then placing the measuring cups so that they're snuggled up together by size. It's kind of soothing, making sure they have each other in the chaos of the drawer.

This is how the day passes until I hear the elementary school bus pull up. The little kids come shrieking out—the blond Riley sisters, six and eight, who always wear pink as if it's an assigned color; and poor J. J. Alvarez, Noah's fifth-grade brother, who walks alone, his backpack dragging on the sidewalk. Mason's school day is done shortly after, but Mom arranged for him to get a ride home with his friend Grace. It's not his favorite thing to do, because Grace sometimes gives him romantic presents (a woven bracelet to match hers, her school photo, et cetera), then gets mad when he doesn't do it back, like they're an old married couple and he forgot their anniversary. When I see him get out of Grace's mom's car, Mason looks weary. And that's the word. Not tired, but weary, as if he has a small invisible pinprick where his energy has been draining out. It seems wrong to look like that at age thirteen, but then, probably 70 percent of thirteen-year-olds feel like this because a) life, and b) junior high.

I saved him half of the macaroni and cheese and put it in the bowl that used to be his favorite, the one with Aladdin on the bottom. You have to remember not to take and take and take without giving back, that's the thing. I pour him a glass of orange juice, too, which is honestly a lot of orange, but he smiles when he sees his place at the table.

"Hey," he says.

"Hey," I say.

"Wow, thanks." I found the matching Aladdin fork in the silverware, too. Even though it's kind of babyish, he holds it up and waggles it, as if we both share a nice memory.

"No problemo," I say, like Mr. Mysterioso. I sure wish we could have found that disappearing coin case. It was his favorite trick in the box, the coolest one for sure. It sometimes seems like it's the best things that vanish, and the worst that never leave.

It's sneaky, but when you get out of your own mind for a while and actually *see* other people and what *they* might need, too, you can feel, even for a minute, like maybe things will be all right after all. At least, I have a split second where I think I might have gotten through that hard day with nothing too terrible happening. I mean, the situation is still there, but it hasn't gotten worse.

I try to hold on to that feeling while scrubbing out the pan with the rusty S.O.S pad, but any optimism begins to slip. It's rusty water, and a memory of the dead and bloody pheasants in *Tess,* and a thin film of grease. Nausea spins up, a swirl, a helix. When the doorbell rings, the good feeling is gone, *poof.* I make a huge mistake because I peek out from the curtains. *Of course* they see me.

Peyton and Faith.

I leap away from the window, my heart pounding. My back is flat against the wall, and I try not to move as they *ding-dong ding-dong* the bell, and as Wilson barks his head off. Mason yells, "Ives, GET THE DOOR," imagining a delivery person, maybe, though when do we get those.

When I open it, they're standing on our step like a pair of FBI agents.

"Can we come in?" Peyton asks, as if it's a ridiculous question, given their rights. I step aside, like *Be my guest.* They actually head straight on over to our couch and sit down and gesture to the chair for me to sit, and I practically forget it's my own house, which is probably how those people feel when the FBI really does come. I feel panicked and trapped, and my mind helpfully scrolls through all the movie scenes where someone escapes through the air-conditioning vent of a building or squeezes through an impossibly small bathroom window in the nick of time. Since I'm generally not that athletic, I just sit where they tell me to.

"Okay. What's going on?" Peyton demands.

There is no way I'm going to tell them what's going on.

"Are you, um, *pregnant*?" Faith asks. She stares at me with her clear blue eyes. She asks this with the sort of shock, disgust, and disbelief she might show if she'd just stumbled upon me in an alley with a heroin needle in my arm, rather than in a situation that her sister, Harmony, was probably once in, too, though her family won't admit it. A situation that is generally possible for most anyone with a uterus.

I open my mouth to lie, but my face turns red and answers for me. I can't even believe all the ways your body can be a traitor.

"Oh no, Ivy . . ." Peyton sighs and shakes her head. Her earrings are little unicorns. One of them is right side up and the other on his back with his feet in the air, a dire sign. She sticks her fingers in the threads of her pre-worn, pre-holed jeans. I remember us trying to play that cat's cradle game at a sleepover when we were little but giving up because the string just got too tangled.

"How did this *happen*?" Faith asks.

I assume Faith knows the basic scientific details, but I'm not entirely sure. Her dad demanded she be excused from health during sex ed, and she's only allowed to watch PG movies. She once admitted that, for the longest time, when guys joked around and made that fast back-and-forth hand motion to indicate jerking off, she thought they were miming a bartender with a cocktail shaker. And she has one of those purity rings her dad gave her that says TRUE LOVE WAITS. She spins this now. It's on the ring finger of her left hand.

"*How* how?" I ask. But no way. Forget it. Besides, I *was* in those classes, and they never covered *this*.

"Are you okay?" Peyton sits over there on the couch and doesn't come to hug me or anything, but maybe that's because I look pissed. I stare out the window. From this chair I can see down the whole street, where J. J. Alvarez is playing with Hot Wheels in the gutter dust. He's only ten, but he looks thirteen at least. He's big enough that the other kids stay away. "Ivy?" Peyton leans forward to get my attention. "I know you've had a rough time lately. With your mom, and then Jason giving you crap every time you turned around . . ."

Yeah, every time I turned around, all right. Teasing, the kind you get when you're in elementary school. *Do you need an IV, Ivy, so you're not so stupid?* But also, hanging out by my locker to look threatening. Sticking his foot out in the cafeteria so I'd have to walk over it to get past him. Nothing I couldn't handle until Drake.

"What are you going to *do*?" Faith asks. "Is Lorenzo going to do the right thing?"

Telling them the truth will mean chaining my ankle to Drake's and the whole Euwing family forever, because if this got out, they'd try to stop any abortion, I'm pretty sure. I can't believe Lorenzo is doing this for me, letting everyone think it's his. *I don't give a shit*, he keeps saying. *These people don't mean anything to me.* He's telling the truth. He doesn't even know how long he'll be staying around here after graduation, and he isn't even going to do the whole cap-and-gown ceremony at our school. That not-knowing, though—Lorenzo's obsessed and, man, practically haunted about not having a life plan. *I need to do something that matters. Something that helps.* Talk about the restless agony of something missing, especially if that something is an answer.

"The right thing?" I say. It's such a weird idea. Like there's only one. I mean, what is the right thing, really? Tell me. What is my right thing? Because I only see wrong things, not right ones. I have to pick the most right wrong thing.

"He sure better stand by you," Peyton says. She's trying to be protective, but it sounds intimidating.

"Please. *Please.* I don't want to talk about this, okay? If you're my friends and you care about me, I'm asking you to just go on about your life as usual. Pretend this isn't happening. Let me just figure it out. Afterward, we'll all just go back to normal."

"*Afterward?* After *what?* I hope you're not going to do anything awful. And by the way, no one's going back to *normal.*" Faith makes a face, huffs out of her nose. It's practically a snort. "After today, normal is long gone."

I think she means the stick, but when she and Peyton give each other *oh my God* eyes, I realize they mean something more. "What?" A shadow feeling slides across my body and presses down. It's hard to breathe.

"It doesn't matter," Peyton says.

"*What?* What happened? Tell me."

"On your locker. Someone drew this big . . ." Faith draws one line down in the air and then a horizontal one over it. It's hard to tell if she's drawing a cross or a plus sign, like the one that appeared on my pregnancy test. It's weird how similar those two things are when you think about it, only the height of the crossbar making the difference. The kids who go to City of Hope Church of God and New Redeemer Christian might say that the height is the important thing, being above, but I'm starting to wonder if it's harder to see from up there.

"A . . ." I put my palms up to say *no idea.*

"Cross," Faith says.

"It wasn't a *cross,*" Peyton says. "It was a plus sign, like the *test.*"

It's so mean that I refuse to cry. I fold my arms in anger at every person who's confident enough to be superior, because if something bad hasn't happened to you, it just hasn't happened *yet.* How easy it is to be smug when you've had it easy. When you've been lucky.

"Who did it?" In spite of my anger, my voice wobbles. If I'm being honest, I'm devastated. Sadness and horror are rushing in. The uglies, for a new reason.

"Probably Hope or someone," Peyton says.

"Probably *Noah,*" Faith says.

"*No!* He wouldn't do that!" Peyton's face flushes.

Right that minute I watch Noah's little (big) brother get up and throw a rock at a tree. Noah *would* do that. He was laughing so hard after Jason fell at that party that he was practically wheezing. Hope, too.

"Is Lorenzo okay?" I ask. I haven't gotten to talk to him yet. "Did they do anything to him?"

"You're seriously thinking about *Lorenzo?*" Peyton spins her bracelet.

"I love him," I say, and immediately regret it. It's private. But I do. I love him, and I left him alone to face those wolves.

Peyton and Faith meet eyes. They think I mean something else, like me and Lorenzo are bonded in baby-making lust. Lorenzo is already an outsider, a guy from *California*, and now any earlier distrust of him has been proven right. They're not FBI agents anymore. No, now they're the family members doing an intervention, and I'm the stubborn addict who refuses to admit I have a problem. To Faith, though, a sexual lapse is way worse than drugs. Once you fall like this, you can never get back up. You can get sober, but you can never get your purity back. *Purity.* It's so weird. Only girls have it apparently.

"You barely know him. None of us do. He's been here, what, nine months?" Peyton says, and then flinches.

It had to be *nine months*, didn't it? Faith gives Peyton an *Ugh!* look, and Peyton gives her an *I'm sorry, okay?* look back. Peyton's control of the situation slips, and she picks at a hangnail and then bites the edge of her finger. Saying the exact wrong thing is probably a universal experience, but it sure doesn't feel like it when you do it.

"He seemed fine, Ivy. No one did anything to him," Faith says. "Well, *Nate.*"

"*Our* Nate?" This hurts. We've been friends for a long time. Way back in third grade, he was so bad at spelling, I'd help him with his words at recess.

"Well, he said, 'Thanks for knocking up my friend,' and then he shoved Lorenzo like it was a big joke. Some other people heard. Jason, Drake. They started laughing, so that probably didn't feel awesome," Peyton says.

Jason. Drake. Perfect. How perfect. I'm sinking. I'm sinking in some gross liquid of anger and embarrassment and a surreal horror.

"So funny, hahaha," Faith says.

"Yeah, congratulations for not using protection." Peyton looks so mad. Mad enough to cry. And it's confusing, you know. Because when they blame the guy, they say he got the girl pregnant, like on his end, the pregnant is the worst part, not the sex. When they blame the girl, she should have kept her legs shut, like the sex is the worst part, not the pregnant.

"I'm sorry . . . ," I plead. "Can you . . . I mean . . ." I don't know how to say it, but I want them to leave. I wave my hand helplessly. None of this is doing any good, and none of it will change a thing. And it's so strange, but with me in this chair and them over on that couch, I see it, this wide, wide space between us. It wasn't there just a few weeks ago, but now it is. We're so far apart already. There's that expression, *You're not in Kansas anymore,* and I'm suddenly aware that I'm not in childhood anymore.

"You want us to *go?*" Now Peyton looks hurt.

"I'm sorry. I'm just overwhelmed. And my mom is going to be home soon, and I haven't told her yet."

It's a total lie, and I don't have a clue why I said it.

"Oh my God, she doesn't *know?*" Peyton tells her mom everything. They're best friends, even more than her and me, or her and Faith. Every Mother's Day they go to one of those paint-your-own pottery places and make something for their collection. They've done so many of them, they're down to those little dishes you put your cooking spoon on so the counter doesn't get tomato sauce on it.

"Your mom is going to be *devastated*," Faith says. "I feel *so bad* for her! And oh my God! What about dance team next year?" For a minute Faith is forgetting that she's doing dance team, not me.

"I just . . . maybe need some time alone to figure out how to tell her before she hears."

Lies and more lies. My spirit lifts from my body, and I see the girl acting a part below. It's a bad movie on the Hallmark Channel. Maybe I'm just trying to give them something, since they came over. Inside information. An important role. A parting gift before they leave, or else, hinting at a larger mess and an imminent disaster that will send them fleeing.

"Oh geez, Faith, we should let her . . . you know, *think*." Peyton grabs Faith's knee and gives it a little shake, same as my father does when he's decided something. My father. I'm definitely not going to tell him. Maybe someday, but not now. There's no guilty indecision about this. He keeps things from us, too—girlfriends, especially. Lots of them.

Faith loops her handbag over her shoulder. Peyton does the same with hers. I picture them years later, here in Paris, Texas, doing that same thing after having lunch together at Colombo's Italian Café.

They hug me. In my mind I wave goodbye from the other side of the canyon.

"Lorenzo better get a job, at least, and fast," Faith says.

After they walk out the front door, I think about that bumper sticker I saw a few months ago, on a shit car at Save A Lot, the one that said DON'T BELIEVE EVERYTHING YOU THINK. It stuck with me. It just keeps looping and looping in my mind.

When my friends head to their car, Diesel springs out and rages against the chain link, and Faith grabs Peyton's arm in alarm. She always sees Diesel do this, but it still scares her every time, too. I watch until Peyton's mom's car—a new Hyundai, not a shit car—vanishes down our street.

"It's safe. You can come out now," I yell to Mase. I know he's been listening to every word.

"Whew," he says when he pops out of the kitchen. "I need a drink." He twists the top off of a Dr Pepper and takes a long swig.

9

THAT CROSS ON MY LOCKER—IT FEELS LIKE AN anchor pulling me down, down, into a permanent humiliation. I can't stop imagining Jason and Drake laughing, hahaha, like vicious hyenas circling. I want to hide, maybe forever. I go to my room, get in bed, and pull the covers over my head. It's hot under there, and I have to keep popping out to breathe, but I don't want to be anywhere else ever again. I'm too tired to move. Every piece of me is embarrassed, all of my skin is, and my traitor hands, and my horrible mouth.

I stay in there until Mom comes home. She tries to lure me out, but I can only moan a *nooooo*. She pleads, and I tell her I just wish me and Lorenzo could get in the car and go to Oregon right now. Nothing has the chance to get on a right road again until then. She sighs because that's never going to happen.

She leaves me alone. I go back under. I hear her talking to Mase, and I hear the *dink dink dinkdinkdink* of dog kibble dropping into Wilson's metal bowl. The faucet goes on and then off, his water, probably. I hear Mom talking to someone on the phone now. Mumble, mumble, serious. A spell of quiet listening, and then more mumbling. Grave tones. Think of that word, *grave*. It's a Tess word. Mom better not be telling anyone else. Already, Mase knows, and Grandma Lottie knows, and our whole school, basically. Who's left? Might as well rent a billboard.

Usually, I can barely sleep when I'm stressed by something silly like a final, but now sleep is so insistent, it keeps pulling me under. When I wake up, I have to pee, bad, and I'm super hungry, and I smell butter. Mase is making dinner, so I finally drag myself up and out to the kitchen. Even when you vanish, you need to eat. I hear voices. Well, one voice that's not usually there.

"What are you doing here?" I ask Lorenzo.

Mom's sitting at the table with a bottle of Shiner beer, picking at the yellow label, and he's sitting across from her, looking like he's been to our house a million times. He's got an open bag of chips in front of him, and orange fingers from barbecue flavoring.

"Well, good morning, glory," Mom says, even though it's getting dark. "I thought you might like some company. I thought . . . This was a bad day, you know. A very bad day."

"Hey, Ives," Lorenzo says. "What a shit thing that happened. Man. I'm so sorry. People *suck*. But we're here to turn this ship around." He licks the orange off his thumb. He never talks like this, the ship thing, I mean. I see a couple of empty Coke cans on the table, crushed in half, so maybe it's caffeine-fueled optimism.

"We've been—"

"I don't even want to know," I say, interrupting Mom.

"Croque monsieur!" Mason waves a spatula. Croque monsieur is basically a grilled ham-and-cheese sandwich, which Mason smashes into delicious melty goodness by pressing a pan into another pan. We've had it before, but I'm not complaining, that's for sure. Side dishes: chips, if Lorenzo hasn't eaten them all already, along with a bowl of cantaloupe and honeydew balls I spot on the counter. My mom gave Mase the melon baller (haha, if I were in the mood to laugh) last Christmas. It's like a tiny ice-cream scoop with a long handle, and he, ugh, balls lots of things besides melons—apples, pears, ground beef. "Sit, sit!" Mason urges, like an eccentric, overly enthusiastic chef in the movies.

I do. Lorenzo grabs my hand and gives it a little shake of love, and I'm not even grossed out by the chip dust. Mason slides the sandwiches onto our plates.

"Wow," Lorenzo says. He's never had Mason's croque monsieur before, and after Mase joins us, Lorenzo takes a bite. "Mmm," he says, mouth full. He stretches the sandwich triangle until a string of cheese slaps his chin. I wonder what it would be like to watch a husband eat his meals day after day. Gross, probably. Disgusting enough that you'd eventually forget how cute his butt looks in those jeans.

Mom interrupts dinner to turn on some music. It's one of her favorite albums, and we've heard it countless times, a group called Fleetwood Mac. Mase really likes it. Sometimes he says, *Put on the Mac-a-roni!* and we know what he means.

"*Rumours,*" Mom says to Lorenzo, like they have an understanding. It's the name of the album, but something's happening. Something's going on here, and it's making me nervous.

"So you said your parents weren't married very long?" my mom asks Lorenzo. She opens a second beer. She rarely even drinks. I had no idea we even *had* beer. A lot seems to have happened during that nap.

"They were divorced when he was *three*." I try to sound like I'm an expert in all things Lorenzo, even though he's new to me, too, to be honest.

"Like, four years?" Lorenzo says. "I barely remember, so whenever I see them together, you might as well take two random strangers in Kroger and imagine them married."

"They don't match *at all*," I say, as if my experience extends beyond meeting his mom for lunch once, and seeing his dad for a few uncomfortable minutes in their kitchen. But this seems true. His dad is kind of tough but handsome for an old guy, like one of those actors in the sort of movie where his family is kidnapped and he needs to save them and the world as the clock ticks. What is that man's name who's in all of those? I can never remember. Harrison something. Koster? Kostner? And Lorenzo's mom is all professional and outgoing, polished, with a businessperson's manicure and not a Maureen-manicure with sparkles and holiday themes. She's "in sales" but something medical, and Lorenzo lives with his dad because she travels so much for work.

"He kind of keeps to himself, but, you know, he's more of a passionate guy than you'd think." Lorenzo laughs. Such a great laugh. It always makes you want to laugh, too. You can tell he really loves his dad, even if his dad is so quiet that their relationship seems like a mystery. He's the sort of quiet where he barely speaks, so you just want to get out of there. "Funny story. When he was in college, he once rode a bull to impress a girl. Just, like, got in the ring, no experience on a horse, nothing, let alone bull-riding."

"Oh geez, was he okay?" Mom asks.

"Broke his nose."

"What about the girl?" I ask, but then Mom interrupts and tells him the story we've heard a million times, about how she and her girlfriend, Mom's oldest friend, Esilda, decided they were going to try to get onstage when they went to a Hootie & the Blowfish concert.

"Hootie and the Blowfish, sick name," Lorenzo says.

"Tootie and the Blowfish," Mase says. He obviously thinks Lorenzo is amazing, because one minute he's acting all grown up, and the next like he's a five-year-old trying to get attention.

My mom strums her imaginary guitar, swinging her head. " 'There's nothing I can do. . . . I only wanna be with you-ooo.' Es had one knee on the stage, and I was pushing her rear end up when security came."

"Busted," Lorenzo says.

Now Mom raises her hand to quiet us. She tilts an ear so that we listen, too. " 'Dreams,' " she says to Lorenzo.

He nods and just pulls the strings of his hoodie, because you can't miss them, those words. Someone is telling someone else that if they want their freedom, they won't hold them back. There are a few lines that I never really heard before, and now they make my throat tighten with emotion.

What you had, and what you lost . . . I know, I know. I can't look at anyone. I separate the balls of fruit by color with my fork.

"Ivy?" Mom says.

"Hmm."

"We've got something to tell you."

"*We?*" I pop my head up.

"I've been thinking. Thinking *a lot*. But after today . . . it just keeps pounding on me, how much has been taken from you. And, you know, I realized that this *choice* shouldn't be. Your choice, what you want right now. I can't even believe I'm saying this."

"What?" I have no idea what's coming.

"You keep telling me that you wish you could do this with Lorenzo. Drive to Oregon. The two of you."

"You're *letting* me?"

"I'm letting you."

"Wait, what? Do you even *want* this?" I ask Lorenzo. He offered, but this was before the cross. This was before it could actually *happen.*

"Hell yeah, I want this."

What about Lorenzo and the law? It's one thing to wish for it and another thing to actually *do* it. "What about you and . . . ? *You* could get arrested! For *helping.*"

"I have choices, too," he says.

"Choice," Mom says, like the word is sacred. "Choice is the thing."

The last crust of croque monsieur is gone, and only the smooshiest fruit is left in the bottom of the bowl. The songs have moved through "Never Going Back Again" to "Go

Your Own Way," and I have the anxious feeling of actually getting something questionable that you said you wanted. "Are you *sure*?" I ask Mom.

"Don't give me a chance to change my mind," she says.

"As long as you don't get married on the way," Mase says again. He starts cleaning up, by which I mean crumpling up the chip bag.

"Wait, wait," Lorenzo says. "Hang tight." He lifts one finger, scoots out of his chair, and then, *poof,* he's gone, like Mr. Mysterioso.

I have no idea what's happening. "Just wait," Mase says, but he doesn't have a clue, either. Wilson Phillips picks up on the edgy energy in the room and starts hopping up on my legs.

When Lorenzo returns, he's carrying a notebook. The flat spiral kind, green, the ones you get at Euwing's for a dollar thirty-nine, and at CVS for a buck, as soon as the school supplies appear. A pen is stuck in the coil, and when Lorenzo sits back down, he plucks it out and opens the notebook, and a map slips out. An old-fashioned map. Long rectangular paper, which he proceeds to unfold and unfold again, like Mr. Mysterioso pulling out endless scarves from a hat. The music has turned seriously upbeat. A hopeful energy fills me, same as the song about a you who makes loving fun. Mom scooches the fruit bowl, and Mase moves the milk carton.

"That's so cool," Mase says.

"Tell me you have seen a map before," Mom says.

"On your *phone*," he says, and she groans. Ever since Mase saw a music CD and thought it was a tiny record,

Mom insists on showing us things from days gone by—fax machines, calculators, the Violent Femmes. She once crossed two lanes of a highway when she saw a pay phone and made us get out and look at it, and she told us about the time she needed a ride home after a bad date and had no money, but she did have luck, because she found a quarter in the little metal tray. Another time, we went all the way to the Galaxy Drive-In in Ennis, Texas, *before drive-ins go extinct,* she said. She used to go when she was little, and she and her sister, Aunt Betts, would wear their pajamas and watch from the back seat, with Grandma Lottie and Grandpa Larry in the front. We drove a full two hours just to see *Ghostbusters,* which you can see on TV pretty much anytime you want if you have all the big cable channels like Peyton and Faith do. That pay phone—it had scratched-up plastic walls and smelled like pee, and the drive-in speakers kept cutting out, but to her it was like seeing mastodons in a museum. Things that were monumental and are now gone.

This map, though—it's a living thing. It's come out from the glove box of Lorenzo's shit car and is showing us how it's done. There are circles around various places, and when I look closer, I see that they form a route from Paris, Texas, to Manhattan Beach, Oregon, where Grandma Lottie lives.

"Oh wow," Mom says. "You said you planned the trip, but *damn.*"

Lorenzo smooths the map and then watches my face. He stares until I get it, too, until I see. Paris, Texas, to Lima, Oklahoma, to Moscow, Kansas, to Genoa, Colorado, to Naples, Utah. From there it's Manila, Utah, to Geneva, Idaho.

Then, in Oregon, from Rome to Glasgow, and on to Manhattan. Manhattan Beach in Oregon, that is.

My heart starts to fill, the taps turned on full blast. I've told him so often how I wanted this, and bad. And Lorenzo—he heard.

"We're going to travel the world, Ives," he says.

That night, around the kitchen table, I go through every emotion. Despair, fear, hope, joy, because there's that song playing called "The Chain," which makes me think of chain-link fences and cages and Diesel, barely held back, but there's also one called "Songbird," a song that brings tears to your eyes but is all about love. And about there being no more crying, and the sun shining down.

The itinerary changes a bit because Mom says, "Hey, my sister lives in Florence, Oregon. You two can stay with her. Florence! Right here, right by Manhattan," which makes Lorenzo so happy that his eyes light up. Mase gets a pen out of the can by the wall phone (not used anymore but still up, another mastodon), and he hands it to Lorenzo, who crosses out Glasgow and circles Florence. Mase also spots Limon, Colorado, right by Genoa, so we add that one in, too.

I am so full of gratitude, I'm not big enough to hold it all.

It's getting late, and Lorenzo's heading home, gathering up the papers, the plans for Plan A. I feel shivery with emotion, and I race to my room to grab a hoodie so I can walk him to his shit truck to say goodbye.

My mom's voice is low, but I hear her. "And you still don't want to tell your dad yet?"

"Yeah, I've gone over it in my head a bunch of times. It's going to be easier if he just thinks we're going on a road trip. He's all in favor of a road trip, I'll tell you. Otherwise I'd have to tell him the truth, and I *promised* Ivy. It'll get complicated."

"Right," she says, but Mom's voice is worried. Lorenzo's dad—he's the kind of guy who doesn't say much and stays to himself, but if someone tells him about me, this will get messy. Any fool anywhere who has watched absolutely any film knows that a secret like this is a Recipe for Disaster.

"God. I hope I'm doing the right thing," Mom says. "This doesn't feel like the right thing. What about—"

"If we're choosing choice, we're doing choice all the way," Lorenzo says.

They shut up when I appear, and I walk Lorenzo outside. We stand under the beautiful old moon. It's weird, but the night is quiet, so quiet. Diesel is inside. The silence is almost more nerve-racking than Diesel's snarling and barking. When you can see him, you know where he is; you know how to gauge the danger.

Lorenzo kisses me. I forgot how good it is, just us doing this. The anxiety steps aside and glee tap-dances out, because Lorenzo and I are going to get to be alone. Alone, for days. For *nights*. Lorenzo, see—we haven't even had sex yet. And I never have. Not the sex you see in movies like *Rockaway Weekend*, anyway. Two people in bed, actually in love and making love and wanting each other. I haven't had anything close to that with him or anyone.

Lorenzo looks at me like someone cherished and not ruined.

"Songbird," he says, and taps my nose.

10

THE PLAN GETS MORE SOLID OVER THE NEXT COUPLE
of days, with places to stay and final details to help us save
money. Mom's oldest friend, Esilda, lives in Dodge City,
near Moscow, Kansas, and Mom arranges our overnight
visit. Mom's second cousin, who I met, like, once, has a
B and B in Utah near our route, too. This cuts our motel vis-
its down to three each way. Mom has done all the financial
calculations—gas, lodging, food, et cetera (THE et cetera).
She's compared it to the price of flying, and it's much cheaper,
if we keep our lodging costs down. I feel so bad about the
money. I keep saying, *Let me use what I've saved,* and she
keeps saying, *No, Ives, absolutely not. This is a health-care
issue. This is a medical expense.*

I stay home from school again that day. I go to work,
though. Mase is mad about it, and Mom keeps pressing me
about my *options,* quitting being the first one. I won't listen,
and her impatience is showing. She blows breath out like
I'm being unreasonable. I hear her talking to herself. Maybe

I am being unreasonable, I don't know, I don't know. I just know that school is gone, and this is a piece of me and my life and my plan for the future that's still here. This is me, the responsible one, the go-getter. The one who became an assistant manager way earlier than anyone else. I want to hold on to it. So? So what.

The bell of the door dings my arrival. I'm so anxious because maybe they know already. I have no idea what might happen when I show my face there. I pass Buddy and Missy in their cage. I stick my finger in to be friendly, but I don't want to, okay? I don't want to be friendly to them. Buddy is pick-pick-picking his wing, and Missy is staring at me with those fake eyes from the bin at Shelley's Craft and Quilt, and the newspapers at the bottom have shit on them and smell sour and pulpy. My stomach swirls. I wish someone would let those birds out, but I've heard that if you're in a cage like that for so long, you sometimes fly right back in. It makes me sad to think about. And then I wonder, you know, if Harmony feels this way about the Belle Vista apartments, living there with Abraham.

My heart starts pounding hard when I see the top of Maureen's head, bent over some boxes. "Hi!" I call, my voice dripping sweetness. This is the *Have they heard?* test, right here in aisle 2B, next to SHAVING NEEDS.

But Maureen only says, "Hello, Ivy. Was it you who left your yogurt in the fridge? It's *expired.*"

And I only answer, "No. Must be Evan's."

Evan hasn't heard anything about me, either. At least, he's whistling as annoyingly as usual, and Mr. Euwing waves at me from the back. I'm in the clear, I'm in the clear! Still,

I'm so anxious during my whole shift that I forget to scan Mrs. Dean's coupons, and I mark down all the garden supplies (*all* of them—gloves, trowels, ceramic frogs, little metal signs in the shape of sunflowers and watering cans that read CARDINALS APPEAR WHEN ANGELS ARE NEAR and PARDON THE WEEDS) when I was supposed to discount the summer toys (water guns, blow-up pools, floatie rings).

"Can I speak with you?" I finally ask Maureen near the end of the day. I can't put this off any longer. She's in the break room, rinsing out her coffee thermos for tomorrow.

"Now?" she asks.

"If you don't mind."

She obviously minds. She sighs as if she's a Sherpa going up Everest. She places the thermos in her purse, one of those QVC types with fourteen thousand pockets that bulge with the importance of burden. She zips it dramatically to indicate that I'm delaying her imminent and much-deserved rest. It's true, I am, and it's true, too, that she does deserve it. She works so hard. She'll be the first to tell you that, but still.

"I have a family emergency." I give her a general pained expression. It's real, that's for sure. "I'm so, so sorry to do this, but I'm going to need to take some time off, starting Saturday."

She scans my face as if she has an internal lie detector, which, obviously, she does not. Even Maureen isn't awful enough to give me trouble if my family is hurting. She rubs her forehead. "Ooookay. Well, Bob and the Mrs. are taking Drake to Six Flags, so she can't fill in."

I have a brief flash of a baby's father, riding in a log down pretend rapids, his skinny arms up, screaming. Uglies,

uglies. My hands make fists; my nails dig in. "Oh shoot," I manage to say.

"I can maybe ask Cheyenne, though I am fully aware how she'll feel about *that.*" Maureen actually seems sort of happy about this, forcing Cheyenne to do something she'll hate, maybe because Cheyenne *lacks initiative* and *has a thin résumé, one temp job, if you can believe it* and *has to be practically given opportunities on a silver platter.*

The biggest thing, though—Maureen has *still* not heard anything from anyone about that stick, and when she heads straight on in to the pharmacy to convey the new staffing crisis to Mr. Euwing before he leaves, he still hasn't, either. When the lights are down, just before we lock up, Mr. Euwing places the cover over Missy and Buddy and then takes my hands. This is one of those times I was talking about, where the old guys don't seem to know they shouldn't do this.

"I hope you'll let me know if there's anything I can do," he says. I want to take my hands back, wipe all of the gross-ness of off them, but I force myself to keep them there. He's done so much for me. His hands are cool, and I feel the edge of his wedding ring pressing into my skin. I try not to look away from his small pale eyes, hidden behind his glasses, staring into mine from his wide, blocky face.

"Thank you."

"Come right back to us." He takes a tiny tube of Carmex from his pocket (aisle 5, near the front), unscrews the cap, then slides the bulb across his chapped lips.

"I will," I say.

When he leaves, I can still smell the waxy, medicated

scent. Maureen locks up, and I head to the parking lot. I see the dome light of their truck go on as Mr. Euwing opens the passenger door. Drake is driving again. Mrs. Euwing is in the back, where, according to many, the wife belongs.

Come right back to us.

I will.

It was wrong of me, feeling all sad about Harmony being like Missy the lovebird, freed from her cage, but returning. I'm probably no different.

I spend the next day packing, and reading *Tess of the D'Urbervilles*. I wish I could just get that paper done, but I can't. I hit a wall whenever I try. The question that Ms. La Costa asked, *Why does history matter?*—I have no clue. Or else my head is in too much of a spin to think straight. It's a leaf in a storm, rising, twirling, dropping, landing on someone's garbage can, lifting again.

Lorenzo finishes school. In the afternoon, I go over to his house. I try not to think about what I missed, because I love the last day of school. It's the best day. Everyone's so jazzed and happy and the hall floors get covered with paper from everyone cleaning out their lockers and it just feels like the summer is so long, all stretched out ahead of you, full of promise. Anything can happen in those beautiful days before the school supplies appear on the store shelves. You're in the bliss of future flip-flops and floaties and end aisles of sun lotion and Otter Pops, and the little kids come off the bus and run home, screaming and chasing each other. I haven't been back to school since the stick and the cross, and in the car heading to Lorenzo's, I try to imagine my return in the fall. All I can see are eyes, and all I can feel is bad.

Lorenzo lives closer to town, and his house is small but bigger than ours, and it has a garage and a driveway. He's there, and I can only see his legs, sticking out from under the truck. My first thought is that the truck has broken down. Now that we have a plan, I keep worrying that it'll be destroyed at any minute. I try to make a lot of noise as I approach so my voice doesn't startle him. He might suddenly sit up and get a concussion or something.

"Hey, Lor." I'm trying out the nickname, since we're about to spend two whole weeks together, and I don't even have one for him yet. It's a no-go. He's not a Lor or a Zo or any other combo of letters. He's just himself.

He scoot-scoot-scoots out. His hair is all a mess, and it's so cute, and I wonder if that's what he looks like in the morning. I'm going to find out, and this makes me a nervous wreck, to be honest. Like, will we stay in the same bed? I mean, of course we will, but what if I drool? Can I somehow manage to brush my teeth before he wakes up? There's only going to be one bathroom. Farting will require self-confidence I do not possess.

"Ivy!"

Based on limited information, sure, I have another opinion: you know someone loves you when their face lights up whenever they see you.

"Is the truck okay?"

"Oh yeah, it's great. I mean, it's got a shit ton of miles on it, but I'm just making sure the oil's changed, and we're in good shape to go."

I loop my arms around him. It's strange, but we haven't been kissing a ton since I found out. I worry about this, like maybe he doesn't want me anymore, or want me like he used to. It's hard to know if it's me or him, though, because the Ivy who wanted him, too, seems separate from the me now, in this particular body. The old Ivy was way younger than I feel lately, and she was carefree and hopeful about all the great things that kisses could lead to. I miss it. I miss when things were just hot between us, and I hope it comes back.

"Is Chloe home?" Chloe, Lorenzo's sister, is a great little kid who's still interested in plants and bugs and birds, unlike a lot of the girls in her and Mase's class who've replaced those things with boys. I like her a lot, but I'm kind of hoping I don't have to see her sticker collection or hear facts about rabbits right now. It hits me—oh God, I hope *she* never finds out. She looks at me like she looks *up* to me. She once gave me her favorite rock, a polished purple one with a milky universe inside.

"Nah. She's getting a jump on summer at Frances's house. My dad should pay those people child support."

"Oh good." It makes me wish Mase had a best friend. "I just wanted to see you before tomorrow. To ask, you know, if you're *sure-sure* that you want to do this? Because I can totally handle it myself." I *can*. I'm a DeVries, a girl with her hands on her hips, fierce—at least at this moment I am.

"Yeah, Ives. Yeah. Of course. Are you having doubts?"

"No, I'm fine, just . . . It feels like we're . . ." It feels like we're going on a honeymoon or something, a big trip for an important reason, which we are, but not that reason. "It's big."

"Hey. We got this all planned out, but we can also just straight-shoot it over there. The fastest way possible. We don't need all this world-tour crap if you don't want it."

"I want it. I mean, I love the way you're trying to make this . . . more than just a trip to get . . . Making lemons out of lemonade."

"The other way around."

"It is?" He nods. I've always said it that way, but of course he's right. What was I thinking? God! I'm too clueless to be someone's mother, that's for sure. "Well, I mean, you're making a fun road trip out of a . . . Out of lemons."

The lemon-abortion thing doesn't work at all, and we both just stand there. Things get awkward fast, and I wonder how, how, how we're going to do okay for hours and hours in the car. This sounded like a dream before, but now it seems full of possible moments like this. The unspoken word sits between us, all sharp and ugly, surrounded by barbed wire.

"I meant to ask you something important," he says. "Before we go." His eyes are serious. The bird above us is not reading the room and chirps cheerfully. An airplane whooshes overhead, full of people who get to leave this place. My stomach starts to hurt. I picture an abandoned map, me and Mom and Mase making this trip.

"Okay." I brace myself.

"Do you mind if we stop in Dinosaur, Colorado?"

I laugh. Oh my God. Oh my God. I'm so relieved, I almost pinch him.

"I mean, we *have* to, right?" he says.

Lorenzo and I are leaving in the morning, so Mom's big old blue Samsonite suitcase sits by my bedroom door. That suitcase is another thing that's almost extinct but is still hanging in there. It has a ruffly pocket inside and a bumper sticker she tried to take off but couldn't all the way. It used to say CLINTON GORE '92 but now says TON GORE.

It's pretty much half-empty. I tried to look up what the weather was going to be like in all those states, but I got tired and just figured *summer*. Lately, my mind feels fuzzy sometimes, like it's wrapped in a down duvet.

It's close to midnight, and I'm still awake. It's unusual, not being yanked into that deep sleep, but I guess anxiety is winning the battle over my consciousness. God, thoughts take a lot of work, worries do. Managing them. Keeping stuff away—what happened to me, yeah, and also the fact that, in so many ways, my body isn't entirely mine. In spite of getting all this time alone with Lorenzo (a *dream*, I keep reminding myself), I just want it to be over with. *All* of it over with. The trip, the procedure, going back to school and work, facing the people here afterward. I want so much *all* to be in the past that I wish I could wake up in my first year at Paris Junior College, where most people won't know me. I'll have a chance to be new then. My body will be only mine again. In junior high I had this friend, Javier, who lived down the street before he moved away, and he used to go to St. Mary's. He told me that Catholics confess all their sins, and then the sins get wiped away after you say a certain number of prayers. A clean slate, wow. It sounds like such an awesome idea, but I'd probably be doing prayers until I was eighty.

There's a knock at my door, and Mom pokes her head in. "Ivy?" she whispers.

"I'm awake," I say. She opens the door, and Wilson Phillips comes running in. He's been woken up and is suddenly back on dog duty. Poor guy, his work hours have been totally off lately. He takes a flying leap onto the bed and licks my face, and his tongue actually touches my tongue, and gross. Gross. This brings to mind a horrible image, and uglies, uglies. I push him off. Mom sits by my bed.

"Ivy? Are you sure about this? Going with Lorenzo, I mean?" There are a lot of people asking each other if they're sure about this plan, which is not a good sign. "I feel so weird about it. It seems . . . reckless and irresponsible. Of me, I mean. As your mom. I want to respect your decisions around this, but it's killing me. I should be with you." Her mouth is solemn, her eyes distressed. And this is the exact reason I don't want her with me. I can't deal with her pain and worry when I'm trying to deal with my pain and worry. I can't take care of her taking care of me.

"My choice," I say. I've discovered that *choice* is the magic word with Mom on this, and it's true again, because when I say it, it's a power shield, and she backs off. It seems like it should be a power shield for every human being, but it isn't.

"I need . . . I want to . . . God, why is this so hard? I want to tell you something," she says.

At first she doesn't say more. She just traces the diagonal stitching of my bedspread with her finger. She's in her green robe with the quilted collar, the one me and Mase gave her for Christmas when I was, like, ten. The cuffs are frayed, and her toe polish is chipping, and gray is showing through her hair, so, you know, beauty and high style are not a priority in our house. Getting through stuff is the priority.

Dread slinks around in my body. I'm afraid of what's coming. "What?"

"I've never told anyone this before."

I suddenly understand what she's about to say. I don't know when or how, but I know what. I'm shocked. Like, really shocked. I'm not sure if I want her to tell me. No wonder she's been so understanding. No wonder, no wonder. "Okay."

"So you remember Terry. . . ."

"*Terry?*" Now I'm completely stunned. And horrified, to be honest. If this story involves Terry, it means it basically just happened. Like, a year and a half ago. I was expecting, what, a teen thing? Not a grown-adult-woman thing.

"Tall guy, dark hair, bad temper?"

"*Of course* I remember. I just . . . I wasn't expecting you to say his name."

"And remember the year before last, right around when I just got diagnosed, and Terry and I had broken up?"

"Kinda hard to forget."

"Right after I heard I had to have a biopsy, I stopped my birth-control pills. Just cold, out of fear. I'd been on them for years, and with the estrogen and breast cancer link, I was full of terror, and I stopped. I'd maybe missed three of them, four at the most, and I just figured, I don't know. I'm old, too. The chances of getting pregnant at my age, practically in menopause . . . So Terry and I . . ."

"I got it. You don't have to explain this part."

"And when I later realized I was pregnant on top of everything else . . . cancer, an upcoming surgery, radiation . . . Terry gone, Terry, with his anger and his, uh, fondness for alcohol . . . I didn't see any other choice. Not a choice that would be healthy for a baby, or remotely wise for me, or you both . . ."

"Yeah, *no.*"

"So I ordered some pills online. To induce a miscarriage. Ivy, I had an abortion, too."

Her face is focused, but her voice is solid and unwavering. She doesn't cry or seem racked with guilt. She isn't troubled to the point of despair, but she doesn't seem fierce to the point of hands on her hips, either. Both of those things require a similar energy, or maybe rise up from a similar ground. Aside from the way she watches me to see how I'm taking in this news, though, she's just calm and matter-of-fact.

"Why can't I just get those pills?"

"It's illegal now. You could get prosecuted. And I want you to see an actual doctor."

"Okay," I say.

"This is a health-care matter."

"Okay, okay."

"I just . . . I wanted you to know. It seemed wrong to sit here and hold my secret and pretend we're somehow different. We're two women, you know. We have bodies. Bodies that require all kinds of health care, Ives. Mammograms, antibiotics, sometimes chemotherapy. Sometimes an abortion."

I lean forward and hug her. It's wild—me and Mase, we had no idea. Man, what she was going through on top of what she was going through . . . I'm kind of grossed out about Terry, but hey, when haven't I been. Mom and I separate. I *do* see her anew. How do I explain it? She seems like her own individual self. A woman, yeah, who's experienced things.

She squeezes my leg. "It's going to be okay," she says. And even if I don't believe her, her hands are more like my hands when they open the door to leave. And her shoulders are more like my shoulders when they disappear down the hall. She, too, had counted and counted and counted again the days on her calendar. She, too, had made trips and trips and trips to the bathroom, hoping for her period. She, too, had peed on that stick and watched the clock as the minutes ticked to her future. She, too, had looked at that plus sign and thought, *I never imagined this would happen to me.*

11

"MASON!" I YELL. HE'S TAKEN A SHARPIE AND written *of* between the words *Ton* and *Gore* on the suitcase bumper sticker, so it now reads TON OF GORE.

"What?" He pops his head in from the kitchen. He's still in his pajamas, and the house smells like pancakes even though it's only seven a.m. Lorenzo and I have eight hours of driving ahead, so we're getting an early start. Also, Mason totally knows what. He tries to look innocent of any suitcase graffiti, but the corner of his mouth goes up in the suppressed joy of mischief. I don't really care about the *of,* but that kind of wrongdoing is no fun at all unless someone gives a good show of pretend outrage.

"Thanks *a lot.*"

And then I hear the rumble coming down the street. Is it louder than before? It seems louder. I hope Lorenzo's shit truck will get us to Oregon.

"He's here!" I shout.

I asked Lorenzo to keep the truck running when he

arrives so there won't be long goodbyes. I've got this full cup of emotion, and it just might spill over. I want to get going. But, damn, when Mom dashes out of her bedroom in her shorts and Bon Jovi T-shirt, I see how wrong I am, wanting to rush away from meaningful hugs and supportive glances and any and all of the gestures of love available to us sorry humans. Give me all the meaning. Give me all the hugs. Mase lifts the suitcase and hauls it out the door, looking like one of those ants carrying an enormous bread crumb. Mom's holding a shiny gift bag, the red foil one. It probably started off as a Christmas bag years ago, but it's appeared at every gift-giving event since.

"Here," she says. "My favorite prescription drug."

I shake it like I don't already have a solid guess what it is. I lift my eyebrows, pretending the contents are a mystery. Pretend outrage, pretend mystery—you've got to do a little innocent pretending when you love people.

"Open it on the way."

We all exchange *I love you*s, and Mom slips me some money that she can't really spare, and a credit card for emergencies, too. Mase tells Lorenzo to drive carefully, sounding like those dads in the car commercials when the daughter and the guy go to prom. I get in and Lorenzo honks goodbye. Mase gives a thumbs-up, and Mom folds her arms, the worry-squinch on her face, though maybe she just needs glasses. Diesel barks and flings himself against the chain-link fence, baring his fangs as we pass. J. J. Alvarez, wearing striped pajamas, stares at the morning out his window like he's seeing it through prison bars.

I dare to look over my shoulder, and I see my mom and my brother getting smaller in the distance, and my heart does one of its biggest magic tricks, where it's filling and breaking at the same time. Even Mr. Mysterioso can't do that one.

"Let's get out of here," Lorenzo says when we reach the end of our street. I look at him, really look at him, for the first time that morning. Dark curly hair, a beat-up KANSAS IS FOR LOVERS T-shirt. Soft ragged jeans, that smirk-smile that just kills me every time.

"Where'd you get that?" I point to his shirt. We're staying in Kansas tonight, at Esilda's house.

"Found it in my dad's drawer. Handsome, huh? *GQ* model is what you're thinking."

"So hot," I say. I pretend-touch a fire. "Eyow!"

"Tell me it's Raisinets." He nods his chin toward the red foil bag.

"Wait. Raisinets? You've got to be kidding me. You *like* those? Are we going to have our first fight of the trip? I didn't think anyone really ate Raisinets. You know they look like rabbit pellets."

"The appearance of something has never deterred me from loving it."

"Which is why you love *me*—is that what you're going to say?"

He rolls his eyes like that's the most nonsense thing ever. "I was thinking of my dad's old bulldog, Buster."

"I'm guessing a solid seventy percent of bulldogs are named Buster." I roll down my window. I suddenly remember

Mrs. Leroy from seventh grade, teaching us transitional phrases. *Fresh air* could be a transitional phrase. I feel myself moving through it, from home to wherever we'll end up next.

"What's in there? I can't stand an unopened present." This is one thing I already knew about Lorenzo. He had a birthday right after we started dating and practically ripped open my gift with his teeth. It was an Oakland A's baseball cap, and his eyes filled with tears when he saw it. His best friend in California, Mateo, had given him one, and Lorenzo lost it, he'd told me. Whenever he talks about Mateo, he gets that bromance-y wistfulness, and that hat had meant a lot. He couldn't believe I'd remembered.

I peek into the bag and move the tissue paper around. At the bottom, I spot a fleck of green plastic Easter grass from the bag's brief role as a basket. I smile—I was right. I shake the CD like a maraca. "Playlist."

"Oh awesome! Hey, how'd she know I had a CD player in the truck?"

"Because it's at least ten years old? Hey, Hootie and the Blowfish, 'Hold My Hand.'"

"Hoo-teee! My buds!"

"Bon Jovi, 'It's My Life'; Alanis Morissette, 'You Learn' . . . ," I read. And then a few songs down, I see Miley Cyrus, "The Climb," from that old *Hannah Montana* movie Mom, Mase, and I used to watch over and over on the couch, and "Love Lasts" by Hunter Eden, which plays at the end of *Rockaway Weekend*. Gloria Gaynor, "I Will Survive"— that song we all danced to in the kitchen during the worst of

The Beast. I see the last song—"Hold On," Wilson Phillips. Mom may not be here, but she'll be here. "Let's save it," I say, or try to say, because my voice is suddenly a tight violin string.

"Okay. Onward! Paris to Lima. Bypassing Cobb, Oklahoma, and going straight to Corn, and then ending up in Dodge City, near Moscow, and staying with . . . I always forget her name."

"Esilda. Mom's friend from age twelve."

"Esilda, Mom's friend from age twelve, who works at the Boot Hill Museum."

"Exactamundo."

I have a hard moment when we pass Faith's house. The garage door is up, and I've been in that garage tons of times, that's the thing. They keep the bottled water out there, and a bike pump, and it smells like a lawn mower that's just been used. But I remember the disgust on Faith's face, too, when she sat in our living room, and that disgust feels like a wall between us. She might have put up the wall, but we each have a side, and the wall belongs to us both. I tell myself I'm only hurt, but maybe *I* also feel a tiny bit of disgust toward Faith right then. It's an awful, awful thing to feel about a friend, someone you love. But where is her kindness and support when I need her most? I feel that pull of longing again, to feel what they do for God, to love him and be loved back. They're so confident about it. So certain about what's right and wrong. It seems nice, in lots of ways, not to see all the other sides about what you believe. A whole lot less confusing, for sure.

"You two will be okay," Lorenzo says, reading my mind. "She's your *friend*." He says it like Mom says "choice," like that word is sacred. Like that word is permanent.

And then, before you know it, we're getting on 271. The highway is stretching so forward, you can't see the end of it. If you didn't know better, you might think that it just kept on going, a ribbon around the earth. A ribbon you can hop right on and ride, starting in our very own Texas. There are miracles already: a passing trailer with two llamas inside, a silo gleaming like the biggest tin can ever, a lone cow, a billboard featuring a giant waffle. I stick my head way out the window like a dog, taking in the air, the wind, the world. Here's another opinion: I'm a very lucky unlucky person.

12

AFTER A HALF HOUR OR SO, THERE'S THE BRIEF THRILL
of crossing the state line into Oklahoma. It's dry tan grass
on one side, and dry tan grass on the other. Honestly, why
not spruce up the state line a bit? Why not make it an occasion, especially when it's the major thrill for little kids (okay,
me) on long car rides? How about a festive row of those plastic flags you see at used-car lots? Or one of those supertall air
people that wave and sway wherever there's a mattress sale?

"Hey, there was a sign," Lorenzo says after I make these
suggestions aloud. "And just wait. When you come back to
Texas, you'll get a marker on an awesome rock pile."

Rapidly, I'm realizing that there may be certain pesky
irritations now mine for miles while I'm in this truck with
Lorenzo. He has an insistent love for names, which I notice is a
thing sometime after we're officially in Oklahoma. A real love.
Like, the kind where you can't stop reciting any mildly quirky,
humorous, or intriguing one you see, to the point where your
fellow passenger may one day begin to scream silently.

"Stoned 4 Survival," he says, and looks at me as we pass a low-lying green building with a tin roof and a marijuana leaf painted on the top. This is after he's already called out Love's Travel Stop (accompanied by an eyebrow wiggle), Wholly Cow Mobile Home Park, Brennan's Bass Shop, and A Little Piece of Heaven RV Resort.

"You sure do like names," I say.

"You remember where I used to live, right?"

"Southern California?"

"*Avocado*. We could have lived in Gravesboro, but my dad couldn't resist."

"Him, too, then." I can't really imagine it. He seems so serious.

"Him, too. It's kind of our thing. Take special notice of the fact that we are right near Cobb, Oklahoma," he says.

"Will do."

And a while later: "Hey, Antlers! We're in Antlers!"

"Mostly, I see more dry tan grass," I say.

"That's all you see *from the highway*. There is so much more out there! And just wait," he says again, because if I'm seeing his pesky irritants, he's also seeing mine. "In a few miles we get to see Lima. First stamp in our passport."

"Is this it? I think we missed the turnoff. Or maybe we're not there yet."

"Here *is* there," Lorenzo says. It sounds vaguely philosophical, but if it has meaning, I have no idea what it is. He mostly sounds like our friend Ian, the time Ian ate his brother's pot brownie by mistake.

We're standing outside, leaning against his truck, parked in a high school lot. We drove around, and aside from a few churches, a brick factory, and a meat-processing plant, this is pretty much Lima. It's hot. A trickle of sweat actually rolls from my armpit down my side, like a giant armpit tear. For the millionth time I'm mad that men get to take off their shirts but women can't. I shift my bra around for some air and get a jab of pain, along with a reminder of why we're even here. You'd think being pregnant would be on your mind every single second, but it isn't. Right now, for me, anyway, the signs aren't giant and shouting, and I can understand, I really can, how some people might not even know it's happening until later.

Lorenzo opens his phone and reads. " 'Lima, Peru, is an architectural marvel, with fascinating Incan sites, extravagant palaces, and beautiful cathedrals. Founded by Francisco Pizarro in 1535, Lima is a must for history buffs.' Et cetera, et cetera. 'Downtown Lima is popular and generally overflowing with people, and you may prefer . . .' La la la. 'Beach areas, high-end shopping, five-star hotels.' "

"This is a really nice high school," I say. "Way nicer than ours, even."

Lorenzo kisses me. He pushes me up against the truck, but I worry we're being watched in such a small place. I give him a little shove, and Lorenzo—he listens to it. "Wait just a sec," he says, and opens the back door of the Avalanche. He fishes around in the real avalanche of our stuff, a slide that occurred after Lorenzo hit the brakes for a lone wild turkey who must have left his flock to seek adventure the way some people join the Peace Corps. Oh wow, wow. Lorenzo hands me an icy cold Mountain Dew.

"You are a cola angel," I say.

"In terms of thirst-quenching options, Mountain Dew is the peak experience. Maybe it's the color. Get it? Peak experience?" He laughs at his own joke, one obviously made entirely by accident, even though he's pretending otherwise.

"Peak, haha." I roll my eyes, as any bad joke requires. "Same, though. But I think it's because 'mountain' and 'dew' both sound so refreshing."

"Agreed." He cracks the top of his, takes a long drink, burps. I giggle like a child and shove him again.

"Buuurp," I say. I'd better be careful making fun of bodily sounds, so I cool it fast. I take a long, delicious, glorious, fantastic drink. Man, that's good. "What are tho—"

But he's a step ahead of me. He sets his bottle on the hood and hands over two small booklets covered in blue construction paper.

Now I see—I understand the blue construction paper. *Passport* written in his blocky handwriting on the front.

My throat pinches with emotion as we stand in that lot in front of a VISITORS ONLY parking sign, and as I scratch my ankle with the toe of my sneaker from some insect bite.

"You," I say. I never noticed it before, but his eyes have green flecks in them. How could I have missed this? Well, I saw it in Lima, Oklahoma.

He takes one of those self-inking rubber stamps and sets it on our first page. The paper is blank, aside from where he's labeled it *Lima*. He presses down. Now the paper is adorned with a red *PAID* stamp.

"All I had on short notice," he says.

"The *kashunk* sound is the important thing anyway," I say.

"Exactly! *Exactly.*" He smiles so big, and he shakes his head like maybe he noticed something about me, too, same as I did with those green flecks.

First stamp in our passport, he'd said a while back, but I had no idea he'd meant an actual one. A handmade one, stapled at the crease. There are no ancient ruins or fancy hotels here, but I feel proud of my stamp. I hold it at arm's length and admire it, as if I've really been somewhere.

I *have* been somewhere. Back on the road again, I open my phone and read aloud from the first site I find. " 'Lima is a town in Seminole County, in the state of Oklahoma, in the United States. At the last census in 2010, the population was fifty-three. This was a twenty-eight-point-four percent decline from 2000, when there were seventy-four residents.' Wow. Fifty-three!"

"Two different Limas," Lorenzo says.

"I bet the people in each Lima couldn't imagine living in the other Lima."

"Can you imagine if they had to swap? Like, if they had no choice, and suddenly the Lima Peruvians had to work at Butch's Custom Meat Processing, and the Lima Oklahomans had to live in a city with, what did it say, eleven million people."

I look down, stare at my fingernails. I mean, I *can* imagine being forced to live a life I didn't choose.

When Lorenzo glances over at me, he reads my face. "Oh yeah," he says. "Yeah."

"Do you remember when I told you to take special notice of Cobb?"

"Yes, indeed I do." I shift around in my seat. Four and a half hours in, I'm reminded of when we drive to see my dad in Odessa, a seven-hour trip, nothing anyone wants to repeat very often. Namely, my butt hurts, and every time after we stop to pee, like we just did in Mustang, Oklahoma, I'm sure I have to go again. Maybe because of you-know-why, but maybe because this is what always happens anyway. *When do you ever get to pee in Mustang?* Lorenzo had said, and so we found Mustang Old City Park, where we guessed right that there was a public bathroom. It had a single stall and one of those murky mirrors you can't actually see yourself in. I was thankful for that. I'm afraid to face the truth of what Lorenzo sees when he looks over at me, especially with the heat and the open windows. I used a paper towel to turn on the faucet, and another to open the door, and then I wadded them up and shot toward the garbage can and actually made it, which would've astonished my sophomore PE teacher, Mr. Roberts.

"Well, I told you to remember Cobb, because the town of

Corn is coming up, and tell me—when have you ever been in Corn and Cobb on the same day?"

Oh my God, Lorenzo is the cutest, especially when he has one elbow out his window. It's out his window a lot, because we have to keep turning off the air conditioner. It blasts to freezing without warning, and my nose becomes a small, icy peak, though it's eighty-two outside. It's just like home.

"That's a never," I say. He's the cutest, the sweetest, and also the most relentlessly cheerful. Hopefully not so relentless that it gives me murderous thoughts, but I'm wondering.

"Um, Lorenzo? I hate to even say this, but I have to pee."

"Again?" I see the slightest flicker of irritation. The first of the trip. "You just went."

"I'm . . ." I gesture to the general area of my middle. I don't know why, but I suddenly feel like I could burst into tears.

Lorenzo sees my face and comes to the rescue. "Oh right. Well, great, because when can you ever say you peed in Corn?"

It's elementary school humor, but we both crack up.

Lorenzo takes the exit, and we're soon greeted with a squat WELCOME TO CORN water tower. There's also one of those gas stations like the one at the real Rockaway Auto Supply and Repair, featured in *Rockaway Weekend*, with the old red pumps and the winged Mobil horse. There's also a second WELCOME TO CORN sign, swirling on the outside wall of Corn Hardware, which makes it the friendliest town we've been to so far. We head into the Corn Museum next to the town hall. It's not a museum exactly, more a room with photos of the old Corn, which looks a lot like today's Corn. We pretend to be interested so I can use the bathroom.

When I come out, Lorenzo's already in the truck. He's

got a couple of sandwiches wrapped in waxed paper, and two more Mountain Dews. I tell myself that one day, when I really am going to be a mother, I won't drink soda and will eat every healthy thing possible. I will be so good, I promise you that.

"You hungry?" Lorenzo asks. "Your brother packed lunch."

"My brother packed lunch?" I didn't even see him sneak it to Lorenzo.

"Cevapcici? No idea." He peeks into the smashed-flat hamburger bun. "Sausage, and maybe cream cheese?"

Lorenzo hands me my sandwich, and I am all at once overwhelmed with homesickness. This makes no sense whatsoever, since we're not even that far from home, but sense or not, I am. We're only halfway to Dodge City, and the panic of a midpoint floods in, the *going forward is as long as going back* paralysis. And then I remind myself that this is only the first day. The many days ahead, not just ending at the procedure, but ahead-ahead, scroll out like a coil of wire pulled tight.

"Are you a stop-and-eat road-trip person, or an eat-while-you-drive one?"

I shrug. "I don't really know who I am." I don't mean it that way, some dramatic statement about my whole being; it just pops out. Still, I realize it's true. Maybe because I all at once see myself from afar—a girl sitting in front of the Corn Museum with a boy she barely knows, holding a drippy Paris, Texas, cevapcici in rapidly failing waxed paper. I have no idea how I got here.

"Let's eat, then drive. This is pretty messy." Lorenzo licks his thumb.

"Sure."

Who am I? The kind of person who does what other people want, I guess.

Uglies, uglies, uglies.

13

AFTER WE FUEL UP, I TAKE OVER THE DRIVING FOR A
while. I'm concentrating so hard, I miss that we've crossed
over into Kansas until I see a LAND FOR SALE sign reading SITKA, KANSAS. It looks like that sign has been there a
long, long time. My eyes blur with endless fields and fields
and fields, tan-yellow and tan-yellow, a flat world, inter-
rupted only by grain silos and brief drives through towns
featuring the essentials: stoplight, church, gas station, store.
Lorenzo is asleep beside me, his mouth open. I see a filling.
I wonder when he got it. I wonder if he hates the dentist
or doesn't mind. I wonder a lot of things about him—what
he was like as a boy, and if he thinks animals have people thoughts, and if Sundays make him sad. I wonder if
he likes Halloween or Christmas better, or if he's like me
and just prefers a regular day. I wonder the same thing
he does, the thing that frustrates him to no end—what he's
going to do as a grown man, who he'll *be*.

We haven't *really* talked in all of these seven hours.

We've joked and told funny stories. I offered the one about me and Javier during PE, where we hid under the bleachers during a whole season of baseball and no one noticed, and Lorenzo told me some Lorenzo-and-Mateo adventures, a lot of them involving beer and horses and laughing so hard, they couldn't breathe. The most serious thing we spoke about was Dad, about how strange it is that he's in my baby pictures and he taught me how to tie my shoes and all, but how I don't really know who his friends are or what his life is like in Odessa, aside from how he goes to work and watches sports and loves Hot Dog on a Stick, so much that he even has the beach towel and visor with the logo on it. Lorenzo and I, though—we haven't talk-talked. Not about *this*. Not about what we're doing.

I try to remember what deep stuff we've discussed in the short time I've known him. I mean, my mom being sick, of course. His mom being gone, my dad being gone, yeah. How terrible it can feel when you realize you haven't even thought about them in a long while, or even worse, when it doesn't seem like they've thought about you. I remember what Lorenzo said about his dad, how he sometimes seems like a TV with the sound off, something you forget is even on until you catch a flicker. And I remember what my mom said about my dad, too, how she never saw him cry, not once.

I pass another grain silo, standing there as lonely as you can get, the very picture of loneliness.

I rustle around, kind of loud, trying to wake up Lorenzo without actually waking him up. I reach for my Mountain Dew, drink the last warm, flat swallow of it.

Lorenzo stirs. Sits up. "Hey," he says.

"Hey."

"Dang." He stretches his neck, does a trunk twist.

"We're almost there."

"Where are we?"

"Oklahoma," I say. His eyes bug. "Kansas, joking."

"I'm not going to diss these fine states by saying they all look the same."

"Respect, always," I say. "We have to remember that our city has an Eiffel Tower wearing a cowboy hat. You missed the town of Buffalo. Also, Protection." I pause. "Or maybe I missed protection."

"Ivy." He grimaces. "Wait, were you just waiting for me to wake up to tell me that joke?" He takes his phone out, scrolls. I'm surprised he can get service.

"Are you the strong, silent type?" I ask. That's what my mother always said my father was.

"I'm not that strong." He's still looking at his phone.

"No, seriously. Do you ever talk about your feelings and stuff? I mean, do I know the real, deep-down you?"

"Are you okay?" He puts his phone on the seat. When I see the screen, I can tell there are a ton of messages, text after text.

"It just hits me every now and then, what we're doing."

"Yeah."

"And I don't know how you're even feeling about all this. People at school, the whole thing. What *you're* doing. You seem . . . so okay. Cheerful."

The light is changing. It's turning that gold tint of dusk. In spite of his nap, Lorenzo looks tired. I'm tired. I feel like we've been together forever, like a married couple, getting on each other's nerves. It's hard to believe I was just thinking that I didn't know him.

"Look, Ivy. I'm trying to be here for you, and we didn't expect any of this, and it's all just . . . I'm holding my shit together best I can."

"I'm sorry," I say. I am. I am so, so sorry. That little blue construction-paper booklet with his handwriting on it and in it—*Passport, Lima, Moscow* . . . All of this. People speak in so many ways. And sometimes silence is kindness.

"Country Club Drive," I say to Lorenzo, who's behind the wheel now. "Next right. Here, here."

"Whoa," he says.

"Man, oh man." We see this big brick mansion, basically, and then another giant modern white house, like something you'd see in a movie taking place in Hollywood. But then the houses get a little more regular. I mean, they're big, with beautiful grass and large lots, and they're across from a parking lot and then a golf course, but they're not mansion-huge. Esilda might be Mom's oldest friend, but mansion-huge was making me nervous.

"I look like crap." Lorenzo takes a sniff of his T-shirt's armpit. He's getting nervous, too.

"This one," I say. It's funny, but if you took our house and stretched it and made it bigger and way nicer and added three garages and a huge yard, you'd have Esilda and Dave's house. Mom told me we'd been there before when Mase and I were little, but I don't remember it. Esilda visited us when Mom was sick, and a few times when we were younger, but mostly their friendship is just theirs. Esilda, this house—they're parts of Mom's life, familiar but not.

Lorenzo pulls up, turns off the engine. He's looking in the little mirror in his visor, trying to pat down his curls.

"You look great," I say.

"Serious doubts about the T-shirt right now."

"*GQ* model," I say, but his swagger is gone. I've never seen him this self-conscious before. "Hey. It's fine. It's great. Just be yourself."

"Which self?" he says, which is an excellent point.

"The one in the KANSAS IS FOR LOVERS shirt. Until further updates."

He smiles, but then there's no more time for prep or pep talks. The front door opens, and a little dog races out, and there's Esilda and Dave. We saw Esilda last year during The Beast, but her long dark hair, worn in a braid, has some new gray strands. She's wearing a loose denim dress and chunky jewelry, and she's already hugging me. "Sweet girl!" she says.

"Doc!" Dave yells at the dog, and jogs down the grass. Dave's wearing cargo shorts and a plaid shirt, and socks with sandals, and he has thinning hair and a handlebar mustache. I've met Dave once or twice, but clearly not enough to recall that he looks like a sheriff in an old Western. "Doc! Get back here!"

"He's a beagle. You know what that means," Esilda says.

I have no idea what that means, but Lorenzo races after that canine bullet, too. The dog is already speeding through the neighbor's yard, but Lorenzo outpaces both Dave and the beagle and lunges. Wow—he practically looks athletic. He returns to Esilda's house, a conquering hero with the dog under his arm. Dave is slapping his back and pouring thanks, and Lorenzo is *in*.

"You must run track," Dave says.

I want to laugh. The idea of Lorenzo in organized sports is a crack-up.

"Sophomore year, two hundred meters all-state in California."

"No way," I say. I'm shocked. I suddenly see him in satin shorts and a satin tank, his long legs racing on a red pebble loop, people cheering, a different boy altogether.

"Our son Robbie ran track," Dave says as he and Lorenzo disappear into the house.

"You're looking more and more like your mom." Esilda has her arm around my waist.

"I am?" Shocked again. All I see is my father's nose.

"Peas in a pod."

Lorenzo follows Dave into the family room, where a game is playing. I hear sports sounds on the TV, and the words "major league." Dave's giving him a tour of a shelf of trophies belonging to Robbie and Todd, their sons. From the adjoining kitchen I spot a painting of a horse in there, and a large framed photo of a ranch. Then Dave opens the sliding glass door to the backyard, and out they go. I have a moment of panic and, oh dear, realize I've come to rely on Lorenzo already, even here, where I should be the expert.

Esilda's showing me a sour cream–raisin pie she made and asking about the trip over, and how my mom is. I feel shy with her, without Mom there. Mom says that they have the kind of history where you can pick up wherever you left off no matter how much time has passed. But also, it seems to me right then, the kind of history that holds so many stories that I feel like an outsider, a child.

"I promised your mom we'd FaceTime later, 'kay? So we can all be together again? I just can't get over it. You've become a grown woman practically. In a *year*."

But then I blush, because *grown woman* and *pregnant*. I gave Mom permission to tell Esilda why we're on this trip, but I'm not sure if she knows I know she knows (ugh), so I just say, "More than I wish," to get us on the same page.

"You doing okay?" she asks. She takes my hand and squeezes. A gray cat, who I later learn is Miss Kitty, curls around my legs.

I shrug.

We both stare out at her huge backyard. It has a deck with steps and a cute toolshed and a barbecue spilling smoke. Lorenzo and Dave stand next to it, drinking Cokes from a cooler on the patio.

"He seems great," Esilda says.

"He's definitely great." We pivot the conversation as

Esilda clinks ice straight from her fridge into two glasses and offers me a soda, too. An ice-pouring fridge officially becomes a dream of mine. "I couldn't remember your house, but wow, it's amazing."

Esilda starts removing big, generous salad bowls from the fridge and a sheet pan from the oven. The kitchen has wood cabinets and flower tiles around the counters, and one of those islands like Jason Maxwell's house has. She points up to a stencil that circles the top of the kitchen walls, a row of dancing cowboy boots. "Your mom helped do that."

"She did?"

"You and your brother went to see your dad over the summer, and she came here."

"Before or after Terry?" She probably knows more about Terry than Mase and I do. Maybe even about Mom getting . . . Gross. I don't even want to think about it.

"Before. She did a much neater job than I did." Esilda laughs. "She's the artsy one."

Esilda studied accounting and is now the business manager of the Boot Hill Museum. She and my mom met in sixth grade, when Grandma Lottie and Grandpa Larry and Mom and Aunt Betts lived in Medford, Oregon. Before Rockaway Auto Supply and Repair, and definitely before *Rockaway Weekend*. Esilda and her mom and siblings moved to Medford from Cusco, Peru, to live with an uncle. At the time, Grandpa Larry worked at a plywood-processing plant, and Grandma Lottie worked at Fran's Fabrics. They did okay, and they had a house and everything, but Esilda lived in an apartment with lots of her family. She'd come over to hang out and use the shower before school sometimes. One of their favorite things to do as kids was to look at catalogs and pick out the stuff they'd buy if they had money.

"She always says you're the smart one." My mom seems so proud of Esilda when she says it.

"That is such a lie," Esilda says. "She never gives herself enough credit!"

"You're her . . . like, *dream*. She wants me to try to get a scholarship like you did, instead of going to Paris Junior College. But I don't think my grades are good enough."

"We'll talk," she says, because right then Dave is yelling that the ribs are done, and when we head out, Lorenzo's getting compliments on his shirt.

There's so much food: barbecue ribs and coleslaw and this layered mashed potato–like spicy salad that Esilda says is causa. Yuca fries, and Dave's favorite rolls called zwieback that he makes from his mom's recipe. Sour cream–raisin pie sounded gross, to be honest, but it's delicious—custardy, with meringue on top, though I can see that Lorenzo is accumulating a tiny pile of raisins on the side of his plate. We FaceTime Mom and Mase after we eat, and Mom and Esilda giggle and laugh like they're sixteen, and we have to hear the Hootie concert story for the jillionth time. Also one featuring Dave at this concert venue called the Gorge in the town of George, Washington, where Mom and Esilda went to see the Dave Matthews Band. Call it the story of two Daves,

I guess, and, boy, does Lorenzo's face ever light up at the George, Washington, part. Mom thought the concert was boring, but Esilda loved it, and here's when Esilda met her future husband. Her own non-singing Dave was working as a parking attendant for the summer, on break from Washington State University, where he was a student in the beef program. When Esilda drove up in her shit car, it was love at first and second and third sight.

"She'd seen this movie—" Dave says.

But Esilda is someone who tells her own story. "I'd seen this movie. A few years back. *The Horse Whisperer*? Robert Redford, on a ranch, big sky country, sexy guy who has a special way with wild horses?" She smiles, shrugs. "It stayed with me for some reason. Like it had . . . I don't know. Clues to my future. The height of romance, right? So when I meet this guy in his cowboy hat and find out he's studying to be a rancher . . . somehow I knew I found my hot horse whisperer."

It's not your first thought when you see him wearing his socks and sandals.

"It was my baby blues," Dave says, blinking his eyes.

Well, it was something. And judging by the way she looks at him right then and the way he looks at her, it still is.

After dinner, dessert, the call, and cleanup, Esilda and Dave make us promise to visit the Boot Hill Museum in the morning, where Esilda works. Dave gives us two tickets that read

MARSHAL PASS. ENJOY EVERYTHING BOOT HILL MUSEUM HAS TO OFFER! Esilda shows us to our rooms. I'll be in Todd's, and Lorenzo is in Robbie's—they'll both be home from college the next weekend. All down the long hall, there are framed photos of Todd and Robbie—little guys with dark, blunt-cut bangs, moving up to the awkward, big-toothed phase in elementary school when Robbie got glasses, and on up again to junior high and high school, looking handsome and serious in caps and gowns. My mom's got those, too, of Mase and me, minus the caps and gowns, but my dad's hallway is just plain.

Esilda says good night and hugs me long and hard. Lorenzo and I meet in the adjoining bathroom to brush our teeth. It's such a nice bathroom—powder blue with framed pictures of seashells, a shower stall with a sliding door and not a plastic sheet that sticks to your legs, and, wow, two sinks.

Lorenzo's wearing a pair of soft shorts and a straight-up blue T-shirt, and I have on my *T. rex* nightshirt. *T* is definitely fierce, even if his arms are too short relative to his body size. You always feel a little embarrassed for him, but, boy, it doesn't affect his self-esteem. It's me and Lorenzo's first night together, our first mutual teeth-brushing, and it's strangely intimate. As Lorenzo squirts Crest on his blue brush and I squirt Ultrabrite on my green one, I feel like I've known him my whole life. Esilda and Dave started their together life story in George, Washington, in a parking lot. I wonder if Lorenzo and I started ours at a science fair in Paris, Texas.

"The beef program?" he whispers.

We giggle.

"Shh!" I say, and shake his arm. "For ranchers-to-be, I guess. I think he ran his family's ranch here until he semi-retired or something. Have *you* been waiting this whole time to tell *that* joke?"

We brush. Lorenzo waits until his mouth is frothy and then *grr*s like a rabid dog.

Lorenzo rinses and spits. "They are the sweetest people," he says.

I rinse and spit. "I wonder if there's a separate pork program."

We giggle some more. I feel bad wiping my mouth on the white guest towels, set out in a little pile for us.

Lorenzo leans against the counter and pulls me to him. Wow, I keep forgetting how attractive he is. Now his mouth is all minty, and he's clearly just rolled on some deodorant, because a fake pine smell surrounds us. Man, I want him bad. I want him like I've wanted him before all this, those times in the car, or on the couch at his house when his dad and Chloe weren't home. Also, that time out by the Eiffel Tower on his blanket. I crave him like I'm the old Ivy, with a body that's just awake and alive and mine, what a relief. All of me is an electric buzz, and I feel him hard against me, another relief, a big relief, because maybe he does still want me like he used to. Maybe those moments where I'm sure he's treating me differently, like I'm breakable or not desirable anymore, are just me feeling different and breakable and not desirable.

Still, there's no way we can do anything here. I swear, I can sense Esilda and Dave listening to our silence. Lorenzo gives a little groan, and I put my hand over his mouth. No. No, no. I remove it.

"We can't," I say.

"We definitely can't," he says.

He kisses me. Boy, I wish we could.

He pulls away. Gives my butt a squeeze. "Waiting is good, too," he says.

"Not as good, but okay," I say. Though, I mean, how would I know? "Before you go . . ."

"Yes?"

"There's a raisin mystery."

"A raisin mystery?"

"You picked them out of the pie but claim to love Raisinets. Explain."

"Loving one kind of raisin does not mean loving every raisin. Or nut, or dog, or person, or *anything*."

"Fair point."

"Raisinets are delicious chocolate-covered morsels. The other raisins are puffy and liquidy and . . . plump. Like . . . the eye of a small animal."

"Oh gross." I swat him.

"A hamster. A baby raccoon." He shivers dramatically. Makes a creepy face. He doesn't look like a possible future husband then. He looks more like a kid.

"Say good night, Lorenzo," I say. I pinch his butt.

He gives my hair a sexy tug. "Good night, Lorenzo."

14

IN THE DARK I LOOK ALL AROUND AT THE STUFF IN
Todd's room—photos of friends on a corkboard, his graduation cap tassel, and a few concert tickets stuck there with
pushpins, too. On his bookshelf there's lots of sci-fi and Stephen King, an antique car model, a large silver cowboy belt
buckle, and the kind of giant seashell you blow into. I sort
of want to try it, but you shouldn't go around blowing into
shells that aren't yours, haha. My last opinion for the day.

More details: a llama doll, a wooden whistle in the shape
of a bird, a framed photo of him and a girl who I also spot
in the corkboard photos. On the nightstand under the lamp
and beside the slim, high-tech clock is a carved gourd. It's
probably from Peru, same as the beautiful, brightly colored
tapestry above the bed, which shows scenes from life in the
Andes. It seems like a room filled with lots of experiences.
If Todd slept in mine, he'd see my dresser crammed with lotion bottles (on sale, plus employee discount at Euwing's), a
DON'T MESS WITH TEXAS shot glass filled with cheap rings,

and a photo of my dad and us when we were little, the one where he's lying on the floor and Mase and me are sitting on him like a horse and he's laughing. Also, my pile of clothes, since I hate hanging things up, and a poster of a beautiful beach I thought was Hawaii but Peyton once told me was actually California, because she'd been there.

This room gives me an ache of loneliness. Or maybe it's longing. Something pulling on my heart in a way that makes you want things. The room and the person who lives in it are so alive, so *in* life. I can't explain this very well, just that I can never imagine Todd in the back room at Euwing's Drugs. I mean, he's not, like, a Hollywood actor or anything, but he's going to Cal State University in Long Beach, where Esilda's sister lives, and he's studying psychology. This seems like another planet from Paris Junior College, where I think I might study writing because of one single comment Ms. La Costa made. For a minute I'm so lonely that I imagine one of those scenes you always see in the movies where a person sneaks into the other person's room during a visit to the relatives for a wedding or a holiday. I would tiptoe into Lorenzo's room, just on the other side of the adjoining bathroom, and I would get into bed with him. If it were like those movies, we'd oversleep or not hear the alarm and then have a bumbling near miss of getting caught.

I'm lying in bed, playing the *Wait, was that a cramp?* game that always starts up the minute I'm still and quiet and horizontal. But that game is just cruel, so I get up and rummage around in my bag for my Tess book. I want to finish. As hard as it was to get into, that Hardy guy has me hooked.

There are lines that I can relate to, believe it or not. Beautiful ones about a night under the stars and moon. Sentences that just squeeze my heart. Like the one right now: *Tess hoped for some accident that might favour her, but nothing favoured her.* And the one after that, talking about her being in the residence of a near relation, just as I am this very minute. *Yet nothing essential, in nature or emotion, divided her from them: in pains, pleasures, thoughts, birth, death, and after-death, they were the same. . . .* I *wish* I were the same as Esilda.

Now there's the softest tap on my (Todd's) door. I sit up and clutch my blanket to my chest like a prudish Victorian lady, even though I'm in my T-shirt. I'm suddenly super embarrassed because Lorenzo has never seen me in bed-bed before. He's seen me half naked on a couch, and stretched out on top of his bed in his room, but not in a bed under some sheets. I'm also suddenly nervous, and clearly not fit for this particular rom-com, because I truly don't want us to get caught.

The doorknob slowly turns, and then Esilda pops her head in. "Ivy? Are you asleep?"

"Hi! Oh hi! No."

Esilda's wearing a pretty robe with lots of colors, and she smells like orange lotion, and she's the I-don't-know-you-very-well relative who is still a relative regardless. She's also Mom's age and Mom's best friend, so it's almost like Mom herself coming over to sit on the bed.

"You doing okay?"

"I'm okay. I really appreciate you having us."

"Oh, honey. Anytime. *Anytime.*" Esilda takes my hand and squeezes and then lets it go. "Honey, I wanted to . . . just talk for a second."

The nice mom feeling vanishes. Alarm shoots up my body. Maybe it's the two "honeys" or that I'm suddenly remembering that Peru is a mostly Catholic country, and remembering, too, a story we heard many times, about Esilda and Dave's wedding, Catholic again, where the priest drank too much before the service. Also, the fact that we are still in the Bible Belt, which right this minute is cinching tighter and tighter. Dave grew up here, a rancher. Could Mom and Esilda have such different views of something that divides people so dramatically? Of course they could. I'm friends with Faith, who's completely antiabortion, and with Peyton, who wavers.

I stare down at Esilda's big diamond ring, steeling myself for stern words about how abortion is murder. I want to protect my body. Under the sheets I cross my legs, and I fold my arms, too.

"Okay," I say. I'm in her house, in her son's bed, and the door is closed, and there's no way out. I'm alone, and my voice is cold.

"I just . . . There are only two people who know this story," she says. "My husband, the love of my life, and your mom."

"Okay," I say again. But when I look in her kind brown eyes, I see pain.

"When I was in high school, this friend of our family, this friend of my dad's . . ."

I got this so wrong. So, so wrong. I guess when you're judged and judged, you're on constant alert for judgment. But I'm still protecting my body. My legs and my arms are still trying to keep someone away. "Oh no."

"You can probably guess what I'm about to say. And the details might be, um, triggering, so you don't need them. But this guy . . . He did a lot for us. For my family. Money, food, a job for one of my brothers. And so one day, when I brought this bag of clothes to his house for his son, some of my brother's shirts my mom wanted him to have because we couldn't give him nearly what he gave us, and he wanted to have sex . . . I don't know. I thought I'd better. I didn't want to cause trouble, to cut off the flow of help, to seem *ungrateful*. I tried to get out of it at first, shoved him away, because of, well, the awful details of him. His breath, his whiskers, his hangy neck, my disgust, my horror. But then I just did it."

I dig my fingernails into my arms. I feel so gross. I stare down at the bedspread.

"Your mom tried to tell me that if he forced himself, if I hadn't said *yes*, then he raped me. I couldn't believe that or understand that, and I didn't want to. That was not a fact I wanted for myself. And I hadn't screamed or kicked or all the things you imagine with that word. It seemed complicated. It still does. When I ended up getting pregnant . . ."

I think I might be sick.

"Are you okay? Is this okay for me to say? I might want to tell you this, but it's your choice if you want to hear it. We should have all the choices, every possible choice, when so much hasn't been our choice. For centuries, you know?

Me, you, every woman, honestly—so much hasn't been our choice. Agency over your own body is, like, the smallest, most basic right."

She says that word again and again, *choice*. It's a billboard, it's a headline, it's in neon lights. It's quiet, firm, dignified, self-respecting, a shout suppressed. And, hey, ignored enough that it can seem like a gift instead of a right.

"I want to hear."

I do. It's hard, but I do.

"We lived in Oregon, so abortion was legal. It was a different time—there wasn't this new wave of legislation happening everywhere. Your mom came with me. I didn't feel guilty or torn, in spite of my upbringing. I only felt nervous about people finding out, my family, especially. And relieved. So relieved! Your mom wanted me to tell my own mom about what happened, but I couldn't. I didn't want to risk what she might say. Where we're from, in Cusco, back then and still now—unless your life is in danger, anyone who gets an abortion can go to prison, same as a lot of places here today. Even if you've been *raped*—jail. Many of the women there don't even have access to contraception. Men have God-given rights, supposedly. And back then, too, where we were from? Women were even sterilized against their will. Held down and *forced*. An abortion . . . I couldn't tell them. And I didn't want my mom or my brothers to confront that man, either. I just wanted it all to go away. And right or wrong, that was my choice. And like your mom said to me then, and as I just said to you, that, at least, should be in your hands."

"I'm sorry," I say.

"Those words belong to so many other people, but not you," she says. "I just wanted you to know, Ivy, that I understand. And that you're not alone. We're family. You'll get through this, and your own, *meant* life is waiting on the other side."

She looks up at the tapestry above Todd's bed. "He romanticizes," she says. "All that beautiful work that women do . . . But he also understands these issues are not only women's issues. These are human issues. And his children must understand the same thing, and their children."

It's hard to speak. "Thank you for telling me."

"There are so many girls and women who have been here, before you've been here. So many, we're like a secret underground network."

I can't imagine that. I feel more like the single, solitary Tess in a town full of righteous parishioners. It's strange, though, that both my mom and Esilda had an unwanted pregnancy and I never even knew it before. I guess we're an underground network of three, at least. Esilda hugs me, and I'm enveloped in the smell of oranges. She kisses the top of my head, and after she closes the door behind her again, I see the room differently. The llama, the gourd, the tapestry; the hands that likely made the llama, the gourd, the tapestry. I see Esilda differently, as her own self, not just Mom's friend. I admire her so much, her kindness, her hard work, her choices. The choices that brought her this life with her rancher. The choices that brought her these sons, with the big teeth at age seven and the tassel at graduation, and the future ahead of them, and them, and them.

15

IT'S SO, SO WRONG TO BE EATING COTTON CANDY before you've even had lunch, but try telling Lorenzo that. God, he's happy. We're standing on a long patch of grass in front of a Western-looking street, with Western-looking storefronts labeled LONG BRANCH SALOON, DRY GOODS AND CLOTHING, GENERAL OUTFITTING STORE, G. M. HOOVER CIGARS AND LIQUORS, and more. The minute we walked past the Boot Hill Museum's RELIVE THE LEGEND! sign, he was all jazzed, wanting to do everything at once. We took photos of each other at antique school desks and climbed into a stagecoach. We looked at some stuffed cattle and fraying old clothes on mannequins and pretended to be in jail. Now, even though it's almost noon and we should be on the road, we're waiting in the hot sun for a gunfight. I fan myself with a Boot Hill map, because heat seems hotter lately. Lorenzo's got Marge Simpson's beehive on a stick, color: blue. He takes a pinch of it, tilts his head back, and drops it in, licking the crystals off his fingers.

"Are you sure?" He offers it to me.

"I'm sure."

Well, we've already had curly fries and a sarsaparilla at the saloon, where a piano player who looked like an insurance salesman wearing suspenders and a bowler hat played fast, tinkly tunes. Next to us, also waiting for the gunfight, there's a family. The mom and dad are young, and they have a little girl, and a baby in a backpack. I look away because seeing them makes a tight string inside of me go loose. One day maybe, but not now. One day when it's good and right and I can be her, that woman now leaning down to explain to the child that she might want to cover her ears.

I'm all involved in their story, that mom, that child, the baby grabbing a few fistfuls of the dad's hair, and so— *Bang!* The sound startles me so bad, I give a screech and jump back, and Lorenzo puts his arm around me, and out they come. "Townspeople" first—the saloon ladies in their frilly dresses and feather hats, shopkeepers in their suspenders, and then the six bad guys from one direction, and a sheriff and a deputy from the other, all dressed in leather chaps and vests, boots and hats and red bandannas. The baby starts to fuss, and the dad wanders off with the baby to avoid a meltdown. I see him looking into F. C. Zimmerman's Lumber and Hardware.

"Ivy!" Lorenzo grabs my arm. "Look! Look who it is!"

"The piano player?"

"Not that one. *That* one."

He points to the sheriff. And then I see it, the long mustache under the brim of that hat. He's not sporting socks with sandals now. Nope, he's wearing dusty cowboy boots and a stern expression, and he's saying something he's probably said a hundred times or more. No *wonder* I thought he looks like a sheriff in a Western.

"I expect law and order in Dodge City now," Dave says. "We're not putting up with any trouble from any Texans."

One of the bad guys is wearing Nikes, and one flubs his lines, but my heart blooms like one of those flowers in a time-lapse science movie. It feels so good, him saying that. Dave, saying those words. Like it's maybe actually even possible, that someone larger has their eye on things, and that they won't allow bullies.

"Why didn't they tell us?" Lorenzo asks, his teeth dyed light blue.

"Mom always says Esilda loves a surprise."

And now here she comes, Esilda herself, heading our way from the parking lot as the *pop-snap* of guns goes off, and the bright flicks of fake gunpowder *snap-crackle* on the dusty ground. She waves, and she's wearing her work clothes, slacks and a blouse and low heels. Off in the distance, I can see an apartment building, and a jet flies overhead, because, like everywhere and with everything, the long-ago is smack in the middle of the today. Esilda and the airplane give me an unexpected surge of hope, like when you've caught a sunrise.

Esilda's out of breath when she reaches us. Her eyes gleam. "Did you see?"

"That sheriff deserves an Oscar," Lorenzo says. Dave is stepping around a few pretend-dead bodies and is handcuffing the dude in the Nikes as his deputy wrangles the rest of the group away, like a rancher with a small herd of obedient calves. The dad with the baby and the mom with the little girl have disappeared through the saloon doors. It's too much real even in this much pretend, maybe.

"Surprised?" Esilda says.

"Totally shocked! That was amazing. Dave was great! I almost didn't recognize him," I say.

Esilda's looking his way. She's got love in her eyes. Still. The flower in my chest blooms again, and I am so happy for her and for them, for having this life they built from their own decisions and hard work. So happy that I could almost cry. Where would Esilda be now if she'd made other choices? Where would Dave be? And Todd and Robbie? Not here. Dave takes off his sheriff's hat, wipes his forehead with his bandanna, like a hard day's work has been done. He looks our way and winks, gives a thumbs-up.

Esilda smiles. "My hot horse whisperer turned sheriff," she says.

I make sure to take a last trip through the swinging doors that read LADIES AND GENTS so we don't have to make any extra bathroom stops. We say goodbye to Esilda and Dave in the parking lot of the Boot Hill Museum, though we'll be seeing them on the way back home, too. Esilda's packed us some sandwiches made with the leftover pork from last night. I peek in the bag, and there's more stuff—cookies and fruit and chips. I remember all the food she brought when she came to stay with us during The Beast.

The meaningful glances of love join the food of love, and now come the long hugs of love.

"You're going to be okay," Esilda whispers. *She* looks okay. She looks strong and happy and like her very own self.

Dave pretend-twirls a pair of six-shooters. He tips his hat as we drive away. Dodge City is safe, thank goodness. I practically see the swirling words *The End* on the screen of our back window.

"Next time, we're staying later, 'kay?" Lorenzo says. "I can't believe we missed the Country Style Dinner. It's part of our ticket! Kansas-raised beef roast and mashed potatoes and brown gravy."

On my lap I'm holding the sepia-toned image of me and Lorenzo, wearing serious expressions and old-timey costumes, that we got taken at the Old West Photo Parlor. We're posed in front of a pretend corral scene. I wave it at him.

"My sexy horse whisperer," I say.

"Neighhhh," Lorenzo whinnies as we get on Highway 56 and head out of Dodge.

The windows are rolled down, and our hair whips around our faces. I take off my sandals and put my feet up on the dash. I wish I could tell Lorenzo about Esilda, but I don't. It's her story, one she shared with me.

"Time for that CD yet?" Lorenzo asks. "Day two is a big day. Three major cities, three countries. Moscow, Limon, Genoa. And"—he makes the sound of a drumroll, palms on the wheel—"the Wonder Tower!"

Lorenzo's dying to see the World's Wonder View Tower. For a guy who has a thing with names, that name is a promise. He spotted it on the map, and we vowed not to look it up so it will be a surprise. I'm excited, too, if I'm being honest, even though I make a pretend *Get ahold of yourself* face to his wild-child one. "I can't believe this is only day two. It seems like we've been gone forever."

"Is it my scintillating company?" Lorenzo says. "I never know if it's skin-tillating or sin-tillating."

"Whoa. Skin, sin." I wiggle my eyebrows. I feel sort of embarrassed after I do it, because that's the extent of me trying to be sexy. Tonight's our first night in a motel together. Alone, the two of us, all night—I can hardly believe it. I'm nervous, but I can't wait. For a minute there, lost in the dream of it, I completely forget I'm pregnant, until the buzzing pain in the sides of my breasts reminds me. I unhook my bra and slip it through the sleeve of my T-shirt. Ahh. Maybe one day, if we're lucky, bras will be extinct, and we'll only see them on display somewhere, like those medieval torture museums.

"Magic trick," Lorenzo says when I remove it with a flourish. Mr. Mysterioso would be envious.

"Where's Limon again?"

"Colorado."

"No, in the world."

"Costa Rica. Come on, music?" Lorenzo bobs his head to a nonexistent beat.

"Sure."

I lean way over into the back, and Lorenzo gives my butt a squeeze. Motel, skin, butt squeeze. I suddenly remember ninth grade, when we had to recite the Gettysburg Address, and Nate mistakenly said, *Foreplay and seven years ago.* Five hours until that motel—it sounds like a lot of hours. I fish around in my pack for the CD.

Lorenzo's phone makes the *whoosh* sound of a text. And then he gets another one. I remember all those texts on the screen the day before, too. My own phone has been weirdly quiet. No texts or calls from Peyton or Faith, when I usually get a bunch. I called Peyton before we left and told her what we were doing, because I couldn't face Faith. The silence is either them leaving us alone, or something worse.

My fingertips reach the CD, and my butt returns to the seat.

Whoosh!

Instead of reading it, though, Lorenzo shuts the sound off.

"What's that?" I ask.

"No big. Just, uh, Ian. Asking if he can borrow my, uh, bike."

"You have a bike?"

"*Of course* I have a bike."

"That's not an *of course.*" It's also so obviously a lie, I can't even stand it. My good mood is vanishing fast. I feel pissed. Maybe even more than pissed. I feel worried, and there's nothing like worry to make you pissed. Ugh! "I saw all those other texts, Lorenzo. A big bunch of them yesterday."

"It's no big deal, Ivy."

"Small deals don't require lies." I stare at him, showing him I mean business. He keeps his eyes on the road and says nothing. I bet if Peyton were here, using her mom voice, she'd get him to talk in two seconds flat.

Instead we sit in silence until it's so uncomfortable that the silence might as well be an actual thing instead of the absence of a thing.

Finally, Lorenzo sighs. "It's just my dad."

"Wait, what?" I don't know what I was imagining. Another girl, maybe, even if I know that's ridiculous. Those worries about being unwanted, you know, they just keep popping back up. Like maybe he might want someone less complicated. Less *used*. We're not supposed to be that, right? Used? And used things get thrown away. When someone paints a cross/positive pregnancy test on your locker, when you're heading across seven states to get an abortion, you can feel vulnerable, I guess. Like you're small and naked, wrong and bad, a target.

"You don't need this, Ives," he says. "Let's just put on some music, huh?"

"What I don't need are secrets. All of me is a secret. I don't need outside ones, too."

He sighs. Puts on his turn signal and changes lanes because there's a hay truck in front of us going, like, twenty miles an hour. Every time we've seen a hay truck before this, Lorenzo would shout out a cheery "Hey!" but not this time.

"I don't want to hurt you. Hurt you *more*."

"Just tell me! God!"

"Um, Faith's mom—"

"*Faith's* mom?" I don't even know what he's going to say, but I'm so mad. So mad, if this involves Faith somehow. My friend. My supposed friend.

"She went to see my dad—"

"Oh my God." I'm so furious, my teeth clench and my face turns red. My fury is a ball of scorching energy, and there's no room for it in the cabin of this Chevy Avalanche.

"She told him, okay? About you being pregnant. She assumed he didn't know. Why she assumed that—no idea. I mean, yeah, she was right, but still. Anyway, she asked him if he was aware of where I was and what I was doing, and he said, 'Road trip,' and she said, 'Do you know what *kind* of road trip?'"

"I can't believe this. I just can't. Did she go and see *my* mom, too? She couldn't have. Mom sounded fine on the phone last night."

"No idea. Maybe she knows your mom will back you no matter what." The little muscle in Lorenzo's cheek tightens and loosens and tightens again. His eyes—well, I can almost see what he'll look like when he's thirty-five.

"She thinks she knows everything, doesn't she? She just thinks she knows every little thing. What does she want, me to be another Harmony? You and me, Harmony and Abraham at the Belle Vista apartments, poor as shit, stuck?" I think of Esilda, what would have happened to her in that apartment with her family.

"Harmony?"

"Faith's sister! *She* got pregnant."

"No way."

"Yes way. So what's your dad going to do? What's he saying in all those texts?"

"He's just mad."

"Everyone thinks they know everything."

"I don't care," he says. The traffic is heavy where we are now, heavier than it's been before, and he sneaks a look at me and then holds my hand. I'm the kind of mad that doesn't want to be held. I'm the throwing-and-slamming kind of mad.

"Lorenzo! Maybe you should just tell him the truth. This isn't fair to him and definitely not to you."

"No, Ivy. I won't. This is a small unfair compared to the big one if you end up stuck with that fucking family for the rest of your life."

"You don't have to tell him who it is. Just tell him, I don't know . . . that it's not you. That it's someone else, and you're just helping me."

"That's not going to work, Ives. I can't protect you if *he* protects *me*. He's going to want to do that. He's going to want to set people straight, and then *that* truth will get around, and you'll be completely open to whatever happens next. This makes me even more sure."

"He cares what Faith's mom thinks?"

"Not just Faith's mom, Ivy! Paris, that whole town . . . God, everyone knows everyone. What the hell. Do you know who he works with at Turner? Huh? Noah Alvarez's mom."

He glances at me for my reaction, but I don't say anything. If the Euwings found out, if they tried to stop me, if they made me have this baby . . . I feel sick. More sick. Sick on top of the furious. And scared. Really scared. It's a bad, bad combination.

"That's right," he says. "He's in heavy hauling and she's in pipe fabrication. I swear, that whole place . . . It's like that game where there's only a few degrees of separation between you and that movie star guy, whatever his name is. Everyone's practically fucking related."

He's furious, too. I get a glimpse at *how* furious he is— I actually hear the chilling sound of his teeth grinding, like rock against rock, about to start a fire. I look out my window and fume. It's wrong, but I snatch my hand back. Wrong because the guy sitting beside me, his foot on that accelerator, carefully glancing in his rearview mirror, he's *beside* me. One hundred percent. And he's pure kindness, like if you looked up the word in the dictionary, you'd see his picture.

I watch a grain silo whiz past. Another grain silo. And then a low-lying motel, just a single long building with brown doors and a smattering of cars, the kind of motel you'd see in a movie with a drug cartel or a murderer on the run. Then fields, fields, fields, farmland, farmland, telephone poles, so lonely looking, tilted and sad. Why do telephone poles out here look so lonely? A solitary figure in a vast landscape, going it alone. Even a row of them, alone, alone, alone.

Lorenzo is tap-tap-tapping the steering wheel with his fingertips. It's not the fun kind of tapping, like when we have music on. It's like a woodpecker. An anxious woodpecker, searching and searching and not finding.

"What?" I say.

"What, what?"

"Lorenzo." I make my face stern. But then there's an avalanche in the Avalanche again, because the sternness slides right down my face and I start to cry. "Tell me," I plead. "What else is he saying? There's something else. Come *on*."

"He found my notes. All the places we're gonna stop. He found the world tour."

"Okay, okay." I wipe my eyes. "What does that mean?" Then it hits me. Then I know. "Oh my God. Is he, like, *coming after us*? Lorenzo, is he, like, on his way to stop us or something?"

"No. I mean, not right now—"

"What do you mean 'not right now'?"

"He's home! He's texting from home. Ivy, stop yelling. This isn't helping."

A giant dairy truck zooms past us, and the windows rattle. I breathe. My heart . . . Well, that expression *pounding out of your chest* sounds about right. It's leaping around in there like a caught animal. If Lorenzo's dad comes after us, I'll be a caught animal.

"Is he going to, like, follow us or something? Do we need to change our route? Like, throw him off our scent?"

"I can't believe you just said 'throw him off our scent,'" Lorenzo says. He starts to giggle, an irrational giggle, and I can see right there on his face what he's feeling, that out-of-body shock at finding yourself in a situation you never imagined, flying down a highway with a pregnant girl in your truck, the windshield a pointillism canvas of smashed gnats.

"Do we need to, though? You told me how he felt about . . . this issue, too." It's still hard for me to say the word.

"He's home, Ives. He's still there."

"I mean, what's he going to do to stop me anyway, huh? Wrestle me down and sit on me?"

"Let's just try to relax, okay? Let's put in the CD and try to relax."

I do, mostly because I need my mom right now. I need her bad, and this is all suddenly the very worst idea, me and Lorenzo, doing this together, Lorenzo with a dad who might try to stop him—me—from doing what he thinks he's—I'm—doing. I need my own mom, an adult, a woman who's been through stuff, who is actually fierce, hands on her hips, who was fierce even when she got down to a hundred pounds.

Hootie & the Blowfish, "Hold My Hand." First an upbeat instrumental, and then, dang, Hootie's voice is like hot chocolate with marshmallows and a graham cracker—smooth, husky, bittersweet—and I can't help myself; my spirits lift a little. Hootie is telling me the truth. That there's a mess and a crying girl, but someone reaching out, too, willing to take her to a different place. Saying that maybe they can't change the world, but they can still love each other the best they can. Lorenzo is here with me, and Mom is here with me, and so is Hootie, and so is everyone who ever heard this song and felt it, really felt it. Music is medicine, my mom always says.

Lorenzo takes my hand, and I let him. He's also feeling the medicine.

And then comes Bon Jovi—"It's My Life." It begins with a heartbeat, ba bum, ba bum, and I think of the other heartbeat that will form inside of me if we don't hurry, and I think of my own heartbeat, and I hear the words that are furious and defiant, and now there's a different medicine. The angry voice expresses the anger in my body, because it's *not* my life, not really, not if other people can make decisions about it that aren't mine at all.

Now Lorenzo's feeling this, too. His face, his profile, has turned hard. He rolls his window all the way down. He sticks his head out. "FUCK!" he yells to the gas station and mini-mart we pass. "FUCK!" he yells again, to the tractor rumbling slow along the side of Highway 56. Maybe it's not the right word; who knows what the best one would be. It's just the angriest one, so that's what I yell now, too. "FUCK!" I yell, defiant, as the wind snaps my hair and fills my throat and then my lungs and then my whole body.

"FUCK!" we yell to the long, long train riding parallel to us. "FUCK!" we yell, drowning out the sound of the wheels on the track as they roll, roll, roll along.

16

MOSCOW, KANSAS. WE PULL OVER NEXT TO THE
water tower that reads MOSCOW in big yellow letters. We
get out, stretch our legs, and Lorenzo stamps our passports,
kashunk. It seems a little sad after this afternoon, after the
truth of Faith and his dad and Faith's mom. But no, I tell
myself. No. The *kashunk* is defiant, Bon Jovi defiant, *my
heart is like an open highway,* and we are living our story.
I will put my hands on my hips against all the people who
want to force my whole life onto one road, when I want to be
here on this world tour, and maybe many more world tours
afterward.

We take our photo with the tower behind us, and I
send it to Mom, and she sends back the emoji with the
love eyes, times ten. Lorenzo and I sit in the gazebo that's
right near the tower, and we eat a couple of Esilda's cookies and drink some Mountain Dew. If this were a movie,
we'd be hauling ourselves over that chain-link fence, and

we'd climb that tower, and we'd maybe write something on it to prove we were there. Instead, I think *chain-link fence*, and fight back a wave of uglies along with a wave of nausea, though what do you expect, chocolate chips and Mountain Dew.

"Moscow looks kinda like Lima, and Corn, and Cobb," Lorenzo says.

"Not to the people of Lima and Corn and Cobb and Moscow, population two hundred seventy-two," I remind him.

We drive through Ulysses, Kansas, and Coolidge, Kansas. If I remember right from Ms. La Costa's class when we read *Little Women*, both Ulysses S. Grant and Calvin Coolidge were supporters of the suffrage movement. Those old dudes are maybe a glimpse into the future, just a short distance from the state line into Colorado. It doesn't feel any different yet, but it will be, even if the trees just look like trees, and building like buildings.

We gas up, and once we're in Colorado, we stop to eat Esilda's sandwiches for dinner in Kit Carson. It's a town that looks like the real version of the fake Dodge City—at least, all of the buildings have signs in that elaborate and blocky Western-town writing. We park in front of the Kit Carson Museum, where there's a train and a plaque all about Kit Carson, the guy. We stand there and pretend to read it—at least I do.

It's almost eight before we get to Limon, population one thousand one hundred. We're losing steam, and we still haven't reached the Wonder Tower at our last stop of the day, Genoa, where we're staying the night, so we only get out to take our photo next to this big mural near the

Limon Heritage Museum. The mural features a huge on-coming train and a creepy Old West family of four, the kind of family that some people think of as traditional but that probably rarely exists in real life—mom, dad, son, daughter. Well, ours was like that for a brief period of time before my parents got divorced, though divorces aren't on murals. I have a brief self-pitying pang about not being close to my dad. Like, I have no clue what he might be doing right now, and he definitely has no clue what I'm doing. In the movies he and I would bond after I shared my news, but in real life I'm not going to tell him. Maybe when years pass and we know each other better.

Lorenzo and I stand by the painted family and make it less traditional for our photo, and then Lorenzo takes way too long trying to get me to look like I'm stopping the train with my hand, the way people do with those shots at the Leaning Tower of Pisa.

Back in the truck, Lorenzo's tired. I see that look he gets, the skin under his eyes drooping like the valance of a cur-tain. I'm worn out, too, but I have enough energy for the fun thing that's coming. It's like when people say they always have room for dessert, because I always have room for something exciting. I've been eyeing those words ever since I saw them on the list, words that jump out with a roadside promise: THE WONDER TOWER. I'm imagining something straight from Mr. Mysterioso, secret surprises and magic revealed, awe.

"The Wonder Tower!" I say to Lorenzo.

But instead of giving me some dancing fists or other sign of enthusiasm, he looks over at me and scrunches his face to say, *Not so much.*

"You peeked."

He shrugs. "I couldn't stand it."

"It's bad?"

"You maybe shouldn't get your hopes up." It's a warning I wish I'd had before my hopes already got up.

Ugh, hopes are probably one of the most stubborn things, because once they're down, they take some convincing to go up, and once they're up, they take some convincing to go down. In spite of what Lorenzo's said, I still imagine a column reaching skyward, filled with the marvels of nature. My mom sometimes says, *Ivy, you see with wishes.*

We take the exit. The tower isn't much farther—I spot it right away, and from a distance it still holds possibilities. It's red and white, and it looks like a lighthouse set in the middle of a wide field, something from a children's book, made up, constructed from imagination and filled in with story. Windows rise up the column, and there's a square observation deck just below the top. But when we get closer and closer still, following the low billboards that read SEE MUSEUM! WONDER VIEW! SEE TOWER! COINS! BOTTLES! LOOK! TWO-HEADED CALF! the gloom gets closer, too. There's an old red ticket booth that reads SEE SIX STATES! but it's abandoned, like a long-ago carnival, crumbling through time. The tower itself is all peeling paint and tattered brick, with busted windows. It's surrounded with barbed wire and KEEP OUT signs.

Lorenzo drives across the lot, bumping over gravel. A few old shit cars are parked in front of the ticket booth in a permanent fashion, and Lorenzo parks beside them. "Want to get out?" he asks, and I nod, but I don't want to, not really. I'm just being polite since we drove all the way out here, and I always feel bad when people's good intentions go awry. Maybe I'm trying to prove that my own optimism wasn't foolish, too, even though this place can't prove anything but how bad things can get when you stop taking care of them.

We do get out, and the evening is cooling down, but I'm kind of scared here. There's nothing to be scared of, but I am. Some birds are eyeing us, and the sky seems to press down. It's unnerving. Lorenzo is looking into one of the shit trucks, his hand cupped around his eyes to see better, but they're just rusting bodies, extinct, with only their skeletons left.

"It could have been so great? I was hoping maybe it might be better in person?" Lorenzo says, using an abundance of question marks. "I read that this was a big attraction in its day. The original owner used to stand at the top of the tower, shouting at passing cars through a megaphone, trying to get them to stop. It was jammed full of odd stuff, like the skeleton of a woolly mammoth."

I picture the house of a hoarder, the smell of an antique store, the dusty decay. "I can't believe they'd have a woolly mammoth." God, that's sad. Imagine the trip he took, that mammoth, all the places he'd been, the life he'd had, only to end up in this place. I'm trying to be a good sport, but my voice is full of sorrow. I guess I'm thinking of all the things deserving of wonder, now stuck somewhere by fanatical ringmasters—woolly mammoths, birds in cages, *girls*, now trapped in the decrepit Belle Vista apartments, that past-tense motor inn with the HEATED POOL, COLOR TV, A/C sign still out front. We don't always remember what belongs to us and what doesn't.

Lorenzo reads my face. I don't know how, but he sees all of it. "Let's get out of here," he says.

"We should take a picture anyway," I say, "because this also happened," and we do. It could have been great, this old roadside attraction; maybe it could have, on a day where we hadn't had news of his dad and Faith and Faith's mom, gawkers themselves, with their big eyes and their judgments. Maybe not, though. This is probably one of those places that *should* be gone, places where people look in at other people and animals in order to see their otherness, their not-me-ness. Places where you can be smug in your own rightness, convinced that only you are what a living being should be.

"Slapping a name on something doesn't make it true," Lorenzo says.

⌐

The sun has set by the time we get to the Sahara Dunes Motel. It's a two-story pink building, with a low-lying, one-story pink tail. The sign glows red in the dark: CONT. BREAKFA, WI-F.

Lorenzo pulls the brake. "I'll check us in."

I duck down in the truck. Lorenzo is eighteen and he can rent a room, but me, just sixteen, here with him . . . I feel like a criminal. I am one, in my state, with what I'm about to do. I'm not sure who I'm ducking from. Maybe some nice family with kids who shouldn't see the pregnant girl, or the vice squad or something. Maybe the motel lady, who might call the cops.

I scooch up and peek. Lorenzo is so brave, just walking in there. He's never done anything like this before, checked in to a motel, but you wouldn't guess it. I mean, wow. He goes right up to the woman behind the desk, and I can only see his back, looking like a very grown-up back, knowing what to do. If it were me, I would have watched a YouTube video or something, so I wouldn't make any slipups. The only times I've been in a motel have been with Mom and once with Dad, and they did the checking-in, but now here I am, going to a motel with a guy. I'm waiting in that truck, and I can suddenly smell the inside-car-ness of it, like you can when you're waiting and it gets cool in there. It's dark and we're in another state, and I have one of those moments where my body is mine but my insides aren't, the me I am very separate, which is hard to explain. But then Lorenzo comes running outside and back to the truck. All of his know-how is completely gone, and he looks frazzled.

"Wallet, wallet!" he says, rummaging around.

"You didn't bring it?" I hate to say it—I would have at least done that.

"Just my credit card. I need ID!" ID, for what? Does this get registered somewhere governmental, like, these people were in this motel at this time? It adds to my nerves, but then I frantically locate the wallet under a Doritos bag and hand it over. Lorenzo jogs back. I picture, I don't know, like maybe when the officer goes back to his squad car in the movies and checks the registration and discovers he's pulled over the most-wanted man, but only because he had a broken taillight. But no. Lorenzo's back in a minute, dangling a key attached to a pink plastic diamond, *206* painted in gold.

We lug our bags up a narrow pink stairway and to our door. When he unlocks it, I smell ancient smoke and Pine-Sol. I crinkle my nose and try to think of cold, clear things like rain and icebergs, fast, as the nausea elevator rises. There's one queen bed with a shiny floral spread, and I can see one of those foldout things where you put a suitcase, and a mysterious door to the adjacent room, which is sort of scary. Also, a TV on a dresser and a chair in scratchy plaid. Lorenzo shuts the door, and it feels so quiet suddenly, and we're more alone than I ever felt with him in the car. If this were a movie, there'd be a drug deal or a murder here, for sure, or we'd listen to the couple next door having sex all night, but instead Lorenzo just says, "I have to pee so bad."

Yes, I do realize there has been much discussion on my part about bathroom use, but this is an unfortunate life truth, and an outsized issue on any road trip. So he hurries to the bathroom, and I hear a flood, an absolute waterfall. Man, it goes on forever—how big can a guy bladder be? I mean, no wonder I'm the one always asking to stop. He's like a camel, with his own built-in storage for liquids.

I first check that the mystery door is for sure locked, because if anyone walked through there, I would have an absolute heart attack. Then I sit at the edge of the bed and pull out my phone. I'm about to text Mom to tell her we got here, but instead I see that I missed one phone call and three texts. The ringer was off, maybe from way back at the gunfight show, so I didn't hear it. I suddenly start to worry, because when the screen is all full like that, you know there's trouble. And yeah, there's a voicemail from Mom, checking in: *You okay? Let me know, but call me tomorrow.*

But the three texts—they're from Faith.

I can't look. I just can't. I send Mom a cheery message telling her that we've arrived safely and that we'll talk in the morning. Faith's words are right there on the screen, though, and there's no way to avoid them.

I'm sorry, but I can't accept the decision you're making.

And then:

Jesus asks us to hate the sin but love the sinner, but I'm struggling to find forgiveness in my heart.

And then:

Abortion is murder, Ivy.

My stomach aches. Or maybe the pain is in my chest; it's hard to tell—my whole body just feels taken over by *hurt.* I'm having one of those film flashbacks of my friendship with Faith, mostly of the times I'd been there for her—during a breakup with this guy from another school, Matthew, and when she had a bad flu, and throughout the weeks of her sprained right arm when I carried her books and stuff around. The sweeter things—laughing together, little love notes of encouragement she'd secretly write in our notebooks, the way she'd tug my ponytail—I can't even get close to those thoughts. Other images shove in, bad ones, ones that Faith is pressing into my face like a smothering pillow. Images I've seen on those signs—the fetuses in the womb with their sea-creature tails and tiny paddle-finger hands—which are burned into my brain from protests and political ads and even that billboard in the desert on the way to visiting my dad. And there it is again, that longing. A longing for God, a connection to a larger goodness, something simple like that. A deep desire to love God and be loved back, a desire that seems more and more impossible. I'm just not sure I trust him when the people who claim him the loudest can be so cruel.

There's a flush, finally, and the bathroom door opens. Lorenzo pops out, and he's wearing the plastic shower cap.

"Sahara Dunes, baby!" he says, and then sees my face. He flings off the cap, and I show him my phone.

"Get rid of those texts, Ivy. Delete them. Seriously. And hey, FYI, Jesus never said that, unless he speaks through tacky pillows from the Gift Barn. That's not in the Bible anywhere."

"Is that true?"

"I looked it up." And then he reluctantly admits, "When that jackass Noah Alvarez said it to me. The last day of school."

"I hate him," I say. My face heats up again with anger and shame. I see Noah laughing at Jason Maxwell at that party, and laughing every time Jason taunted me, and I can imagine him laughing, too, when Jason told Drake Euwing the thing that would make sure I'd never get rid of him. *She has a crush on you! She does! Her friend told Noah. She thinks you're HOT.* Wow, he must be laughing now, too. He and Jason must think I got what was coming to me, even if they blame Lorenzo.

"There *is* something in the Bible that says, 'Do not judge, or you, too, will be judged,' though." Lorenzo looks pissed. Any idea of this being a romantic or sexy night with me and Lorenzo under those sheets is gone. After we brush our teeth and pretend to watch some TV and turn off the lights, Lorenzo kisses my cheek, and we turn our backs to each other. I'm not angry at him and he's not angry at me, but we're both so angry in general that touching feels too kind and soft and loving. We don't even have to talk about it. He sets his toes against mine at one point, and I have my hand on his hip at another, but neither one of us wants our first time together to be tonight, not after this.

At around midnight the couple next door starts having sex, and the headboard bangs against the wall, just like you always see. One thing you can count on—if a couple is having sex in a motel in the movies, there will be another couple on the other side of the wall who isn't, and I guess this is true.

What they never show—a girl on the other side of the wall, wondering if both people in that bed really want to be there.

I wake up just after two, according to the bedside flip clock, circa the 1990s. The pillow is super stuffed to the point that my head is on a separate floor from where my body is. I'm also near the window and can see the occasional swoop of car lights when they go past. I even see them with my eyes closed, which is a strange and inexplicable science thing about eyelids. I'm convinced I haven't slept at all, but I must be wrong because I realize that Lorenzo's not beside me. He must have gotten up in the night, and it's irrational, but I fly up in alarm and then breathe a sigh of relief when I see his bag still here, in the same disheveled state it was in when we went to bed.

I pull on a sweatshirt, slip on my flip-flops. When I open the door and lean over the pink railing, I see Lorenzo down there, in the parking lot, sitting on the hood of the Avalanche. I walk down the narrow steps, my flip-flops smack-smacking my heel in this quiet night. The only other sounds are the murmurs of a TV in someone's room, and the chirp of crickets, and as I get closer to Lorenzo, the crinkle of a wrapper.

"Hey," I say.

"Oh hey!" he says, and startles. "Bite?" He offers me the Butterfinger. In the movies he'd be out here smoking a cigarette, the orange tip glowing in the darkness, but Lorenzo's smarter than that.

"No thanks."

"Probably holding out for Raisinets."

"Scoot over, you butthead."

He does. I climb up and join him.

"You cold?" he asks.

"Not really."

"Look." He gestures upward with his chin.

I do look. "Wow."

It is *wow*. Really wow. We see a lot of stars in Paris, but here, even with the light of the Sahara Dunes behind us, they're spread out above us, an immense and endless glitter blanket.

"Two hundred billion trillion," Lorenzo says.

"Did you just make that up?"

"No!" he laughs. "I took astronomy in California."

"I can't believe we go around forgetting stars."

He looks at me, and with such love, too. "Your eyes are stars."

I roll mine.

"I mean it," he says.

"It's just the light from the Sahara Dunes."

He kisses me, because kindness and softness and love have returned. They're ours. No one can take them away, I think, though that kind of certainty in a movie means *Watch out*. Lorenzo tastes like chocolate and fake peanut butter. When the kiss is over, he leans back against the windshield, and so do I. He pops the last of the Butterfinger into his mouth; that's what happens to the food. He crumples the wrapper and sticks it in his pocket.

"You'd never litter," I say, because I want to talk about goodness.

He makes a face at me like, *Are you kidding? Of course not.*

We're quiet, just looking at stars. Two hundred billion trillion of them out there. Maybe this is the real Wonder Tower, the hood of this Chevy Avalanche.

"You know when you asked me if you knew the deep-down me?" Lorenzo finally says.

"Yeah."

"Here's a thing. A big thing."

I take his hand and wait. I think about Mom's and Esilda's hands working the quilt lines before they spoke to me, about the way big stories require you to sit quietly until they arrive.

"Remember Mateo?"

"Of course. How could I not? You guys got stuck in six feet of snow in his shit Datsun. Chased by a horse one time. His mischief eyes . . ."

"He was like a brother to me."

Lorenzo stops, so I wait again, but I start to get worried. Really worried. I've come to love Mateo, too, just through Lorenzo's stories. "*Was?*" I finally say.

"He got, um, shot. Murdered. Right on his front lawn. His stepdad—killed his mom inside after an argument, and shot Mateo in his back as he was, uh—" Lorenzo's voice strangles with tears. "Trying to get away."

"Oh my God, Lorenzo." I feel struck. I can barely breathe. "*No.*"

"I know. It happened right before we moved here. I was so glad we were leaving. Getting the hell out of there. I passed his house every day, that lawn."

"Oh my God, Lorenzo," I say again. I'm so shocked that I feel suddenly cold, trembly. "I'm so sorry." My arms are shaking, but I hold his hand hard. I don't know what to do. I've never heard anything so awful happening to someone we know. "You never said. You never told me."

"I don't like to talk about it. It makes me imagine it, and only it, him running. I like to remember the other things about him. Looking up there, you know, at the stars like this, I think about him."

"I bet. Of course. Oh my God."

"And I thought about him just tonight, right? When Faith used the word *murder*? I just don't get it, you know, how people say having an abortion is murder and will do anything to stop it, but guns are murder, too, and they won't do a thing to stop those."

I never really put those things together before, but he's right.

"And they're usually the same people saying both things."

There's no good answer to this, so I just keep holding his hand.

"I just wish there was something I could have *done*," he says.

A car speeds past with two people inside, strangers living out their own big stories and struggling with their own big questions. Above us there's something so much larger, that universe, that forever. And right then my deep desire to believe in God folds and rises, and folds and rises again. I wish so hard that I could. I want to believe so badly. For me and Lorenzo, and for Mateo. For my mom and Mase. But the God who belongs to my friend Faith, that punishing and withholding and cruel one? I don't know, I don't know. It's like my mom said after her boyfriend Terry left: *Don't be with a guy like that. Don't do what I did. You deserve better.* The God who's supposed to be about love—that's the one I want. The love one. The one I can feel the presence of when

I look at those stars and sense all the magnitude, and the awe, and the mystery. I don't want a Wonder Tower God, available to only those with a certain ticket, a walled-off being surrounded with barbs and wire. I want the one who offers wonder to every person, just by giving them a sky.

17

I'M SLEEPING DEEPLY WHEN A SOUND WAKES ME UP. *Kashunk*. And then again: *kashunk*. I shake off the strangeness of my surroundings and sit up. I see Lorenzo sitting at the fake wood table, stamping our passports from yesterday. He's dressed already, and there are two cardboard cups with white lids. Coffee, I'm guessing, and a box of powdered-sugar doughnuts.

"Genoa!" Lorenzo holds up the passport for me to see. "We didn't do it yesterday, after all of the, uh, excitement-slash-condemning."

"Powdered sugar," I say. I'm suddenly starving. "I didn't even hear you leave." And I didn't even feel him there in the bed with me, I realize, not much, not even after we finally came inside and slipped under the sheets. There was an arm around me at one point, leg against leg, but then sleep pulled me under. I get a pinch of insecurity again. Like, if I were just a regular girl, *unmarked* by all this, undamaged, would we have been going at it all night? Would there ever have been just a leg against a leg? That condemning, though. It seeps into you, goes deep. I hope it doesn't stay. I hope it isn't mine forever.

"Dang," Lorenzo says. "You are so beautiful even just sitting in the shit bed of the Sahara Dunes. It's like I see your soul shining."

He's seeing me right here in the morning, before I've had the chance to brush my teeth or survey my face for possible disasters, and his face is just so full of love and acceptance, I can barely believe it. I want to cry when he says that about my soul. The love and acceptance—it just washes away the marks and the damage and the insecurity, at least for now. "*Your* soul shines," I say, and then I swallow hard because my voice is wavery. I know Tess isn't a real person, but I wish someone could have done that for her.

"We should probably get going, huh?" he says. I look at the clock. It's not even seven, but it's one of our biggest days of driving, and Lorenzo wants to stop in Dinosaur.

"I'm the fastest getting-readier ever," I say.

"I'm really happy you don't take hours, because I've been waiting for you to open these doughnuts."

I hop out of bed. In the bathroom of the Sahara Dunes, Lorenzo has already hung his wet towel back up, and has put the second bar of soap in the little shower tray. I turn the shower on so he won't hear me use the bathroom. I'm in and out of there in fifteen minutes, even though the room keeps steaming back up when I put on my makeup, even though I have to keep trying and trying to clear it away to see myself.

"Let's get out of here," I say. I jam my stuff in my bag and zip it up like an ending. We're done with this place. It's maybe a goodbye to Faith, too.

"Man, it's pretty out here."

"I'm so glad you've said that a hundred times now," Lorenzo says, plucking some fries out of the bag and tipping them into his mouth as he drives. "Ives? Are you sure you don't just want to get on the freeway and go? Like, straight there, forget all this world-tour shit I made up? I mean, they've just basically been small towns."

I would never admit this to him, but honestly, *yeah,* I've had that thought so often. Not about the freeway exactly, but just . . . if we flew there or something, this could all be over with by now. I thought it all last night, because every day, you know, every single day there is still this unwanted thing happening, not just *to* me, but *in* me. Inside my very own body. I want it *gone.* I can only imagine how Mom felt during her cancer, how desperately she wanted *that* gone. But I want to be on this world tour with Lorenzo *so bad,* too. How do I explain? I guess—it's what a regular girl might do during a regular summer. A regular girl just busy being alive. Maybe that's why Mom needed to take us on those trips during her treatment—one to Nacogdoches because it was in a Lucinda Williams song, and one to Hot Springs National Park since she couldn't remember the last time she saw a waterfall. She probably wanted to feel like a regular woman just busy being alive.

"No!" I tell Lorenzo. "Are you kidding? This is the only thing I *do* want, being here with you. What's been great . . . We don't know what we're going to get. That always seemed like a bad thing before. But now . . . the best thing about a surprise isn't what it turns out to be. The best thing about a surprise is the excitement of a surprise." I'm not sure I'm even making sense.

"Yeah, I get it. The time before the vacation is sometimes better than the vacation."

"Not that you're doomed to be disappointed or anything. Just, I was really looking forward to the Wonder Tower, and it wasn't what we expected at all. And look. Out here—this is *incredible*."

We're suddenly in a whole different land compared to the endless dry fields, the pastures, as flat and forever as a quilt over the world. It started shortly after we drove through Denver and began entering the mountains: rocky hills at first, and then trees, a few and then many, ponderosa pines, spruce, and fir. They dotted the scenery, but then rapidly became waves and waves of trees, the spiky back of a giant green sea monster, up and down and up. And then there were places where rivers ran right next to the road, with tumbling white water and huge boulders, nothing I'd ever seen before. Sometimes, too, a bridge right over those rivers, where looking down was a nervous thrill. Beautiful words appeared on the map: Clear Creek and Foothill Road. Golden and Evergreen and Silver Plume.

"The surprise is the surprise," Lorenzo says, and he's

exactly right. And then I tell Lorenzo not to be a French-fry hog, and he tells me I'm a Red Vines hog, and then we get into a pretend squabble about who's the *biggest* hog, because that's what a regular girl would do, too.

~

We drive through Vail, a name I'd only heard on TV. It's a magic place that looks like an Alpine town, not like I'd seen the Alps, either, but it all looks like a life-sized cuckoo clock. There are pointy brown roofs, windows with shutters, thick lacy balconies. There are rows of flags hanging across the tops of buildings, too, and clock towers, and flower baskets everywhere. Charming, like you could lift the lid and music would play. The hills are painted with yellow wildflowers, and there's the occasional glimpse of pure, clear water— a small lake, a creek, a waterfall. No wonder people with money claimed this place.

"Imagine it with snow everywhere," Lorenzo says, and when I do, I see a fairy tale.

But there are suddenly people everywhere, also, ducking into shops and eating at cafés and trying to find parking places. I'm not sure where they all came from. The roads have been roomy, mostly free of traffic, unless we got stuck behind a semi. But now it's like a crowd has appeared, everyone in this one small place.

We finally find a spot to put our shit car among the Land

Rovers and Mercedes SUVs and tour buses. Past the jewelry stores and shops of cowgirl clothing and stores with names ending in *ologie,* we find a place to pee and spend five bucks on a Sprite. Not everyone can afford a fairy tale.

I feel like the foreigner that I am, just a few states away from my own. I wonder what it would be like to go into one of those places and spend hundreds of dollars on a sweater, or order whatever smelled so delicious back there, grilling meat, garlic. Sometimes I don't understand how we're all the same country.

We take a photo of us where you can see the clock tower in the back and the mountains beyond. We catch it at a moment when it looks like there's just us, even though that's far from the truth. In it we look uncomfortable. Lorenzo has a ketchup stain on his shirt, and I'm in my old tank top and shorts, hot and pregnant and thirsty.

We get gas. While Lorenzo is filling up the tank, I call Mom. I tell her how great it's all going and skip the stuff about Faith so she doesn't get upset. She reminds me for the millionth time that her cousin Nadine, our next stop, has a good heart, but that her husband, Dwight . . . She always trails off, which means he's an asshole. I tell her we have it handled and not to worry, and after we hang up, I text Peyton. *Are you forsaking me, too?* I type, and then press Send. *Forsaking.* I don't think it's a word I've ever used in my whole life, and I don't even know where it came from. It's vaguely religious, Bible-y, and I want to change it, but it's too late. Regret and guilt rush in the minute I send that message. I wait, though. I look at my phone and say, *Please*

please please, but it sits there all silent. If my very own Peyton turns her back on me, it means they'll all fall like dominoes. I can't even imagine being that alone.

Lorenzo pops into the truck. "Whoa. I didn't even get snacks. Four bucks for Red Vines."

"No way." We should have gotten gas anywhere but here. It's so expensive.

"This really does feel like a world tour, you know what I mean?" Lorenzo says when we're on the road again.

"Like visiting a town so different from ours?"

"A town, a way of life. You look at all that money. . . . You kinda understand people holding so tight to their beliefs, when beliefs are the things they have the most of."

I stare out my window, out at a ribbon of haze in the blue sky, a FALLING ROCKS warning sign, and an SUV passing us. It's got a mom and a dad sipping out of cardboard cups in the front, and children watching a movie in the back. I spot a mountain filled with ski lifts, something I've never seen before. The chairs swing, empty. I want to point it out to Lorenzo, but my mind is too crowded with what he said. He's right, probably. Money is power, but what do you do when you don't have much of it? Beliefs are free.

We descend. From high mountains, some with snow still at the very top, we move down to slopes of trees, and lower again to rocky hills, and lower still to towns where the mountains only serve as a distant backdrop.

"And now comes a sad story," Lorenzo says. "Antlers to Rifle."

"Eek." I picture the elk head in Jason Maxwell's rec room. I think of Mateo and check Lorenzo's face for any signs of upset, but he's only mindlessly drumming his fingers on the steering wheel and watching the road. I shift around in my seat for the millionth time. Aside from that brief stop in Vail, we've been in the car for four and a half hours. For a while there, the scenery was a film to sit back and watch, but even a beautiful film makes your butt hurt when you've been in one place too long.

We stop in Rifle, just to stretch our legs. Also, Lorenzo buys a bag of chips and a can of bean dip, some ranch Corn Nuts, and some Funyuns. I never met anyone who ate Funyuns before, and I truly wonder if he is the sole individual responsible for keeping the Funyuns factory going. You have no idea how much guys eat. I had no idea how much guys eat.

We get out at Rifle's town square. It's small and features an iron statue of a cowboy riding a fish as if it's a bucking bronco. No idea. We scoot in together and take a selfie. In the photo I look tired, but more relaxed than in the one from Vail. When you look at a photo like that—you in front of a fish-riding cowboy—you have one of those moments where you're struck again with the truth of where you are and why.

"Do me," Lorenzo says. He plops down on a bench

where a life-sized iron statue of Mark Twain also sits and puts his arm around him like they're pals. I snap his photo. It's funny, but after riding around for hours in the car like this, Lorenzo's getting so familiar, I sometimes forget to notice him. But sitting beside him on that bench, I do. God, he's cute. That grin of his.

"I'd like to do you," I say, and kiss him. It's becoming pretty clear that the old Ivy, the one who wants him bad, is still here, all right. It's strange, though. I wonder if maybe I should be more traumatized about sex after what happened, and in my "condition." Like, in the movies I'd be crying or pushing him away instead of going right over to him and straddling him, like I do now. Somehow the uglies, the cringing grossness of my awful hand and Drake Euwing and that night of the concert just don't belong near Lorenzo, though. They're separate, and I can keep them separate. It might be different for other people, but this is how it is for me.

"Same," Lorenzo says. "You have the cutest little ass." He grabs it. But then he thinks better of it and gives me a little shove. I get off of his lap. One little friendly shove and, boom, the worries are back. I know we have to talk about this, because telling someone they're beautiful or getting an erection doesn't necessarily mean they *want you*, want you. I'm scared to ask, to even say the worry out loud, because if Lorenzo thinks I'm too wrecked to have sex with, he's going to break my heart.

I hear Lorenzo's phone buzz in his pocket. He's got it on vibrate, which means he doesn't want me to hear it ring.

"Your dad?" I ask. "Has he been calling?"

"Nah."

"Lorenzo, don't lie." He always scratches his chin like that when he lies.

"It doesn't matter."

"It does. You have to tell me what's happening. Is he going to swoop in with a SWAT team or something?"

"He's just making empty threats."

"Like what?" I'm getting nervous. I don't believe that there's such a thing as an empty threat. An empty threat is still a threat, and a threat is a possibility.

"He's not coming out here, Ivy. He couldn't catch up to us if he did, and he's afraid to fly."

"Lorenzo! Come on. I think you should tell him the truth. I mean, not the whole truth," I say. The thought of the Euwings finding out fills me with panic. "You don't have to tell him everything. You don't have to say *who*, just not *you*. He won't even care what I do then."

"I'll tell him, okay? Someday. But not now, when people are writing shit on your locker. When your best friend sends you texts like that, when her mom . . ." He shakes his head. "What are we going to say, it's some random guy? My dad won't believe that. He'll think we're lying to protect me. And all those other people . . . They *will* believe it. Random guy, man. They'll have their fucking torches lit." The tips of his ears turn scarlet.

"It's better than what's happening to you. And if people believe it's some guy from, I don't know, out of state, out of town, anything, the Euwings will never guess. Drake was *laughing* when he heard about me. He's not going to figure it out! It won't even occur to him. Honestly, why would it? You're not going to think a person could get pregnant that way. *I* didn't even think so. It won't be anyone's first thought, anyway. First thought is *you,* my boyfriend. If it's not you, they'll just think I sleep around."

Lorenzo groans. "Ivy. *Just?* These people, it's like the Middle Ages."

It's like *all* ages, I want to tell him as a vision of Tess appears in my mind.

"And, Ives, really. It *doesn't* occur to him? Drake? Not just a tiny bit? Then why didn't he tell his parents about you being pregnant, huh? Why didn't he run right home to tell them the juicy gossip about Euwing's Drugs' star employee? You went into work, and they were clueless. Some part of his twit brain didn't have a *second* of wondering?"

God, I get the uglies, big-time. Gross, shivery, sickening uglies. The idea of dweeby Drake, maybe, alone in his room during that second of wondering, thinking he might have had the power to change my life. And he *did* have the power. *Does.* "You don't have to protect me. You don't have to try to save me." I don't mention Mateo, but after that story, I sure do understand Lorenzo better. I understand that lone Converse and maybe this whole trip.

"Do you *want* my help, Ivy? It sometimes doesn't seem like it. It's okay if you don't. Just tell me."

"I do want it." I do, oh, I do. "But look what's happening to *you.*" And it's not very fierce, is it, getting help like this? I don't say that part.

"How my dad is acting—it's also good to see. Well, not *good,* but eye-opening, right? The way he's not respecting me? Like, if this *were* my choice, let alone *your* choice?"

"Esilda—she said these issues aren't only women's issues. They're human issues."

"For sure. And I tell you, if someone was forcing me to do something with my body that maybe put my health at risk, or changed my whole life . . ." He shakes his head.

"And hey, we should get away from *this* guy." I flick Mark Twain. "He thought that women voting was disgusting. He said the 'natural bosses,' men, should do it. For a lot of years, anyway, he was a big misogynistic butthead." It's another thing I suddenly remember from Ms. La Costa's class and the suffrage unit.

Lorenzo stands up, like he's been burned. "Racist, too. What the hell was I thinking."

As we head to the truck, without looking back, Lorenzo raises his arm and gives Mark the finger.

The closer we get to Dinosaur, the giddier Lorenzo gets. Dinosaur National Monument has two entrances, one in Utah and one in Colorado, but Lorenzo wants the bigger thrills of the Utah side, so we drive a couple of miles over the state line to park.

"So cool, right? One attraction in two states! When have you ever done that, huh?" he says.

"Absolutely never."

It's so hot out here. The Quarry Exhibit Hall is a huge

glass building built around a rock wall that has actual fossils embedded in it. There are huge dinosaur skulls and skeletons in there, too, and Lorenzo makes me take a hundred pictures of him and of us, our faces jammed together, the bones of ferocious creatures behind us.

"'Allosaurus,'" I read. "'Common predator.'" It has more teeth than the common predators of today, at least the ones in Paris. A longer neck and larger body, too, but the same dull and unreadable eyes.

The heat hits again as we leave the air-conditioned building. We meander down the Fossil Discovery Trail, a triangle path that loops around the dry canyon valley.

"One and a half miles?" Lorenzo asks.

"Sure."

"'Open-toed shoes not recommended,'" he reads, and looks down at our sandals. "'There is no shade on this trail.'"

"No problemo," I say, though all I really want is a nap someplace cool.

"'All natural areas pose risks. Your safety depends on your good judgment.'"

"We're screwed," I say.

⌐

It's hard not to think about rattlesnakes. Our feet are so exposed that I have to keep shaking the pebbles from my sandals. But I stop thinking about snakes and my mind turns to larger predators when we reach the lookout point. It's a

200

prehistoric land—harsh, rocky, moonlike—but it's right here, in front of our eyes. You can imagine the dinosaurs we just saw, stomping around, being powerful, eating each other or being eaten.

"Just like *The Land Before Time*," I say. Mase and I used to love that movie. I don't remember much about it, aside from the big earthquake, and young dinosaurs running from danger, fighting the odds, and struggling to get to the Great Valley—a tale of survival and teamwork and love, pretty much like this road trip.

"Sharptooth," Lorenzo says. He makes a claw and forks it my direction. "When I was a kid, my dad put me in these religion classes on Sundays. Pretty sure it was mostly because he had to work and they were free. We were studying dinosaurs at school, and I'd just made this awesome diorama with a *T. rex* and some plastic palm trees we got at the dollar store. So I asked the religion teacher where the dinosaurs were in the Bible."

I laugh. "What'd she say?"

"Something like, 'It's a mystery of faith,' but she never gave me an actual answer. I remember feeling so disappointed. Like that moment where you realize adults don't know everything, so you're basically up shit creek."

"*Someone* should know everything."

"Yeah, exactly."

"But no one can even agree on what's *true,* let alone what's right or wrong."

When I look out over that land, where long, long ago dinosaurs lived, and where just a few minutes ago we took selfies with their bones . . . the story, the whole story, seems so much older and more complicated than I ever understood. And more frightening, too. Eat or be eaten, predators and power.

"*Triceratops* are the cutest ones," I say. God, I do love having an opinion, even if beliefs are really just you, trying hard to be sure of something.

But I know this. I know it so completely as I stand in the heat, my shoulders turning red, pebbles in my sandals, staring out at history and the present and the future—opinions aren't truth, even if a whole lot of people have them.

"*Stegosaurus* second place," Lorenzo says.

18

TURNS OUT, MOM'S COUSIN NADINE AND HER husband, Dwight, don't actually have a B and B in Vernal, Utah, like we thought. They have a KOA campground. I was sure we were lost, which could have easily happened, with Lorenzo shouting every time he saw a dinosaur statue as I was driving and trying to navigate. Vernal loves its dinosaurs, all right. An extra-large pink one even greets you as you enter the town. She's got a wide smile and movie star eyelashes and holds a sign that reads, VERNAL, UTAH'S DINOSAUR LAND.

At the entrance of the campground, I pull over and double-check the address. Lorenzo stamps our passports for Naples, the town just before Vernal. "This is definitely the address she gave us," I say. "But, whoa, when my mom said 'B and B,' I was picturing some gingerbread-type Victorian with lace curtains and teddy bears on the bed."

"Teddy bears on beds give me the creeps anyway," Lorenzo says as I find a parking spot. The campground is huge, grassy, and sprawling, spotted with some cabins and a few classic Airstream trailers, which sit like enormous silver bullets shot from a sci-fi gun. A few RVs are hooked up at various sites, too, along with some tents. There's a playground and a pool, picnic tables and sandy pits for horseshoes. "And, wow, look at this place. It's awesome. Ives! Ives, look! A *geodesic dome*!"

"Where?"

"There! How can you miss that, seriously?"

"That white thing? It looks like big half golf ball."

"Are you kidding? It looks amazing. Like a lunar landing something. Do you think it's one of the places people can stay? This would be the best day of my life if we got to sleep in that."

It's the best day of his life.

"I hope you don't mind staying in the dome," Nadine says, walking us toward it. "It was the only thing we had available when your mom called."

"Mind? No way! This is incredible!" Lorenzo is practically skipping. "Why would it be *available*?"

"Well, there's no actual bathroom, and it gets pretty hot, just to warn you. Dwight had it built to grow tomatoes, but that didn't last long." Nadine seems about as different from Mom as you can get, even though she's her second cousin. I always get confused about what that actually even means, grandfather's sister's daughter, ugh, who can keep track when family trees are more like family forests. The point is, she and Mom are related and keep up with each other through Christmas cards and social media. I remember meeting her and her husband, Dwight, and their three sons maybe once when we were little, so it's one of those times when your relatives are strangers. Nadine has short brown helmet hair laced with gray and a wide, troubled face. Her clothes—baggy shorts and an oversized V-neck T-shirt—seem tired, maybe from a lot of years working hard to hide her body. Nadine . . . How to put it? She seems like the visual equivalent of an apology, weary from overuse. I wonder if she ever danced at a concert or felt the way music can free you and fill you.

"We really appreciate you having us," I say.

"Just as long as one of you stays in the bunk beds, and the other in the queen."

"Of course."

"Dwight would kill me if you two kids were messing around in there. He wanted one of you to stay with us, but I told him Ivy was always a good girl."

Lorenzo and I meet eyes. He's smirking a little. I mean, he's one half step from a snort, and so I give him a *behave yourself* glare.

"No, no, absolutely," I say.

"Dwight's house, Dwight's rules," she says.

"Dwight's geodesic dome, Dwight's ru—"

I shoot Lorenzo another look, and he shuts up.

"Here we are."

We duck inside. It's supercute in that small circle, with

the golf-ball ceiling and golf-ball walls made out of some parachute-like material. There's a pine bed and a pine bunk bed, large enough for a pair of ten-year-olds. There's a small stall at the foot of the bunk beds, next to a tiny sink on a pine box. Wow, though. It's hot-shower humid in here.

"The toilet is new," Nadine says, nodding toward the stall. "So you don't want to go flushing any . . . female products."

"You don't have to worry about that," I say, and then kick myself, because Nadine and Dwight don't know why we're going to Oregon. If I thought the Sahara Dunes bathroom was a challenge, the stakes have just been upped.

"This is great. This is so great," Lorenzo says. Perspiration is gathering on his forehead and upper lip.

"You're coming for dinner?" Nadine asks without much enthusiasm, as if she's hoping we'll say no.

I'm stuck. If I say no, it might be rude, and if I say yes, a burden. "Only if it works for you?"

"Of course it does. You're family. How often do we see each other, huh? The last time was what? I don't even remember. You were tiny. I'll just have to stop at the store and make some chicken or something for us, since my kids don't like meat, and something with bacon for Dwight. He's been doing keto for the last month. He hasn't lost a pound, but he keeps telling me I should do it." She pinches some flab at her side. If that's what Dwight does to her, I hate him already.

Dwight leaves the table after he eats and goes to the living room to watch TV. It's a game of some kind, and sport sounds aggressively charge into the dining room and tackle me. Their small ranch house smells musty and has scuff marks on the walls, but it tries to be cheery with all of Nadine's crafts—folk-art light-switch plates, crocheted owls with felt eyes, a cross-stitched pillow with the words WELCOME TO DOWNTON ABBEY, and a chalkboard with a hand-lettered sign that reads DREAMS ARE FREE.

A huge platter of fried chicken sits mostly untouched, since Thomas and Tate went out with friends instead of having dinner with us, and the third, Bryan, the oldest, never showed. He lives in one of the Airstreams on the property, Nadine told us, but you can tell there's a lot of tension about him, because whenever his name comes up, Dwight drops in little disapproving comments, like *He'll have a car when playing video games is a job* and *Bryan prefers to be alone,* as if that's a bad thing. Dwight is a big guy with big judgments and a hard face, the kind of man who lives in the world in his own head and not the real one that has other people in it. Even their dog seems unhappy, and I want to get out of there so bad, but Lorenzo insists on doing the dishes because he doesn't want Nadine to get stuck with them. I dry while Nadine finds the fried chicken recipe for me to give Mase. It was really good, but even more, I just want to give Nadine *something,* because all of it—the dinner, the husband, the kids—makes me feel so bad. When we leave, Nadine gives me a pom-pom ponytail holder she made, and then the door shuts, and thankfully, thankfully, we are alone under the beautiful Utah sky.

"Let's get out of here," Lorenzo says.

"Shh, shh!" I already feel so guilty, and I don't even know why. But if Nadine heard and thought we didn't appreciate her, I'd never forgive myself.

"How do you open this thing?" Lorenzo's clanging the latch of the chain-link gate. That sound is a memory. I can suddenly feel my fingers gripping metal, and the press of chain-link diagonals in my skin. The uglies plus this guilt are an enormous hand pressing on my chest. It's hard to even breathe.

"Here," I say. I lift the metal hook and swivel it to free us. I latch it carefully so the dog doesn't get out.

"I'm so depressed," Lorenzo says as we get in the truck and he starts the engine.

"I know, I know. Hit it," I say, and he does.

"Find me a grocery store, Ives," he says.

"You can't possibly be hungry," I say. "You ate your portion, plus poor Bryan's, at least."

"Hunger is the point." His voice is urgent. "I want to be so hungry, I'm hungry for life itself."

"Okay, okay." I type into my phone. "Davis Food and Drug, on Main Street. Take a right up ahead, and then it's a half mile."

He parks in the lot. Inside we're smacked with bright fluorescent lights, and Lorenzo grabs a cart. He drives it like a race car, straight to the freezer section. We stare at the ice cream. "Cookie dough," I say, and reach for a pint.

"We each get our own," Lorenzo says. We tumble them into the cart. "Hop on," he commands.

"On?"

"*On.*"

I do. I'm too big for this, but I hold on to the metal edge, and Lorenzo rumbles a pretend motor and takes off.

"Vree-oom!" he says, much too loudly, and a woman looks at us disapprovingly, and he nearly tips us going around the corner to the cookie aisle. I get those Keeblers with the caramel and chocolate and coconut, and he gets Oreo Thins, plus those peanut-shaped cookies with the peanut butter centers, and then he tosses in some Milk Duds and Red Vines, and, heck, why not, why not just be happy, I add a box of Reese's Pieces.

"Water," I croak, like I'm dying in the desert, or maybe in the desserts.

"Right. And spoons."

We veer and screech, Lorenzo's sandals squeaking on the floor as the Muzak version of "Hey, Soul Sister" plays. We narrowly miss a Fourth of July display, a flag made from soda cans. On the way out the door, Lorenzo uses the quarters in his pocket to buy two giant gumballs from a machine. By the time we're out of there, under the bright lights of the Davis Food & Drug parking lot, the despair has dimmed, but only barely.

⌐

Sometime after one a.m. the vibration buzz of my phone wakes me. It's a text from Peyton. *Please don't put me in the middle,* it says. Now I'll never get back to sleep. It was hard enough to drift off in the first place. Sure, we gorged on sugar when we got back, but it's so hot in there, too. If I were a tomato plant, I'd have grown a half inch, at least. Lorenzo is crammed into one of the bunk beds, his feet sticking off the end, and he's ditched all his clothes. I take advantage and get a good look at the sexy moon curves of his ass.

I locate my sandals, duck under the small dome door, and, once outside, I slip them on and head to the KOA bathroom. I don't want to wake Lorenzo by using ours, and besides, wow, the air feels amazing. The sky is a star blanket. It's the same one that covered the land of the dinosaurs, and still covers the Sahara Dunes, and home, too, though this can be hard to believe.

I aim toward the light outside the concrete block of restrooms. I head for the chick in a triangle dress, and not the dude in a uni-suit, and think for the millionth time how weird it is that this—a dress—is the chosen symbol for girls and women. I pee and wash my hands as fast as I can because campground bathrooms are a potential murder site, according to most movies, and because the scratched-up stall (*Cassie was her,* no *e*), mottled mirror, and slimy-sudsy counter unnerve me. I'm heading out, tossing my paper towel into the garbage can, when a figure comes around the corner and I scream.

"Jesus, Ivy," Nadine says.

"Oh my God, you scared me to death."

"What are you doing out here?"

"What are *you* doing out here? You're still working, even this late?"

"We've been getting all these complaints about the men's

toilet." She lifts a plunger in evidence. "Don't tell me. Something's wrong with yours."

"No, I just didn't want to wake Lorenzo." There's a funny silence between us. Awkward. "Lorenzo, in his own bed." I don't know why she makes me feel so guilty.

"Ivy," she says.

"Yeah?"

"I know this is none of my business, but . . . the two of you . . . You . . . Are you, uh, *pregnant*?"

We're standing in the circle of light from the cement bunker of bathrooms. I fold my arms over my T-shirt, covering my breasts. Nadine should be paying attention to that guy trying to get into the pool after hours, not me. "What?" I say, because it's not a yes or a lie.

"I was just wondering if you were going to your grandma's in Oregon for a, uh, different reason than just a visit."

My mouth gapes. I feel struck. I want to flee, but there's nowhere to go.

"I can guess what you're probably thinking," she says. "Me, Utah, whatever . . . But no. I'm not going to try to stop you. I only . . . I felt like it was important to say something."

Nadine—well, it's hard to explain, but all at once I just see a woman standing there. A woman who isn't going to hurt me, or maybe even judge me. Another woman, another actual human being I never really *saw* before. "How did you know?"

"You kept . . ." She indicates pulling at her bra, this way, that. "Like it hurt. You seem, I don't know, tired, more tired than a girl your age should be, too. A certain kind of tired.

And your mom's voice . . . It was just . . . different. You don't have to know someone well to realize when they're hiding something. And when I saw you do that, with your bra . . . Well, I never told anyone this before, but it all came back to me. Lorenzo, he's so sweet and careful with you, and I never had that, but the rest of it, the memories came whooshing in."

"You? The same thing happened? You had an . . ." I don't say it. No matter how quiet I am, that word is too loud with all of those sleeping people around us, in cabins and tents and RVs. But I can't believe it. I truly can't. Another woman is going to tell me about her abortion. How is this possible? Is there, like, a sea of women who've had them and I've never known it?

"Well, yeah, I got pregnant, but I had the baby."

"Oh." Okay. Never mind the whole sea idea.

"I'm not saying this to change your mind. I'm just kind of glad I caught you out here. What happened, as I said . . . I've never told anyone."

"Was it Dwight?"

"Before Dwight. I was just a few years older than you. I had this boyfriend, Mike. He didn't want to use contraception. He was religious and said he was against it, and that he didn't like condoms. He said, you know, he'd pull out. I don't know why I didn't stick up for myself. He was just moody and kind of controlling, and I just went along. And then . . ."

She shakes her head. Looks off into the star blanket.

"You got pregnant."

"And he didn't want me to have an abortion. He forbid

it. Forbade it, whatever. I went to this clinic anyway. But in Utah—you have to get counseling, you know?"

I shrug. I have no idea.

"Yeah. Counseling to discourage you from getting an abortion, and then you have to wait seventy-two hours before going back. For me . . . To go back there again, to stand up for what I wanted—it was too much. I was legally an adult, but I just couldn't do it. I could barely talk back to my mother, you know? And Mike said he'd be around to help."

"And he wasn't?"

"God, no. After Bryan was born . . . Oh, my parents, my mom especially, she was furious! I was trying to hold it all together. I had this job at a motel . . . cleaning. So when I met Dwight, it was a godsend. He came in and took control of everything. But he also . . ."

"Took control of everything?"

She shrugs and then sighs. "Right. And Bryan—Dwight hated him. Bryan was just a kid, but Dwight treated him really bad. I have so many regrets. I never regret Bryan, not for a minute, but I wonder, I often wonder, what my life would have been if I'd made my own choices. I mean, truly made my own choices."

After we say goodbye, I feel close to Nadine. And I feel incredibly sad. I'm so lost in thought as I walk back to the dome, watching my step in the dark, that I almost miss it.

Up there, in that black glitter sky, a shooting star briefly flares.

You're supposed to make a wish. But it's a strange thing to do, when you think about it. Especially since a shooting star isn't a star at all, just a bit of dust or rock, burning up as it falls into Earth's atmosphere.

For a second I want to go back to that bathroom stall. *Cassie was her.* I want to write my own message. *Ivy will never be her.* She will never be Nadine, burning and tumbling, pulled with a gravity not her own.

19

"I TOLD HER IT WAS NONE OF HER BUSINESS," MOM says during our morning check-in. We've already driven past Manila, Utah (Manila, *kashunk*), with its gorgeous red canyons and deep blue rivers, and through the mountainous roads of Geneva, Idaho (Geneva, *kashunk*). We're quickly approaching the refreshing-sounding Soda Springs. It was supposed to be a four-hour drive, but Lorenzo's been speeding the whole way, and it's only eleven-thirty. I've told him to slow down a thousand times, I swear, but he's in his own world this morning. Not the world of Manila, Philippines, or Geneva, Switzerland, or even Manila, Utah, and Geneva, Idaho, but somewhere completely inaccessible.

"Mom! A 'none of your business' is not a no! A 'none of your business' is definitely more a 'yes, but I won't admit it.'" What she's just told me—it's awful, awful. Lorenzo gives me a *What the hell is happening?* face and then speeds up again. "Lorenzo, Jesus!"

"He'd better not be driving too fast," Mom says.

"Did she go in there just to ask about me? I mean, why was she even at the store?"

"Well, she's not exactly a regular, Ivy. She had a brief spell with puff paint a few years ago, but that's it. She pretended to look at the stencils. Maybe I shouldn't have told you. I don't want you to be in the dark, is all! God, it pissed me off. Can you imagine if that righteous busybody knew the *whole* truth?"

I go cold. I suddenly shiver. "Don't even say that. Oh my God, don't even. You've got to fix this!" I moan. "They can't know *any*thing. They just can't. Plus, *my job.*"

"Honey! That is the *last* thing you should be thinking about. There are other jobs! *Lots* of other jobs."

"No, there aren't. And I'm an assistant manager! I have to think about *college.*"

"We'll work it out, Ivy, I promise."

"That is so vague. That is totally meaningless. My job isn't meaningless. It's a *plan.*"

"At your age it can be hard to see past what's happening at this moment—"

"You never 'at your age' me, Mom. Nev—"

"But there are lots of possibilities and moments beyond this one. What you see right now isn't all there is. It's not all and everything, even though it feels that way. God, I can't stand the thought of you even in that place."

"You are not helping!"

"We're doing the best we can here, okay?"

Wait a second. Wait just a second. Like Nadine said, you know when a person is hiding something. "What else happened?" On this three-lane highway, Lorenzo's riding the butt of a Camry, and then he passes the first chance he gets. The driver honks, a long, loud protest of Lorenzo's obnoxiousness.

"Was that a honk? Is he driving safely?"

"Lorenzo, relax," I say.

"Is anyone relaxed in this car?" he says.

"Tell me what happened," I say to Mom.

"It's nothing, really! Just that Alvarez kid."

"Noah?"

"No, his little brother. Mase was out riding his bike, and the kid balled up his sports coat and stuck it under his T-shirt and yelled, 'Who am I?' "

I'm so confused. "Sports coat?"

"They just got back from church."

"Mase, riding a *bike*?"

"I bought him one at the thrift shop and made him go out. I'm worried about him."

Fury fills me. J. J. Alvarez—I have an ugly moment where I imagine opening Diesel's gate when that kid is digging in the gutter. Mom, standing behind the counter at Shelley's Craft and Quilt—she was a sitting duck for Mrs. Euwing when she waltzed in there to find out about me. Look what I've done, though. Look what I've done to my people. "I just hope you—"

I don't get the chance to finish. The signal drops. I try to call back, with no luck. I send a text but get an *unsent* message. I wave my arm around to get a signal, but it's hopeless. Out here there's nothing but dry grass and more dry grass, and a row of snail-shaped clouds above.

"Shit," I say.

"Dwight would send you to your room for your dirty mouth," Lorenzo says. Ever since we left that geodesic hothouse and the city of Vernal, we've been making jokes about Controlling Dwight. *Dwight would disapprove of your speeding. Dwight does not like doughnut crumbs in his car.* I didn't tell him about Nadine, the story of her non-abortion. She shared her secret, and same as with Esilda and Mom, I'd keep it. How many women have a story they never told? A lot, I'm beginning to think.

"I hate Dwight," I say.

"God, Ives. What's going on? It sounded really bad. *Who* was asking if you're pregnant?"

"Just Mrs. Euwing."

He gives me a look that could be five conversations, at least.

"I am so tired," I say. I remember what Nadine said, about how I looked more tired than a girl my age should. I lay my cheek against the glass, because we're on the air-conditioning part of our drive, before the engine overheats and we switch to open windows. Fatigue feels like it has tendrils, swirling and reaching, wrapping around my ankles.

"Buckskin Mountain, School House Inn, Petticoat Peak. We're in those Laura Ingalls Wilder books," Lorenzo says, but he sounds spent, too. When I look at the speedometer, he's going eighty.

"Slow down! You're going to kill us. Seriously."

He doesn't answer. It makes me think something *else* has happened that he hasn't told me yet. The something elses are piling up, another avalanche in the Avalanche. I don't know if I can take hearing whatever it is.

"Lava Family Sanctuary. Look it up, would you? What could *that* be?"

"No signal." I wave my phone at him.

"Hey, a weigh station," he says. "If you're overweight, Dwight will make you eat bacon and only bacon."

We reach the town of Inkom, and my service returns. "Lava Family Sanctuary . . . They have tepees, too. It's a campground. A 'place of safety and refuge.'"

"Let's go back," Lorenzo says. "And stay there forever."

It sounds good to me. *Safety* and *refuge* are two of the most beautiful words ever.

"Is that it? Is that the lava?" I ask. We're still a few miles away from Craters of the Moon, but I think I see the beginnings of a long field of hardened black. "Or maybe just the shadow of a cloud?" I look toward the sky, but there is no cloud. I glance at Lorenzo. He's off in space somewhere. His head is inside his own private helmet, adrift from Earth and all its beings, or at least adrift from me, here in our own little capsule. "Do you see it?" I ask again.

"Yeah, yeah."

"You're not even looking in the right direction." Lorenzo's been so excited for Craters of the Moon, one of the special stops on his world-tour itinerary. Something definitely is going on. A shadow crosses my own sky. A sickening sense of doom descends. Bad news is coming. More bad news. I remember when Mom told us about The Beast, cancer, how I wished for just one more day of not knowing, the kind of perfect day we used to have before we did. They weren't actually perfect, of course, but they didn't have The Beast in them.

"Right. Yeah, lava, I think."

We take the road that heads toward the park. The land gets darker and darker. The blackness seems to spill toward us. By the time we reach the visitor center, we're surrounded. All you can see for miles and miles are lava beds and lava spires in lava rivers.

It's eerie. And it's hard to explain, but if Dinosaur National Monument looked like the past, Craters of the Moon looks like the future. You can almost imagine this lava continuing to spread, farther and farther, an unstoppable force.

"Should we just drive the loop?" Lorenzo asks.

"You're kidding, right? You've been dying to get here! What's going on? The whole time we were in that sweaty golf-ball dome, you talked about this."

"It seems really hot out there," he says.

I stick my arm out the window, and the wind pushes against it. "No hotter than Dinosaur. Plus, we got *this*." I swing the six-pack of Mountain Dew by the plastic ring.

"We should stop buying those. Those plastic rings strangle sea animals."

Lorenzo's mood is darkening by the minute, same as that landscape had. Maybe this is just him, the way he is when he's in a really bad mood. How would I even know? I thought his bad mood was when he turned into a grumpy toddler, like when we'd wait too long to eat. I was unaware that this morose, end-of-the-world bleakness existed in him. "Look. There's a place to park." I slide neatly into a spot right next to a big old RV. It has a license plate that reads CAPTAIN ED and a peeling bumper sticker, HOME OF THE REDWOODS.

Lorenzo runs his hand through his hair. I picture him at age thirty-five, and forty, and on and on, doing these same things—descending into a mood, the hand, the hair—because maybe one day we'd get married. After a bonding experience like this, we could.

He sighs. We could also break up. Before we get home, even. Guilt floods my whole body, and my cheeks blaze. No one should ask their boyfriend to do something like this. I should have just gone with Mom and Mase, like Mom wanted. Lorenzo could be at home, having a great summer, hanging out at the pool or something, not going on a weeks-long trip to help his pregnant girlfriend get an abortion. Not doing something illegal, and taking on a responsibility and a reputation that aren't his. What did you do on your summer vacation, wow.

It's my turn to go silent. The sudden shift into anguish is overwhelming, and his mood is weighty enough that I start to sink, too. I try hard not to do the wrong thing. We're about to have a really bad fight, I think. A fight so bad that I might be left on the moon.

"Come on," he says. "One short trail?"

After we get out, he offers his hand. His fingers reach across the bleakness, and I remember that he loves me. It's weird how quickly that fact can seem to vanish. One bad mood plus all of your wrongdoings, and boom.

The short trek to Inferno Cone is steep, and we huff and puff on the lava path that winds up the high black hill. And then—wow, a great view. A magnificent vista of this strange place created when lava spewed and oozed out of the deep fissures in the earth. Awe brings Lorenzo back to me.

"It's out of this world," he keeps saying. His eyes shine.

Oh, I love when they do that. I am so relieved and happy that they're doing it again now.

On the way back, we climb onto big lava-bomb pieces, ejected during the eruptions, and we take the stairs that descend into a lava tube cave.

"I wish we could stay all night," I say when we're back in the truck. Craters of the Moon is a Dark Sky Park, meaning no city light reaches it. This sky blanket will be even more glittering than the last one at Nadine's campground.

"Maybe on the way home?" he says. "I was thinking, we should maybe hurry this up? Like, use the main highways? Drive past Bliss tonight, and take turns driving to get into Oregon?"

"Lorenzo! We can't go past Bliss!" If the Wonder Tower was *our* thing, and Dinosaur and Craters of the Moon were *Lorenzo's* things, Bliss is *my* thing. It'll be our second stay in a motel, and Lorenzo chose Bliss because it sounded romantic. Lorenzo and romance and Bliss—I want it. I *need* it. It's what we should have, what we would have had, if this had never happened. Not a stay in a motel, but the two of us being in love, being alone, having sex. It's silly, but I picture

Lorenzo lifting me up over the threshold and plopping me onto the bed and climbing on top of me. We'd wrestle playfully, and then things would get serious, passionate.

We're still in the parking lot of Craters of the Moon. Lava surrounds us in all directions. Lorenzo runs his hand through his hair again. Oh man. He looks exhausted. Way more exhausted than a guy *his* age should look. I've asked way too much of him. I see it for sure. He's done. He wants this over with. He wants to get away from me and this ugly situation, like, go eighty miles an hour away. I fold my arms and stare out my window at the black earth.

"Shouldn't we maybe just *get* there?" he says.

"Well, you think so, obviously."

"I just can't imagine waking up another day and then another still pregnant, as we tromp around like we're on some fun road trip."

"We're *also* on a fun road trip. Aren't we? I mean, this is awful. Why can't we have two seconds of seeing stuff along the way? We can't just have, like, a regular summer, too?" I'm getting more worried by the minute. My mind searches for a plan if he leaves me, but I only see hot, oozing rock now cooled to a permanent hardness.

"This is stressful, Ivy. I mean . . ." He gestures toward my middle, like my body is a bomb. And right then, I am a bomb. I hear a *tick tick tick,* an urgency. We do have to hurry. Not enough to skip Bliss, but we do. "Don't you just want to get this *done*? All this shit happening at home . . ."

At the word "done," a wall crumbles, and fear gushes in. Feelings do, so many that *I* could be a done thing after this is over. I wrap my arms around my knees, bury my face. I make myself into a ball, a rock on fire, heading toward Earth. My face is hidden, but I shut my eyes, too, because I don't want to see me crash.

"I'm scared," I mumble to my knees. How do I explain? As long as we keep driving, we're not there yet.

"Ives, what? I can't hear you."

"I'm scared!" I say, and I look up, and it's a mistake. I see that wrecked landscape for miles, a vision of the end of the world. Maybe my insides will feel like that afterward—scorched, empty. Maybe I will *be* like that, ruined. So many things are gone—telephone booths, woolly mammoths, friendships, and drive-in theaters. I picture this bundle of cells inside of me gone, too, but I also picture my right to do this gone, narrowing until it disappears altogether. My right, my choice, buried by a lava that is inching out in every direction, with a wave of girls and women running to the coasts before they're buried, like in those movies about an apocalypse.

I start to cry. My chest heaves, and I sob like I haven't ever sobbed before. I sob like I've stopped holding on. I miss Mom and Mase so much right now that my whole body aches.

Lorenzo's arms are around me, regular Lorenzo, my Lorenzo. I'm mad at him, though. It's his fault I felt all that fear. I'd been doing great, keeping it away. I learned this from The Beast—once the fear gets out, once you look at it, it takes on a life of its own.

"It's going to be okay," Lorenzo says.

It's hard to believe him when he doesn't sound so sure. And it's even harder to believe when he turns the key of the truck and it just makes a *rrrrr rrrr* sound but doesn't start.

That's what always happens in those disaster films. A car won't start, and they have to get out and run, or else they're doomed.

But then he tries again, and the engine kicks to life. It takes a while for my heart to slow. In this disaster movie we get out of here, but barely. I worry, though, I sure do, for all the folks behind me.

20

I DUCK MY HEAD DOWN AGAIN WHEN LORENZO
checks in to the Sure Bliss Motel, a low-slung building in the
shape of a U with a pool in the middle. It's not what I was expecting. It's not what it sounds like, for sure. I'm beginning
to think that all these places are conspiring to speak to me,
to tell me that it's easy to slap a name on something. What
it truly is—well, that's a whole other thing, and lots more
complicated, besides. The sign reads FREE WI-FI, PANCY,
which sounds wrongly playful. Here, Bliss seems sad.

Lorenzo and I are still semifighting, or rather, *I'm* still
mad, whether Lorenzo knows it or not. I have no idea why
I am exactly, other than he seems like he wants to get the
heck away from me and this whole situation—being stuck in
a hot truck with a moody pregnant girlfriend who cries all
the time and who's put him in legal jeopardy just by being in
that truck. *I* want to get away from me.

After he gets the key, we go to our room. Lorenzo does

not carry me over the threshold or wrestle me on the bed, and all my romantic ideas just seem silly now.

The room smells like a grandma's attic, plus the former occupant's perfume, and there are two beds with shiny floral spreads, with twin paintings of barns hung above them. I drop my bag and head to the bathroom, and I splash cold water on my face so I don't puke. The only good thing so far in Bliss is that I get to be the one who breaks the little gold seal from the toilet-paper roll. I pee so much lately that it's shocking. I can't help but think of *all* the shocking changes that would happen to me if I wasn't able to take this trip, if I had to stay in Texas and have a baby when I didn't want to. If I were forced to because I had no other option.

"Ready?" Lorenzo says. We're heading out to dinner because we're both starved. He hasn't even taken off his coat.

"Yep. Let's go." And then, because I'm a passive-aggressive butt, I say, "Bliss is so romantic," under my breath.

"What?"

"Nothing," I say.

There's a dinosaur in front of the Oxbow Diner, but Lorenzo just walks right past it. It's one of those places that would usually make him super happy. It has a tall sign that truckers can see from the freeway, featuring a steer head lit up in red. A couple of semis are parked in front. Inside, I see Formica tables with swivel stools anchored down around them, and baskets of food on red-and-white-checked paper. Red-and-white-checked paper means get ready, because the food is going to be awesome.

After we both order the Original Classic Chicken-Fried Steak and sodas, Lorenzo studies the wrinkled snake of his straw wrapper, and I try not to look at a baby in a high chair, with those bits of hamburger bun strewn on the floor around her.

"Ivy—" Lorenzo says, at the very same moment that I say, "Lorenzo—"

"Go ahead," he says.

I press the tines of my fork into my napkin. "It's fine by me if you just want to get to Oregon as soon as possible. You don't even have to wait for me once we get there. I'm sure my grandma can help me get home. You've been . . ." It's hard to talk. My voice gets all wavery. I swallow. I don't want to cry again. "Incredible."

"Wait, what?"

"You've done more than anyone else ever would have. You've made this whole thing okay somehow. And I'll always thank you for that."

"Are you breaking up with me?" He looks shocked.

"Aren't you breaking up with me?"

"No! Of course not."

"No?"

"No. I'm head over heels for you, Ivy. You're sure you're not breaking up with me?"

"Lorenzo, would I be that big of an idiot? I'm so in love with you, I can barely stand it."

"God, you scared me." He has his hand to his chest.

"Wait, though. If you're not breaking up with me, what was going on?" Our sodas arrive. I've never been so glad to see a Mountain Dew. Sometimes the neon shade looks radioactive, but now it looks like the most refreshing and thirst-quenching dream green. I'm so relieved. Whatever was going on, we'll be okay, Lorenzo and me. God, I love the Oxbow.

"*Is* going on. Is, not was. Don't be mad. I was trying to protect you? But it's not right. I mean, you deserve to know everything. I shouldn't keep things away from you like you're a little kid. You're a strong, fierce almost-grown woman."

My face flushes. I feel proud that he said that, even if it's a total lie. He knows all about the DeVrieses and what I think I'm supposed to be, so this is him telling me what he thinks I want to hear. To be honest, him protecting me sounds kind of nice, too. The truth is, I'm not fierce and I'm not frail. I'm just me, somewhere in the middle. "Okay. What?"

"My dad is on his way."

The cheer of the diner vanishes. The plastic-covered menus, and the smell of fried stuff, and even the baby, now being lifted from her chair by the tired-looking mom—it all seems full of peril. "On his way, like, to the Oxbow?"

"No! No, I mean, he told me this morning he was getting on an airplane."

"To where?"

"Boise. I didn't believe him at first, because he wouldn't leave Chloe. And then he told me she was staying with her friend Frances. Chloe hates staying the night at other people's houses, but he made her." The chicken-fried steak arrives. We both fake-smile at the server and say thanks, and she smiles back like we're two cute kids on a date instead of a pair of fugitives seeking an illegal-in-their-state abortion. "Fuck, this looks good," Lorenzo says. It's huge and crunchy, and gravy spills around the plate like the lava from Craters of the Moon.

"Lorenzo! Nooo," I moan. "You should have stopped him! You should have told him it's not even yours."

Lorenzo takes a bite. Talks with his mouth full. "I'm not going to. You know, it's really beginning to piss me off, how he's not respecting what I want to do here, let alone what you want to do. Really pissing me off." He saws at his chicken. This is the picture of a guy digging his heels in.

"I cannot tell you how weird this is, that there are suddenly all these people who have strong opinions about my body."

"It's weird, it's so weird. If I had some private health thing, and people were coming at me from every direction . . ."

"Boise is how far away from Bliss?"

"An hour, hour and a half. But his plane has been stuck in Minneapolis for hours. He's not even in Boise yet."

"But once he is, he's headed *here*? And we'll be fast asleep at the Sure Bliss?" I can't believe it. And it's disappointing, really, that Lorenzo's dad has turned out to be a rabid anti-choice guy.

"Now that I told you, I doubt either of us will be asleep."

"Lorenzo, we've got to get out of here."

"I've gone over it a hundred times in my head. I mean, what's he even going to do if he finds us, huh? So he talks to us. Whatever. It won't change anything. What would he do that would be so persuasive? What could he do that would stop this?"

"Why just wait and find out? Let's just go to Rome tonight. Let's get ahead of him."

"It's a three-hour drive, Ives. We won't be there until . . ." He looks at the diner clock. It's in the shape of a pie, with a fork as the hour hand and a knife as the minute hand. "Midnight, at least. We don't have anywhere to stay, and we paid for the Sure Bliss."

"It doesn't matter. We'll figure it out." I sound like Mom when she doesn't have a great plan, either. "All I know is, Bliss isn't bliss, like Wonder wasn't wonder."

⟍

We go back to the Sure Bliss and get our stuff. I feel bad about the sixty-eight bucks, too, but Lorenzo tells me now not to worry about it. We can car-camp at the Pillars of Rome, he says. *Car-camp* sounds more glamorous than just sleeping in the truck. I text Aunt Betts to ask her if she'd mind if we came a day early. *The sooner the better,* she answers. I text Mom and tell her we're driving on because Bliss is awful, and she says, *Stay safe.* It seems like an impossible request.

After the other headlights of late-night drivers fall away, the drive to Rome gets dark, dark, the kind of endless dark you feel in the car at night when you're little, sure it doesn't have an end and will go on forever. I was sleepy back in Nampa, where it was safe to be sleepy, where you could still feel other humans alive on the earth with you. But I'm alert again now, focused on our two beams doing their best to illuminate the dry grass and flat orange rock on either side of us, and the endless V of the highway.

"I think these are farms?" I say. I've been afraid Lorenzo might fall asleep, so I keep saying stuff to keep him awake. He's actually as alert as I am, though, his jaw stern and his eyes fixed.

He doesn't answer.

"Pillars of Rome, look!" I say.

Lorenzo sighs in relief. "Great."

"We're looking for Rome Road." It's so hard to see. I even roll my window down and squinch my eyes, but it doesn't help. It's surprisingly cool out there. On our left we pass a small café, which features a large sign that reads, well, CAFÉ, and another sign that reads ICE. It's next to a gas station, both closed. "Lorenzo, we passed it. The restaurant is after Rome Road on the map, not before."

He veers into the lot of the café to turn around. It's more than a café, I see now. The sign also reads GAS RV PARK STORE MOTEL. I spot a few tiny shedlike buildings back there, but all the lights are off. It's the whole town of Rome in one spot.

Lorenzo loops back.

"There, there," I say, jabbing my finger toward the road that appears immediately to our left.

It's wide and graded but unpaved. We've gone from a pitch-dark two-lane highway to a pitch-dark unpaved road.

In a film we'd definitely run out of gas, or run into a killer whose face would pop up in our rear window.

"None of what we're doing makes sense right now," Lorenzo says, stating the obvious.

"Are there bats out here? Tell me there are no bats," I say.

"There could be elephants, for all I can see." Lorenzo's nose is practically against the windshield. "Is this a dream? Because I can't even tell what's real. We should just stop. Let's just go back to that motel place and park."

"This is a road that takes trust," I say. I'm trying to sound brave because I really want to cry. I'm tired and have to pee again, and it's impossible to know where we even are, or where we're heading.

"Wait," Lorenzo says. "I think I see them. Unless it's a mirage, which seems entirely possible. Do you see them?"

I lean forward, too, and now both of our noses are basically touching the windshield. "I see them. I see them!" Up ahead there are cliffs that rise to the sky. It looks like an enormous wall, cut with pillars and pinnacles that resemble Roman ruins, all set here in this unlikely spot, the Oregon desert. The Pillars of Rome. They seem to go on for miles and miles. I could swear that we've stumbled on an ancient city, still and asleep in the middle of the night.

Lorenzo drives as close to the pillars as we can, veering off the graded road. He stops and then reverses, so the truck bed of the Avalanche faces the ruins. He yanks the parking brake. "Whew," he says.

"Whew is right." Just staring into the dark like that is exhausting.

Lorenzo opens the door and hops out. He rolls his neck in a circle to get out the kinks but stops midway, his chin up. "Holy shit," he says. "Ivy, get out here!"

I hurry to join him, sliding on my flip-flops. The night air and those ruins up ahead cure me instantly. My anxiety has vanished, replaced with the thrill and relief of arrival. But then I look up, too. I see what we haven't been able to see, just driving inside that truck, trying so hard to look ahead. Above us, all around, is a deep purple sky with so many stars, they're spilled sugar crystals on glass. Lorenzo puts his arms around me from behind. He scoots my body a few degrees until I am looking toward a granite palace at a far corner of an ancient city. Above it, in the sky, a swath of yellow marble spills down.

I'm awestruck. "What is that?"

"The Milky Way."

"It's unbelievable. None of this looks real. Lorenzo! We went on a world tour, but we're seeing the universe."

"It took us a while, but we found Bliss," Lorenzo says.

I yell, "Don't look, don't look!" to Lorenzo as I pee. I don't go far from the truck, because it's scary dark out there, with only the stars for light. When I return, he's gathering up a few blankets, and our packs to use as pillows. The truck bed has a mat and a slab of foam that Lorenzo's rolled out. I use half of a water bottle to wash up and brush my teeth, and

Lorenzo uses the other half. It's warm enough out there for us to wear shorts and a T-shirt. He pats my spot in the truck bed, and I get under the blankets, and Lorenzo does, too. It's pretty comfy. Well, maybe not comfy, but not as hard as you'd think.

It's so, so late, and I'm sleepy, but there's the miracle of an ancient city in front of us, and the miracle of a Milky Way above us, and there is love between us, and so things that last are everywhere. All the stress and fear and questions rise up into the dark and long-witnessing sky and become immaterial, shattering into a million pinpricks of light. I can breathe out here in this night air that has been night air forever. I trail my hand under Lorenzo's T-shirt, and then he trails his hand up mine, and then we are kissing softly, and then not softly at all, and Lorenzo puts his hand between my legs, and I tug him so he'll get on top of me.

I scoot out of my shorts and underwear and grab the elastic of his and yank down. It's gotten so hot, I toss the covers off, and Lorenzo scoots the rest of the way out of his shorts, his bare ass up to the sky.

"Are you sure?" he whispers.

"Yes, I'm sure. I'm so sure. Are *you*? I sometimes worry you don't want—"

He interrupts me with a kiss. "Oh, Ivy, I *want*. If it ever seemed like that, I was just worried that *you* might not want to, after—"

Now I interrupt him with a kiss. I thought we needed to have some big talk, but it turns out we don't. He cared about me, I cared about him; that's what was going on. And he's *still* caring about me. He leans over to rummage in the pocket of his shorts for a condom, because protection means *all* protection.

"You're okay?" he asks.

"I'm so okay," I say. "I'm great." I don't want to even think about bad things. I just want to be with him, here. I'm the old Ivy, the new Ivy, the right-this-minute Ivy. He's making me impatient with all this talking. I wrap my legs around him and pull him toward me.

And there, that night, in the real Bliss, I have sex—sex that I want and with a guy I love—for the first time.

They were as sublime as the moon and stars above them, and the moon and stars were as ardent as they. That line from *Tess of the D'Urbervilles.* Yes, and yes.

21

I NUDGE LORENZO AWAKE BECAUSE THE SUN IS RIS-
ing. A ridge of pink clouds stretches drowsily along the top
of the stone city, and above it the sky blazes orange. This
morning I can really see the ancient columns and doorways
of ruins that aren't ruins. Nothing is gone here. It's just the
way it's always been, this rock. The majestic formations, this
mystical Roman city—it's orange, too, practically glowing,
like it's lit from within, and the morning rays paint hopeful
light down the sheer walls and along the pinnacle tips. I can
imagine it, the learned, robed people from long ago, walking
up those steps, disappearing through those doorways to talk
about philosophy and art and humanity. It's so beautiful
that my heart fills. How can life be bad, or at least forever
bad, when things like this exist?

Lorenzo sits up on his elbows. The morning light is so
golden, and it bathes him, too, and me, I see. I hold my
golden arms out and turn them, golden palms up.

"Wow," he says. We both just gaze at this triumphant

place. There's not a soul in sight. Not a single other soul. It's so wild to think of Mom and Mase at home, missing this. It's so wild to think of Faith and Mrs. Euwing and Jason Maxwell and his brother and Lorenzo's father, all of them, wrapped up in the drama of one girl's life instead of this. It's so wild to think of the leaders of City of Hope Church of God, and Fellowship Pointe, and New Redeemer, lawmakers and leaders, even, wrapped up in the business of girls' bodies instead of this. And it's so wild, too, to think of me, wrapped up in the drama of my own body instead of this. That desire for God I have? For something larger than me? It's filled in this place.

"Come on," I say. I tug on Lorenzo's shirt, and then we hop from the truck bed and slip on our sandals, and then we run. It's harder than it sounds with the scrubby ground, the plants wet with dew, and the pebbles underfoot. Here, there's the urge to go as fast as you can, like you did when you were a kid, ready, set, go.

We're right up next to it, that dinosaur rock, those vertical walls and pillars and pinnacles made of fossil-embedded ash from Pliocene volcanoes. I look at the spot way, way up where our old earth meets sky. It makes me feel so strong, being there. Lava pours and wrecks, but ash rises and makes a city. I put my hands on my hips, and I am the girl who is sometimes fierce and strong and sometimes not, who gets through hard things and who is in charge of her own future, even if some people don't want her to be. I am not a rock pulled down by gravity. I am the regular girl whose magic meets the morning sun.

I pat the rock. "Hey, big guy," I say to it.

"Wow again," Lorenzo says, but his rumpled self means me this time. He's staring at me like I'm a fine sight. Sometimes I don't want to be wow, I just want to be me, but I kiss him anyway.

We climb around a few walls and peer into crevices, and we see how it's all real and an illusion. How this astonishing place also looks like one thing but is really another—holding beautiful secrets, though, instead of disappointments.

"We'd better get going," Lorenzo says, and my normal life returns with a yank and a whoosh. Then Lorenzo says, "I'm starved," and the facts of the body, troubling and miraculous and mundane, plain old nature mostly, return, too.

We stamp our passports, *kashunk,* and then we stop at the café for breakfast on the way out of Rome. Last night I had sex for the first time, or what felt like sex for the first time, miraculous and plain old nature also, with someone I love, always miraculous. I'm mostly unchanged, aside from being absolutely starving and a little more in love. Lorenzo pours syrup like his pancakes have erupted, and it's the end of time for his white plate, and splotches of his place mat, too. He uses so much syrup, his fork drips, and maybe after years of loving him this would turn into something annoying, but now it's just another adorable thing. I cut my fork into the stack and see the layers, and they're so thick and delicious, I eat ten bites and then I'm stuffed.

"We're ahead of him now for sure," Lorenzo says. His dad is out there somewhere, and it's like all the enemies, the men who head the churches, the men who make the laws, are one man, Lorenzo's dad, trying to stop us. I hate him. I hate Lorenzo's dad for trying to be some strong-arm bully. "And when he finds out we're not in Bliss, he'll think we're staying in Glasgow. From my first map, before your mom told me about your aunt who lives in Florence."

If this were a movie, he'd find us. Would there be a shotgun or what? Maybe he'd drag us to a church for a wedding. I'd have to tell him the truth then. Maybe even the whole truth, not a weak and unbelievable "random guy" lie. The truth about Jason Maxwell and Drake Euwing. About all the assumptions people are making, because assumptions are so easy when something isn't your business.

"If he goes all the way to Manhattan Beach, my grandma will eat him alive," I say. Grandma—now she for sure is fierce. She might have come that way, DeVries DNA, but I think it's more that she's had a lot of practice defending her territory. After *Rockaway Weekend* was such a hit, tourists would try to pry a hubcap off the wall outside their place, or they'd pretend to work in the shop for a photo, picking up one of the wrenches to replay that scene. Sometimes they'd even get behind the counter. They wanted all of it to be theirs, to own it. Why is it that boundaries always make some people want to cross them? Why is it so hard to understand what is yours and what isn't?

Lorenzo's dad can't force me to do (or not do) anything,

can he? Yet the idea of him finding us is making me anxious. No. Scared. I know how I am. I mean, I could bend to someone's will just because the fight seems worse than doing what other people want. That's what got me into this mess in the first place.

"Hey," Lorenzo says. He reaches across the table and runs a finger between my eyebrows and down my nose. "Don't look so worried." He looks worried, too. He tips the last of his coffee back, sets his cup down, and reaches for his wallet.

When we walk back outside into the already-warm sun, I feel the sticky path of syrup on my nose from Lorenzo's finger, and I can't help it. I smile.

"Fuck, fuck, FUCK!" Lorenzo says. He pounds the steering wheel.

I drop my face into my hands.

Lorenzo takes a big breath. Tries again. *Rrr, rrr, rrr,* the engine says, but doesn't start.

"Shit car! You shit car!" Lorenzo pounds again.

"Don't say that!" Another opinion I have is that appliances can hear, especially cars. Maybe it's more a worry than an opinion, because look what Lorenzo's car has done for us so far. It brought us all this way, and we barely gave it a thought or a thanks. If it hears this slew of insults and lack of gratitude, I wouldn't blame it if it refused to budge.

Lorenzo silently fumes. That's the expression in books, but his is not really silent. Fury shoots through his nostrils, the sound of a nose blow without the blow.

"Are we out of gas?" I ask.

"No, we're not out of gas!" I'm learning something new about Lorenzo—high levels of frustration cause him to snap and huff and swear, though maybe this only comes when his pregnant girlfriend is racing to get an abortion as his father closes in on them. "Look! It says we've got half a tank."

"Mr. Smiley used to say we had gas when we didn't, until we got the thingy fixed."

"My thingy is fixed," Lorenzo says. This sounds kind of funny, and I want to get the nervous giggles, but trust me, now is not the time.

Rrr, rrr, rrr. Screeeeek.

"FUCKING HELL!"

"Maybe the battery?" I offer.

"I got a new one before we left!"

I roll down my window. It's getting hot already. Aside from this Café/Gas Station/Motel/Store/Entire Town, there's not a single building in sight. Lorenzo hunts around in his glove box for a manual or something, but that manual was gone a long time ago.

He takes a deep cleansing breath, the same kind that Yogi Barb had us take on the Freedom Flex yoga videos Mase and I did with Mom during The Beast. Mase always called her Yogi Bear and farted whenever we did the Happy Baby pose.

SCREEEEK!

"Maybe a bad distributor cap?" I suggest. When you've always had shit cars, you learn way more about this stuff than you ever wanted to know.

"That is not what a bad distributor cap sounds like." He shakes his head and looks out the window as if an answer might appear in the café parking lot. His lips are moving, like his brain is playing out a film, maybe the confrontation with his dad when we're stuck here in Rome and he finds us, boom, no problem. It's the only possible place in Rome we *could* be, because this *is* Rome.

But then an answer does appear in the parking lot. A big man with saggy jeans and a shirt that reads #1 DAD heads over and ducks his head toward Lorenzo's window. "Sounds like a bad distributor cap?" he says.

I shoot Lorenzo a *told you so* look, but he doesn't see it. He's already popping the hood, and out of nowhere someone has a towel, and they're wiping the inside of the cap. Lorenzo tries the engine, and it starts right up, and he hops out again, leaving it running. Their voices get all big and victorious, and they slap each other on the back like they just won a war or a football game, as I sit in my seat like the little woman.

Lorenzo returns. "It's messed up," he says. He means the cap, but there's so much more that is, so much more, little moments, and big ones, and life ones.

"That's for sure," I say.

He looks over at me, and he realizes. "Oh, oh," he says. "I get it. I'm an asshole." But he doesn't say this sarcastically, like a lot of guys would, like my mom's old boyfriend Terry, or my dad, even, or Jason Maxwell, for sure. He says it like he *does* get it. Like he *is* an asshole, which was true a few minutes ago, but not forever.

In the film I would have taken off right then, when the engine was running and I was the only one in the truck. But films don't often show the boring parts. Where you screw up for a second, or hours, or days, but love each other anyway, times a million.

We're a pair of fugitives, past the police barricades, on the road to freedom, overconfident and blaring the tunes. Thelma and Louis, no Louise. My feet are on the dash, and we've got two new Mountain Dews in the cup holders, and some Corn Nuts we got at the Café/Gas Station/Motel/Store/Entire Town back in Rome. We just finished praising ourselves for not saying "when in Rome" when we were in Rome, not even once. Now we are singing along with Gloria Gaynor, "I Will Survive." Mom would know the words, but we don't, so we just shout-sing stuff that sort of sounds right.

" 'At first I was a-brave, I was 'lectrified!' " Lorenzo sings. He's warbling so loud that when he looks my way, I can see his tonsils.

" 'I never knew how I would love so I was by my side!' " I sing. Damn, we're awesome. We are so good that a crowd would be on their feet, screaming and throwing us flowers.

We car-dance, a spectacular shimmy that involves only

the upper body, which we discovered back in Genoa but are clearly now perfecting.

" 'I will survive, I will survive!' " We finish with a flourish and then applaud ourselves. Lorenzo hoots for us, handling the dual roles of performer and audience with skill and gusto. I may have given myself a sore throat.

Lorenzo presses Pause. "We're gonna have to get gas soon," he says.

"Want me to look for a place?" I wave my phone.

"No need. Probably won't get Wi-Fi out here anyway, and I totally know where we have to stop." His eyes gleam with glee. "Did you see the signs?"

"Nope," I say. I was busy watching him, and thinking about last night, and how bad I want to do that again.

"Christmas Valley."

"No way."

"How can we pass that up?"

If you're Lorenzo, the answer is, we can't.

⌁

"Huh," Lorenzo says when we take the turnoff to Christmas Valley. There's not much to it, mostly the same scrubby ground stretching for miles in every direction again. There are a couple of small cafés, but that's about it. "Christmas Road in Christmas Valley. I was at least expecting a Santa Claus statue. Or those stores full of nutcrackers and Christmas shit even though it's summer."

"Not an elf in sight," I agree.

"Not a single candy cane. A candy cane is bare-minimum Christmas."

It's so true. Especially those tiny ones in rectangular cellophane wrappers, strung together like an endless chain of bad ideas. "They've got sand dunes somewhere around here," I report from my phone, since Wi-Fi has, *poof,* appeared. "Also, a place called Crack-in-the-Ground."

We giggle.

"The shining beacon of a Chevron!" Lorenzo announces. Yep, I see it. I'm always so glad when we arrive at a gas station. Out in places like this, a full tank of gas is road-trip reassurance. All that land and land and land and no Wi-Fi. Running out of gas would be a disaster.

He pulls in next to the pumps. "Red Vines?" he asks. He puts up crossed fingers on both hands, like he's hoping I'll say yes.

"Well, *of course,*" I say.

He pops out, grinning at me. There's a white Toyota Corolla parked at the curb next to the store, and the driver's-side door opens.

"Hey, Lorenzo," Lorenzo's dad says.

22

"DAD."

I panic. I'm so shocked seeing Lorenzo's dad standing right there talking to Lorenzo that I consider scooting over to the driver's seat and flooring it. But the flip side of shock is feeling suddenly paralyzed, like it's all a movie scene I'm watching. I'm waiting for . . . what? Lorenzo's dad to grab Lorenzo, haul him off in his white Toyota Corolla? For a minute I forget that I'm the one holding the goods. The fetus he wants to save is in my body, not Lorenzo's. It's me he'd have to force. Men don't often force men. Men force people they can force.

But there's no struggle or shotgun or whatever else you might imagine. No real show of power. Actually, Lorenzo's dad, in his loose jeans and old tennis shoes, his dark thinning hair, his sad eyes—he doesn't look capable of making anyone do anything.

"I'm . . . I don't know why I'm . . ."

"Yeah, Dad," Lorenzo says. You can see Lorenzo's fury

rising. "*Why* is the question. What are you doing here? How did you even find me?"

"Christmas Valley," Lorenzo's dad says. "When I learned you left Bliss, I thought, 'Where would he stop? Where of all these places would Lorenzo just have to see?' I looked at the map, and . . . well, there it was."

I've scooted so far down in my seat that only my eyes peek above the doorframe. When I hear Lorenzo's dad say this, I realize all that I've forgotten. The only thing I saw in my mind when I thought of Lorenzo Xavier Bastimentos's dad was *parent*. I saw his dad's silence when I was in their kitchen, his unease with me. I saw his firm belief that abortion is wrong, and how he wants to stop mine. But I didn't see the guy, a real guy, who knows Lorenzo so well that he can look at a map and pinpoint exactly where his son would stop. I didn't see their relationship, their conversations. Their private jokes, and battles, and history.

Lorenzo rubs his eyes and then his forehead, like he's a hundred steps past exhaustion. Being known is the best, but also sometimes the worst.

"Remember when we moved to Montana and we took the weekend to go to both Big Arm and Big Foot?" I've never heard Lorenzo's dad talk so much. I also realize that I don't even know his name.

"Sure, after you wanted to go to both Tobacco and Stoner Place," Lorenzo says.

Lorenzo's dad hikes his belt. He looks shy and embarrassed. Awkward, even. He glances over at me, and I don't duck down this time. I meet his eyes. He should know I won't be pushed around. However, this is definitely easier to say now that I see he is shy and embarrassed and awkward.

"You could have saved yourself a lot of time and trouble and money, Dad, because you being here isn't going to change a thing. You riding in, like the . . . whatever the word is."

"Cavalry," his dad says.

"What the fuck ever," Lorenzo says. "And you may have forgotten, but I'm eighteen."

"*She* isn't," he says.

"Don't even. Don't you even." Lorenzo gets all narrow-eyed again. I suddenly remember something Lorenzo told me, about the time he and his dad once got in a fight over who was going to choose which movie to watch, an argument that led to days of silence until his dad came home with a couple of steaks, and then they never referred to it again.

"I just want to *talk*."

"You couldn't do that on the phone?"

"Not when you keep hanging up! Not when you don't even answer." Lorenzo doesn't reply. He always understands when someone has a fair point. It's one of his best qualities. "This all makes no sense." Lorenzo's dad gestures to the white car and the Avalanche and the general area of Christmas Valley.

"It doesn't have to make sense to you. Only to Ivy."

"I don't mean what she's doing, or what you're doing. I mean *me*. Being here. It's so fucking ridiculous, getting on an airplane! I just . . . Fuck." He shakes his head. He has big hands, and he looks like the kind of guy who can fix things, but not this. "I wanted to tell you about . . . my regrets. Big regrets. I wanted to tell you, you know, *now.* I never told you before."

There are no SWAT teams, and no police swarm in, and there isn't even a furious father making demands, really. Just a guy with a story. And I don't want to hear another person's pregnancy-abortion story, at least not his. But we agree to meet at a coffee shop a few blocks from the Chevron. I shouldn't have agreed. I should just let them talk while I call Mom or something, but I don't. I seriously need to stop giving people things only because they want them. I'm pretty much a boat going down a river at the mercy of the rapids— not *in* the boat, managing the oars.

We first stop at this restaurant right across from the gas station, but it has a Confederate flag in the window, and Lorenzo's dad rolls down his window and points to it, then hitches his thumb in the other direction to indicate *No way.*

"I'm so sorry about this, Ivy," Lorenzo keeps saying.

I want to say *That's okay,* but it isn't, so I don't. I just stare out the window, letting my blank face speak.

"Why don't you just stay in the truck and wait for me?" he says another fourteen times, but I'd rather make a show of my misery. As we get out of the truck at the coffee shop, I give my shorts a little yank and adjust my tank top. Suddenly, I feel very pregnant. I mean, I've felt pregnant this whole time, but all at once I feel visibly full-breasted, the button of my shorts straining for closure. I hate every piece of me—my body, that betrayer. I wish I were wearing a giant coat and long pants.

"What's your dad's name, even?" I shrug to indicate how little his father matters to me, but it's a lie. He matters a lot. I feel his judgment creeping around inside of me like a poisonous creature.

"Gene. His name is Gene. His last name used to be Pool, but he got so much shit for it when he was in high school that after his dad left, he changed it to Bastimentos, his mom's last name."

These human pieces of Mr. Bastimentos are hard to take. It was easier when I thought of him only as a rabid anti-abortion dude, like all the others. Ugh! Easy assumptions and judgments go both ways, and, God, I hate when things go both ways.

Gene is already inside, getting us a table. Three plastic menus have been set down, along with three squat glasses of water with half-melted ice floating at the top. Man, I don't want my bare legs on that red vinyl seat. I just don't.

My stomach feels sick. Pregnant sick, the kind of nausea that takes over your whole body. It's a gross, swimming surge, same as the anger that's swirling inside. I'm not me, I'm a vessel. For the millionth time, it feels unfair, so *unfair,* that our bodies do things against our will. All bodies do, but it feels more unfair as a female, having the outside world forcing its will on you along with your insides doing the same.

One day, Mom said to me, *you'll feel the joy and miracle of this, but not now.* The joy and the miracle are supposedly the payoffs for the five days every month for years and years that you have to deal with your period. And the pain and cramps and emotional outbursts and worry about blood and seepage and white pants and white sheets, pulling that string, again and again. Let alone the massive physical transformation and toll of being pregnant. I have a flash of those films of a woman giving birth, the power in her body, the sheer physical force, and I think, *No wonder.* No wonder early man going back and back looked at that power and force and said, that shit better be squashed, or we won't be in charge. We better get on top of that power, and fast. We better use all we got, physical strength and control and shame, because, man, oh man, she is lightning and thunder, the bearer of all things, right there. She's massive, so we better make her feel small ASAP.

Those Bastimentos men sure can eat. Gene orders pancakes, which we already ate back in Rome, and Lorenzo orders a burger and onion rings, and it's, like, eleven a.m. I order a soda, because who can manage food when some dude is going to tell you what you should do with your life. And he's going to tell you what to do when he doesn't know a thing about it. But hey, why should the circumstances matter to him when it won't affect him one bit.

The server collects the menus, and Gene folds his hands on the table. He looks across at us. "Kids," he says, and this thread of anger I feel spooling makes a few more loops. Lorenzo takes my hand under the table, but I shake it free.

"Dad, come on. Can we just do this?"

Gene jabs the end of his straw against the paper place

mat, crinkles the paper down to expose the plastic. "I was a senior. She was a junior. In high school."

"Was it that girl Patty? The one you had sex with for the first time?"

"Nah. Patty didn't mean anything to me. This was someone I loved. Like I said, I've never even mentioned her name. Too painful. But . . . Rosemary."

I stare down at the scalloped edge of the place mat, follow its curves with my eyes. God, I wish I hadn't come. I'm sitting by the window, and Lorenzo is blocking my exit, or else I might get up and go. It's just beyond belief, when you think about it. Three people are here discussing something I should do with my entire life, three people are here discussing my pregnancy, which means we are discussing what happened because a guy stuck his penis near enough my vagina for sperm to make their unwanted journey to my egg. Three people are discussing my very own internal organs. Well, three people aren't discussing, actually. One guy who thinks he knows best is.

Their food arrives. Gene pours syrup on his pancakes, same as Lorenzo, as if he's a syrup god, dispensing abundance. It drips onto his place mat. "Rosemary. *Man . . . ,*" he continues. It's the kind of pause that says how extraordinary she was, how crazy about her he was. "She just understood me like no one else ever has. She had these bright eyes, and the softest skin, and this pure, sweet singing voice—she was in choir. Always got the solos because she sung like an angel. We were in love. Like you two are. I had a, um, condom, but we got, uh, carried away. When she got pregnant . . . I wanted to get married. I would have, in a *second.* Her parents, though. Her mom and dad—they pushed her to get an abortion. Pushed, I mean, they *told* her that's what she was going to do. Her dad and her mom—there was no discussion."

"What did *she* want to do?" Lorenzo asks.

"I don't even know. They wouldn't let me talk to her. I tried. I tried everything I could. I had no say. *I* had no choice."

"Choice," I say. My voice—I don't even know if it's sarcastic or sad or resigned. The word just sits there. It could mean a hundred things or absolutely nothing.

"I regret it. She was . . . maybe the love of my life. And I don't want *you* to regret it," he says to Lorenzo. "Either of you. I mean, if you love each other . . ."

There's this window, a slice of a moment, where I understand. I hear how helpless his voice sounds, how it must have felt to be part of something but have no say in what got decided. I look up at him, and I see how this still pains him. I see sorrow, a life that could have been, his whole existence, different. I get the way a guy could be left out here. I even get how a story of choice can be the reverse of what we expect— a girl being told by her parents that she would *not* have a baby, because who knows what Rosemary wanted. Choice, *choices*, all the ones a person could make for themself— respect goes both ways. But that thread of anger just makes a larger, tighter, more certain loop, a loop that goes from anger to fury. I feel the lava rising under my own earth. It's not angel Rosemary I'm thinking of. It's Patty. It's Patty, the other girl he had sex with, the one who didn't matter.

Right then, right then . . . I see it all with such clarity.

Why does it suddenly seem like there's a sea of abortion stories? Because there's *always* been a sea of stories about women and sex. Stories about women and the choices they make, and *don't* make—those, too. There are the stories she's never told, but there are the stories *he* does tell, that *they* tell, *about* her.

Lorenzo is so right about the torches and the Middle Ages, but hey, I can fix this. I'm going to. It's easy. It's so very easy. I'm furious about how easy this is, how clear it is. I'll be his Patty, I'll be their Tess, their Bethany "B.J." Grigg. I'll be the slut, the one who sleeps around, the one who is condemned and then discarded. Lorenzo's dad, people at home, the kids at school, their parents, Peyton, the Euwings, Drake himself—they will fall into this story with glee; they'll wear their contempt with a satisfied moral righteousness, because they *love* this story. People have always loved this particular story.

"Well, you don't have to worry. You wasted a trip," I say.

"Ivy," Lorenzo says. "Don't."

"You wasted a trip," I say again, gritting my teeth. "You made assumptions about me. You decided how things should be without even knowing the facts. You were sure you knew, enough to get on an airplane, but you *don't* know. This"— I point with both fingers to my abdomen—"isn't even Lorenzo's, okay? Do you see how wrong you were?"

My face is flushing. I feel a lava flow of rage. But I see that Gene's mouth gapes like a dark tunnel on a mountain road. One of his eyes starts to twitch.

"Ivy, you don't have to—" Lorenzo is holding my arm. Holding me back.

I vowed I would never tell anyone aside from the people closest to me, and I'm not going to tell this man. I'll be the slutty slut, I don't care. I *choose* it. I want to stand right there with Tess, with Patty. I stare hard at Gene, with his one eye betraying his shock. Whenever that happens, whenever your eye twitches like that, you try to tell yourself that people don't notice, but you're wrong. Everyone sees. "You can relax, okay? Lorenzo won't live a life of regret. It has nothing to do with him. Scoot," I say, and shove Lorenzo's leg.

I vowed I would never tell because it wasn't anyone's business what happened with awful Drake Euwing—how Jason Maxwell, deep in his battle plan to torment me after I embarrassed him, told Drake I thought he was hot. How he encouraged Drake to make his move, because he knew Drake basically stalked girls, his tongue hanging out all the time. How Drake asked me to that Jesus concert at City of Hope Church of God, and how I thought I'd better just go. Just go and get it over with. What was I thinking? I was thinking he's the boss's son, Mrs. Euwing's beloved boy. A situation to be managed carefully if I wanted to keep my job. I would say yes and then no, which would be better than just no. Yes, so he'd feel good enough to not get me fired, and I'd figure out a no from there. Jason had already taught me, and taught me good, that the egos of some boys had better be handled with care, because punishment would come to those who didn't.

Even the people who love me will never know everything about that night, not the gruesome details. How I wanted to get out of there so bad, that concert, how Hope Mathias and Trevor Lively and his girlfriend, Jayna, saw me with Drake, and how I just wanted to disappear. How I sat through all those songs about He and Him and Glory and Highest, words hidden in loud lyrics and a rock beat. How I sat through that intermission, too, where—just like the time with Caleb Baylor—the preacher urged the audience to come down and be saved, only this time Drake was trailing his fingers up and down my leg. How all I could think about was how to get away. How, when it was over and the crowd was leaving, I told him I had to get home by ten or my mom would kill me. I told him all kinds of stuff, just piling it on—how I couldn't date anyone, how I liked him, how I thought he was so great, so, so great, but, but, but. I even threw in this completely silly and dramatic statement, *It can never be,* and he *loved* it.

I would especially never tell anyone what happened next. How I thought we were headed to the back parking lot where Mr. Smiley was and where Drake would be picked up because he couldn't even drive yet, but how he yanked me toward the baseball fields. How he backed me up against the chain-link fence and started kissing me, gross, gross, and I just went along because Drake said some laughable, ridiculous thing, like *I'll give you something to remember me by,* which meant this was the end of it, thank God. How he had somehow already unzipped his pants, and his penis was out, and he jammed my hand on it, gross, his hip bone locked hard against me. How I gave him a little shove and said, *Drake!* but he was panting hard, so I thought, fine, whatever, just get this over with, he's going to come any minute, I could tell, because he sounded just like Caleb when we fooled around once or twice. How I thought, this is going to be over with, just get through it, and then I can leave and forget all about this humiliating experience and still keep my job, but how he stuck his penis through the leg of my underwear, up against me, not in me, and in seconds, seriously seconds, I felt the wet stickiness all over me. How Drake said, *That was awesome,* and how embarrassed and ashamed I felt, God. How horrible and disgusted I felt, especially because I was just starting to fall for this guy named Lorenzo who moved here from California, but how this night felt completely separate, since Drake was just an awful task I had to check off to move on with my life, and Lorenzo was love.

How, when I got home, I did the thing you see in the movies where a girl washes her hands over and over again. How I used a washcloth between my legs but got in the shower, too. How the uglies descended while the water poured over me. How I'd finally managed to shove it all into a corner of my brain, when my period was late and I couldn't even imagine why. How I looked up *Can you get pregnant without having sex?* How it said, yes, yes, yes, but it was difficult, though easier if you were young. How I was young. How it *all* was difficult, difficult, difficult. How it all seemed impossible and impossible and impossible. How I'd just wanted it over with, and how maybe it would never be over with.

And I would never tell Lorenzo's dad or anyone else, either, how I told Lorenzo at the Eiffel Tower, and how he didn't blame me, which seemed like a miracle. Or how my mom said, *That's not consent, Ivy,* after I told her. How I answered, *I never said no, though,* and she said, *You never said yes.* How she explained this Planned Parenthood thing, where consent has this acronym, *FRIES.* She couldn't remember what all the letters stood for, except *freely given, reversible, enthusiastic,* and not because someone has power. How I said, *Drake is a dweeby sophomore, he doesn't have power,* and she said, *Anytime you think,* I'd better not say no, *someone has power over you.* How I said, *No awful acronym should be paired with something people love so much, like fries,* but I was crying. How I kept saying, *I'm sorry,* and she kept saying, *It's not your fault.*

How, whenever I remember it, I feel my fingers gripping that chain-link fence.

I stand there at the table, glaring at Lorenzo's dad, and then I turn and head for the door. People are staring, I don't care. I leave the smell of onions and frying burgers behind me, and the air-conditioning, too. The heat hits. I actually retch but manage to get my stomach under control by sheer will.

I can barely touch the door handle, and inside will be intolerable, so I just stand around near the truck with the door open, letting it cool before I get in. I had vowed I would never tell anyone else that entire story, but as I stand there with the sun burning my shoulders and with kicked-up dust in my sandals, I think about Mom not telling anyone and Esilda not telling anyone and Nadine not telling anyone, and I wonder how many women there are, holding a similar secret, *secrets.* Secrets about getting pregnant or having an abortion, yeah, but more than that, way more. Not telling a soul about a moment that was confusing or forced or painful or nauseating. Or maybe even glorious or full of desire. Not telling anyone about their choice to not have a single moment define and change or even become their life. Instead of a river of lava destroying and flattening everything in sight, I imagine the secrets rising, tier after tier, an immense and physical creation, something magical in the moonlight, stunning in the orange sunrise. Something that looks like a Roman city but is really just nature, Mother Earth surviving the volcano. So many stories in the layers, even if the rock is silent.

23

HERE'S WHAT HAPPENS TO THE FOOD: LORENZO leaves his half-eaten burger and a few onion rings. I can see this from where I now sit, the driver's side of the Avalanche. The server brings a Styrofoam container, and the rest of the pancakes are slid in, the lid closed. Lorenzo and Gene hug. This pisses me off, even if it's unfair. I want Lorenzo to choose sides, and that side is me. Nothing is that simple, absolutely nothing, where you can draw a line down the middle and everything stays on its side. Not even this, this forever debate about abortion.

Lorenzo and his dad chat a little outside, standing next to Gene's white rental car. I hunt around in my bag for my phone so I can poke on it angrily. Instead, I see that I have a message. The ringer was off while we were in the café, and I missed a call. It's not a number I recognize, but it's a Paris area code. My heart lurches. My first panicked thought is that something has happened to Mase or Mom. The last person I expect is Mr. Euwing. But here's his voice, with the screeching of Missy and Buddy in the background.

I'm calling for Ivy DeVries. This is Bob Euwing, from Euwing's Drugs. . . . His voice turns my stomach. I can feel his fingers on my wrist, and the press of his hand on my back, and I can see his small eyes staring at me behind his glasses. *We've recently become aware of your, uh, circumstances, and as you know, as I made clear when you were hired, this is a family company, with family values. We don't see these aligning with your, uh, circumstances, and so we're, uh, terminating your employ—*

I stop the recording. I'm so full of fury that I stab the little garbage can, deleting the message. I realize my mistake, because it's illegal or something, isn't it, what he's doing? But whatever. Whatever! Illegal, immoral, what a mess, because, let me tell you, he's immoral in a hundred ways, and so is Mrs. Euwing, and so is Drake, an immoral core in a righteous cocoon. Oh my God. I am so full of rage, I'm a furnace. My face is radiating heat, and a trickle of sweat goes straight down my forehead.

Lorenzo—he's automatically heading over to the truck's driver's side now, because, yeah, he always drives. The car is his car. The road is his road. The laws are his laws and the world is his world; at least, that's the mood I'm in. He sees me there and makes a correction, but I give him, that dad hugger, that twitchy-eyed-dad hugger, no leeway. I don't see how cute he is right then, or how sweet, or how thoughtful. I see him as part of Gene/Bob Euwing/Jason Maxwell/Drake/Dwight/Terry/church leader dudes/senator dudes. There are no clear sides on this line I'm drawing, for sure, but fuck it.

"You driving?" He gets in.

"What's it look like?" I want to boss him around. I want to be in control, to be the one who gets to say. It feels kind of good, to be honest. Dang, imagine if you got to do that all the time.

"Hey, I'm really so—" He puts his hand on my arm, and I shake it off, hard. Hard enough for him to hear *back off*. I yank the car into reverse and speed out. The tires spit gravel. I've decided to skip Glasgow. Who cares. I want to see my aunt. I need my people. I need my own people so bad, I want to cry, but I'll be furious at myself if I cry. I don't want to be the soft, vulnerable girl he gets to comfort.

He's silent. I can't tell if it's the kind of silent where he feels in the wrong, or the kind of silent where he's pissed now, too. Between us there's that ugly, electric tension that's like we're fighting without words. I'm practically hyperventilating, I'm so mad. I grip the steering wheel and vow not to speak, but that lasts about ten minutes until I turn onto County Highway 5-10, like the GPS tells me to.

"Patty," I say.

Lorenzo looks completely baffled.

"The girl he had sex with, the one who didn't matter."

"Is *that* what you're—"

"Not 'what.' *Who*." Imagine *her* secret story. That's what I'm doing, all right.

"Ivy. Come on. I'm not my dad. I'm not all men. I get it."

"Not until I said it."

"I had other things on my mind. Like you feeling you needed to tell my dad it wasn't me."

"Probably being all huggy-lovey with Pops was on your mind, too."

"You didn't have to tell him anything, Ives. I would have stood by and kept your secret for however long you wanted. Forever."

I wish so bad I were home. With Mom and Mase and Wilson Phillips. Or rather, I wish they were here with me. Not in the Avalanche, but on our way to Oregon. *Your secret* makes me feel so alone. "You just want to rescue me. You just want to save me because you couldn't save Mateo." From the moment he told me about him, as we lay on the hood of the truck in the parking lot of the Sahara Dunes that night, I knew that. He can deny it all he wants, but I feel this truth. So sorry, guy, but I don't want to be your small, rescued girl. There's so much to be mad at, I have no idea what it all is.

Lorenzo sighs. He just stares out the window at the same scenery we've been looking at most of the way. A highway with farmland on each side. Less Lima and Genoa, Geneva and Rome, more Corn and Cobb, Antlers and Rifle. With my foot on the gas, my jaw clenched, I feel a new determination. I don't want to go to Paris Junior College, and on to Texas State. Somewhere, yeah, but not there, and I'm going to see those cities, the big ones, the real ones. I will see them, I swear.

Lorenzo dares to speak. "So what, Ivy? So what if I want to rescue you. You don't need it. I know that. You can handle this and anything else. Rescue isn't always just about some dude being all chivalrous. I just love you, is all. And I can't stand to see you hurt, because you're a beautiful person."

Fuck. Fuck! My throat gets all tight, and it's hard to swallow, and my eyes feel hot, and they get watery, and I have to blink back tears. I sniff a big noisy sniff, too, and it's kind of gross, but he's only looking at me over there so tender. He looks kind of cute again. Just a little, but he does.

The silence between us, it's weird, but I can feel it get hazier and softer, and we're not arguing wordlessly anymore. He opens his palm in the space between the seats, same as a dog shows you his tummy, and I put my hand in his.

"He fired me," I say as I stare down that long, empty two-lane highway. Where is everybody, huh? Not out here, that's for sure.

"What?"

"Bob Euwing. He just called and left a message. He fired me. He kept using the word 'circumstances.' Your 'circumstances.' Family values."

"Oh fuck no, Ivy. Fuck no! Family values, like the ones they taught *Drake*?"

"I can't even believe this. I just *cannot*."

"I can. Bob Euwing, that slime bag. He's a creep, Ivy, him with all his *my little go-getter*. The creep raised a creep! He can't fire you for this. You should go after him. You should tell him *the truth*."

"I'm not going to tell him the truth. I don't want anything more to do with those people."

"God damn it!" Lorenzo is furious now, too.

"He said he was, uh, 'terminating' me."

"Terminating?"

"Terminating!"

I have no idea why it happens, maybe because this is all just so awful, but when I say the word *terminating*, the one so often used instead of the other, unsaid word, the secret word, I scoff a little. It's sort of a scoff-snort. The scoff-snort is almost a half laugh, and Lorenzo—well, his mouth rises ever so slightly at the corner. Bob Euwing being such an idiot, using that word as he fires me, it's so ridiculous, so shocking, that fury tumbles into its nearest neighbor, hysteria. I laugh. I laugh, and Lorenzo laughs, and then I am laughing so hard, I'm making choky, gaspy sounds.

"Termina—" Lorenzo says again, and I have to hold my hand up because I can't take it. His face is all scrunched, and he barely manages to strangle out an "Oh my God, oh my God." My stomach hurts, and I am rocking with such hard laughter, I can barely see.

"I gotta pull over," I say. Once I do, we repeat the word again, or try to, and burst into hysterics again, and then, God, it's just so incredible and terrible, all of the assumptions people make about each other, that I start to cry. Hard. Really hard, and Lorenzo puts his arms around me.

He holds me, because I can be angry and devastated, full of fury and vulnerable, fierce and broken, capable and cared for. Longing for my family but mostly okay where I am. Ugly and beautiful and lost and determined and shame-filled and good. I can be good.

When we separate, I wipe my eyes with my palms. Lorenzo puts his hands on either side of my face. "Abortion road trip love story," he says. This expression of his—it sounds kind of awful, it doesn't seem right, but it's not entirely wrong, either. How do I even explain? It's a *whole,* and it tells me he loves me wholly. "You never use the word, Ivy. *We* barely do, and, you know, we should be able to say it. One in four women gets one."

"One in *four*? Is that true? How do you know?"

"I looked it up. One in four. We should *all* be able to say it."

"Abortion road trip love story," I say. And, hey, I don't crumble into a pile of dust. Look at that. Abortion—I'm still here. Abortion, abortion, so are one in four women. "You drive now?"

"Your choice," Lorenzo says, and I couldn't agree more.

24

I'VE BEEN TO AUNT BETTS'S HOUSE IN FLORENCE, Oregon, a few times before. It's not far from Manhattan Beach and my grandma's house. Mom, Mase, and I visited just two Christmases ago. We also went there for my cousin Jack's wedding, but I somehow forgot how beautiful it is. Florence is a harbor town on the far edge of the Oregon Coast, and you have to drive over this big bridge to get there. When you're crossing it, the water of the river is all around you, and the ocean is in front of you, and the small, charming town sits like a little island as your destination. It all feels like you're descending straight into a vacation, or into another life where your parents own the fish-and-chips place in town and you'll eventually fall in love with a fisherman. Well, this is what Aunt Betts did and does. She fell in love with a fisherman, Uncle Jess, and they owned the fish-and-chips and chowder place until last year, when they retired. In the film version you and your successful fiancé would come here from the big city for the big wedding, and your first love from your small-town high school would still live here, causing romantic complications. Which is what happened with my cousin Jack, minus the complications, as far as we know. We met his old girlfriend, Amy, who worked at Captain Ahoy's Chips and Chowder until it closed, but Jack and Raquel went back to New York to their jobs in finance after the celebration.

"Dang," Lorenzo says when we go over the bridge, because wow. Our windows are down. The A/C seems to have given up entirely, though it's hard to tell with the Avalanche. The smell out here is the best—salty air, deepwater fishy who-knows-what—and the sun is perfect, all summery but not hot-hot. This place is not like anywhere else we've been on this trip. On the one hand it's hard to believe you can just get in your car in Paris and end up in Florence, but on the other, it feels like we've earned it. After all those endless, dull miles of highway and dust, with only the occasional passing of a semi for excitement . . . we get the reward of *the coast.*

"It's a mirage," I say. It sure seems like one. After this day it seems like a haven.

"Can you even believe all the places you could live?" Lorenzo says.

It's so true. I mean, I live in Paris, but you can start to think you'll always stay where you are. Home seems permanent, but I suddenly feel like home could be one of Mr. Mysterioso's tricks, a coin appearing here and then there. Like, the cover on the jigsaw puzzle box was always a farm, but now it's an ocean.

"See that tiny row of houses just past town, sitting right over the bay?"

"Yeah?" He looks at me hopefully.

"My aunt doesn't live anywhere near there," I say, and Lorenzo pretend-scowls. "Haha, just kidding. That teeny, beat-up blue one between the fancy ones—that's her house."

"Argh." Lorenzo grabs my knee and shakes it. It's fun to be the one who knows this area. "Who needs fancy?" he says. "I mean, on the water like that? Pretty fucking fancy."

"Not when you see all the cat hair." He's not sure if I'm serious. "Kidding again!" I'm so excited to be here.

We drop down into town. The vacation vibe ratchets up a few notches. The sidewalks are busy with people eating ice cream and couples strolling into places like the Wind Drift Gallery, and Books 'n' Bears, and Kitchen Klutter. There are hanging flower baskets here, too, but it's nothing like Vail. The galleries and shops here don't have sparse walls with jillion-dollar paintings or extravagant clothing or expensive jewelry. Instead they're jammed with the stuff local artisans make—hanging clay fish, and lighthouses made out of stained glass, and wood wall art in the shape of seagulls. This is a town that has classic car shows and wiener-dog races.

"All About Olives!" Lorenzo practically shouts, gesturing to a small shop. "Free olive tasting!"

"I can't think of anything I'd like more," I lie.

"What do they have besides the black ones, and the green-with-the-red-in-it?"

"Greek, I guess? Flavors."

"Vanilla and chocolate," Lorenzo snorts.

I pretend-stick a finger down my throat. "Madagascar Lime, and Salt and Vinegar Special Spice."

"Garlic Chimichurri, and Burrito Rotunda!"

"Hair of the Dog, and Linguine Maximilian!" We could play this game all day.

"What does 'hair of the dog' even mean?" he asks.

"No idea. Hey, maybe a half mile or so, and it's on the right. Look for a driveway with a seagull on a stump. Seagulls are big here." I shrug.

"Yeah, well, seagulls rule this place," Lorenzo says. He flicks the lever for wiper fluid to wash away a splotch of white that's appeared on his windshield, but it only makes an empty *vvvv vvvv* sound, and the blades smear it to a rainbow-shaped white.

"There, there!" I point.

As we head down the gravel drive to my aunt's house, set there on the narrow slice of water, I feel the embolden-ing power of family again. Of love, the way even the near-ness of it lifts you and holds you up. After the devastating morning, it's hard to believe I can feel something so entirely different—excitement, joy. It reminds me for the millionth time that feelings aren't permanent, even if they seem like it. You've got to keep trusting in that, I realize, the truth that a feeling will pass. Your helpless boat might be bump-ing and sloshing and thrusting you forward, but, you know, you aren't going to stay in the same place.

Lorenzo gets out of the truck, and so do I. He kisses me, and I remember full-on how cute he is, and how much I want him. I remember his skin against mine in Rome. I remember how kind he is, too. Feelings about people you love—even those don't stay in one place. The guy I was furious at is gone, and there's just total Lorenzo now. I get that magical feeling, like that scene in *Rockaway Weekend*. Lorenzo lifts me up, right off my feet, but we almost fall over, and we both make a *Whoa!* sound at the same time. When he sets me down, I give his butt a playful pinch. I know, I do that a lot, and who could blame me.

"That's the Siuslaw River," I tell Lorenzo.

"Coleslaw River?" he says, which means we've moved from anger to excitement and have now skidded and plopped smack into the ball pit of silliness.

My aunt heard us pull into the driveway, and out she comes. She looks like a tougher, older version of Mom, with her short hair and thick body. She's wearing jeans and a Captain Ahoy's T-shirt, which features a piece of fried fish with legs, wearing a jaunty hat and a big smile, dancing alongside a mug of beer. Aunt Betts tosses her arms out. She looks even happier than that halibut.

"Iv-eeee!" It's the second time I've been lifted off my feet in the space of minutes.

"Aunt Betts!"

"Damn, I'm happy to see you, girl! And you must be Lorenzo," she says. "We sure appreciate you bringing our Ivy to us. How are you feeling, huh?" She knows why I'm here. Grandma needs to know, so I agreed to let Mom tell Aunt Betts, too.

"I'm okay," I say.

"Grandma can't wait to see you, but I'm so glad you

decided to spend a night with us first. Man, I wanted that bad. I can't wait to catch up! Let's get you settled."

Their house is small but has big windows featuring a view of the narrow river, and on its other side the narrow lip of sand dunes that lead to the Pacific Ocean. The living room is a mix of styles, with leather recliners and a leather couch, and modern white wood bookshelves, but with an antique china cabinet and a painting of a forest scene in a heavy, elaborate frame. She leads us to the same bedroom Mase and I shared last time, which used to belong to my cousin Savannah. It's now Aunt Betts's sewing room, since Savannah moved to California, but the only evidence of any sewing is a machine folded beneath a table. There's just one bed, and I assume Lorenzo's going to sleep where Mom usually does, in Jack's room. Instead, though, Aunt Betts says, "You both can stay here."

"Both of us?" I'm shocked, and when I look over at Lorenzo, I almost crack up because he's turning red like you wouldn't believe. But Aunt Betts only waves her hand and makes a face.

"We don't need to pretend," she says. "You took this whole trip together! I'm a lousy pretender. News flash, people sleep together, huh? Hey, when Jess and I were just a little older than you two . . . let's just say I understood the lyrics to bad seventies songs about doing it in Chevy vans, because Jess was hot. *Is* hot. Bathroom across the hall."

She isn't embarrassed, so I don't know why I am. Lorenzo, though, he's grinning like he's just met the coolest person on earth. "Thank you so much."

"You sick of my clam chowder?" she asks me.

"Are you kidding? I love that stuff."

"I thought I'd never want to see another bowl of it after we sold the restaurant, but it turns out I was wrong."

Lorenzo has made his way over to the wall above the desk. I was so wrapped up in the whole sharing-a-room thing that I didn't even notice what's covering that wall—a sprawling chart, with photos and pieces of connecting string and bits of paper with handwriting. Wait. Not a chart—a tree. It looks a little deranged, like those films where a person decides to find the murderer from an unsolved crime years ago.

"This is cool," Lorenzo says.

"Genealogy. I needed a hobby after I retired. Jess said that stalking the new management of Captain Ahoy's wasn't cutting it, so I decided to stalk something else."

"Old relatives, huh?" Lorenzo leans forward to get a closer look at the small black-and-white images.

"That there is the illustrious, dark, and convoluted history of the DeVries family," she says, and puts her arm around me. "The prologue of this girl right here."

Mom always says that three women who are so similar need space, same as lionesses with their territories on the savanna, but it seems unfair that Aunt Betts and Grandma are here, right by the ocean, Florence and Manhattan Beach, while we have Paris, Texas. There are other reasons they've butted heads over the years, something about sibling rivalry and playing favorites, Aunt Betts taking or being given money to open Captain Ahoy's when Mom never took or was given money. Something else about them ganging up and not approving of my dad, thinking he was aloof and arrogant and controlling, which maybe turned out to be true, but who wants to admit it. That early evening, though, when we're out on the small deck by the river, Mom and Aunt Betts are laughing on FaceTime, totally and forever on the same team. They're joking about their mom, Grandma Lottie, how she sometimes pretends that she cooked the Trader Joe's frozen dinners from scratch, and no one calls her on it. Joking, too, about how Grandma Lottie always says that she doesn't give a shit anymore now that she's old, that she'll say whatever she wants, when, in truth, she always has.

Maybe I do see their sibling rivalry, though, when Aunt Betts puts her arm around me and holds the phone out and says, "I got this girl, now. For a whole night, all to ourselves. Look at us, same eyes, same nose," and Mom just answers, "Her eyes are green, like mine," and Aunt Betts says, "Whatever you say," as if it's not true.

I let them talk, and say goodbye to Mom, and head down to the river. I'm glad they're busy catching up, because I don't want to tell Mom all about Lorenzo's dad, and Mr. Euwing firing me. It's summer, and I just want to enjoy summer, being barefoot on this grass, watching Lorenzo trying to get into the small kayak Uncle Jess built. He's all baby-calf wobbly legs, if a baby calf were trying to get into a one-man boat, and Uncle Jess is saying, "Steady, steady."

Uncle Jess is up to his knees in the water, and the hem of his shorts is getting wet. His tiny gray ponytail is escaping out of the bright pink band he maybe snitched from Aunt Betts.

"You got it, you got it!" I shriek to Lorenzo, because he does. God, summer is just so great when you can forget you're pregnant and on a road trip to get an abortion that's illegal in your state. It smells so good out here, like warm blackberries. A neighbor is barbecuing, and a polite ribbon of smoke drifts over, bringing the promise of grilled steak. I swat a mosquito trying to nip my leg, and I don't even mind, because even that means it's a normal summer evening. Lorenzo is so tall, and now he goes from baby calf to giraffe, sticking up out of that kayak, wearing a goofy, victorious grin, like a character from *Mario Kart*.

Uncle Jess gives the boat a little shove and turns to me with a clenched-teeth, wide-eyed *oh shit* look. "He can swim, right?"

"I think so," I say, because I don't even know.

"Watch me, I'm the river master!" Lorenzo shouts. He holds the oar in the air, gives a shimmy, a new version of our car dance with a kayak.

"Inadvisable," Uncle Jess says. Uncle Jess has that ponytail and a bit of a beer paunch, like he's seen a lot of life but it's mostly treated him okay. He looks a little like a biker, but he's really a boater. He worked on fishing boats, and now that he and Aunt Betts are retired, he builds kayaks and canoes. Mase and I always liked him. Even when we were little kids, he never treated us the way some adults did, talking in high-pitched voices and asking what our favorite subjects in school were. He'd just ask us to help him do something adult and slightly dangerous—light the barbecue, use his sander on a boat he was refinishing in their garage.

I cup my hand around my mouth because Lorenzo is getting pretty far out there. "Way to go!" I shout. "Will he be able to come back?" I ask Uncle Jess.

"No way to tell without it happening." Which is true about most things, I guess.

Lorenzo gives a couple of adept paddles, then shows off some more. He lifts the oars out of the water and rocks to a beat, bobbing his head. "Pa-ddle man, pa-ddle man. See you around, suckers!" And then in he plops. The boat just rolls right over, turning a circle like a green bean in a bowl of minestrone.

"Oh my God!" I shriek again while Uncle Jess just watches calmly, as if my beloved Lorenzo is in one of those YouTube videos where some cocky dude does something zany and foolish and gets what's coming to him.

Lorenzo's head pops up. He looks drowned and flat-haired and somehow unrecognizable, same as when we give Wilson a bath and he's totally soaked and looks super-thin and has new bangs. Except Wilson always looks miserable, and Lorenzo looks so darn happy. "I'm all right!" He waves.

I wave back. He tries to hook a leg back in, and then the other one, with no luck. I'm worried but also wish I had a video of this, because what I'm witnessing would get a jillion hits. It's better than those guys falling off trampolines or making a dramatic flip and then crashing off a skateboard.

"He's a natural," Uncle Jess says deadpan.

I snort. I forgot that Uncle Jess is pretty funny, too. It's the kind of funny you've got to listen for, though, not the show-off kind. "I keep telling myself he's got a life jacket."

But now, in a flash moment of the unexpected, Lorenzo transforms from the object of ridicule into an athlete. He's somehow gotten ahold of the boat and is doing this graceful, strong, one-armed crawl stroke. Uncle Jess makes an impressed *huh* sound beside me. Lorenzo's back at the bank in no time, and he emerges from the water dripping wet but with confidence, and he hauls that heavy boat to shore like it's . . . only a green bean in a bowl of minestrone.

"Look at you," I say. In a film his muscles would be popping, and he'd have seaweed around his neck. In real life he's still his skinny-ish self, and his hair is all smooshed Chia Pet, but I'm in awe. "Wow."

"I used to be a lifeguard." He shrugs, adding another chapter to the half-read book of Lorenzo.

"Rescuer," I realize.

"Hey, that kayak could have drowned," he says.

25

"HERE *YOU* ARE," I SAY TO AUNT BETTS. I TAP THE photo of her on the family tree. It's an image of her sitting in a lawn chair by this very river, the one I can see out the window, glinting in the moonlight as if it has secrets. I'm in my pajama shirt already, teeth brushed, ready for bed, but Aunt Betts is lingering in the room. Lorenzo is still with Uncle Jess in the garage, checking out a new boat he's building. I wonder if it's an excuse so that Aunt Betts can be alone with me to talk.

"Gor-geous." She rolls her eyes. She looks just like Mom when she does it.

"You are." Maybe not in a traditional way, but she's beautiful like a real tree is, sturdy and unique and grounded. "And who is this?" I ask. "Must be your . . ." I follow my finger up the line of the trunk. "Great-grandma on your mom's side? My great-great-grandma?"

"Yep. Check out that fur." The woman is wearing a stern expression and a dark dress and blocky shoes, but her chin is ducked into some sort of fox or mink. She's holding on to the arm of a man next her, who's smoking a cigar with a flourish. He's shorter than she is, and he's sporting a hat tipped at a confident angle. He's got a grin that looks like trouble.

"Glamorous, huh?"

"Who was he? He seems like a gangster."

"More like a common criminal. Husband number three. Pretty sure he stole that fur she's wearing."

I follow the branches up, up . . . "Wow, look at *her* mom." It's wild to realize—that woman right there is my great-great-great-grandma. She's large and imposing, as serious as a concrete bunker, and probably poor. At least, in that yellowed photograph, the kids lined up on either side of her look dirty and unkempt.

"She had eighteen children."

"Eighteen?"

"Can't imagine doing that on purpose, can you?"

"Geez, no. Was it a religious thing?"

"Probably a we-don't-have-a-lot-of-options thing."

"Eighteen, wow." It doesn't even seem possible for one body.

"Go back down a generation for a sec."

"The great-great-grandma in the fur?"

"Yeah. That's Mary. Grandma Lottie's grandma. Do you know anything about her?"

"Not really. Only that she married a lot. Three times, like you said. That's about it."

"Well, I'll tell you something else about her." Aunt Betts pauses. "I hope you don't mind. Like I said, I'm not very good at pretending."

"Okay."

"She had several abortions."

"Several?" Oh wow. Poor Mary.

"Several. Look, her own mom had eighteen kids. And Mary—sometimes married, sometimes not, working in manufacturing, barely making enough to survive . . . She already had Grandma Lottie's mom, and a little boy. How would she have taken care of more? At least, this is what I heard from a cousin of mine. You think *I'm* into genealogy? She traced her dad's side of the family back to a king or something."

"Still. *Several.* It seems shocking. I mean, it was illegal then, right? Like, everywhere?"

"You probably shouldn't get me started on this stuff."

"Genealogy?"

"Abortion!"

I make a face.

"I'm not kidding," she says. "I read all about it when I heard Mary's story, because *several* seemed shocking to me, too. It's fascinating, you know, how woven into our history abortion is."

I *don't* know. I just stand there, because the history she's referring to is happening to me right now. Will happen, in two days. "Woven into our history, like how? Like we have a DeVries abortion curse?"

She laughs. "Our history, DeVries, yeah, but the larger 'our,' too. History-history. We didn't have a curse, and Mary wasn't even shocking; it's just how things were. *Are.* So yeah, us, too."

"You're saying people have just been getting abortions forever?"

"Pretty much, yeah. I mean, look." Aunt Betts waves her hand at our tree. "When you have lots of people having sex, you get lots of people getting pregnant, and lots of people who don't want to be. Basically, the human race from the beginning of time. And in terms of it being illegal? It *wasn't* in half the states in Mary's day, and in all places—you had what was illegal, and then you had what was commonplace. We're talking about Mary in the 1920s to 1930s, but even before, back to the 1900s, even 1800s . . . abortion was simply a part of everyday female life. That's what I learned. Most ordinary people? They didn't think of it as a criminal act or anything. It was just a tolerated fact of life. Women talked about it to each other, giving advice, passing on information. Friends, daughters, nieces, granddaughters—you told her where the abortionist lived. You went with her if she had to get one, took care of her after. It was what women did for each other. Do still."

"Mom's friend Esilda?" I stopped for a second. I had to think about how to say this without sharing Esilda's private business. "She said that all the women who have abortions are like a secret underground network."

"Yeah. And you find out about networks like that when you're suddenly in one."

"Oh my God! It's so true. You wouldn't believe it. I just keep hearing all these stories now."

"I haven't had an abortion," Aunt Betts says, "but the same thing happened when I had a miscarriage. So many people told me they'd had one, I was shocked. I had no idea it was so common." Aunt Betts shakes her head. "All the shame women hold in their bodies . . . Damn. Which reminds me, something *else* surprising about Grandma Mary's time? Well, the abortion story line is usually about shameful single girls having sinful sex and getting pregnant, like they somehow do it by themselves, right?"

"Right."

"In those days, it was mostly married women who got them. Women trying to do the best thing for their families, worried that their other children would suffer with another mouth to feed. And the women getting abortions then, and even way before, they were from all walks of life, too. The poorest of the poor, the wealthiest of the wealthy. Same as now. And women from every religion. Every single one. Same as now. But the *biggest* thing that's the same? *The numbers.* From the time people ever first thought to keep track, around the 1900s on . . . twenty to thirty-five percent of women had abortions. Can you believe it? Those are the numbers now! One out of four, twenty-five percent."

"It's been like that for *a hundred years?*"

"A hundred *plus* years, same, same, same."

"One out of four, forever." It's hard to imagine. I mean, I had no idea.

"The number that changes? How many women *die* when they don't have legal options, because women have *always* found a way to get what they need, laws or no. Which brings me to . . ."

Now she taps a different image. A separate branch. We'd been looking at Grandma Lottie's line, and now we go to Grandpa Larry's, who died when I was little. I recognize his photo. My mom has the same one in a little frame on our bookcase. Grandpa Larry's line rises and then branches to his own father and mother, where Aunt Betts has placed her finger.

I squinch to read Aunt Betts's handwriting. "Alice?"

"Alice."

I am suddenly very worried for Alice.

"So, in terms of *illegal* . . . Just a generation up, when Mary was having her abortions, it was mostly the abortionists who went on trial if they got caught, usually if a woman died. *Her* punishment was death itself, obviously, but also public shame, because they'd put her name in the paper. Her picture, too. Sometimes, they *would* go after the abortionist's other patients. God, honey, they'd barge in there and question women who were on their deathbeds, searching for evidence against the doctors. They'd track down a patient's mother or sister, too. Picture some chump dude with authority, demanding that you tell him when you last menstruated, who you had sex with, if the doctor put various instruments inside of you. Asking your sister what your flow was like when you menstruated."

"Why do I hate the word 'flow'?"

"Ditto. All of it was a way of disciplining the woman, though, right? Those shaming articles, wow. Keeping women in check."

"So gross."

"Fast forward to the 1940s, when your grandma was a little girl, Mary *her* grandma now, and in the 1950s, too . . . That discipline—it wasn't *enough,* apparently, because around then they started *really* going after the women, raiding clinics. Abortion was becoming safer, it wasn't killing as many people, so, damn, those women were really getting out of line. So officers would storm in, sometimes catching and arresting the patients who were right there on the tables, grabbing the records of all the others."

I imagine it, girls and women, feet in stirrups, already scared, now terrified. It's horrific. So horrific, I only shake my head.

"They'd scare you, threaten to expose you by forcing you to testify. Jail you if you didn't. Any doctor who referred a woman to a clinic was threatened, too, and viewed as equally guilty. I've got to tell you, reading about this stuff is hard and sad. I mean, *the fear.* And women dying, you know. Doing it themselves. This history—it's mine, and yours, and all of ours, because *Alice.* So many Alices! None of us knew her. Grandpa Larry barely knew her. She died when he and his brother were just little boys. Trying to give herself an abortion."

"Oh my God." I feel sick. I look at her picture. She's a real woman, with a plain face and hair pulled back. A real woman with no options doing a desperate thing. Two boys with no mother.

"Ivy, I hope that isn't an awful thing to tell you right now. Because the first thing you need to understand is that abortion as a health-care procedure . . . it's safer than childbirth. It's safer than dental procedures and colonoscopies. Safer than getting your tonsils out. But I just wanted to say . . . Well, you know how I told you about grandmas and aunts and moms passing on information about being a woman? I want to do that now. For you. I want to tell you where you, *we,* came from. Information about being a woman? How about *this?* We get a load of shame as females. But look at us all, connected here." She points to the great-great-great-grandmother. "She had eighteen children." Next she points to Mary. "*She* had several abortions." Now she points to Grandma Lottie's mom, Lana. "*She* had a baby out of wedlock when she was just seventeen. A baby she named Lottie." She moves over to Grandpa's mom. "She had an abortion after having two children and didn't make it. Left two little dudes without a mom. Look at this family history. This is just truth. The plain old truth of being a woman and having a body. And truth should be stronger than shame."

I do look. I see all the limbs and branches. I see all the old images of women, in furs, on farms, in a lawn chair by a river. I see my mom's photo, and I know her story, one that Aunt Betts may or may not even be aware of. I see my photo, my sophomore-year school photo, and I'm standing right here living mine. I want to cry. What shame I feel, what fear, what confusion, they felt, too.

"Sometimes," Aunt Betts says, "I look at this tree, and I think our whole family history is people having sex, women and girls getting pregnant, having or not having babies. But then I realize, that's every family's history."

26

THAT NIGHT, LORENZO AND I SPEND THE NIGHT IN the bed in Aunt Betts's sewing room because Aunt Betts doesn't like to pretend that people don't have sex, and that girls and women don't get pregnant, and that girls and women don't have abortions, a jillion million girls and women, across centuries. I'm aware, very aware, of Lorenzo's body there next to me. I want to roll right over and start kissing him, but I'm also aware of the noises in the house—Uncle Jess clearing his throat, coughing, like maybe he once smoked cigarettes. The hum of the dishwasher, Aunt Betts's low voice saying stuff to her husband. I trail my fingers along Lorenzo's chest, slip my fingers under the waistband of his pajama shorts. He moans and says, "Ivy. We can't."

In the film version we wouldn't be able to help ourselves, and we'd do it anyway, as quietly as possible, barely moving, but this isn't what happens. I take my hand back because it feels too weird doing anything like that in my aunt's house, with them right down the hall. So we only touch bare toes under the sheets, and Lorenzo holds my hand, giving attention to each and every finger. I learn that holding back can be just as hot as giving in.

"I have a confession," he whispers. My body is buzzing, and I have to kick one leg from the sheets, it's so warm under there, so I expect a confession about sex or desire, but no. "When that kayak went over my head? I thought for a second I might die," he says.

"Oh geez, Lorenzo," I whisper back.

"I didn't want you to think I'm one of those assholes who pretend to never be scared."

"Thanks," I say, though this sounds wrong, like the truth is a special gift instead of what just is, something stronger than any humiliation. And then I have a confession of my own. It's been bugging me ever since his dad went home, his life back in order, relieved that this is my possible regret, not Lorenzo's. Free of parental duty, since this was some other dude's doing, not the guy I loved, who loved me back. "I've got to tell you something," I whisper.

"Okay." He stops all the stuff with my fingers and lies still.

"This is going to sound strange maybe, but I just need you to know that . . . even if this was you and me being pregnant? Not because of some awful moment with Drake Euwing, but because of love? I'd still want to do the same thing. The abortion." I say the word, because those women are above me. In their furs and on their farms and on their lawn chairs by the river.

"Of course," Lorenzo says. "We're not ready to be parents." He rubs his toe on mine, and for whatever reason I feel an immense sense of relief. "I can't even cook."

I burst out laughing. I forget to care that my aunt and uncle can hear. "You can't even *cook*?" Of all the responsibilities of having a kid—money, shelter, basic needs—he's worried about making meals.

"I can maybe do a grilled cheese sandwich. Some eggs. I once made some shit pancakes. Dads should at least be able to do good pancakes. Excellent pancakes, with ears and stuff."

Oh man, my heart fills with rainbows and balloons and those great fluffy clouds, the best ones, impossible and beautiful and up, up, up. I feel happier than in my happiest kid memory, when my mom bought me those light-up tennis shoes and I thought I was magic. Impossible, beautiful, happy, magic—it's all filling me to bursting because, somehow, a strange series of events has led me here, insistently and purposefully, to love. To lying next to my favorite person, next to a river, next to the ocean. I realize it's as good a definition of life as any—a strange series of events that lead you, insistently and purposefully, to love.

And I realize something else. Whenever Lorenzo does become a dad, he's going to be a fantastic one.

"Hey, when we get home? Mase can teach you. He makes ears, and chocolate-chip smiles."

"Chocolate-chip smiles are next level."

When we get home. It's hard to understand how something can fill you with both longing and dread. It crosses my mind—no, more than crosses, *settles into* my mind—that the world is big, much bigger than Paris, Texas. It's Lima and Moscow, Geneva and Rome. It's Florence and Manhattan. It's Antlers and Dinosaur and Corn.

Lorenzo gives me a sweet kiss and closes his eyes. I don't tell Lorenzo about my family history, not yet. I just want to spend some time with those women. I sleep under the tree. My mother, my grandmothers and aunts—they keep me company, in my dream world and in the real one. They tell me, we understand. They tell me, it happened to us, too. They tell me, you'll be okay. They tell me, we're here, you are. The story belongs to all of us.

Before we head out, after a breakfast of eggs and bacon and coffee strong enough to curl your hair, according to Uncle Jess, we stamp our passports. Florence, *kashunk*. We haul our bags to the Avalanche. Lorenzo and I are both wearing the Captain Ahoy's T-shirts that Aunt Betts gave us from the box in the garage. Lorenzo's happy dancing halibut smiles at my happy dancing halibut, who smiles back.

Aunt Betts gives me a long hug. "You won't be coming through on your way home?" She sounds sad.

"We're driving straight back on the freeways," I say. "I've got to get home to—" I almost say "work," and then I remember I don't have a job anymore. "Mom and Mase.

And Lorenzo's got to get home, too. He's got to figure out school, or a job, or whatever, he's not exactly sure."

The words *job* and *home*—they make me regret those eggs and bacon. I feel sick. Ever since I started working at Euwing's Drugs, I put on my vest and felt the possibilities of my future, felt myself heading toward something. But that vest with my name on it is still tucked in my work cubby. My mug with the two kissing Scottie dogs that Faith gave me is still at work, too. My favorite customers are still going in, I'm sure, too—Mrs. Peony; and old Mrs. Ivers, picking up her prescriptions and her box of coffee Nips; and Olive Wey, the barista at Java Lane, with her purple hair and nose ring; and Mr. Fartso, which is what Evan and I named Mr. Farling for obvious reasons. We like him anyway. Sometimes he slips us a few bucks, and we take it even though we probably shouldn't, because it makes him happy. *Get yourself a little treat,* he says.

I wonder what they'll all think when they hear about me. I'll be someone totally different to them when I go back. I guess a place, if it's small enough, can define you, and maybe define you forever. I should have realized this before now. We still think of Gina Delgavio as the girl who barfed during the second-grade play, even though Gina Delgavio is in math club, and drives her dad's vintage Mustang, and writes songs that she sometimes plays at the Shrimp House happy hour. I have a brief fantasy of walking straight into Euwing's, straight to the cage of Buddy and Missy, and flinging open the door. But it's total fantasy, the idea that they might fly free. They've been in there so long, it's all they know. Even when they come out to get their cage cleaned, they stay right on the perch beside Mr. Euwing and then hop right back into that . . . I was going to say *chain link,* but it's not chain link. That wire cage.

"Gonna miss you. You give my love to your mom, huh?"

"You bet. I'm going to miss you, too. I'm not going to forget the tree," I say.

"There's a whole forest of those trees." She smiles but looks like she might cry. Instead she just thumps Lorenzo on the back and squeezes my shoulder one last time.

"Hey, remember. When you're in the boat, look ahead to keep your balance," Uncle Jess says to Lorenzo.

There's a lot of honking and waving, and then we're off.

"The tree? The forest? What'd I miss?" Lorenzo asks. It's a blue-sky day, and the air through our windows is gloriously salty.

"Tell you later. It's a long story," I say. Really long. Going back centuries long. "Hey." I take a pinch of my shirt. "We look like a couple of retirees."

"Those people back there," Lorenzo says. "Life goals."

"Highway 101! Icon, man," Lorenzo says. We've played a few of Lorenzo's CDs, but now we're back to Mom's for the jillionth time, and this super oldie is blaring, Marvin Gaye singing "Got to Give It Up." You can't tell what the heck he's singing, to be honest, so I looked up the lyrics way back in

Kansas. It's about a guy who used to be all nervous and self-conscious until he finally just lets it all go and starts dancing. It's got a lot of "ooh, babys" in it, and it's a Lorenzo favorite, probably because you can car-dance your butt off to it. It also gives him the excuse to sing in this super-high-pitched way that makes him both look and sound like he got his balls caught in a sliding glass door.

We shimmy and bounce, and Lorenzo pours his heart out to a pretend audience. If Lorenzo is right, it's easy to see why Highway 101 is iconic. It's gorgeous beyond belief. I mean, sometimes the road just winds through regular old land, some farms or something, little towns of one stoplight and then another stoplight. But then you get a peek of ocean, and a whiff of salt water. You feel the nose of the truck rise, and the road lifts, and wow, just wow—there's the ocean, spread out in front of you in the most extravagant panorama of sky and water and waves, with sheer cliffs dropping straight down to a frothy surf.

"'Groovy partee!'" Lorenzo sings. Those probably aren't even the words, but who cares. Lorenzo's head is tilted back, and his eyes are semisquinched with a fullhearted, give-it-all-you-got performance.

"Uh, can you unsquinch your eyes? This road is making me nervous." There's that, too—the way the road gets so narrow, you could fall right off. It's all beautiful and breathtaking and perilous. Hey, another life definition.

Lorenzo turns down the music. "Sorry, foxy mama." After "Got to Give It Up," I'm always foxy mama for a few miles. Usually until "Everybody Hurts" by R.E.M. comes on, which sobers us up and even makes Lorenzo go quiet.

Apologies to Mom, but after a few times of us moodily staring out at barns and rest stops after that song played, we've since agreed to skip that track.

"How can you even imagine the ocean when you're not by the ocean?" I ask.

"I want to put my feet in there so bad," Lorenzo says. "I've only been to the ocean once, when I won a speech competition and got to go to San Diego."

"Wait. You won a speech competition? What was your speech?" I can't even imagine it. Lorenzo just keeps on surprising me. He has more layers than the Pillars of Rome.

"A Rotary Club thing in California. 'The Leader Inside Me.'"

I snort. He glares, as if I have no right to doubt his leadership abilities, which is the absolute truth. I mean, he's been leading us around the world on our abortion road trip love story. He's a winner in my book, that's for sure.

"I hope they gave you a great big trophy, too," I say.

"A little gold man holding his arm out. I think it's supposed to be a gesture of oratory grandness, but he looks like he's hailing a taxi. Oh dang. Look at that. It's downright majestic," he says of the ocean. "Do you think it's warm enough to swim? I do." He sticks his arm out the window, and the little hairs on it wave in the wind like a wheat field on a breezy day.

"We can splash around for sure. Just wait until we get to my grandma's." Grandma Lottie's house is super small, and the paint is always peeling from wind and salt water, but who cares. It's right on the beach.

"I'm sick of waiting." Lorenzo pouts. I hand him some Red Vines and a Mountain Dew to cheer him up. Sometimes I look at Lorenzo and can totally see who he was as a little kid. Or who he'd *have* as a little kid.

I pull my licorice until it stretches and breaks. It feels weird and wrong to be in such a good mood. I'm a pregnant teenager, about to be not pregnant anymore. I should be suffering, according to the movies, but the closer we get, the more relief starts to fill me. It opens inside of me like that vista—a sky getting larger, the sea stretching out. You can make your own cage, can't you? Just by your thoughts? I won't have to be the pregnant girl much longer, the girl who got pregnant, because the *getting* seems to be worse than the *being* in people's minds. I'll be returned to myself. No, I'll be a *new* self, who now understands about the cage and the Pillars of Rome both.

Lorenzo suddenly brightens. I mean, gets even brighter, and it's not just because Mom's CD has moved on to "Go Your Own Way" by Fleetwood Mac, which he usually sings by repeating the title over and over again. "Hey, we need gas!" he says.

"Do we really need gas?" Sometimes Lorenzo just says that so we can go see something besides road. I lean to look at the gauge. We really need gas.

After we fill up, though, Lorenzo doesn't get back on the highway. He takes a different turn, and then another.

"What? Where are we going?" I moan. I want to get to Grandma's, not see some Tower of Tires or whatever.

"Please," he dangerously begs, with clutching hands not on the wheel. "A *lighthouse*." He says it like he's Mr.

Mysterioso and it's a magic word. Since way back in Colorado, after the creepy Wonder Tower, he's been telling me lighthouse facts, like how the southernmost lighthouse in Britain is called Lizard Lighthouse, and how the Statue of Liberty was originally a lighthouse, but it was a crappy one, so they said never mind. How the tallest one is in Saudi Arabia and is 133 meters tall. *How many feet is that? I asked. I don't know. Tall, okay? Very,* he answered.

"Only for a sec?" I say.

He just smiles. Like a Buddha, silent with truth and wisdom.

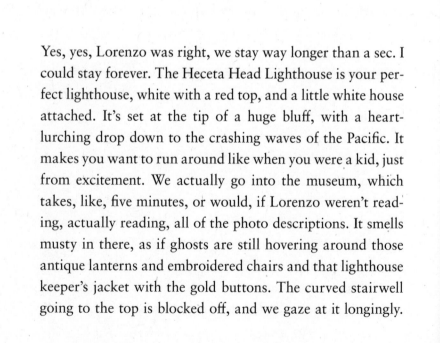

Yes, yes, Lorenzo was right, we stay way longer than a sec. I could stay forever. The Heceta Head Lighthouse is your perfect lighthouse, white with a red top, and a little white house attached. It's set at the tip of a huge bluff, with a heart-lurching drop down to the crashing waves of the Pacific. It makes you want to run around like when you were a kid, just from excitement. We actually go into the museum, which takes, like, five minutes, or would, if Lorenzo weren't reading, actually reading, all of the photo descriptions. It smells musty in there, as if ghosts are still hovering around those antique lanterns and embroidered chairs and that lighthouse keeper's jacket with the gold buttons. The curved stairwell going to the top is blocked off, and we gaze at it longingly.

There are dreams up there, though maybe your imagination is better.

"Did you know that being a lighthouse keeper was one of the first government jobs given to females?" Lorenzo says when we're outside again.

"I do now. I'd take that job." In a minute. That would beat Euwing's Drugs any day. God, it occurs to me, all the jobs I could have, too, along with all the places I could live in. I mean, I could actually be a lighthouse keeper.

We wander over to the lookout point. The ocean goes out, out, and around and disappears to the point that you get it, how it once seemed like the world was flat. That if you went too far, you could fall off. But you can't fall off. The smell of the sun plus the sea smell is so good, you want to eat it.

"This was one of the ones I sketched. It's awesome to see it in person," Lorenzo says.

"What do you mean, one of the ones you sketched?"

"In my drawing pad? With the lighthouses? I didn't tell you about that?"

"You didn't tell me about that."

"I swear I did. Maybe I was just telling you in my head, back in Colorado, after the Wonder Tower. On a road trip it's kind of hard to remember what you say out loud and what you don't."

"A drawing pad? You draw?"

"Just for fun. I'm kind of crap at it, but I like it."

He draws. It's weird, you know, that I fell in love with Lorenzo before I even knew him. So weird, because what was I even in love with? But wow, I made a good choice back then. It's reassuring, to know that I can make really good decisions, along with the really bad ones. The uglies can make me forget that. And given how many decisions we have to make in even just a single day, let alone a life, we're bound to get a ton of bad ones in there. Even some *big* bad ones, along with the big good ones. That couple walking in the lighthouse museum door, the old dude behind the counter . . . All the men and women on that tree, me and Lorenzo ourselves . . . We were just going to have to screw some stuff up, and have some terrible luck, and awful encounters with bad people, along with the great encounters with amazing people.

"Hey," I say. "We found the real Wonder Tower."

"Real bliss, and now real wonder," Lorenzo says. He pulls me to him, and I kiss him, and he grabs the back of my head like he really means that kiss, and if we weren't there at the lighthouse, we'd be rolling around right on the ground.

"Wow," I say, to all of it. Ocean, sun, mouth. Guy wearing a Captain Ahoy T-shirt, smashed against girl wearing a Captain Ahoy T-shirt.

"Ivy?" Lorenzo is suddenly serious. He takes my hands. "Should I be asking you to marry me?"

"Are you out of your mind? Of course not."

"Are you sure? I feel like that's what they'd do in the movies at a moment like this."

"Oh my God. Oh my God! I think that way all the time!" I can't believe he's even saying that. Tell me we aren't made for each other. Tell me he's not my guy. "But, Lorenzo . . . do you know how much *crap stuff* is in movies? I mean, if all of it were true, we'd never enter a parking garage without a car screaming around a pillar. Or a bad guy about to leap as soon as the main actor *bleep bleep*ed her keys. Or, wait, another parking-garage one. A night meeting with a secret informant."

"And the woman would *always* run away from the altar in the nick of time to marry the good guy instead of marrying the creep."

"Just once, I want to see her marry no one."

"Just once," Lorenzo says, "*I* want to see people drive in a car that isn't about to get in an accident."

"Oh my God! I always think that exact same thing!" See what I'm saying? See? We are looking deep into each other's eyes. "I love you so much," I say. "Maybe someday I'll ask you to marry me."

"In the movies I'd shriek with joy, but only after looking down at the ring first. But in real life maybe we wouldn't even ask, you know? Like, *why?* Like, maybe it would be a decision we'd just make together."

"You are so right," I say. He is. He is, he is.

"Damn, you are fucking beautiful in that T-shirt," he says to me.

"You are," I say.

In the movies a pregnant girl would never go to a lighthouse and stand on a magnificent bluff with a fantastic guy and, for a few minutes, totally forget she was pregnant, and totally forget that her life was supposed to be over. She would never just stand there, feeling so hopeful, feeling so *grateful,* smiling as big as a halibut in a hat.

27

"IT'S RIGHT ON THE BEACH!" LORENZO SAYS AS WE pull up to Grandma Lottie's.

"I told you a hundred times."

"But you can't imagine a house on the beach until you see a house on the beach."

Grandma Lottie must hear the crunch of our tires on gravel, or else she's been watching for us all afternoon, because the front door flings open and here she comes.

"Every person in your life has run out the front door to see you, Ives," Lorenzo says, and it's true.

Grandma Lottie—she's not what the movies say is a little old lady. There's no soft pouf of gray hair, or pearls, or a cardigan. She's stout, and her gray hair is short and spiky, and she's wearing denim shorts and a tank top, arm flab free to the world, along with a pair of Birkenstocks she's probably had since the 1960s. "Iv-eeee," she says, sounding just like Aunt Betts. I get out of the truck, and she's already hugging me hard. And now she's hugging Lorenzo, too, and we're an odd trio, a hub of humans who have found ourselves in this one same spot, sharing this exact same moment. Zeke, Grandma Lottie's big old German shepherd, suddenly comes barreling out of the house and basically smashes into us, like a storm into a pier, and we almost lose our balance.

"Who are you? Who are you, you, you?" Lorenzo croons in a lovey baby voice. Oh boy. He's a goner, I can tell. He scruffs the dog behind his ears, pats his big side.

"This is Zeke. It looks like you two were made for each other," Grandma Lottie says, and somehow she's right on. Lorenzo and Zeke—Zeke is like the dog version of Lorenzo. "You want him, you can have him. He's nothing but trouble." She doesn't mean it. Well, yeah, about the trouble part. Zeke does everything a hundred percent, which means he runs a hundred percent, and loves a hundred percent, and eats garbage a hundred percent, and knocks over Christmas trees a hundred percent. But that dog is her best guy, even after all those shattered ornaments the last time we were here. "You both hungry? If ocean air doesn't make you hungry, something's probably broken."

Grandma Lottie—well, as I mentioned, she has opinions about everything, too.

Grandma Lottie's house is shaped like a barn, with a loft on top that's her bedroom, and a larger space below where the living room and kitchen are. Mom and Mase and I usually stay at the Surf and Shore Inn when we come, because there's just not a lot of room. Grandma Lottie's house is stuffed full of books, with stacks that lean and sometimes topple, especially when Zeke blasts through the room to bark at the UPS guy. Other things seem about to tip, too—a mountain of CDs and old records, cups in the cupboard set inside one another to form a tilting tower.

A few years after Grandpa Larry died, Grandma sold Rockaway Auto Supply and Repair and bought this place. She sold the shop to the Hank's Gas Station guy for *beaucoup bucks,* as Grandma always says, thanks to *Rockaway Weekend* and the steady stream of tourists. People who go there—they just want to believe in that scene so bad, even though the movies get so much wrong. In real life, Grandma Lottie will tell you, it's not a romantic place, just one filled with tired and cranky customers whose shit cars have finally had enough. There isn't a lot of forever love in the air when your Camry is beyond saving, I guess. But, boy, who doesn't wish so hard for something larger and lasting when life is full of oil leaks and bad engines.

"You two will sleep here," Grandma Lottie says, and she lifts a couch cushion to reveal the handle of a pullout bed.

"Cool!" Lorenzo says.

"Don't you just love it when an ordinary object has a secret?" Grandma Lottie doesn't wait for an answer. "My grandma Mary used to have a desk with a hidden drawer, and wasn't *that* intriguing. How 'bout we bring lunch to the beach." She opens the fridge, where Tupperware containers are stacked on oranges, and yogurt cartons balance on those. She removes a package of turkey and another of cheese, and an apple tumbles out. She chases it, and it's probably a little bruised now, but it's coming to the beach, too.

The thing is—here things might tip, things might tumble, but you can always set them right again. So what if that apple is bruised. So what.

After we eat lunch on that big old quilt I remember from other picnics, Lorenzo races around the beach with Zeke, tossing a Frisbee into the surf. I've never seen a dog run so fast. He's a blur, and Lorenzo's hair is getting all wiry and damp from the salt air. The sun is out, but it feels breezy and cool, so you've got to watch for sunburn. On the higher ridge of sand, Grandma's house in that row of them gets farther and farther away as Grandma Lottie and I walk. Grandma Lottie holds her Birkenstocks and I drag a stick, because that's what you do on a beach. In the movies if you see an evil guy and a dog in the same scene, something awful is going to happen to the dog. And if you see a guy on a beach playing with a dog, he's a good guy, worthy of being the love interest.

"So, tomorrow," Grandma Lottie says. "Our appointment is at the Tillamook Women's Center. Ten a.m. We still good?"

"We're still good." I don't meet her eyes. I watch the long line the stick has made in the sand. It goes so far back behind me now.

"Okay!" Grandma Lottie says. "You hanging in there, kid?"

"I'm hanging in there. And . . . thanks, Grandma." It's such a weird thing to say. I'm usually thanking her for, you know, birthday money or something.

"I've got to tell you something." She doesn't stop me, or even take my elbow. We just keep walking. She has her sweatshirt tied around her waist, and her hair has gone Einstein.

I know what's coming. I know this will be a story about a woman and sex and pregnancy, another story, because one out of four, and like Aunt Betts said, you don't know about the secret network until you're in it.

"I had an abortion," she says.

There—another woman on that family tree. I wonder if Aunt Betts or Mom even knows it.

"You did?"

"Back in the early sixties, in Chicago. Before I met your grandpa. My girlfriend Betty, she introduced me to this guy, Joey." Grandma Lottie puts her hand to her chest, and her eyes even light up a little. She purses her lips and blows out a *whew,* like Joey must have really been something.

"Cute?"

"Oh my God," she says. "But, wait, before I get to him, I've got to go back to Betty. Betty! She looked like a prissy two-shoes, but that girl was something! I wish you knew her. She was always standing up against some kind of injustice, at a time when people didn't do much of that yet. One thing she used to do . . . It took balls. Back in the late fifties, early sixties, when Betty and I were close, if you went to a bar as a single woman, you could get *arrested*."

"What?" I've never heard of this. I look over at her, because maybe she's making this up or exaggerating. "Like, arrested-arrested?"

"Arrested-arrested. Harassed by police, jailed without bail. If you were out, drinking or socializing with a male stranger, you were violating not just some moral order but actual *law*."

"What about *him*?"

"Him? What*ever* about him? He got to do what he wanted, same as always. The laws were *for* him. To *protect* him. A woman who did that, went to a bar, maybe even flirted, God forbid—men were in danger from her! She might exploit you, right, with her deviousness and sexuality? This law, it was called the American Plan. Perfect, huh? So patriotic. Government policing female bodies and female sexuality, it has a long history. Just that law, it went way back, like 1910 or something, but it got all spun up again after the war. It was enforced in some places well into the 1970s. You know what else that law did? If you were even suspected of having a sexually transmitted disease, they could detain you and *check*, Ivy. Forcibly. All these dirty women might infect our glorious troops, you know?"

"I have never heard of this."

"Yeah? Well, look it up. If women were in bars, or not acting proper, or 'misbehaving'"—Grandma Lottie makes air quotes—"they could be forcibly 'examined.'" More air quotes. "Also beaten and thrown into solitary confinement.

Tens of thousands, maybe even *hundreds* of thousands of women, this happened to. But Betty—she grew up with these progressive parents. I think they were even named as communists at one point, something, can't remember exactly. But in their house, they encouraged going up against the system. So she'd go to these bars with a friend, just to make a point, and this was before 1969, 1970, when women started really protesting this shit."

"Were you a friend that went with her?"

"Hell no! I was too scared for that. But one time she went to this bar in Chicago. It had a sign in the window that said, 'No unescorted ladies will be served.' These weren't uncommon, right? But they might as well have put a sign up that read, 'Betty, enter here.' When she and her friend were about to get kicked out, two guys, they worked in 'finance'—"

"This story has a lot of air quotes."

"Air quotes are about secrets and lies, looking like one thing but being another, so, yeah, it does. You know what 'finance' meant?"

"I don't."

"Neither did we. Betty met these guys at that bar, and later introduced me to one of them, Joey. Let's just say, Chicago, finance, an Italian guy who had money but never really told you how he got it. . . . It wasn't too far-fetched to make the leap that his business wasn't exactly legal."

"Joey, huh."

"Joey. And I got pregnant because neither of us was thinking about birth control. We were just too carried away. Both of us were. I wanted it, *him,* and bad. I would have never admitted that then, and, hey, with shit like the American Plan all around, no wonder."

"I wanted Lorenzo, but I didn't want what happened with that, um, other boy."

"No. I'm sure not."

"Mom said she told you?"

"Yep. How are you doing with all that?"

"I'm just . . ." I want to tell her, because she loves me and nothing will change that, and because all her wrinkles make me think she'll understand. "So grossed out when I think about it. When I remember anything about it, just, ugh. Bad, ugly feeling." *Uglies.* The uglies, here and then gone and then here again. "But I'm not . . . like, crying and having nightmares or anything. Is that weird? I mean, if *this* didn't happen"—I gesture toward my middle—"I could have maybe just locked that whole incident into my attic brain and forgotten about it eventually, you know?"

"Oh, honey. I know. Wow, we got a lot locked into those attic brains of ours. Not weird at all. *At all.*" She looks at me hard, telling me with her eyes that I'm okay. That I'm as whole as anyone.

"I *am* mad, though. God! At him, but at myself, too. Why did I allow it? Why, why, why did this happen? But mostly I want to push it away in my mind and never look at it again. After tomorrow, I want this *over.* I just . . . God. Get the whole thing away! I don't even want to *think* that person's name."

"Well, sure. Why would you?"

"I just . . . I can't even *imagine* if I had to go through

with this. I mean, if I were forced to keep it . . . and, you know, *he* would never be forced. It would be me, my body, going through it, not his."

"Can you imagine, either, making those male lawmakers go through a pregnancy? They'd change their tune in two seconds."

"Did you tell anyone about Joey?"

"A few people."

"Does Mom know? Or Aunt Betts?"

"Nah. Not really. I didn't want to make them uncomfortable." Her mouth tightens at the corners. It feels like one of those lies you tell yourself, but if there's one thing I've learned for sure, how she wants to handle it is up to her. "A couple times, even as a married woman, I worried I was pregnant, too, after the girls were born. Funny, because we think about these big moments when you find out you're pregnant, but every month, if you're sexually active, every single darn month, it's *yes, I am; no, I'm not.* You have plenty of scares, let me tell you. That's a lot of months, Ivy, for half the population, and a lot of things happen that we don't say."

I think of that tree again, again. All the women, all the lives. I think of Grandma Lottie not telling Mom and Aunt Betts, and Mom not telling Grandma and Aunt Betts. I always thought of us as a close family, as an open one, a trusting and accepting one. But this is still something that's hard to talk about.

"Wait. Wait! I get it. Betty. Aunt Betts! You named her after your friend?"

Grandma Lottie smiles. "I did."

Zeke comes shooting past us, wet sand from beard to tail and up to his dog elbows. He leaps up on me and I'm dirtied, completely. He almost knocks me over. I give him a big shove down and wipe the sand from my shorts and T-shirt. "Do you and Betty still keep in touch?"

"No. Too bad. Friends sometimes just fall away over the years. They're the most important person to you ever at a given time, and then . . . you just fade into your own thing."

I think of Faith, not so much fading as abruptly gone. And Peyton, too. I've tried and tried to answer that text, *Don't put me in the middle,* but everything I write does just that. We're going to have to talk when I get home, when she'll see my face and, hopefully, remember who I am.

Behind us Lorenzo whistles and claps his hands for Zeke, and Zeke goes speeding back, head down, haunches pumping like a racehorse. "Do you know what happened to her?"

"I looked her up once," Grandma Lottie says. "Years ago. She lived in Michigan. Had a couple of kids, worked as a mail carrier, looked happy as hell. Everyone has stories you don't know about, right? Your grandma, your mail carrier, your *everyone.* Stories you'd never dream of. So many people are going through stuff, and have gone through stuff. So many people are quiet heroes. That woman next to you in an elevator, or the one walking her dog, or bringing you your water bill and coupons for roof cleaning . . . She is."

Grandma orders pizza that night. She's done with cooking, she says. Lorenzo flips through her albums. He can't believe she has a turntable. It's another nearly extinct thing, and he's so thrilled that I spot him taking a selfie with it, same as we did with the *Allosaurus*. I think of Mom with her drive-ins and phone booths. I think, too, of the American Plan and abortion laws. Some things should have faded into the past long, long ago, but not this record player.

"*No way!*" Lorenzo shouts. It's so loud that Zeke leaps to his feet as if there's an intruder. Grandma and I look up from the kitchen, where I'm eating a pizza crust she doesn't want, because that's my favorite part.

"God, Lorenzo. You scared me," I say.

"Check it *out.*" He holds up an album—Wilson Phillips, their first, the one with "Hold On." Three women on a beach, the ocean behind them. If you look out the windows of Grandma Lottie's house right this minute, it looks pretty much the same—the sun setting, a stripe of yellow light crossing the sky.

"Is that Mom's?" I ask.

"Your mom's?" Grandma Lottie says. "No, it's *mine.*"

"It was one of her favorite concerts. Reunion Tour 2004. She was there, singing with her girlfriends, happier than she'd ever been in her life." I'd heard that story a hundred times.

"Well, she loved them so much because *I* played it all the time. I always had music on. I probably got it from *my* grandma. She used to play the radio, and we'd dance."

Me and Mase, we never thought to look through

Grandma Lottie's albums before. We always thought that music was Mom's thing. But it started even before her. With Grandma Mary, and maybe before *her*, even.

"We've been listening to 'Hold On' our whole trip," Lorenzo tells her. "Ivy's mom made us a CD. Can I play this?"

"Of course you can play it," Grandma Lottie says.

Lorenzo seems to know just how to handle the album. He slides it from its inside paper cover and holds it at the edges using only his palms. He places it over the—whatever, the little thingy in the middle. He moves the long arm across and sets the needle down. There's a tiny *crickle*, and then come the familiar clear voices, singing about chains and change and holding on for one more day.

One more day, they urge, and I can do that. I can hold on until then, and even beyond.

The music fills me, and so does hope, and love, and that big ocean. The glass doors are wide open, and the smell drifts in, and it's just freedom out there. It goes on and on, no chain-link fence, no cage, nothing that says you can't, you won't, you must. It's just nature and our big old earth, doing all the natural stuff that it's always done, waves in, waves out.

"I've got to call Mom," I say. I picture her at that concert, and Grandma Lottie in some record store, sliding the album across the counter, and Great-Great-Grandma Mary, turning up the volume on the radio.

I take my phone out to the deck. Mom picks up on the first ring. There's her face, looking worried. "You okay?" she says, instead of "hello."

"I'm okay. I'm here." I hold out my phone and make an arc so she can see the big, wide Pacific.

"You sure are."

I bring her back. "Listen," I say.

"I know that album." She laughs.

"I'll fill you in on everything later, but I just wanted you to be here with us." I feel all teary again. It's music, and love. It's music and love and hormones, probably. After tomorrow I'll be on my way to my old self. Goodbye, hormones. Except, wait. I remember what Grandma Lottie said about every month, every single month, the possibility of yes or no, the thing you want or the thing you don't. We carry that—that responsibility, that fear, that promise. We do, inside our own bodies, day after day. I think of those protests, where you see the people with signs chanting, "My body, my choice," and I suddenly feel what they mean. *Really* feel it, because *my body.*

"It's weird. I'm the one at home, and yet I feel far away," Mom says.

"I love it here," I say.

"Yeah?"

"I mean, look." I hold the phone out again, this time just so she sees how far that beach goes. It's like the endless rainbow of Mr. Mysterioso's scarves, going on and on. "There's so much *room.*"

"I guess there is," Mom says. "Let me just see your face." She looks at me and I look at her. Her thoughts seem to have a hundred layers, same as the Pillars of Rome. "Precious you. I love you, Ivy."

"I love you, too."

"Can you put Grandma on?"

I do. They're out there for a long, long time, talking. A whole album long.

That night Lorenzo and I have another fingers-only touching under the sheets of the foldout bed. We leave the doors open, and there's cool air around us. I can see Lorenzo's beautiful brown eyes in the moonlight, and his freshly showered body, and his wet curls. There's a metal bar right under our backs, and the mattress is about an inch thick, but if Grandma weren't right there above us, and if Zeke weren't across the room staring, I'd pull Lorenzo right on top of me. Lorenzo . . . man, oh man. As Grandma said about Joey, as people have been saying about each other for eons, *whew.*

28

ALL NIGHT I HAVE BAD DREAMS ABOUT GOING ON A trip and getting lost. I wake up nervous. Lorenzo kisses me good morning. It's not a kiss like we had at the lighthouse—it's a sweet, *I'm not going anywhere* one. Grandma is already up. I hear the shower turn on upstairs. We get up, too, and Lorenzo folds the bed back in. So many things can feel like a before and an after, a beginning or an ending, when you're in that mood. The bed does.

At the last minute I decide that I don't want Lorenzo to come. I keep imagining everyone's eyes on him, thinking he's some wrongdoer. I also keep imagining what always happens in the movies, and happens in real life, too—a bunch of protesters at the entrance, spitting venom, threatening, making you feel ashamed or terrified so you'll change your mind. I see a girl rushing in, me, a coat over her head to protect her identity. I just want to be with Grandma, someone who knows, a woman connected to all the other women on that tree. Women who survived venom and fear and threats and shame. They'll be my protective coat, surrounding me and preserving my identity.

"You positive?" he asks.

"Yep."

"Okay. I'll be here," he says.

There's no big drama. In the movies—if he got me pregnant and wanted me to have an abortion, it would only be to show what an awful guy he is. Some other guy, a good guy, would save the day and become a dad.

"All right, Ivy, bus is leaving," Grandma says. It's what she always says when she drives us anywhere. I love that. It occurs to me just how much I love that, the way that the people you love just keep on being the people you love.

It doesn't take long to get there. The whole way, I stare out the window at the ocean, and then at the town of Rockaway Beach, and all the little houses, and all the lives you could have, as Grandma chats away about nothing.

When we reach the Tillamook Women's Center, there are no angry protesters. There's just a boring old building, a woman going in, a woman coming out. A shit car parked in one space, a really nice one in another. There's no drama here.

Right before I get out, it happens. I have a moment where I feel uneasy. I worry if I'm doing the right thing. I worry that maybe God will hate me.

In the movies we're at the part where no "good girl" would go through with it. She'd decide to have the baby after all, or something would happen so she wouldn't *have* to go through with it. Something to preserve her goodness. Right then she'd start bleeding or something. A miscarriage to save the day.

Instead Grandma opens her door, and so do I.

I peek my head in, expecting . . . I don't know what. But there's only a regular old doctor's waiting room, with padded chairs and magazines and an aquarium. We check in, same as at any other doctor's appointment. Everyone is friendly and matter-of-fact in the Tillamook Women's Center. There is no evil antiabortion figure, a fake nurse, shoving pamphlets at me, and there are no evil or heroic proabortion figures, either. There are just kind women, doing their jobs. There are objects that demonstrate care and calm, like framed photos of the nearby coastal beaches, and soothing music, and Kleenex boxes, just in case. A girl about my age sits next to her mother. She's doing stuff on her phone and doesn't look up. There's another woman dressed in business clothes, a suit and heels. She has manicured fingernails, highlighted hair, and she looks at her phone, too.

The teen goes in. And then the businesswoman. A couple enters, the guy about Lorenzo's dad's age, the woman a bit younger. A nurse calls me back, and Grandma squeezes my arm. "Love you, bunny," she says.

I follow the nurse, and the door to the waiting room closes behind me. The nurse tells me that her name is Marjorie and asks me how I'm doing in a way that seems like she really wants to know. She's about Mom's age, and her black hair is pulled up. She has glasses and friendly brown eyes. There's a paper-covered table, with the silver stirrups that I remember from my one trip to the gynecologist Mom brought me to when I turned sixteen. The stirrups are cozily tucked into a pair of socks, so they'll be warm. Marjorie shuts the door.

I fight the urge to explain myself, why I'm here, all my reasons. Instead Marjorie just places a blood pressure cuff on my arm and pumps the little bulb. "Perfect," she says, and removes it. "This is for you." She pats a gown, folded on the table. "Fashion statement, for sure."

I change into the blue-and-white gown. It smells clean, and the ties are slightly frayed, reminding me again of all the people who were here before me. The doctor knocks. She has short blond hair and crinkly smile wrinkles by her eyes. She squeezes my hand. When I lie back, there's a poster of a tropical island with a palm tree on the ceiling. The nurse returns, and she gives me a blanket that's been warmed and that has a comforting bleach-y smell. I get some medicine that makes me sleepy but not asleep. I scoot my butt to the end of the table, place my heels in the stirrups. I look at the clock: ten-thirty. Drowsy, pleasant palm-tree island, the vague awareness of a machine, and the nurse asking if I'm okay. And then I'm sitting up. The clock reads ten-forty-five. It's over.

A short while later Grandma and I are back in the car. In the film version I'd be tormented, crying, racked with a guilt that would never leave me. I'd start to bleed, maybe bleed to death. The scene would happen in a Victorian bed with blood-soaked sheets, or on the gory floor of a motel bathroom. But I'm only a little drowsy, vaguely crampy, and I'm wearing a pad, and there's regular old blood, nothing theatrical, nothing unfamiliar, even. What I feel is a quiet understanding that it's over, and that I am mine again. What I am is hungry. Starved. It's barely eleven-thirty, but Grandma stops at the Dockside Drive-In, and we get enormous cheeseburgers and fries and onion rings and vanilla malts, and Grandma stirs her with the straw and tells me about the book she's reading, about a woman who befriends an octopus.

Can a story without drama be a good story? Can a film without drama be a good film? Can we just have a story about love and being human, about making our way as best we can in the period of history in which we live? Because that story is every story, that story is plenty dramatic enough. Dramatic and awful and glorious and dark and hilarious; painful, too, and full of relief. So much relief that when a grandma slurps to the end of her milkshake, starts the engine of the car, and asks, "Music, or no?" you answer, "Music."

29

YOU ALSO THINK THE STORY IS DONE, BUT IT'S NOT. You are relieved it's over, but it's not over. I'm sure I've put the worst of this behind me, but the worst is coming. You can think that trauma is the big thing that happened, when it's really what comes after that. In the film version the decision is always the end of the story. There's a satisfying conclusion, and the credits roll.

In real life I go back to Grandma's house. I get in my pajamas. The day is all beautiful blue, and the doors are open, and the ocean is out there waiting, but I curl up on the couch under one of Grandma's quilts, the ones you need here by the ocean when the summer passes and winter storms kick up. I sleep. I hear their voices occasionally, Grandma's and Lorenzo's. I hear Grandma on the phone, too, with Mom, probably. But sleep just pulls me under, sleep like down feathers, sleep like meringue, soft and comforting. It's the medicine, but not just. It's relief. All of the knots that have been inside of me untie. All of the things I've been gripping let loose. I rest. I'm certain. I'm safe, I think.

I'm wrong.

We stay at Grandma's for a few days. At first I feel crampy and awkward with that pad, undesiring, undesirable, a body registering all that's happened to it. Emotional, too. I fight with Lorenzo because he mentions the sand in the house, and I think he's blaming me because I forgot to towel off my feet. *It's my sand as much as your sand,* he says, but I'm ready for blame, so I see it everywhere. When I talk to Mom, I snap at her for reminding me to wear sunblock. I think she's saying that I'm a child who makes bad decisions, when she's really saying that it's hard to take good care of yourself after you've been through something.

But then time and care and the wide Pacific do their jobs, and I feel better. I haven't gotten the uglies in two whole days. Love is doing battle with the traumatic stuff, and it's winning. On a beach walk with Lorenzo, I watch the water from a wave fill a tide pool. That's how I feel, right there, I think. Myself returning, spreading to the outermost edges.

Another time, Lorenzo and I walk all the way to the farthest point, where the tide has come in and we can't go any farther.

"We made it," Lorenzo says, looking at the distance we've come.

"We better hurry before we can't get back," I say. Already, the beach is narrowing, and we'll have to wade in a few spots.

"We'll get back," Lorenzo says. "Don't worry."

And then I ask him one of those things I hate myself for asking. It's Tess's fault, probably. It's hard to forget how Angel, her husband, the guy she loved, left her after finding out that Alec D'Urberville raped her. *You were one person; now you are another,* he said. I'm different now, too. "Do you still love me?"

"Ivy, Ivy. How can you ask that?" Right there and then he lifts me up. Me, with that pad, those mistakes, those insecurities. "Of course I do. You're my best everything."

⁓

The night before we leave, Grandma orders Thai food. In our house back in Paris, takeout is such a treat that you'd think you'd never get tired of it, but after so many nights of restaurant food, all I want are oranges and maybe Mase's Gai Lan Oyster Sauce Stir-Fry, which is really just broccoli in soy sauce. Grandma Lottie tries to make it a party. She puts on music, some of Mom's favorites, and her own favorites, too. Grandma Lottie doesn't have Nirvana and Pink and the Black Keys, but Mom doesn't have Martha and the Vandellas, and Sly and the Family Stone.

In spite of the thumping beat, and Grandma Lottie doing some shimmies as Zeke jumps up all wild, and in spite of eating off of paper plates balanced on our knees, and noodles spun around our forks, I feel sadness inching in. I'm going to miss her, Grandma Lottie, and I'm going to miss this place. We still have five more days of the trip home, but I'm worried about what will happen when we get back. Here, the ocean is so old, and it has seen so much that it makes you feel like you, too, can endure. There, we have a fake Eiffel Tower surrounded by churches, the City of Hope Church of God, in particular, with that chain-link fence around the baseball field.

Grandma Lottie catches me staring off. "Ivy," she says. "There's the world inside your head and the real one going on outside of it. It's better to spend your time in this one."

That night Lorenzo stamps our passports. *Kashunk.*

It's not an arrival, but an ending.

It's actually chilly the next morning when we leave. Fog lies along the beach as far as you can see. Grandma Lottie tosses on her jacket to say goodbye. Lorenzo and I are wearing our new Oregon Coast hoodies that he got us on a trip into town, featuring a whale's tail emerging from a wave. *Twins, like a couple of retirees,* he said when he gave mine to me, just as I had said in Florence.

Outside the Avalanche, Grandma Lottie hugs Lorenzo hard, and then me. When we separate, and I look into her blue eyes, I wish she knew Mom's secret, and that Mom knew hers. I wish they could have talked about true things that can bring people closer together. But I'll never say a word. Respecting other people, that's the main thing.

"I have something for you," Grandma Lottie says. It's tucked into the pocket of her coat. She hands it to Lorenzo. A CD.

"Road trip music!" Lorenzo says. "One for the way there, one for the way home. This is awesome."

"When did you make it?" I ask. I lean toward Lorenzo, and we look on the back, the song names written out in Grandma Lottie's small, bold writing. "These Boots Are Made for Walkin'" by Nancy Sinatra; "Women Is Losers," Janis Joplin; "I'm Every Woman," Chaka Khan; "Bad Reputation," Joan Jett; and more.

"The two of you took a lot of walks. One last hug," she says, and so we do.

"Thank you for everything. So much."

"Onward," she says.

We promised Mom that we'd head home the straightest, fastest way possible, major freeways only, and I'm running low on money, even with the cash Grandma Lottie shoved in my hand on our way out. But this is a coast full of lighthouses, so we've decided we'll stop at Cape Meares. At least,

Lorenzo has decided we'll stop at Cape Meares, and I give in after some pleading. We fly down Highway 101, Lorenzo singing, "Sis-tahs are doing it for themselves!" at the top of his lungs as I crack open a cold Mountain Dew for us to share. We get off at Bayocean Road, a narrow two-lane highway that hugs the coast with nerve-racking chummi-ness. I turn the music down. It's scary to even peek out my window, the drop-off is so steep.

"The exit is a mile ahead," I report. I can't wait to get there, off of this terrifying road.

The screaming of a siren barrels toward us, approaching fast, and my mind fills with horrible thoughts of cliffs and cars, murderous husbands and falling women. Lorenzo pulls over. There's not much room, that's for sure. The ambulance disappears up the road, but Lorenzo is still staring, watching it in his rearview mirror.

"Lorenzo? We can go." We're hanging on to that cliff by its own goodwill. If I opened my door, I could fall right out.

"You know, I've been thinking."

"Can we think when we're not about to fall into the ocean?"

"Right," Lorenzo says. He pulls back into the lane, and I exhale. A minute ago that two-lane highway was petrifying, but compared to the shoulder, this now feels safe.

"Okay, what were you thinking?"

"EMT," he says.

"Wait, wait. There's the turnoff."

Lorenzo takes it. Trees fold in on either side of us until they clear again. It takes a minute to realize we're on a high,

high cliff, a long jutting finger of land that ends with a drop-off to the sea.

"EMT?"

"That's what I'm going to do."

"Rescue."

"Rescue. As a job! A paid position. I've been thinking and thinking, and that's it. That's what I want to do. I bet there are hundreds of places I can get certified."

"You'd be so great at that," I say. He would. I try not to get all worried about those other words, "hundreds of places I can get certified." I try to remember what Grandma Lottie said, about the world I'm in right now, instead of the one in my head.

"I think it's the answer about what to do next. This whole way, every time I see an ambulance, it crosses my mind. And when I envision it, it just feels . . . *right.*"

"Well, sure. You'd be amazing," I say. "Up ahead. Half mile, turn off."

We drive until the road ends at a parking lot. "Hey, where's the lighthouse?" Lorenzo says.

"Down that little path." I point.

We park. Lorenzo takes my hand, and we run like little kids on a field trip. The path is forest and more forest, until straight ahead we see the tip of the lighthouse. It's squatty and white, with a lamp as big as its column.

"This is the shortest lighthouse in . . . I forget," Lorenzo says.

"It's pretty short, for sure. But wow." The Pacific that surrounds us—it seems so wise, as nature does sometimes, as if it holds all of life's truths, if only you could get to them. The waves break against the rocks below, and the spray rises high and splatters down again, splashy fun and serious business both.

"Hundreds of places *we* could go," Lorenzo says, out of nowhere.

"The real Rome, the real Paris, the real Manhattan," I say, even though the one thing I know for sure is that they are *all* real, especially to the people who live in them. When the people of Rome, Oregon, say *Rome,* they don't think of ancient ruins and the Colosseum; they think of one gas station/motel/restaurant. That should be respected, is my opinion. Same as the way the people of Rome, Italy, could never imagine a Rome where the whole town is one building, and that should be respected, too.

"The real right here," Lorenzo says, and holds me close.

We head back to the parking lot and our shit car, the Avalanche, but then something catches my eye. To our left there's a sign featuring an intriguing word and a large arrow pointing toward another path, one that disappears into the forest. Oh man—I veer Lorenzo toward our car because if he sees the sign, he'll make us go down there.

Too late.

"Octopus tree!" he shouts. He's already tugging on my arm, and yeah, okay, he's right, because you really shouldn't pass that up.

"What do you think it is?" I ask.

"Something cool." After all the disappointments of the Wonder Tower and Christmas Valley, Lorenzo is still optimistic. I guess he sees through wishes, too.

Down the path it's easy to tell when we've reached it. Fenced off in a patch of grass, there it is—this strange beast, an enormous Sitka spruce with no central trunk. Instead, *many* trunks extend and then rise from a singular spot, resembling an octopus, sure, but maybe even more, an entire forest in one tree. It's ancient, the sign says, and the forces that have shaped it are a mystery.

"Two hundred and fifty to three hundred years old," Lorenzo says.

Of course I think of it, that tree on Aunt Betts's wall, a single trunk with many branches, while here, it's many trees all in one. I think of all the women of my tree who stand or have stood as silent as this one, standing next to other silent trees in other families, and on and on and on, in Rome and in Rome, Lima and Lima, Paris and Paris.

"My great-great-grandma Mary . . . ," I say, and then I tell Lorenzo everything, about her and Alice and Betty. I don't tell him about Grandma Lottie or Mom, though, because privacy is a right, too. I try to explain, without the specifics, how women keep telling me their stories when they know my story. It's hard to find the words. "There's just so much silence," I say.

"One in four," Lorenzo says again.

"For hundreds of years, same."

"I had no idea it went back that far. This might sound weird, but after I read that, whenever I see a group of women, I count."

"I've been doing that, too, since you told me."

As we head back to the car, Lorenzo's humming "Sisters Are Doin' It for Themselves," because it's one of those songs that can get stuck in your head. He's a guy I know, really know, one who used to be a lifeguard, and who lost someone he loved, and who likes to draw lighthouses. Who can't pass up a place with an intriguing name. A guy who wants to rescue people for a living, and learn to cook, and who does a mean car dance. One I couldn't love more. A guy I'd go anywhere with, Rome or Rome.

"Pass me some Red Vines and let's get out of here," Lorenzo says. I fish around in my bag until, bingo, my fingers hit the familiar corner of cellophane.

He turns the key.

Nothing.

"Aw, *crap*!" he says.

He tries again.

Not even a *rrrr, rrrr, rrrr.*

"Shit!" he says. I just sit there, not saying a word.

One more time.

Nothing.

"Fuck!" After this swift ride up the hierarchy of swear words, Lorenzo pounds the steering wheel. I sigh.

"It doesn't even sound like a dead battery," I say. I know what it sounds like. Like our old Toyota Corolla that we had before Mr. Smiley. "It sounds—"

"Dead."

"Yup."

Lorenzo gets out anyway and looks under the hood. It's as pointless as looking in our refrigerator on a Monday, the day before Mom goes grocery shopping. There's not much to see. He slams the hood back down. He pops his head back in and shrugs. "We're not going anywhere. At least not in this shit car."

I call Grandma. We wait for her outside. Lorenzo and I lean our backs against the truck and look out toward the tip of the lighthouse. I try to remind Lorenzo that this shit car has been good to us, really good. I try to remind him to be generous, because we don't even know all she's been through, before she was his, even. She had all kinds of stories, long before she played a starring role in our own.

30

"MISSED ME ALREADY, HUH?" GRANDMA SAYS AFTER she pulls up.

"We're just lucky I took *this* out right before I turned off the truck," Lorenzo says, waving the CD. "I have no idea why I even did it."

"Some part of you must have known," Grandma Lottie says. She believes in those kinds of things. Don't even bother challenging her. You know how we DeVries women are with our opinions.

We pack up all our stuff and transfer it to Grandma Lottie's car. I'm worried about leaving the truck. It's like we're abandoning a friend, but, hooray, a tow truck's already coming down the road. Lorenzo's anger has vanished, and now he has his hand on the hood, saying a private good-bye. Grandma Lottie is thumping the tow truck driver on the back, and they're laughing like old friends, which, of course, they are. Grandma Lottie and Grandpa Larry were in the auto supply and repair business for years.

"She looks so sad on that hook," I say as the tow truck heads out.

"Man, this *sucks*," Lorenzo says from the back seat of Grandma Lottie's car. "Do you think she can be repaired?"

"Hell no," Grandma Lottie says. "But we're going to sell it for parts, and she'll have a whole new life, or lives. And you'll get a big fat check to buy another good shit car."

We say a second goodbye to Grandma Lottie. This time, at the departures gate of Portland International Airport.

"If you call me because your flight's been canceled, I'm going to think that the fates are trying to tell you something," Grandma Lottie says.

But in a short while, Lorenzo and I are sitting next to each other, in an airplane this time, with a woman who looks a little like Lorenzo's mom already on her laptop sitting in our aisle seat. We clutch hands as if it's our last day on earth as the nose lifts and we go skyward.

"She paid me way too much for that truck," Lorenzo says again. He told Grandma Lottie the same thing, but she was having none of it.

"You can't budge Grandma Lottie from something she wants to do."

"Sounds like someone else I know."

He looks at me again the same way he did in the Sahara Dunes that morning, with a face full of love and acceptance.

Wow, that stuff is powerful, that love, that acceptance. Some people—they can make you think differently about yourself in an awful and shameful way, and others . . . Well, let's just say Lorenzo makes me think that what happened with Drake Euwing was one understandable experience, and not who I am. I'm sure of it right then, as Lorenzo studies the laminated airplane safety card, and as I study him. I'm pretty sure, too, that this certainty will soon come tumbling right down, as fast as that cartoon figure on the inflatable slide. Up, down, hundreds of times, probably. That's just us being human, I guess, doing our best to figure it out—tiny person, huge cosmos, too many confusing experiences to truly make sense of them all. If someone is sure of themselves one hundred percent of the time, I'm not sure I want to meet that someone. Just—let's all struggle honestly, please. Let's all try to see the struggle with a little bit of that love and acceptance, huh? That's what I'm feeling as Lorenzo tucks that card back into the seat pocket and takes my hand.

In the film version of this movie, Lorenzo and I would be speeding home across the freeway, windows open, blasting "Hold On." You'd see it in my face, the way relief had replaced fear, and how love fought the bad guys and won. Our truck would disappear down that—wait, not a freeway. You never see those unless something's going to blow up, so a highway. You'd see our truck disappear down a highway in the yellow light of summer, and you wouldn't know what happened to us after that, but you'd feel pretty sure it was going to be good.

In real life the truck is dead, and we're heading back days early, a reentry that feels shocking and sudden. As much as I can't wait to see Mase and Mom and Wilson, I'm full of sorrow. In a matter of hours, Lorenzo will go to his house, and I'll go to mine. I'm also worried. Really worried. At home, what I've done is scandalous. The idea of this being one understandable experience will absolutely and without a doubt disappear. There, what I've done is against the law, and immoral.

"You okay?" Lorenzo asks.

"Anxious."

"Yeah."

"I'm sad it's over."

"So sad," he says.

In real life I've left relief back on Manhattan Beach. In real life Lorenzo is now pushing buttons on the airplane seat arm, wearing the only pair of earbuds we have.

"Hey!" he says. "I found an eighties playlist. Check it out."

This future EMT, he makes this sound accidental. But when I put one earbud in my ear, and he puts the other in his, it's a song from Grandma Lottie's CD. We both listen to Joan Jett scream-singing that she doesn't give a damn about her bad reputation. Lorenzo plays the drums as they go wild. The lady who looks like his mom turns to stare, but who cares. It turns out he does an awesome airplane dance, too.

It's totally strange driving Mr. Smiley again. My hands and feet barely know what to do, and the car seems like someone I used to know but don't anymore.

"It's weird being in your car with you driving," Lorenzo says.

"I was just thinking that exact same thing."

Mom and Mase picked us up at the airport, and now I'm bringing Lorenzo home. Outside the arrivals gate Mom hugged me like she hadn't seen me in years, even though we'd FaceTimed practically every day. As she drove us back, I held Lorenzo's hand and stared out the window, too emotional to look at him. Paris, Texas, looked smaller than I remembered. Our street seemed so narrow. When Diesel went wild and jumped up on the chain-link fence as we passed, I had to turn away. I'd forgotten how scary he was, with those sharp fangs, and his eyes past any point of reason.

"We're almost there already." Lorenzo's voice wobbles. "This was the shortest drive I've ever taken."

My throat is cinching tight, and my chest aches. "I'm going to miss you so bad."

"I'm going to miss *you*, Ives. I've gotten so used to having my favorite person right here." His eyes fill with tears. I pull in front of his house. It feels like a million years since we were last here. I see Lorenzo's sister, Chloe, peek through the drapes.

"Chloe knows about me," I say. Chloe does, and so do my neighbors, the Bransons, probably, and Maureen, and even Maureen's daughter, Cheyenne. So many people. My heartbreak at saying goodbye to Lorenzo is swiftly turning to something else. A deep realization that I am here, at home. That I am this girl, and not the one I thought I'd become.

"So? Chloe should know these things happen."

"I don't want to be her *lesson*."

"That's not what I meant."

"What about *Gene*?" I say sarcastically, and scowl.

"Don't hate him, Ivy. He's just a dude with an opinion."

Opinion. According to Mom, I'm someone who has lots of those. Having them—it always sounded harmless, a quirky character trait. It hits me, I feel it deeply, how brutal and devastating opinions can be. How dangerous, even.

My anxiety kicks up dust and swirls, same as when we sometimes spun around in the Avalanche when we realized we were going the wrong direction.

"And my dad isn't going to talk to anyone about you or me or any of this. He gave me his word," Lorenzo says.

I shrug. I'm trying to hold it together, but *it* is large—fear and grief and missing Lorenzo so bad already.

"It's going to be okay, Ives," Lorenzo says. But he doesn't sound so sure. The guy who proclaimed with such certainty that he wanted to be an EMT, the guy who ran on the beach with Zeke, who car-danced with abandon, whose eyes gleamed so sweetly in the morning light at the Pillars of Rome—he looks worried and tired. We wore our twin sweatshirts on the plane, and his is in a ball under his arm, and mine is tied around my waist, because here, it's too hot for them. When we pull Lorenzo's bags from the trunk, he gives me a long hug. I'm wishing I had a chance to brush my teeth so I can kiss him all minty instead of all airplane-y. But when we finally say goodbye, there is no long kiss to match the hug, only a brief one on my forehead, like people are watching. He hurries inside, as if he feels a hundred eyes.

31

THAT NIGHT MASE MAKES COQ AU VIN AND potatoes dauphinoise. The coq has no vin—it's just chicken with carrots and onions minus the wine, and the dauphinoise are scalloped potatoes from a box, a dollar twenty-nine, with enough garlic to ward off evil. But it's all so good. Wilson is staring up at me, doing his best polite-boy pleading, and he's right to want it.

"You missed me," I say to Mase.

"Not a bit."

"You cried every day I was gone, you missed me so much."

He rolls his eyes. He's cutting his meat funny, his fork upside down. It's something new.

"What are you doing with your fork?"

"It's how they do it in Europe," he says, like I couldn't be more clueless.

"He's been trying to get me to push peas up on my fork

with a knife, but I gave up," Mom says. She's using her extra-cheery voice, the one that sounds like a kindergarten teacher mixed with those annoying wind chimes we sell at Euwing's Drugs alongside the LOVE BLOOMS IN MY GARDEN signs. *Used* to sell. The wind chimes we, I, *sold* at Euwing's Drugs. I don't have a job anymore, and this takes me by surprise every time I remember it.

Mom's bluebirds-and-sunshine voice—it means something is very wrong. She used it a lot during The Beast. Mase is tense, too, and his room is superclean, I noticed, the same way he used to keep it during Mom's illness, with his pillows all lined up equidistant. I realize something else: there's no music on. The house is silent.

"What do you say! How about we all watch a movie together tonight!" Mom burbles. "Some fun rom-com? It just hasn't been the same here without you."

"That's for sure," Mase says.

"You hate rom-coms!" I say. Mase stares out the window, and Mom pushes a carrot around. "What's going on? When I was getting my stuff out of the car, you hurried me in here like the paparazzi were going to leap out any second."

"You need to tell her," Mase says. Something else is different. His voice sounds deeper. He's still the same skinny Mase, but things are changing.

"Ughhh!" Mom says. Whatever it is, they've been fighting about it.

"She can't just go walking around all unaware."

"Unaware of *what*?"

"It's not *safe*." Mase has barely eaten. Maybe two bites of potatoes, because even under stress, potatoes are hard to resist. The word *safe*—it's a rock thrown through a window. Something shatters inside me.

I don't say anything. We sit in silence. I just beam my eyes into Mom's, because knowing is always better than not knowing, even when it's awful. Of all people, she should understand that.

"A woman—" she says.

"*First*, a woman," Mase interrupts.

"Would you just let me—" Mom snaps.

"Ughhh!" he says now.

"First, a woman came into the shop."

"Okay," I say.

"The day after Mrs. Euwing did. The woman . . . She just came right up to me, when I was cutting some fabric for a customer. She plunked down her purse and said, 'I cannot believe what you're doing. Promoting the abortion rights agenda in your own *home,* with your own *daughter.*'"

The chicken swirls with the potatoes in my stomach and with the gross sandwich from the plane and with the Egg McMuffin we had for breakfast. Dread dauphinoise. It seems suddenly shocking, the way flight can bring you from one state to another in a matter of hours.

"Oh, Mom . . ." I groan. "What did you do?"

"I didn't do anything. I didn't have time. She left. The customer was waiting, so I kept cutting, and then I handed her the fabric. I was in shock. I mean, 'the abortion rights agenda,' what the hell."

"And then—" Mase says, and Mom glares at him.

"Wait," I say. "Wait a second. What woman? Did we know her? I mean, was this just some random person?"

Mase and Mom look at each other.

"Oh my God! Who?"

"Mrs. Phelps."

"Mrs. Phelps? Our *principal*, Mrs. Phelps?" I see her, her blond bob and belted dress, handing out honor society awards at the end-of-the-year assemblies. Handing out awards to *me*.

Mom presses her fingers to her eyes.

"No. No way. I can't go back there! There's no *possible* way I can go back there. Our very own principal?" I shove my chair back. I'm having a hard time breathing.

"Ivy, we will work this out, I promise you. We will."

"We should sue her butt," Mase says with his new man-voice. "Aren't we supposed to have freedom of religion? It sure doesn't seem like it when their religion is our laws."

"I can't," I say. "I can't do this." I get out of there. I accidentally knock over my chair, sending Wilson scuffling. I feel so bad, scaring him, making the people I love go through this embarrassment and mess.

I slam my door. I'm breathing so hard, my chest is heaving, as if I'm going up the longest, hardest hill. What flashes in my mind are those women, the tens of thousands of them, who were "examined" against their will, who were suspected of defiling or scamming men because they went out alone. What did they feel inside when that was happening? Did their chests heave as if they were going up the longest, hardest hill? Did they feel dread dauphinoise?

I flop onto my bed. I mash my pillow over my head. I'm so tired. I'm so done.

But wait. Wait. I get up. I rummage madly around and find my Tess book. I flip through the passages I highlighted, until there . . . There.

Let the truth be told—women do as a rule live through such humiliations.

By some miracle, I doze. The pillow is off my head, flung to the floor because it's a jillion degrees. There's a knock at my door.

"Ivy?" It's Mom. I glance at the clock—it's only eleven p.m. With a gross *whoosh,* my life returns to me. Mrs. Phelps, with her calm smile as she walks the halls, with her firm voice when she talks into the microphone at assemblies. *Attention, students!* Everyone listens when she speaks. She has *authority,* and it was wrong of me to think I was only in danger from men who make laws and men who lead churches. We always used to joke about the size of Mrs. Phelps's engagement ring. My mind is being hit with asteroids in every direction, *bam, bam, bam,* because why do we even have those, huh? Jewelry is fun, I get it, but what's the deal about *Ooh! Let me see the ring,* and the size of it, and the dude not getting one. What's it saying, huh? She's valuable because he plunked a bunch of money down? Mrs. Phelps has a big, important job. Maybe Mr. Phelps should've gotten a ring.

Mom sits on the bed.

"Everything feels bad," I say.

"It's going to be okay," she says.

"How?"

"No idea. But it will."

"Why do people hate women so much?"

"Same reason they hate lots of groups of people. They're worried we're powerful."

"This is almost worse than, you know, *that*. What happened with, ugh, *him*." I say it, but I don't know if it's completely true. I flash on that chain-link fence, that smeary wetness on my hand and the rest of me. I push away the gross thought. That was awful, this is awful. The abortion, though, it *wasn't* awful. It was the thing that could heal the awful. I remember the relief I felt, thinking I left the awful behind, but here it is again. "I was starting to be okay, but now I'm not."

"I think that's the idea," Mom says. "I mean, socially ostracizing people is one of the oldest punishments there is. Shame is a powerful deterrent. But it relies on you to participate."

"I'm trying to summon Joan Jett," I say.

"Joan Jett?"

"Not giving a damn about my bad reputation."

"Oh, *I* know the song. But how do *you* know it? Don't tell me. Grandma."

"She made me a CD."

Mom smiles. "She used to play it for me. Pretty much through my entire junior year. The ex-girlfriend of a guy I started dating spread some rumors about me. Why he was with me and not her, I guess."

"You never said."

"I didn't even remember it until just now. But, wow, right then I thought I was going to *die*."

"People have sure been obsessed with the idea of girls having sex," I say. "For eons."

"That's for sure."

She hugs me. When we separate, I feel all choked up again. Not about what's bad, but about how the people you love get you through what's bad. It seems like the most beautiful thing in the world, people being there for each other. "Mom? I just . . ." I can hardly speak.

"I know, Ivy," she says, and she does. "Me too."

I can't sleep.

It's Mrs. Phelps, but not just. It's her and Faith, and Peyton, how we still haven't talked after her *Don't put me in the middle* text, how she hasn't even reached out to see how I am. It's my school, and the town I love, and my whole future. I also just miss Lorenzo. I want to call him right then, but it's after midnight now, so I don't.

Instead I do something I haven't done in a long while, not since The Beast, and those nights I would lie awake, sick with worry. I head out to our backyard and climb up the tree right next to the house. The night air is cooling and smells like hay and earth, and my hands and feet remember what to do. The biggest leap is from the one long branch that, from the ground, appears to end at the roofline but doesn't. It actually heads in its own direction, to the roof and over. If you scoot right across it without looking down, you'll get the greatest view you can imagine.

And so I scoot, and I don't look down, but I don't look over, either. It's dark, and when I finally glimpse that hump of a figure there, I scream.

And then *he* screams. "Jesus, Ivy," Mase says. "You scared the crap out of me."

"*You* scared the crap out of *me*! What are you doing up here?"

"The same thing *you're* doing up here."

"Are you two all right?" Mom shouts from her bedroom window below.

"We're fine!" I shout back. "She knows we come up here?" I say to Mase.

"*She* comes up here."

"She does?" I arrange myself next to my brother. He does first-class roof sitting. He even brought a blanket.

"There was half a pack of wintergreen Life Savers up here last time." Mase and I hate those, but Mom loves them.

We gaze out at the Paris, Texas, Eiffel Tower, with its red, white, and blue lights and red hat tilted at the top. I almost don't want to ask. "So what else happened? After Mrs. Phelps. At dinner you said, 'And then . . .'"

Mason sighs. "It's bad, Ivy."

I grip my toes tight to the roof. How much farther could I fall? "Just say it, Mase. God, I don't need the buildup."

"Don't snap," he scowls. "Someone called CPS on Mom. You know, Child Protective Servic—"

"I know what it is."

"Maybe it was Mrs. Phelps, no idea. But a social worker came over. Apparently, someone was 'worried' that Mom wasn't fit to parent, since she let you go off with Lorenzo to have an abortion. The woman walked around our house and asked questions, and decided it was all bogus, but still. I could've—*we* could've—been taken away from her."

A horrible bitterness rises up my throat. "I'm so sorry, Mase. I'm so, so sorry at what I put you both through." I feel sick.

"*You* didn't put us through that. Mrs. Phelps did. Or whoever else called. *They* did. We've got to get out of here, Ivy," Mase says with his man-voice.

I almost say, *I don't know where we could go,* but I do. I know hundreds of places we could go, as soon as we remember we're not stuck here. We're lucky, though. So lucky, and it's good to remember that. So many people *can't* go. So many people *are* stuck. So many people are more and more stuck because they can't get to Oregon like I just did.

"Someday I want to visit the real Paris," Mase says as we stare at that glowing red cowboy hat suspended in the dark sky. "Maybe I'll even live there and learn French cooking."

"You should," I say. "You will." I want to tell him about the real bliss and the real wonder. I want to tell him how big the world really is. How many people, and places, and possibilities there are, and how badly I wish those possibilities belonged to everyone. Also: how many different ways of thinking and seeing things there are. When I look at Mase, though, he's got this expression of weariness and longing, like he already knows all of this, just from being Mase. So instead of saying anything, I take his hand, and we sit up there, too high, in the dark, at the tip of a branch of our family's tree.

32

WELL, I DID IT. I GOT MY COURAGE UP AND CALLED Peyton, and here we are.

"I'm home," I tell her.

"That's great, Ivy," she says. "I'm super happy you made it back safe."

She picked right up, which is a good sign. But her voice is kind of distant, which is a bad one. This is Peyton, you know. She's my friend, a real friend, someone who loves me. I think she does. It hasn't seemed like it lately, but I'm pretty sure. If she's somehow gone, too . . . everyone's gone. Everyone who isn't family and Lorenzo.

"You're not going to believe what Mrs. Phelps did," I say, and then I tell her. She's really quiet for a long time, and I'm not sure what kind of quiet it is, only that it's very uncomfortable.

"Wow," she says finally.

"Do you want to do something today?" Mom's at work, and Mase is on his bed reading the Julia Child cookbook

Mom got him at the used bookstore last week, and Lorenzo's going to spend the day looking for a car, and, usually, this would be the most normal question ever. It doesn't feel normal, though. So much is weighing on Peyton's answer, it's like I'm asking her to marry me.

"Uh," she says.

"I could come over, and we could play *Mario Kart.*" It's something we do. Or did. Peyton's mom doesn't let her play anything more violent or adult, so we speed around in our cars or little airplanes, crashing into each other on purpose. Suddenly, this seems like a long time ago.

"Oh shoot," she says. "I can't. I've got a doctor's appointment, and then my mom and I are doing some errands after."

I'm not sure if she's lying. I don't think so. I'm trying not to see through wishes, but I think she's really going to the doctor. "Are you okay? The doctor and all?"

"Regular checkup, ugh."

"I miss you," I say. "I want to see your face."

"Me too, Ivy. We will."

She has to go, so we hang up. I don't know who else to call, who is safe to call, but I have people who love me, and I am fierce, you know, on occasion, maybe even now, and I remember Grandma's friend Betty, and the women in my family, and Esilda, and so many women who went through much worse, who still do, all over the world. So I hunt around for my bathing suit and then put it on. My body is still my body. It's not my enemy. I'm kind of proud of it, how hard it works and the stuff it has to endure in order to carry my self around.

"Heading out," I yell to Mase. Wilson gives me a look full of sorrow. For him the saddest sad is people leaving, and the most joyful joy is people returning. He probably has that exactly right.

"Wait! Wait," Mase yells back. He's racing my way. I hear urgent, thumping feet, and then here he is, in that pair of shiny sports shorts that he wore for one unhappy season on a summer basketball team. Also, that tank top he made from cutting off the arms of an old T-shirt, which features a teeth-baring *Tyrannosaurus* and the word SMILE. "Is Lorenzo going with you?"

"No. He's getting a new car, since the Avalanche is finished."

Mase makes a face to say, *Ivy, the avalanche is definitely not finished.* "Do you think you should go alone? How about I come with you?"

I snort. The idea of him protecting me is hilarious. Also, I'm not going to hide forever. So what if anyone makes me feel bad.

⌐

Kids from New Jefferson High hang out at the pool here in the summer, so I tell myself this is good practice for going back to school in September. It's already crowded, with moms sitting on lounge chairs scooted together and little kids screaming in the water. I see that Quentin Giles, who was stoned pretty much throughout all of last year, somehow got a job as a lifeguard. When I walk around the shallow end, heading toward the deep, I remember how Lorenzo used to be a lifeguard. I try to hold that image close to me, because people can be there for you, even if they're somewhere else.

I find a vacant chair and scoot it closer to the edge. I need the shortest walk to the pool possible, because even on a regular day, I feel self-conscious in my bathing suit, unlike, say, Olivia Kneeley, who walks all around in her bikini with such confidence. Olivia Kneeley. Oh God. It all comes rushing back, that test sliding across the floor, landing under her seat. I fight off the uglies, which are back again on this sunny summer day.

I lift my cover-up over my head. I see a couple of kids from school, a year younger than me, in Drake's class. They're not even supposed to matter, younger kids, who cares, but I see their heads bent toward each other. One looks straight at me and starts to laugh.

This was a bad idea, a really bad idea. I'm slowly realizing it, too slowly. My body feels so exposed. More exposed, way more, than it felt when I sat here last year with my friends, goofing around and having fun, when no one knew the most private things about me. Those kids are picturing me and Lorenzo. They're picturing some film version of what just happened to me. I see Trevor Lively, too, and remember him and his girlfriend, Jayna, at the concert that night.

I take out *A Game of Thrones,* which Peyton gave me for my birthday last year. Between work and school, I didn't have time to read anything that thick, but I have the time now. I open the cover, and just past the map, there's a prologue. And it strikes me right then how critical they are, the befores before the start. You can't quite understand the whole story, can you, without that information? *Why does history matter?* Ms. La Costa asked. Well, I'll tell you, but it's going to take a while.

Little kids are waddling around with water wings on, and other ones are jumping in the pool and diving for pennies. Quentin Giles blows his whistle, and I look up. But it's not the running kid who's sharply being told to *Walk!* that gets my attention. It's Faith and Peyton and Noah Alvarez walking through the entrance. They actually join Olivia Kneeley, who was barely friendly to us before. Peyton and Noah are holding hands. She never even mentioned that they're together now.

My face burns. I want to cry, but I don't. I keep trying to read George R. R. Martin, talking about the cold, and about the things that can be learned from the dead. I keep my eyes down. I want to run so bad. I want to be gone, gone, but I realize there's that chain-link fence all around me. Through it, I can see our car and freedom, but I have to get out first. I tell myself to *Hold On*, that I don't give a damn about my bad reputation, but nothing is working.

"Hey."

I glance up. I've known Peyton so long that it hurts to look into her face. I love that face. I clench my teeth so I don't say something ugly, something I'll regret. "How was *the doctor?*"

"Ivy," she says. "I'm sorry." Her face doesn't look sorry. It looks distant. "It's just that my mom thinks—"

"Your mom thinks, your dad thinks, Faith thinks . . . Do you ever have an opinion that's your own?"

"This conversation isn't going to go anywhere." Peyton folds her arms.

"Yeah, probably not," I say.

Peyton turns and walks away, her flip-flops hitting her heels. She turns away, just like that. Can you hate a ponytail? Because I do. I hate the way it swishes back and forth so righteously as she heads toward Faith and Noah.

I force myself to sit there, pretending to read the book she gave me for my birthday. I stay in that spot as my skin crawls with shame and embarrassment and wrongdoing. I force myself to get up, to walk to the edge of the pool, same as Olivia Kneeley would. I swirl my toe in the water, as if testing the temperature. Well, I know the temperature. It's cold.

I sit back down as long as I can stand it. Then I get the heck out of there.

"I wasn't fierce," I say to Lorenzo. We're in his driveway, and he's beaming with appreciation at his new shit car. It's got a wide, flat nose, with headlights that rise up like the eyes of a crocodile rising from water, and it's the color of off-season tomatoes. It looks like something from the past and the future both.

"Seriously, you're supposed to go through all this *and* be fierce?"

"I think so."

"It seems like that's asking a lot. Look at this interior, huh? I've got to show your grandma. She's going to love it."

"It's great, Lorenzo." It smells like cigarettes, and the inside is a tan-gold from days gone by. The driver's seat has one of those beaded seat-cover things that are supposed to massage you while you drive but that look like someone's craft project from the 1970s. "How old is it?"

"You don't want to know. But, Ivy, sometimes I go from fierce to terrified in the space of five minutes."

I suddenly remember. "Like when you kayak."

"Like when I kayak," he says. "Like when I do tons of things. Pretty much when I ever try anything new, let alone go through something like you have. When I tell you the name of this car, you're going to know why I just couldn't resist her."

"Tell me."

"What was I thinking, getting a truck called an Avalanche? What did we expect, huh? The tide is turning, Ivy." He pats the long, flat nose. "This one's called a Triumph."

33

IN SPITE OF THE NEW TRIUMPH, MY MOOD SLIDES down, down over the next few weeks. I try to apply for a few jobs, with no luck. I help Lorenzo fix some problems in the Triumph, problems that cars don't even have anymore, and other problems that we still do. I hang around Mase as he cooks, reading aloud the weirdest recipes from Julia Child, like Waterzooi of Chicken, which is basically a chicken stew with six eggs and cream, gross.

"Mom would kill you if you used up that many of our eggs, and we never have cream."

"Ivy, would you *stop*? You keep losing my place. Find something else to do."

I try a paint-by-numbers that Mom brings home from Shelley's Craft and Quilt, bought from the sale bin with her employee discount, a cat playing a violin. I pull out Mase's old Mr. Mysterioso kit, but I can't make anything disappear. Not the things I most want to, anyway. Not images of Mrs. Phelps, and Faith, and Peyton. Not images of chain link, and of the Euwing family, with Drake driving the family truck, with Mrs. Euwing riding in the back.

"Are you seriously wearing my old cape?" Mase asks.

"It looks dashing," I say, and take a spin, trying to make it fly out, same as when you're four and actually believe that a piece of cloth fastened around your neck gives you powers. Then again, it probably *is* true for a lot of men in their business suits and ties.

Tucked inside our house, in the brilliant blue of summer, I convince myself that boredom is my biggest problem.

It isn't. Not by a long shot.

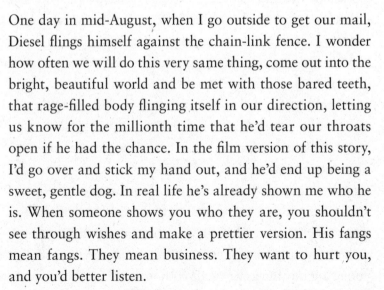

One day in mid-August, when I go outside to get our mail, Diesel flings himself against the chain-link fence. I wonder how often we will do this very same thing, come out into the bright, beautiful world and be met with those bared teeth, that rage-filled body flinging itself in our direction, letting us know for the millionth time that he'd tear our throats open if he had the chance. In the film version of this story, I'd go over and stick my hand out, and he'd end up being a sweet, gentle dog. In real life he's already shown me who he is. When someone shows you who they are, you shouldn't see through wishes and make a prettier version. His fangs mean fangs. They mean business. They want to hurt you, and you'd better listen.

It's so hot out that I can barely touch the little metal

clip on our mailbox. I retrieve our electric bill, and one of those envelopes full of coupons we'll never use—window replacements, carpet, improvements you can make while staying in the same place. J. J. Alvarez is riding a new bike around our street, no helmet on. He spots me, and he starts going superfast, butt up off the seat, legs pumping. I think he's trying to impress me, so when he skids to a stop right there, his tires swerving in a half circle, I smile at him.

"Nice," I say.

But he's not trying to impress me.

"You crimed against God."

His dark eyes drill into mine, and he says this with the sort of utter certainty that always makes you want to punch someone, I swear. " 'Crimed' isn't even a real word."

"Baby murder." And now he says *this* with a dark glee. He sets the words there like a challenge, like he's learned one of the lewd, racy secrets of the adult world and is now taunting with an adult's power. Someone cut his bangs badly; they're as uneven as a mountain range, and he's a kid other kids make fun of, larger than the rest, hurtling into manhood with early body odor and a big head. And he's wearing one of his dad's T-shirts with a Harley on it and old yellowed pit stains. But he has an authority and a dominance over me right then that is hard to explain. Maybe it's just because he took it and is wielding it. Maybe it's because, right then, I am sure that this argument, about women and their bodies, about women and their rights, about abortion in general, won't move an inch from where it is now. Not when kids this young already burn with righteousness.

And not when I burn with shame.

All at once I burn with anger instead. Sure, it's easy to be angry and to stand up to this kid, but whatever.

"Do you think an eleven-year-old girl who gets raped should have to have a baby?" I snarl.

He narrows his eyes. "*That* would never happen." He looks unsure.

"Check your facts, you little twit," I say.

That very same night I get an email. I hardly ever get emails, but I see a little number one by the mailbox on my phone. It looks so friendly, like an invitation, but after J. J. Alvarez, I'm even more afraid to open it. I don't recognize the address, but I recognize the number that makes up the subject heading: *$286.*

It's the same number that used to be on the paychecks that I don't get anymore. The ones that I used to deposit as I smiled at Mrs. Florence, the bank teller who always winked and then gave me a sucker even though they're for little kids. I don't even like those suckers, especially the gross root beer ones, but I liked that she gave them to me. I liked the ordinary kindness, the simple generosity. She seemed proud of me, coming every two weeks to invest in my future. *Investing in your future*—it's what she said once, her fingers tiptipping on the number pad.

Mr. Euwing's email reads like a letter. *Dear Miss DeVries: Your final check is here waiting for you. Signed, Mr. Euwing.* It wasn't just signed; it actually said *Signed.* It looks so childish. Something out of a kids' book, a note written from the badger to the aardvark after a fight that ends their long friendship. In the book they'd learn about seeing another person's point of view and become friends again. In real life I need that $286, but maybe not bad enough to set foot in that place.

"I don't want you going there alone," Mom says when I show her. "I mean, why didn't the guy just put it in the mail? It's not safe."

When I get up to go to the bathroom that night, I see Mom at her laptop, doing something I've seen her do a few times now: looking at houses in Oregon.

"Are we moving?" I ask, and she startles.

"Do you want to?"

How do I explain? *Yeah,* I want to. But also, like just today with J. J. Alvarez, an *I'll show you* fury winds up stubbornly through my body. "*Can* we, even? I mean, what about Dad?"

"You see him over the summer. You could fly. He wouldn't mind." She suddenly looks guilty. Really guilty. Worse than when she accidentally got bleach on my favorite jeans.

"What?" I'm scared. No, panicked. "You talked to him. Oh my God, you talked to Dad. You didn't *tell* him, did you?"

"Of course I didn't tell him! But yeah, okay? I talked to him. I just . . . floated the idea. Of maybe moving."

"What did he say?"

"He was really nice about it, actually. He said, 'Texas was never your home. It was mine.'"

A stone sinks inside me. I'm not sure how I feel about this. I mean, maybe I'd like a little more protest from him. Then again, it's relieving, too. Options are. The stone floats back up. Maybe it's not a stone after all. "Does this mean *you* want to move?"

"I don't know, Ivy. This place just looks different to me now."

I understand exactly what she means. This is our home, you know? Even if my friends and I always complained there isn't much to do here, only go to the movies, or bowl, or whatever . . . I love Paris. I used to love Paris. The town square with the big white fountain in the middle . . . In the summer people hang out and eat ice cream on the steps, and in the winter it's magical, decorated with wreaths, the trees all lit, especially the biggest one with the star on top. The Christmas parade, too, when you watch the floats of snow-men and covered wagons pulled by reindeer, and wait for the big moment when Santa and Mrs. Claus ride by on the fire truck so you can scurry to grab the tiny candy canes they throw . . . And the pumpkin festival, with the pump-kin patch and contests for best costumes. The beautiful American Legion Building, with its white pillars and intri-cate windows. The Grand Theater, which people have been trying to bring back for years. You can tell the leaders care about making this a nice town to live in. You're connected to most everybody.

And I want to think of it like that, as a nice place to live. Even when the patio tables and chairs the city put out around the fountain were stolen. Even when you sometimes saw drug deals there. Even though our history includes a lynching tree at the courthouse, and even though Sam Bell Maxey, owner of that beautiful Victorian house, was a Confederate general. Even though one of our most famous statues is supposedly Jesus in Cowboy Boots in the cemetery but actually looks like a very sad woman slumped over a cross. Even though the Grand Theater is full of asbestos. Even though it's hard to get a picture of the Eiffel Tower without the dumpsters in the back. Even though you're connected to most everybody, in ways that become ugly. Even though there are chain-link fences basically everywhere.

"I'll go with you, if you want to get it," Lorenzo says. He's talking about that check, because I can't stop thinking about it. I imagine a big confrontation, where I'm destroyed. I imagine a big confrontation, where I'm victorious.

"I asked him to mail it, but he ignored me. Mom thinks it's a trap of some kind." We're in Lorenzo's backyard, sitting in a couple of lawn chairs, the sprinkler slowly waving back and forth between us. I'm so hot that I scoot my chair close enough for the water to hit my lap. Lorenzo is farther back, and it only sprinkles his toes. I want that money, money I earned, but I'm afraid to go in there. I used to feel so proud to work at Euwing's, but it scares me now.

"Those people can be dangerous, Ivy. Shit. They threaten women. They blow up clinics."

Still, I feel some pull in me to walk straight in there and . . . I don't know exactly. Just, something. My stomach churns, bad Taco Bell times a thousand, like something needs out. Fury, maybe. Truth, probably.

"I have to show you something," Lorenzo says. He comes over to my side of the sprinkler, waving his phone. "There are these *escorts,* right? At abortion clinics? People who go with patients to their appointments so they can get in there safely. You know, through any protesters? You've gotta see."

"Sure," I say.

"I can't stop watching what's happening. Those people— the protesters, you wouldn't believe what they do. They shout stuff into megaphones . . . Aim their cameras onto private property, filming patients going in. They take their pictures and put them on the *internet.* You see these women, reading from the Bible, or holding signs, screaming about murder . . . and dudes—old dudes, looking like some retiree you'd see on a golf course, posing as a fake doctor, or screaming stuff at the escorts and the women going in, how they should act like ladies. How they've become hard and callous and unfeminine women, wrapping themselves up in 'fake manhood' . . . Young dudes, too. It's scary, man, the way they just stare, all intimidating, or shout threatening stuff about Jesus right in people's faces. . . ."

Maybe I don't want to see. There's so much bad energy in the air. I feel it closing in. I feel it like an electrical storm, or a gas leak, suffocating and dangerous. Lethal. It's all around me right here in my state, in my town, on my street, just when I go get the mail. It's right here in a ten-year-old kid on a bike.

"But look . . . ," Lorenzo says. He pushes the *#clinicescorts* hashtag, and when he does, I don't just see hate and harassment. I see people of all ages and genders wearing rainbow-colored vests, silently and calmly guarding clinic entrances, shielding patients using rainbow-colored umbrellas. I see the people in those rainbow vests dancing to songs, wearing cozy hats and scarves to stay warm in the cold, faces as still as those palace guards in London as people scream that they're going to hell, that they need to repent, screaming about spread legs. Praying that terrible things will happen to them.

Now here's an old, old guy, eighty years old at least, a clinic escort in his rainbow vest. He's playing polka music with an accordion to drown out the protesters.

"Rainbows and accordions," I say. In terms of weapons in a battle, they're sure not violent. They're not even very *fierce*.

"I never knew polka could be so reassuring," Lorenzo says.

⌐

That night I can't sleep again. I fight back images of that paycheck and Drake and Mrs. Phelps. Chain link becomes coat hangers become barbed wire becomes a cage, things that are brutal and inescapable. People won't change their opinions on this, they just won't. And people get to have their own opinions. But they shouldn't get to scream and harass and shame. They shouldn't get to bully and terrify and harm. They shouldn't get to shut down options so other human beings are forced into life-threatening and unbearable corners. I keep seeing the eyes of that man with the red beard and baseball cap in the video, staring, staring, like the most silent and dangerous man hiding in a parking garage in the most frightening films. I keep seeing the clean, righteous faces of the men in tidy polos and slacks, too. I can hear one of their voices in the video, still persistent over the upbeat sound of the polka music. *You need to act like a lady. You're not a lady,* he says to one of the escorts.

I think about Betty, and Tess, and all the women on all the family trees, going back and back, and about the men policing the dangerous, seductive, powerful bodies of women. I think about something else again, too. About how lucky I am, because I, at least, had Lorenzo and the Avalanche, and I had Mom, and I had enough money to buy gas, and to stay at the Sahara Dunes, and I had Grandma Lottie, with her house on the beach, who could bail us out of trouble if we ever decided to let her. So many people didn't have those things, going back and back. We could find a way, we could go somewhere else, but lots and lots of people will never be able to find a way, and that's part of the point, probably.

Keeping women, keeping people with few options, in their place.

Sometimes—no, a lot of times . . . all of this doesn't even seem like it's about babies. It seems like it's about what it's always been about. People using their power, same as always, to keep their power.

34

MOM TURNS DOWN THE MUSIC. I HAVEN'T HEARD this song before. It's all noisy guitars and an angry chorus, the performer screaming, "I hate everything about you."

"Who are you thinking of when you play this?" I ask. "Terry?"

"The Beast," Mase guesses. He's plating up dinner. Chicken with pommes persillade and petits pois. Basically, chicken and potatoes and peas. It's too hot for this kind of food. I'd be fine with a bowl of cereal and a Popsicle, but Mase has got to do what he's got to do.

"Paris," Mom says.

"Don't hate the real one, because I'm going to live there one day," Mase says. A pea rolls off the table and lands on our flaking linoleum. Wilson snatches it. How disappointing for him.

"This is the real one, too," I remind Mase. "Like it or not."

Mom sits at her place at the table, in the very same spot

I've seen her practically every day of my life. "Let the family meeting commence," she says. "Item number one on the agenda . . . Okay. It's the only item."

She looks at me, and so does Mase. They're giving me two votes to one, at least. They're letting me decide, when we should all decide. Stay or go. *Go* is all delicious release. *Go* is a new life. *Go* is giving up and giving in.

Stay, though? Stay is that stubborn swirl inside my body, rising. It's the fierceness of the DeVries women, reminding me that I'm one of them. Stay is *Make these people see and understand*. But it's longing, too. Need. *Stay* is my home. *Stay* is *Make these people look at the Ivy they supposedly* loved. *Make them see and understand* her.

Stay is unfinished business, like it or not.

"Stay," I say.

"Ivy, are you *sure*?"

Mase goes silent.

I've been watching those videos now, too. So *many* videos of girls, women, transgender men, nonbinary people, fierce and brave and up-front about their abortions. They have a mission. I want to be like that. I think I want to be like that. It seems like what I'm supposed to do. "Yeah," I say.

"You can finish school at home, even if we don't move," she says.

"I can do this," I say. I drop a piece of chicken down to Wilson to make up for the pea.

Mase looks like he might cry.

"If I run away, they win." It sounds like something you're supposed to say. I probably saw it in a movie, many, many times.

From the moment we get out of the car, I do it. I scan the area, like the Secret Service before the presidential motorcade arrives. Only, it's just Mase and me locking up Mr. Smiley and heading from the parking lot into Walmart. We have to pass the clothes and the electronics and the sporting goods; the makeup, the toys, the shoes and accessories. So far I don't see anyone we know, but I remain on alert, because a sniper might be hiding behind that display of ninety-nine-cent notebooks. Toward the end of August, this aisle is the most crowded one.

"Remember when getting school supplies used to be exciting?" I ask Mase.

"Whatever," he says. He walks glumly beside me. He's barely spoken to me for the last four days, ever since I said, *Stay.*

"Remember when Mrs. Whipple made you write your name on every single marker and pencil?"

"Can we just get our stuff?"

"Let's be sure to be as miserable as possible when we do it," I say.

My own cheer and confidence are half-fake, but I'll never admit that to him. The days are ticking by, and my sense of doom and panic grows as we get closer and closer to the first day of school. Today Mom gave me forty bucks and said, *I hope it's enough.* I do, too, because Mase needs a backpack along with everything else, even though he says his old one is just fine.

"List, please." He hands it over. " 'One-inch binder, subject dividers, scientific calculator,' " I read. I might as well be gathering ingredients to make a bomb, I'm so anxious.

"Have, have, have," Mase says. "I've highlighted the only things I really need."

"Clearly, you don't need highlighters, then." I scan the paper. "Seriously, Mase? This is all?"

"Do you know how long pencils last? *Years.*" He tosses some glue sticks (a dollar twenty-nine) and some lined notebook paper (two forty) into our cart. "Just get your things so we can get out of here." Mase is looking around nervously, too. I have to remember that he was there that day the social worker came. It's probably something he'll never forget his whole life long.

I add some disinfecting wipes, graph paper, a flash drive, and notebooks from my own list. "Backpack for you," I say.

"I used duck tape. It's fine."

"Duck tape, haha," I punch his arm. He scowls at me. "It's duct tape."

"Whatever," he says.

"Quack quack," I say as I steer the cart to the backpack aisle. We've waited until the last possible minute to come here, so there's not a great selection. "How about this one?" I model an adorable cartoon koala-bear knapsack, suitable for any kindergartner.

He folds his arms, strides down the aisle, scanning the prices, looking like the disgruntled manager. He snatches the cheapest one, no frills, classic navy. There's a ton of them left. "Let's *go.*"

"Get on the end of the cart and I'll zoom you around."

It was fun when Lorenzo and I did it, but Mase glares at me. And that's when it happens. We swing a left out that aisle and almost run smack into Hope Mathias and Olivia Kneeley.

"Oh my *God*," Hope Mathias says. "Look who it *is*." Olivia Kneeley laughs.

I flush red. We keep going, we walk right past them, but whatever confidence and cheer I actually did have are gone. "Ignore them, Ivy. All they have are words," Mase says. We go through the checkout line. He was right; we should have hurried and gotten out of there.

The doors swoosh open. Outside, two guys from my school who graduated last year, Terrence Day and Kevar Manet, are hanging around by the curb. They spot me, and Terrence chuckles. They know, too. How, when they don't even hang out with any of the kids in my class? Same as I know Kevar's mom got two DWIs.

"I'd do her," Kevar says.

"You'd do her homo brother," Terrence says, and Kevar shoves him.

My face feels so hot, and my shorts feel suddenly too short. I glance at Mase, but his face is blank. God, I hate them. I hate them so much. I don't know where she went, the Ivy who liked to see the best in people. We get in the car and leave the cart right there in the lot without taking it back.

"Mase, I'm so sorry."

His face is cinched tight. Now he really looks older. Old enough that I can see him as a grown man.

"You know I'm probably gay, right?" he says.

I shrug. "Yeah." I've thought so pretty much since

forever. "I just figured it's your business unless you wanted to bring it up."

"We didn't have some big reveal that you're straight."

"That's exactly what I mean," I say.

"You and Mom are going to love me no matter who I have sex with in the future." It's not a question. It's a plain old fact.

"You and Mom are going to love me even if I never have sex after all of this."

He snorts.

"God, I'm so sorry about those two horrible idiots. Horrible and ignorant."

"They're just words," he says again. "And 'homo,' really? Why is that bad? If it didn't come out that creep's mouth, I wouldn't mind it. I'd *like* it. There's nothing wrong with that word except for the way assholes say it. Words with double *o*'s actually sound very friendly."

"Probably why you liked 'hoco poco' and 'abrocadabro,'" I say. I'd make those two fuckers disappear if I could.

"I forgot about those."

I pull out of the lot. I try to keep my hands from shaking, I'm so mad. More mad for Mase than for me. He's a beautiful and great kid, and he's going to be a beautiful and great man. I'm so upset that my tire bumps over the curb as we get out of there, and I force myself to concentrate so we don't get into an accident on top of everything else. "Hey, remember those bands Mom likes, too? Poco and Toto. Even if they do that song that makes zero sense. 'Ninety-Nine,' right?"

"Yeah. But what about that one by . . . I don't know who. 'Kokomo.' Triple o's."

"Bermuda, Bahama, blah blah pretty mama. Right up there with that margarita song in terms of cheesy but uplifting."

"The rom-coms of songs," Mase says. He stares out the window for a while, watching the gas stations and nail salons and Subways of Paris pass by. "One of my favorite words has a ton of o's," Mase finally says.

"What?"

"Cookbook."

"That's a great one," I say.

But he's wrong about one thing. Hope Mathias and Olivia Kneeley, Terrence Day and Kevar Manet—words aren't the only thing they have. They have laws, too.

I call Lorenzo when we get home, but he doesn't pick up. It rings once and then goes to voicemail, the way it does when your phone is off. In the movies when someone calls the person they're dating and that person doesn't pick up, they're about to break up. I text instead. *Bad day. Too much to text. Talk?* But there's no response. I try again in an hour, but the phone does that one ring again. I send another message. *You okay?*

No answer.

I start to get worried. An unsettling lump sits in my stomach.

That night, Mase immerses himself in a new recipe. Loco moco. It's Hawaiian, basically a burger on rice with gravy and a fried egg on top. It looks pretty awful, to be honest, but I manage to get a small bite in, and it's delicious, actually. Plus, it's two words with two *o*'s, so how can you not love it? I'm having a hard time eating, though. I'm having a hard time just sitting in my chair and not pacing around.

"Still haven't heard from him?" Mom asks.

"Nope."

"Try not to worry. You will."

I don't.

Not that night, not the next morning. I'd drive over, but I don't want to be someone who chases if he doesn't want to be caught.

Finally, it comes. The text.

Ivy, can we talk?

35

WE MEET AT THE EIFFEL TOWER. THE LAST TIME WE were here, I was telling Lorenzo the story of Drake, and how, against all odds, I was pregnant. It's an awful circle, us coming back now, at the end of this story. I guess I can't escape Tess and Angel. *You were one person; now you are another.*

I get there early. I don't even sit on the grass. I just pace around by our favorite tree. *Our tree,* it seems like there are so many *our* things now. Mountain Dew and real mountains, towers and lighthouses, fake wonder and true wonder, the world. We'd traveled the world together. We'd battled *two different* worlds together.

Oh man, oh, I'm sunk, because here he comes, that lanky guy with that head of hair, and he's so adorable, and I love him so much that I can barely look at him, this guy I'm about to lose. He doesn't carry his blanket. Our blanket. He doesn't carry anything, not even a water bottle. He looks grim. He stands in front of me. His mouth just gapes. And, oh dang, his mouth. His beautiful mouth. His beautiful everything that I won't have in my life anymore.

"Lorenzo?" I can barely speak.

"Ivy," he says, and starts to cry.

"Are we breaking up?"

"Breaking up? No! Oh my God, I hope not." He pulls me to him. "I've got to get out of here, though, Ivy. I do."

I push him away. "What?"

"I need to leave, Ives. Something happened."

"What?"

"I got some papers. From an attorney's office. Someone is suing me. For, um, helping you. Get an abortion."

"Oh my God, you're kidding me, Lorenzo. Oh my God, no. No! I am so sorry. I am so, so sorry! Can they do this? Really? Who is it?"

"It's just some random person, Ives. Not even anyone we know. Just some retired guy who organizes the marriage-and-family retreats at City of Hope. Just some dude. It's part of the new law. If an *Uber driver* takes someone to an appointment, *they* can be sued. *Any* person who helps in *any* way."

"This isn't real. This is like, like . . ." I don't even know what it's like.

"What are they going to do next, huh? Ban birth control?"

"They can't do that," I say. "Why would they do that?"

Lorenzo just makes an *Ivy, don't be naive* face.

"What are we going to *do*?"

"I've got to get out of here," Lorenzo says. "That's all

I know. I've been watching all these videos, and I've been learning so much. *So* much, like I was one person and now I'm another. And I just can't, Ivy, I can't live in a place where it's practically the Middle Ages or something. I'm sorry I didn't call yesterday, but I've been really busy. I had to get a lawyer, and my dad only knew this guy who handles tax stuff, so I called Lottie—"

"Wait. *My* Lottie?"

"Your Lottie. *Our* Lottie. She told me that if I ever needed anything, I should call, and I needed something, Ivy, that's for sure."

"She got you a lawyer?"

"Yeah. She got me a lawyer. He's free, too. There are always people to help, Ives. That's one thing I'm realizing. And Lottie got me something else, too. A job."

A *job?* "What kind of a job? Where?"

"Rockaway Auto Supply and Repair."

"*Oregon?*"

"I can work there and save money for EMT training. Tell me you understand. Please. Tell me we'll figure this out."

"Wait, wait, wait. When is this all happening?" This is moving so fast. And I am so mad at Grandma Lottie, my hands are in little fists at my side. I'm *furious* with her.

"Friday. I've got to get there and start looking for places so I can move in by the first of September. Ivy, *tell me*."

"Friday? Lorenzo! Today is Wednesday!"

"I know. There's so much to do. And in every spare

second, I'm filling out as many forms as I can on the anti-choice whistleblower site."

I'm afraid to ask. Instead I just close my eyes right there. I try to breathe. It probably looks like I'm praying, but I'm not. I wish I could. I wish I could believe in the God of the Pillars of Rome and the beautiful earth. Man, I want to. But these people who claim him, they're making me doubt him, and I don't know what to do about it, and maybe I never will. I slowly open my eyes, hoping I'll see something other than what I do: Lorenzo standing there with dark circles under his eyes. Finally, I manage to speak. "The whistle-blower site?"

"Where people can write in tips about anyone like me who has helped anyone like you. The TikTokers are flooding the site with BS information. I filled out one form using just the word 'butthole' over and over again. I filled out another with Bob Marley lyrics. Then I just started copying lines from the *Junior Paleontologist Activity Book* we got in Dinosaur. Then the ingredients on the back of the Raisinets box, like tapioca dextrin."

"Lorenzo, noooo," I moan. "You can't leave. Can you wait? I'll be done with school in a year. We can both go!"

"I can't. I get it, your choice to stay. But please understand my choice to leave, Ivy. I feel like that scene in *Beauty and the Beast,* where they're coming at me with torches. In Oregon, you got lighthouses, you know? It's a whole different light, do you see? I'm scared. I don't want to live in a place where anyone with a uterus is treated like this. Please, just tell me we'll be okay. I just need to hear that before I start packing."

"Of course we'll be okay. Of course we'll figure it out," I say, but I'm just doing that thing again, saying what people want me to say, doing what other people seem to expect of me, because I don't believe it. We're not going to be okay when we live in separate worlds.

~

I'm crying so much by the time I get home that I can barely speak. Wilson barks with his usual excited greeting but then backs away when he sees me, a nervous look in his eyes.

"Mase!" I yell. I don't see him anywhere. I need a friend. I need something. In the kitchen I look for an answer in the fridge and reach for the neon green of a Mountain Dew. It's nothing like real dew on a real mountain. I read the back. What is erythorbic acid? What is calcium disodium EDTA? My God. I never thought to even look at this before. I never really thought to question what it's made of.

I see Mase out the kitchen window above the sink. He's not looking at the Julia Child cookbook. He's only sitting in a lawn chair with his feet in the baby pool Mom got for really hot days. Mase is gazing off, looking at the place where the tree branch disappears, up toward the roof where you can see for miles and miles. His ankles are surrounded by dolphins and whales. He looks glum.

I wish I could call Peyton or Faith or anyone, but I don't

have any friends. Loneliness fills me, like it's an actual some-thing instead of a nothing. I open the slider. Mase stares straight at me. I must have mascara all over my face, and my hair has pulled from my ponytail like I've been through a storm, but he doesn't say anything about the obvious facts of my upset. "Hey," he says.

"Lorenzo is moving. On Friday. Grandma Lottie helped him get a job at Rockaway Auto Supply and Repair. Some stranger is suing him for taking me to Oregon."

Mase doesn't even reply. It's like he already *knows*.

"What are you *doing*?" I ask.

"Pretending I'm at the beach," he says.

I'll talk to her, my mom says, about Grandma Lottie. That night, Mom retreats to her bedroom and shuts the door. I want to listen in on their call, but I'm too nervous. Instead I hover around in my own room across the hall with my own door open, a compromise, same as the way you peek through your fingers during a scary movie. Mom is going to set her straight, big-time, I'm sure, about getting involved in my life like this. I brace for yelling, or, at the very least, Mom's intense voice vibrating through her closed bedroom door.

Instead, after some low murmurs, I hear laughing. Laughing! What the hell? What the actual hell? I place my ear against the door.

"Shaun Cassidy?" Mom says. "No! It was Donny Osmond!" She pauses. "Yeah! That's why it's even funnier!"

Grandma Lottie must be speaking again, because Mom's quiet. Her voice turns serious when she answers.

"Too long. Much too long," she says.

36

THE TRIUMPH IS PARKED IN FRONT OF OUR HOUSE. Last night it was empty, aside from the two of us, limbs entwined, bare skin against bare skin, except for that condom. My head was wedged up against the back-seat door handle, and his leg got a cramp in it, and the whole time, I was praying that the Paris police wouldn't drive up to that far, dark corner of the Eiffel Tower. Afterward I wanted to cling and cry and beg Lorenzo not to leave, but choice needs to be respected. So, instead, I cleared the steam off the window in a circle and gazed at the tower, glowing red, white, and blue with the jaunty cowboy hat on top. This morning I expected a truck or a U-Haul, something beyond just the back seat of Lorenzo's car now stuffed with a few bags.

"That's it?" I ask. He makes leaving look so easy.

"I can't pack what means the most," he says.

My resolve to stay is wobbling. It's wobbling big-time. In the movies I'd have picked up that check from Euwing's, and I'd have had exactly the right amount of money to get us there. I'd run inside right then and grab a few things and hop in that passenger seat, and we'd drive off, the highway stretching in front of us. Sunrise, hope, cut.

But that's not what happens. Instead Mase and Mom interrupt us to say goodbye to Lorenzo before going in the house again, and Wilson stands on his back legs and stares out from the living room. We kiss. We kiss some more. I try to really remember it.

"I love you, Ivy," he says.

"I love *you*," I say. "So much. Drive careful."

"Hey, I'll be fine. Remember, this isn't an Avalanche, Ives. It's a *Triumph*."

And then he gets in. And he actually does it; he drives off. He rolls down his window and waves, disappearing down our street, as Diesel barks his head off and snarls and throws himself against that fence.

━━━⟋

In the movies Mase and I wouldn't start school, either, but we do. As much as I'm dreading facing everyone there, and even after all that's been done to me and Lorenzo and my mom and Mase, I've lived my whole life here. It seems so much easier to be where you've always been, to do what you've always done, to think how you've always thought.

Until it isn't. Until, if you're lucky, it's harder.

I watch as that navy-blue backpack disappears through the doors of the junior high, and I say a hope. I'm calling it that instead of a prayer, a hope to a higher being who loves everyone, who wouldn't approve of harassment and bullying, let alone threats and shame, and definitely not violence done in her name. *Please protect Mase.*

I park in the high school lot. *And me too.*

I don't even need to play the videos of the fierce TikTokers facing the hate in those clinic protests or talking about their own experiences with such bold bravery. They're in my head now, I've been playing them so often.

The building smells the same—Pine-Sol and body odor and cafeteria gravy, a hint of lunch-box apples. It's noisy, friends chatting with friends. This is supposed to be a great year, the best year, when you're on top, when you get all the fun stuff before you have to face the seriousness of being an adult in the adult world. But that's already happened to me, that bridge-crossing. I'm a changed me in an unchanged hallway. I turn the circle on my locker lock—right, left, right—and I glance around, searching for familiar, kind eyes. The only pair that meets mine belong to a junior girl, and I don't even know her name. She gives me a slight smile, and I give her one back.

I see Faith with some of our friends, and she turns away. Peyton is in my second-period AP English Lit class. She says a terse "hey," but that's all, and I spend the rest of the period filled with sorrow and an embarrassed discomfort. At lunch

I sit alone. I imagine a shield of rainbow umbrellas around me. But I'm doing it, right? I'm facing them, being brave? Showing them I'm still here? I'm doing it.

After fifth period, Noah Alvarez overemphasizes the word *period* when I'm standing right there, and everyone around him snickers. Big deal. Who cares. So creative, so inventive, hahaha, good one. The bell finally rings on the longest day of my life. It's the *ding-ding* in those boxing movies, where the guy is beaten and barely standing but alive.

Nothing too horrible has happened. This is what it means to be fierce, right? To be a warrior is to face your enemy defiantly, right?

I head to Mr. Smiley with relief. Day one. Nine and a half more months to go.

But something's wrong with Mr. Smiley.

The sun is so bright, I can't tell what's actually going on. I just know it doesn't look right. As I get closer, I see, and then it's so surreal, it's hard to believe it's happening. There's red paint dripping down the windshield. Red paint, like blood, because that always equals shame in all the books and movies. I think of Carrie in that old Stephen King film, drenched and humiliated in that pig blood, vengeance for being different and defenseless. And Tess—blood when she is pricked by roses, crimson drops splashed on her skirt when the horse dies, blood on the ceiling after Alec is murdered, blood punishment for all the crimes against her.

The paint drips, sliding into the crevice between the windshield and the hood. I grab a sweatshirt from the back seat and some old fast-food napkins from the glove box. It's mostly a smeared mess, and now so am I. The new school outfit Mom got me at Walmart for a surprise, my jeans and the orange T-shirt, are wrecked. I'm marked, but we don't need paint for that.

I text Mase that I'm going to be late, making blood fingerprints on my phone. I don't want him to see this. It's too frightening, too heavy with ugliness and meaning. *Are you okay? What's wrong? What happened?* Whoosh, whoosh, whoosh, the texts come. *Just wait for me,* I text back.

I head to Jiffy Car Wash. I can see out the windshield, but just barely. The car rides along the tracks, and the water comes down, and then the soap, and the sloppy noodles, and more water, and we're washed clean. Almost clean. There's still a reddish residue on the hood, and in the corners of the windshield. There are stains all over my clothes.

"Why is the car red?" Mase says as he gets in. "Oh my God." He sees me. "Oh my God, oh my God. Are you okay? What happened?"

"They just poured some paint on it," I say. "It's fine. I can handle it."

I expect Mase to sympathize, or maybe even cry, but instead his cheeks blaze, same as mine do when I'm upset or angry. He's both.

"This is just so fucked up," he says. Mase never uses that word.

"I know. I know, I'm sorry."

"You, I mean. This, meaning *you*."

"*Me?*"

"You think you have to be some big, strong—"

"Those are *good* things, Mase."

"Yeah, if it's, like, *healthy* for you. This isn't that. It's like you're taking some punishment. Like you're *supposed* to be punished. You're *taking it*. You're doing something you think other people expect of you. Why do you have to face them, huh? Why do they deserve to be faced? Strength isn't just being . . ." He windmills a hand around, searching for how to explain. But I know what he means.

"Fierce."

"Yeah. Strength isn't being fierce. I don't even think strength is always being strong."

My eyes prick with tears. My throat gets tight with emotion, too, the way it does when someone says something true. *Choice* is strength. Making your own is.

I pull the little lever that squirts the wiper fluid of our shit car, and then I flip on the wipers. I can see so clearly now that our shit car's shit windshield has become a metaphor.

"Let's go," I say.

I turn the engine on. In the film version the battery might be dead, but it isn't, and I'm done facing obstacles and facing obstacles because I feel like I deserve obstacles.

"Where?"

I drive toward Main Street, past the fountain. I see Mr. Fartso sitting on a bench there, sipping coffee out of a cardboard cup. Mrs. Peony is making her way down the sidewalk with her little walker with the basket. Oh, it all makes me sad. So sad.

"Did you hear me? Where are we going?" Mase asks again.

I pull up in front of Euwing's Drugs. There's a free spot right in front, like it's meant to be.

"NO. Ivy! I just told you! No! You don't need to go facing stuff and people like this!"

"Not unless I want to." And I want to. I want that check, too. I need that check, and I earned it. "Will you wait a sec?"

"Oh my God," Mase says, and folds his arms, mad. "You require a lot of patience, you know that?"

I walk past the lovebirds, Buddy and Missy. I forget to hold my nose, and the full force of their rank smell hits. I take it all in. I really look. Inside the cage Missy is losing some feathers. Buddy picks at his skin and preens. I hear his words in my head, too, Mr. Euwing's: *You can change its color. You can stop it from flying, even.* Sure you can. When you force them to live inside a wire cage, you can make them do anything.

The fluorescent lights give everything a sickly blue hue. Evan is behind the counter, replacing a roll of receipt tape, but he looks up when I come in and raises his hand in a wave. When I stride down the candy aisle, I see Maureen, moving stuff around in pain relief. She sees me and turns away, but then does a double take. I must be a sight, in those clothes. There's a sale on shampoo, the kind I like, but everything in here is too expensive. Every single thing. I thought this was my future.

I'm so glad I was wrong.

"Ivy," Maureen says. She's coming toward me like a

linebacker, but I push past and go right through the pharmacy door, where Mr. Euwing is reaching for a box on a high shelf.

"Bob," I say.

He turns in my direction, wearing his big customer smile, until he sees it's me. I watch a film play out on his face—disappointment, disgust, and then, when he sees my clothes, confusion and guardedness.

"I came for my check."

"You're not who I thought you were, Ivy."

"You're sure right about that."

"What you've done is a sin," Bob Euwing says, retrieving my check from the drawer under the counter and handing it to me. "I pray that you repent, and—"

"You ought to pray that Drake keeps his pants zipped."

Bob Euwing's face goes utterly still. For a moment I see it. I know I do. It's right there—a clear understanding of exactly what I mean.

"*Drake,*" I say, just to be sure he does. "I wonder if you would've forced *him* to give birth."

I turn and leave. Maureen is holding that price-checker wand like a gun. Well, sure. They love their guns here. Bob Euwing takes Drake out to the firing range all the time, and Maureen and her husband are avid hunters.

"I'm sorry," I say to Buddy and Missy as I leave.

37

SOME PEOPLE WILL NEVER SEE YOU. SOME UNFINISHED business will always be unfinished. Especially when it's been unfinished for centuries.

We put our house up for sale.

Taking help is strength, too, Ives, my mom keeps telling me, and maybe herself, as well. *Taking help is an act of self-respect.*

We're lucky, I'm lucky, I think again and again, that we have options like this, help like this, when other people don't have a house or a Grandma Lottie or the freedom and ability to make this choice, let alone the one I already made at that clinic. How can this thought not loop and loop again through my brain?

As we sift through our bathroom drawers, tossing out nearly empty lotion bottles and dried-up mascaras, as we wrap newspaper around our cups and silverware and pans, and fold our clothes into garbage bags to the thump of Mom's music, I think about Faith's sister, Harmony, too.

Harmony, living at the Belle Vista apartments, with the sign out front that says HEATED POOL, COLOR TV, A/C. I send a silent hope that she's okay and happy.

"Hey, look what I found," Mase says. He holds up the green disappearing coin case from the magic kit that we thought was lost forever.

"Where was it?"

"Just stuck between my mattress and the wall. I swear, I shoved my hand down there a million times when we were looking for it."

Mase—he's thrilled to be moving. The Oregon Coast has a food trail that you can follow from farms to cafés, and he's got his eye on a culinary program at a community college a few hours away from where we'll be living. He can recite the bios of the instructors like a waiter telling you the specials in detail. I can finish my senior year there for free, too, while getting college credits at the same time. After that, who knows. Maybe I'll study writing there or somewhere else, I'm not sure. These are all the things we say to Dad when he calls to talk about *your upcoming transition*. It sounds so formal, but he wants to ask if we're sure and we're okay and happy about it. We are sure, and okay, and happy about it.

"Well, it's not gone after all," I say. Mase makes the penny disappear, and then flips the case over to make it reappear, then disappear, then reappear, like so many things we think are gone but aren't.

It takes a few weeks, but we finally sell the house and get a closing date. The tension in Mom's face eases, especially after she applies for an assistant manager job at Nat's House of Crafts in Tillamook, Oregon, and gets it. It turns out that Nat is a big bearded guy who went to high school with Mom and who runs the quilt club in town. Finally, she stops sitting over that calculator, looking worried.

We don't pack our portable speaker, so that night, our last night in Paris, it sits on a cardboard box, playing music in a nearly vacant kitchen as we eat Subway sandwiches. Mase criticizes the bun quality. Mom and me, we crumple up the wrappers and toss them at him, and Wilson lunges at the paper balls and runs off, hoping we'll chase him, but we're too tired. With all our stuff in boxes, the house is so bare that our voices echo. It's strange to see our walls stripped of photos and posters. Now there are just nail holes and dark squares of unfaded paint, revealed when we took the pictures down, the real color hidden under there all along. What's weird is how happy we are. The house looks so sad and empty, but the people in it aren't.

"I can't wait," Lorenzo says when I tell him the date we're leaving. It's hard to talk to him when he's at Rockaway Auto. Everything is loud and clanging in the shop. I feel shy with him, too. I haven't seen him in three and a half weeks.

"Attorney news?" I ask.

"Nothing. The guy who reported me probably collected his ten thousand dollars and went on with his life."

That night I go up to the roof. And then I laugh so hard. So, so hard that I have to hold my stomach, because two other people got there before me.

"Careful, Ivy, don't fall," Mase says.

"Sit, sit." Mom scooches over and makes room for me.

The three of us look out toward that Eiffel Tower. Mase shakes a box of Raisinets, and a few tumble into his palm.

"Where did you get *those*?" I ask.

"Parting gift from Lorenzo. I was saving them for a special night."

"I can't believe you're eating those disgusting things," I say.

"I like to keep an open mind," Mase says. "Actually, they're quite tasty." He tilts his head back, pops a few in.

Mom holds out her palm. "Fill her up," she says.

"Okay, fine," I say. I hold out my palm.

The three of us just sit under a brilliant and star-filled sky, gazing out at our past and our future both. Real awe, real wonder. Love.

We're leaving in the morning. I keep hoping that maybe Peyton will come by, or even Faith, or both of them together. In the film version this would happen. We would maybe reach some bittersweet understanding. The best would happen. But in the film version of things, the worst happens, too—if someone is on the deck of a ship, they'll fall in, and if people are driving in a car, it will crash. Life, real life—it usually happens somewhere in the middle and not at either extreme.

The movers are picking up everything in the morning,

thanks to Grandma Lottie, plus a coupon code, plus a discount. Mom says she got such a good deal that we can maybe just kiss all our stuff goodbye because we probably won't see it again.

We're at the cleaning portion of moving. Mom is scraping gunk out of the fridge, and Mase and I are doing the bathroom. When the doorbell rings, Wilson Phillips barks his head off, and the noise echoes in the empty room.

"Can you get it, Ivy?" Mom shouts. She's elbow-deep in old salad dressings and expired mustard.

I peek out. I'm still afraid in this place. I haven't even gone out much, not since that paint. My hopeful heart sinks, because it's not Peyton or Faith, and it never will be. Instead it's Olivia Kneeley. Ultraconfident Olivia Kneeley, of the bikini and the popular group, of the shiny hair, of the pregnancy test sliding directly under her chair. Olivia Kneeley, of the bathroom crying incident, the wad of TP, the peppermint Life Savers.

I put my back against the wall like I'm hiding from the FBI. I hope she didn't see me.

She did.

"Ivy?" she asks. "Can I talk to you?"

There's something in her voice. It's not anger or judgment. It's need.

I open the door.

"I'm sorry," she says. "I just wanted to say I'm so sorry. It was really wrong of me not to stand up for you." Olivia Kneeley's eyes fill with tears.

I don't tell her it's okay, because it isn't. I don't give her something I don't want to give. Instead I just wait.

"My parents are the only ones who know what I'm about to tell you," Olivia Kneeley says.

And this time I'm not shocked when someone tells me this story. I'm not surprised that there's another one. I'm not struck that it keeps on happening, this sharing.

It's what is and always has been.

In the movies Diesel would become a different dog, too. We'd see the softer side of him, the reason he was always so cruel. But this doesn't happen, either. Instead, the next day, when we drive away from our house, the only home Mase and I have ever known, he barks oh so viciously and throws himself against that fence. His fangs are bared, and he looks like he wants to rip out our throats.

But it's the last time I'll be scared.

38

WE TAKE TURNS DRIVING, MOM AND ME, STOPPING
for the night only in Albuquerque and Salt Lake City. We
play "Hold On," but also old songs with a new-life vibe,
songs with names like "Pack It Up," and "Dog Days Are
Over," and "Let It Go," which Mase complains about because it's from a Disney movie and he thinks it's babyish.
Which means, of course, that Mom and I have to sing the
chorus doubly loud to be annoying. Wilson does great on
the ride, except for the time we take two seconds to pee and
grab our takeout at the Ride On In Café in Albuquerque and
he eats half a box of Cheez-Its that Mase left open in the car.
It was practically an invitation. At night I watch Mom's profile both in darkness and in the lights of car beams speeding
past. Light, dark, and I remember everything she's endured.
Yet she's still here, driving forward.

We stop and go again, stop and go, the places and names
an exhausted blur. On our arrival day it's a relief when we

finally see that wide sky that means you're near the ocean. When I roll down my window, I get a glorious hit of sea air, which smells old and deep, like the darkest green if it had a smell. I see Mom's hands tighten on the steering wheel, and she gets a little snappish as we make our way through the small port town of Garibaldi. We're all nervous. We've only seen photos of the rental house online. If it's disappointing, we'll start life out here sliding downward; that's the fear.

But it's sweet, so sweet, the house. My heart just lifts, and my body fills with helium giddiness, because it's small and shingled, with a red door and a patch of very green grass, and a hedge of hydrangeas. It has two stories. It's *pretty*.

Mom pulls the parking brake. She pats the dash of our shit car, Mr. Smiley, who has done a downright admirable job of getting us here. "We made it," she says.

⟶

Inside, the house looks so different from the one in Paris. It has a little sunporch, and wainscot in the living room, and a small bathroom with a claw-foot tub. "Look," I say in the kitchen. Not about the cupboards and nooks painted a pale green, and not about the old-fashioned glass drawer pulls, but about the thin wood planks on the ceiling that make it feel like we're in a ship.

"Shiplap," Mom says. She smiles.

Mase runs his hands across something we didn't see in

the photos. A center island, with a shiny, smooth top. He actually puts his cheek against it and stretches his arms across, like he's hugging the globe.

"Oh wow!" I point. A dog door.

We explore. You can see a sliver of ocean if you stand on your toes in Mom's tiny bedroom, and mine has a view of the apartment complex behind us, and Mase's is so small, it'll barely fit his bed inside, but we love every corner of this place—the triangle nook above the stairs, the built-in cupboards with drawers below, painted white. The wood-burning stove. The uglies will have less of a chance here, I can tell. I take some photos to send to Dad.

Mom grips my hands. "Lease to own," she says, like she can hardly believe it, her eyes glittery. I don't know exactly what that means, lease to own, only that she sees possibilities where she hadn't before.

Mase can't believe something else. "We have two stories," he says.

And, oh, we do.

Mom wants to find the market, and Mase is outside, walking on the grass with his shoes off because the grass is so soft here. He finds an old tennis ball on the lawn and throws it for Wilson. I have something else I need to do.

"Mom?" I say, and that's all I have to say.

"Go," she says.

I've been there before, but Rockaway Auto Supply and Repair is easy to find even if you haven't. If you were here last month, you'd have seen tourists taking photos of that iconic storefront covered in hubcaps, and that beautiful old truck parked there. It's a shit truck—it probably wouldn't take you to the end of the block—but it's still somehow beautiful, though, showing off its history.

It's late afternoon, and there are only three or four cars in the lot, including Lorenzo's Triumph. My anxiety winds up at the sight of it. I don't have butterflies. I have some big scary creature stomping around, like the kind we saw in Dinosaur.

As I head to the entrance, I run my fingers along the hubcaps on the wall. The bells on the door chime as I enter. The store has changed, and you don't see the repair shop right away. I have to wind past old Hank, the gas-station guy, and through a few aisles of auto parts. But when I step through the doorway of the garage, there he is, my Lorenzo. He's cranking the wrench on the engine of a motorcycle, and he looks up, and our eyes meet. It's full-on *Rockaway Weekend*, one hundred percent, oh, my heart. I'm not wearing that dress with the hilarious shoulder pads and crimped eighties hair, and he's not in a leather jacket. Nope. We had the same idea, and we're each wearing our Captain Ahoy's T-shirt, with the happy halibut dancing alongside a mug of beer. I want to crack up, because look at us. I want to cry, because I've missed him so bad. But instead our eyes meet, almost like I'm seeing him for the first time. He just stands there with that wrench, and I just stand there staring back, and there's this deep and magnetic energy between us, magic, and I am certain, so certain, that love is the one most powerful and forever thing.

39

ON A MORNING IN THE LATTER PART OF MAY, I DRIVE
Mr. Smiley over to Lorenzo's place, a small studio apartment
above the Beach Bum, a burger bar where, day or night, you
always smell frying meat and onion rings. I knock. When
Lorenzo answers, I step inside, and he pulls me close, and
we kiss. It's only kissing for now, because I have to study,
and he's got to be at the clinic before it opens. Still, I grab
his butt a good one.

I sling my backpack down. I sink into his couch, which
is as saggy as the back of an old horse. And then I spot it.

"Is that a *ukulele*?"

"Didn't I tell you I played?"

"No." I smile. I'm still finding out so much about him.

He's rushing around. He grabs the keys to the Triumph,
and his own pack, and then remembers his water bottle. He
hurries to the sink to fill it up.

"Okay," he says. "Keep the place warm for me."

It's a joke. The place is always warm. You have to keep

that one window open all the time, and even though he also runs a fan, it's better to hang out here with as few clothes on as possible; don't ask me how I know.

"Wait. Your vest," I say. It's hanging over a kitchen chair—a rainbow vest, with the words CLINIC ESCORT on the front. This is what he wears on Saturdays, on the days he isn't working at Rockaway Auto Supply and Repair. On weekdays he's in class at Tillamook Bay Community College, studying things like airway management and trauma assessment and what medication to administer when.

"Ah, thanks!" he cries. He snatches it, then gives me a quick kiss. "Abortion road trip love story," he says.

"Abortion road trip love story," I say back.

I say the word: *abortion*. That's what *I* do now, say it. Me, I'm strong by getting through what I got through, and I'm fierce by enduring. Lorenzo, he's strong by putting that vest on, and he's fierce by walking beside the women as they go through the doors of the Tillamook clinic.

I lean out the window to wave goodbye to Lorenzo.

"Hey, boyfriend," I shout.

"Stop being so gorgeous," he shouts back.

I was wrong, so wrong, about prefaces and prologues, and that's the problem with easy opinions—you can be wrong until you know more. It's impossible to understand the whole story, any story, without knowing the beginning before the beginning, without acknowledging the long, buried roots that have led us here, held us here. Outside on the street below me, I see a family emerge from Rae's Waffle Hut after a Saturday morning breakfast. A mom and a dad, a grandma, two daughters, one son. Three middle-aged women go inside, too. A car parks, and several young couples pile out. I count. One, two, three, four. See those women? And those and those? Her and her and her and maybe even him. I imagine their mothers and their grandmothers and their great-grandmothers. Her and her and her and *her*, in Paris or Paris, Rome or Rome, Florence or Florence, big city or small, across every continent over the world, and across the generations. Layer upon layer, unspoken stories embedded in earth, embedded in the layers of our body, gone and not gone. Her and her, facing other people's will, facing commands of *Here's what you will do* and saying, *I get to choose. I do.* Saying, *Even if I have to do it unlawfully, even if I have to do it in shame and in secret, I do.* Saying, *I have to,* or *I can't, no matter what you think of me or what happens next.*

Her and her and her, staying silent and holding secrets, or quietly whispering, or loudly shouting. Saying it, the last unspoken word, *abortion,* or doing what I am doing now, after I've moved away from the window—writing it down right here for you, Ms. La Costa. *Why history matters.* You said it could be however long it needs to be, and it needs to be *long.* Very long. Four hundred and two pages long. Thirty-nine chapters.

There's something new in the apartment, or maybe I just haven't noticed it before. It's Lorenzo's passport, twin to mine propped on his bookshelf, a record of all the places we've been so far. The places *I've* been so far—despair and fury and wonder and awe, bliss and the Pillars of Rome.

I am the one and only Ivy DeVries, but I am also Betty, and Tess, and Esilda, and Olivia Kneeley, even. I am the women on the branches of my tree; I am the women outside that window, as I write this story.

As I write *my* story, a real one, not something from the movies with clear villains and heroes. It's a complicated story, with pain and shame, with support and love, with both hard decisions and hope, where the plotline has struggle, but also peace and relief. No wonder it's long and heavy, and why it's taken me forever to set it down here, on my mom's second-hand, thirdhand laptop with the Arcade Fire sticker on it. It's the secret story of so many people, whether we know it or not, one, two, three, four. An old, old and ongoing story, with a foreword and an explanatory note. With a preface and a prologue and an introduction to the 109th edition.

Acknowledgments

I'm incredibly grateful, as ever, to two cherished people: my agent and friend, Michael Bourret, and my editor and friend, Liesa Abrams. There are just not enough words of love and thanks for you both, and I appreciate you every single day. My sincerest and heartfelt thanks also go to Emily Harburg, Rebecca Vitkus, Barbara Bakowski, Angela Carlino, Liz Dresner, Megan Shortt, Shannon Pender, and Sarah Lawrenson, as well as the entire RHCB marketing group, the school and library team (with special gratitude to Adrienne Waintraub, Katie Halata, and Erica Stone), our sales force, our entire production and supply chain, and, truly, the whole remarkable group of people at Random House Children's Books/Labyrinth Road, led by Barbara Marcus. I'm so abundantly fortunate that all of you have shared your talent and your time and your hearts with me.

Readers, librarians, teachers, booksellers, reviewers: We've been doing this together for over twenty years now, and I am so honored that you've held and shared my words with such affection and thoughtfulness. I'm deeply grateful for each one of you. Extra thanks to the early, enthusiastic librarian readers of *Plan A:* Laura Lutz and Danielle Jones-Cartwright.

So very much love and thanks to my parents and my sister: Evie Caletti, Paul and Jan Caletti, Sue Rath—your support and enthusiasm for my books (and for me!) over all these years has meant more than I can ever, ever express. Endless and forever love to my husband, John; to my beloved sunshines, Sam and Nick and Erin and Pat and Myla; and to the little joys of my heart, Charlie and Theo and Riley. You are the light and the meaning, the humor and the sparkle, the all and the everything.